BY THE RIVERS OF BABYLON

MICHAEL D. O'BRIEN

By the Rivers
of Babylon

A Novel

IGNATIUS PRESS   SAN FRANCISCO

Cover art:
The Guardian by Michael O'Brien

© 2022 by Ignatius Press, San Francisco
All rights reserved
ISBN 978-1-62164-611-2
ISBN 978-1-64229-262-6 (eBook)
Library of Congress Control Number 2022940933
Printed in the United States of America ♾

By the rivers of Babylon, there we sat down and wept, when we remembered Zion. On the willows there we hung up our lyres. For there our captors required of us songs, and our tormenters, mirth, saying, ''Sing us one of the songs of Zion!'' How shall we sing the LORD's song in a foreign land?

> — Psalm 137
> *For David, by Jeremiah in the Captivity*

Contents

I

The Shepherd Boy

OUR VILLAGE IS OF LOWLY ESTATE, tucked away in the hill country south of Bethlehem, halfway to Hebron. No teachers, prophets, or kings have ever come from this place. But we are content. Our cluster of ten homes we call Little Bite of Bread, for it is nothing like the large town of Bethlehem, which means "House of Bread". The nearby pastures are just sufficient for our flocks, including my family's forty ewes and their lambs. Despite the weather in this part of Judea, which is hot for most of the year, there is ample grass. We also grow grain in the hillside terraces that our people made long ago. There are wild olives here and there, and acacia and terebinth in ravines. A small stand of dwarf oak caps the rise overlooking our dwellings. Faithfully the clouds rise up from the western sea, climb the hills, and, crossing over to the eastern slopes, sprinkle rain upon us. The village water well never runs dry.

Each house is made of field stones; each yard has its outbuildings and a pen where the sheep are kept at night. Throughout the day, the clamor of playing children never ceases. There are so many mothers and grandmothers among us that the smell of baking bread and barley cake is always in the air. Most of us are related through blood, and those who are not seem more like family than neighbors. Everyone here is friendly. We help each other. It is a peaceful place.

By the Rivers of Babylon

After sunrise, six days a week, I leave the village behind, driving the flock before me toward the upper pastures. Out on the green hills there is silence, with no loud voices calling my name or making me scurry on a task. The silence is broken only by the wind and the little noises of the flock.

Always I am happy, but especially when I can play my flute with no one to hear me and practice with my slingshot, like David the shepherd boy who became a king. There are no Goliaths in these days, and the Philistines and Assyrians were long ago driven back. Now a time of fruitfulness has come upon the land.

There are wolves, of course, but for the most part they are night hunters. Once I saw a bear, which terrified me greatly, though when I hurled a stone at it, it fled. The lions are more dangerous, but they are not plentiful. For six years I have tended my father's flock, the past two years alone, and during all this time I have only once seen lions. Last summer, they came out of the southeast in Moab, close to the desert regions. It was unusually hot and dry that year, and their game was scarce. They ventured near the habitations of man in search of sweet meat. Whenever I saw one, I shouted and used my sling, and the prowler would melt away into the bushes. I did not lose a single lamb. I was very proud of this. My father, Buzi, praised me, and my chest inflated with pride.

"Yezekiel my son," he said, clamping my shoulders and lifting me up onto my tiptoes. "Yezekiel, truly *God strengthens*."

Even so, for days afterward, he would send one of my older brothers to stand watch with me until no more lions came.

I am twelve years of age. I am strong, and my eye is sure. Though I have only my stave and sling, I feel sure that no lion will overcome me, should any again encroach upon our land. Of course, this is day-courage, nothing so fearsome as facing predators in the dark. My father insists that I bring the flock home before nightfall and secure them in their pen by our house. And so I do, without fail.

My stave and my voice are all that are needed to make the sheep obey. They know me. They follow me. If, from time to time, one goes astray on the slopes, greedy for a last nibble of grass, witlessly ignorant of the dangers, I usually know which one is missing. I find it and scold it and give it a tap on its rump, and it runs with guilt back to the flock, which is like a small cloud gently rising and falling as it flows over the earth, following the path toward home and their nightly handful of grain.

Then, before I take my own meal, as lamps are lit in the house, I milk the best ewes and save the milk for my mother's crockery, in which she will make butter and whey and cheese and curds. I am very fond of salted curds. When I stand watch out in the pasture, I drink skins of milk and eat bread and nibble curds.

Often throughout the day, I circle the flock, talking to the sheep, reminding them who is the shepherd, who holds authority over them. They know I will not harm them. They understand that I protect them. If an eagle passing over the crest of a hill makes them startle and huddle together, I yell my battle cry and hurl a stone at the sky; the eagle veers away, the flock grows calm. I sit down on a rock and take my flute from my carry-bag. I play a peace-inducing air, as serene as the empty sky. I like to pretend that I make the sheep sing, for after trouble, after fear and reassurance, they make small baahings as they resume their meals.

"All is well," they sing to each other, "Yehezh is with us."

I, too, like to sing, though my voice is changing, no longer a child's throat-flute but something closer to the sounds made by my silly flock, who have terrible voices. Sometimes I lift my head and give full vent to song, hoping that this practice will help deepen my voice, will turn me into a man more swiftly. I am glad that no other human ears can hear me. I sing one of the songs of David—I call them *king-songs*—which I have learned from the elders when they gather in the village to pray to the Most High. My mother's brother, my uncle Joash, who is a priest of the Temple in Jerusalem, visits us from time to time. He teaches us new songs and reads from the holy writings of our forefathers. I do not like him much, for his eye is cold and he sometimes argues with my father in the presence of our family.

They speak of the division of the Kingdom of Judah and the Kingdom of Israel long ago, who was right and who was wrong, of Samaria and Jerusalem, and of present divisions among the priestly and royal classes. Listening to them, I have learned that our people came out of captivity in Egypt long ago and that we are called Israel because we are all sons of Jacob, who was renamed *Israel* by the Most High himself. The division into two kingdoms was a passing aberration, and while the Kingdom of Israel is no more and we are now called the Kingdom of Judah, our people are forever Israel. My father and uncle and older neighbors are always arguing the minute variations on this question.

Despite their differences, the elders drink wine from small silver cups and praise the Lord and sing together. Uncle is admired by my older brothers, for he is moderately wealthy, with a house in the lower City of David, not far from the Temple. I have been there only once, when I was a baby. Though Uncle is of the tribe of Levi, as are most of us in this region, he is not a member of a high priestly family. Yet because the Temple always has need of more priests, he is engaged to perform sacrifices and join in the offering of prayers for the kingdom. Mainly he studies the five books of Moses and writes commentaries. He teaches a group of students who will one day become priests. He begs my father to send him one of my brothers. My father smiles sagely, as if considering a weighty offer of trade, and points at me. I am seated on the floor by the doorpost, eating curds and sipping from a clay bowl of buttermilk.

"Why don't you take Yezekiel?" he says.

Uncle turns his gaze upon me. I am not handsome like my brothers, who are tall and well formed in body and face. My mother, Naomi, has more than once told me that I am beginning to resemble my sheep.

"*Baaaah*," I usually bleat whenever she says this, making her laugh.

Now, Uncle stares at me with his chilling eyes. I can see his disdain for me, plain in his entire countenance.

He scowls, shrugs, murmurs a word that sounds like "runt".

My mother, who is listening by the bread oven, stares at her brother, then turns her back to him. My father straightens, offended, but quickly covers it. He slowly rises to his feet. With great dignity he says: "Recall, brother Joash, that David was the least of the sons of Jesse."

Uncle snorts. "Yet he was fair of face."

"So was Saul exceedingly fair of face and the tallest of men, indeed, the most comely of all the sons of Israel."

I am feeling very hurt in my soul, with a lump in my throat, though I take care not to show that Uncle's words and expression have pierced me. He is saying that I in no way resemble David and Saul. Later, lying awake in the night, I recall that the kingship of Saul was ruined by his grave sins and betrayals. Now I am consoled by the truth that to have

13

looks pleasing to the eye is a passing thing, and the Most High does not value it. Strength is a greater gift, and intelligence of the mind, with swift thoughts and wise words. And obedience to the one true God.

Well, though I am short and slow of wit, I do have strong muscles and excellent aim. And I seek always to obey the laws of the Lord.

Then I smile and go to sleep.

There is a spring halfway up the pasture hill. It oozes water that collects in a tiny pool I have scooped in the turf, then spills over and runs underground a long way to the valley bottom, where it emerges again on the surface and then dives to the valley's lower reaches, becoming a larger pool where our pasture joins a neighbor's. Here the flocks of both families drink without diminishing the supply.

It is a source of much joy for me to improve my tiny pool, to scoop deeper into the soil until the crack in the stone mountain is exposed. Water is life. My spring is water coming from the rock, like the waters that poured forth in the desert when Moses brought us out of Egypt and struck the rock with his staff and saved the people.

I am not like Moses our forefather, yet I can make a little story with my mind-pictures and my muddy hands. I have searched about the hill for loose stones and carried them to the spring, making a ring wall around the pool, holding the wet soil and mud back, allowing the trickle to run free and pure. It is sweet on the tongue. I build a higher wall around it to keep the sheep from befouling it with their mouths and their black pebble droppings. They can drink from the lower spring, which is deeper and more copious.

Why do I do this? I know only that it gives me pleasure. It may be that I wish to be master of one small thing in this world, to guard it and keep it safe from man and beast. It is not, I think, idle curiosity that makes me dig into the soil all around my spring, at six and ten and twenty paces from the pool. I wish to see if there are other sources, but have found none. Yet I did unearth an old arrowhead, its shaft and feathers long rotted into dust. It was fashioned of metal, not stone. It may have come from an Israelite bow during a battle against Canaanites or Moabites, or it may be older still. Perhaps it felled a lion. Or a deer, for forests once grew on these high places long ago. Iosif told me that farther north and west of here, pine, oak, and terebinth trees still grow in abundance.

I feel the arrowhead linking me to the distant past, tethering me to my ancestors, for whenever I turn it over and over in my fingers, a mood passes through me, like a soft wind from a far land, and I feel most keenly that those people in stories were real, as I am real.

The sling stones I find here on the hills are never round and never quite the right size. I can hurl a sharp stone with my hand, and it may do damage to a marauder or threaten it sufficiently. And though I daily practice throwing these uneven pieces of rock, their various shapes make precision impossible. A perfect, smooth stone is a treasure to me. I speak of this because of my journey to the Jordan River some years ago.

My father took me to Jericho when I was eight years of age. My mother was ill with sickness of the eyes, and he had heard that in the lowlands by the river not only fruit grew in great abundance and size—as all the world knows— but great trees that produced a sap which the people of that region called "the balm of Gilead". It had healing powers when applied as ointment to diseases of the eye. Its aroma was sweet, but very harsh did it burn. Yet the burning was for a little time, and the evil humors that turned the eyes swollen and red and oozing puss were driven away swiftly. It was costly, he knew, and we had no shekels, no silver or gold to purchase it, and thus we drove a choice ewe, very woolly, as it was late winter of the year, and very fat. I carried her two newborn lambs in a back sling. And so we walked the three-day's journey in the hope of making a trade in the city marketplace.

When first I saw it, the region around Jericho was a marvel to me. As far as my eyes could see, it was exceedingly rich in well-watered soil where plentiful grain harvests grew, as well as large vineyards and orchards of fig and olive, date palm and other bounteous trees. I ate my first pomegranate there. I am told that from before the time of Abraham it was always a fruitful land, but the early Israelites who settled in Canaan burned off wild brush to extend the fields of the peoples who once lived there. They also made terraces on the hillsides bordering the valley. On these they planted more vineyards and also beans and lentils, barley and millet. The people of the Jericho region still maintain all of this most carefully, as it is the source of their wealth.

The villages around Little Bite of Bread also have terraces, but ours are very small, and our harvests much less abundant. Even so, we have our flocks of sheep, and Jericho has few, for it is exceedingly hot there, too hard on sheep, which do not prosper in excessive heat. On the whole, I think that Jericho is a wondrous place to visit but not to live.

The merchants of Jericho are greedy and proud, proud mainly because their ancestors under Joshua had destroyed the city walls when Israel came out of the desert and crossed over into the Promised Land. After much haggling that I must admit amazed me, coming from so mild a man as my father, I, the silent observer, was proud to see him obtain a pot of the ointment in exchange for the two lambs. The ewe he sold to a butcher, its wool he sold to a weaver. With the money, he purchased a length of white linen, and for me a small copper knife, and a Persian scarf for my mother, purple and red stripes made of very thin cloth, the like of which I had never seen before. Moreover, there were a few little coins left over to tuck into his purse. He also purchased a basket of dried grapes that he lashed to his back with leather straps. The fruit was sticky on our fingers, as the grapes in that part of the world are immense in size and of great sweetness. I ate a few of these, along with dried figs and dates, and found them to be very tasty, even though they were last year's harvest. One finished, I wanted another, and another—and another.

"That is enough, Yezekiel, or your belly will burst," my father warned. "The rest we will bring home to your mother and brothers."

For himself, he purchased nothing. I thought he would immediately turn us both toward home, but instead, he said to me with great solemnity:

"My son, now we will go to Gilgal, where you will see the twelve stones established by Joshua in memorial of the parting of the Jordan River, when he crossed over into Canaan."

I knew the story well, for it is nearly as great as the parting of the Red Sea. In my boy's mind, I had always thought that a river is less mighty than a sea, not so broad, not so deep. Yet it seemed to me as I walked to Gilgal that there was another difference between the two. The parting of the sea was surely a wondrous act of God. But that is not what was mulling in my mind. I was thinking that the parting of the sea was a great mercy from the Lord, for the people were in flight, and they were shameless grumblers, most of them worshipping idols. The parting of the Jordan was different, for the people had become desert dwellers, purified by trials, and the entrance into the Promised Land was a great gift to them. Trying to make sense of my thoughts, and the odd feelings swirling within them, it came to me that the parting of the Jordan was a going-to, not a running-from, and this is a better thing, though the miracles of the Lord were both very great.

Ah, ah, I thought to myself: When the Most High parted the Red Sea, he was closing a peril gate behind the people, and when he parted the Jordan, he was opening a blessing gate before them.

Thus, my father, Buzi, and I came to Gilgal, and there we approached the twelve stones erected by Joshua in memory of the parting of the river and the twelve tribes of Israel that crossed over dry-shod. Joshua took these stones from the riverbed itself, a man from each tribe carrying a stone on his shoulder. And here they are to this day.

My father stood several paces from the little tower of stone, and I beside him. He covered his head with his prayer cloth, and I covered mine with my dust scarf. In silence we prayed for a time, glorifying the Lord within our own hearts.

"It is good that Joshua heeded the Lord," said my father at last, "and placed these stones here in memory."

"Why is it good, Abba?" I asked. "The people would surely have remembered, even without the stones, for the miracle was very great."

"It is good, above all, because the Lord commanded it. And it is good that Joshua obeyed. Yet it is also good because the people who came forth from Egypt were ever forgetting the wonders of the Lord and turning to idols."

"But we are not like that," I said.

He turned his eyes upon me, saying nothing. Much troubled were his eyes. I dared not speak again.

"Ever are we like that, Yezekiel," he said. "Ever are we forgetting what the Lord has done for us and turning away to invoke the demons."

Forgetting myself, I ran forward and dropped to my knees before the twelve stones. I saw that weeds grew in the cracks between them and that windblown dust had made a drift over the lowest. There were animal and human droppings nearby. Tears filled my eyes, I know not why. I bent and put my forehead into the dust, and I kissed the lowest stone. When I kissed the stone, it felt as if my heart broke open and water gushed from it. I sobbed. I sobbed so loudly, and so without reason, that I felt ashamed of myself. Yet I could not rise from my knees until my father came to me and lifted me to my feet. He brushed the dirt from my face and shook the dust from my robe.

He said nothing about my childish behavior, just walked with me toward the river, which is not very far. His arm was around my shoulders all the while, which is something he had never done before.

We came to the river. Both of us were thirsty, and we drank from it.

"The water is clean," my father said, "for it descends a long distance from Kinneret, the lake of the north in Galilee."

"If the lake is drained by the river, Abba, will it not become empty and dry?"

"Never does it empty, for it is fed always by pure waters from the snows of the sacred mountain, which is Hermon, so high it is like unto a pillar of the heavens."

We sat down by the shore and ate bread and dried figs. My father dozed for a time, while I waded in the shallows.

There I collected twelve little stones, most of them like eggs in shape but some of them spheres, all of them smooth. It pleasured me to think that Joshua might have touched them with his feet as he crossed over. How fine they were, rolling about in the palm of my hand. I secured them safely in my carry-bag, and now they are always with me when I keep my eyes alert for signs of wolf and lion.

The wind is a friend to me, though it has moods. It cools me on hot days. It dries my hair and my robe after rain showers. Sometimes I listen to it, and on occasion I will hear music in it. Why is the wind singing? Where does it come from? Where is it going? Why can we not see it, save when it dresses itself in the yellow dust from the south or the white powder from the Sea of Salt? You cannot pick up wind or air in your hands. You cannot seize it, but you can learn about it by testing and appraisal. Whenever I hold my right arm before me and wave it back and forth, my hand feels its presence. Ah, ah, there is surely something there! It feels like thinnest water, a kind that cannot be contained within any shores. It is motionless at times, and at other times it flows gently, or strongly, going where it wills. I have come to believe that this invisible water in which we live is like the presence of the Most High. Sometimes he is silent; at other times, he moves mightily.

My one worry is that a too-loud wind might one day deafen me to the sounds of encroaching predators. This has not yet happened. I pray that it never does.

There are colors in the world. I like the blue sky very much. The red and blue and yellow wildflowers in the pasture bring surprise and delight, and they have many perfumes. I can admire, though only for a short time before I run for shelter, the clouds' purple and grey when a thunderstorm approaches. The sheep, who are like children to me, are white. Now and then a black one. They eat green, for green is the color of life for them. The tawny goats eat everything, all colors. The hens in our dooryard are orange or black or speckled with both. The brown skins of people's hands and faces, with blood pulsing underneath, is a thing I love. Though I long ago stopped the babyish habit of kissing my mother's cheeks, still I love her face, for she is a person full of love. My father is, too, in a different way.

From time to time, I have cut my fingers on sharp stones, and though it is an accident and I am irritated by my thoughtlessness, still, I think that red is very beautiful to the eyes. Think of red and brown side by side. Or red and green. Or red and yellow.

But why is there color in the world? We do not really need it. Even a boy as stupid as I am can understand important things without colors to tell me what is happening. Nothing much would change if everything were black and white and grey.

Then as I ponder it, I see that I am thinking wrongly. We do need colors. It may be that color is like music. We do not need to sing in order to live. And yet the heart does need it, for when we lift our voices we become full of high feelings, and then we are stronger.

I am thinking of brown again. It is the most common color of all. The soil beneath the pasture grass is brown. The soil in the low pocket where we grow our barley is darker brown. My working robe is light brown and full of patches. It is like an old friend to me. My brown sandal straps are always breaking, but mostly they serve me well and are easily repaired. My brown eyes see clearly—everyone attests that my eyes are brown. They say that in Jerusalem there are people, usually visitors from foreign lands, whose eyes are blue or green. My uncle Joash told my father that he once saw at a distance a princess from Egypt who was visiting the Palace and that the courtiers all swore her eyes were as purple as a rooster's tail. It is hard to believe, yet it may be true. One thing I know for certain is that warm love always comes through brown eyes. Or eyes so dark brown they seem as black as the noses of sheep. What if eyes had no colors? How strange it would be. As cold as snow.

Such are my foolish thoughts, day after day.

One day, as the sun crests its arc and is only beginning its descent, my eyes struggle to stay open, I do not know why. I had difficulty sleeping the night before, which may be the cause. At first I sit down to rest beside my little pool. Then I lie prone beside it to splash cool water on my face. It helps, but then I think I might take a little doze, ten breaths and a snore at the most. I cover my head with my scarf to keep out the bright light. How delicious it feels to close my eyes. Before I know it, I am dreaming.

In the dream I am walking in a strange land. All about me are rivers made by the hand of the Most High and a vast web of lesser rivers, very straight, made by men who are digging in the soil to lengthen the waterways and increase their numbers for the furtherance of growing crops. I am afraid, though at first there seems no reason to fear. Without warning, there arises before my eyes a great gate, as high and wide as a palace, all made of shining blue tiles, and upon it are monstrous lions and dragons roaring at me. I reach into my pouch for my sling and smooth stones, but it is empty.

Now I throw myself onto the ground in terror, hoping for the earth to swallow me, that I might be hidden and not eaten by the monsters. Yet the earth will not swallow me, and I am preparing to die when, behold, a man strides toward me, a man who looks as if he is made entirely of bright-shining light. He bends over me and places his hand upon my brow, and all fear flees from my heart. So great is the peace he gives me—like an unknown river inside me—that I am startled out of the dream, instantly awake. Rubbing my eyes, I sit up and find myself on my own quiet hill with my flock nibbling grass nearby, the pool trickling its sweet water, and the sun lower in the sky than it was before.

All people dream in their sleep, and it is but mind-pictures, worries and pleasures and confusions. And yet there is about this dream something like no other. The man seems very real to me, though I cannot see his face. Sitting beside the pool, I put my fingers on my brow, feeling the warmth of his touch still upon it. And the peace remains with me, fading slowly.

That night, after the evening meal, I tell my father about this dream. He ponders it for some moments, nodding and nodding, turning it over in his mind.

"Yezekiel, is it a mind-picture without meaning? Or is it a dream sent from the Most High? Who can weigh these questions rightly? I cannot see inside the head of a sheep, so how can I see inside yours?"

Still, he closes his eyes and ponders more.

Looking up, he says, "You must understand that in the life of a man, very few are the dreams sent from the Most High. Most people do not have even these. Such dreams are given for a purpose, though the purpose may be hidden from your eyes for a length of days or years."

"If this dream is sent from the Most High, Abba, who then was the man of light who came to me and bathed me in peace?"

Again he falls into silent thought.

"I do not know, Yezekiel. Was it a messenger from the Lord? Was it like the angel Raphael sent to Tobiah in answer to prayer. Have you asked for something in prayer?"

"For many things, Abba, for health for you and mother and my brothers, and all the family and the neighbors, and for Israel, that never again shall invaders come upon us."

"Well, all of us pray for these. I mean, did you ask the Lord for anything unusual for yourself?"

"No," I say, shaking my head, perplexed.

"It may be that he shows you your unseen guardian. It is said that angels guard each soul, though never do we see them with our eyes."

"Did not an angel wrestle with Jacob? Are angels as solid as ordinary men, Abba, or do they merely take on the appearance of men whenever they must wrestle with one?"

My father's brow wrinkles as he figures through the question. Coming to a conclusion, he says:

"The angel Raphael who helped Tobiah told him that he was in the *appearance* of man. On the other hand, the angel who wrestled with Jacob seemed to behave in a different manner. If an angel would wrestle a man and strike his hip on the thigh, he would surely have substance and muscle strength."

"Would he always be like that, or only when he is wrestling?"

"I do not know."

"But if an angel came to me in a dream, why would he do so? Why would he wish to show himself to me?"

My father's face grows troubled.

"Always you have a new *why* on your tongue, Yezekiel." He sighs. "Seldom do I have an answer for you."

Later, lying on my pallet in the dark, I wonder if my father fears for my mind. Or it may be that he believes the dream and fears for my future. I wish to ask the Most High to send me understanding about this, so that I may see the meaning of the dream. I lift up my arms into the space above, reaching for the Most High like a child. It *is* childish of me, I know, but I yearn to do this, do not even think about it. I just do it. Then the peace returns, nearly as strong as the peace I felt in the dream, and water runs from my eyes. It is a glad feeling, not sad.

Even so, no understanding comes. I do not understand why it does not come. I do not understand anything, really. The truth be told, I am stupid. I am, as Uncle said, the runt.

In the pasture the next day, I do not sleep, I do not dream. Yet I feel the presence of the unseen guardian. Like the airs around me.

Like the wind.

2

Youth

I AM THIRTEEN YEARS OLD NOW. I have become a man. It is a great gift from the Lord that this past year I have grown taller by the length of a forefinger. I am hungry all the time. My limbs and joints do not act as they are supposed to behave. But this is no great worry, I am told, because that is what happens when your body stretches. During recent months, I am becoming accustomed to my longer strides and wider shoulders. I can hurl a rock farther and harder than when I was a boy.

My mother, Naomi, smiles at me and places the palm of her hand on top of my head, then moves her hand to the top of her own head, leaving a nice gap. Yes, I am now taller than she is. Still, my brothers remind me that I am shorter than they are. I laugh at this; I tell them I can out-run them all. They chase me around the house and sheep pen and cannot catch me. The eldest, Iosif, though he has long been a grown man, still likes to play with us as if we are all a tumble of frolicking lambs. Their teasing is sometimes a little hard on me, but it is always in good fun, not like the bad brothers who sold the patriarch Iosif into slavery in Egypt. I know my brothers love me, because sometimes they will toss me up into the air and catch me before I fall and get hurt. They will kiss my head afterward. During the past year they can no longer lift me, as I have grown too heavy.

Iosif will inherit our flock when he is of the right age, but for now he is a worker in wood alongside my next brother, Isaac. They must walk a day's journey to purchase a straight, flawless tree length, which they bring home on our donkey's back. With great care and much time, they cut planks from the log, then fashion them into winnowing forks and plows, benches and smaller tools and clever little boxes with sliding lids. These boxes they sell in Jerusalem.

After Isaac comes Asher, who is closest to me in age, and like his name he is always happy, full of laughs and tricks. He fears nothing. He is eighteen now and is betrothed to a woman of a village over the hill to the west of us. Her family has a plot of good soil, well-watered, where they grow wheat and barley. There are no sons in their family, and the girl's mother is a widow, so it has been agreed by both families that Asher will inherit and care for them all.

In our family, I am called Yezekiel when things are formal, and often Yehezh when they are feeling fond of me, but only Asher calls me *Zek* or *Zeki*.

Today he says, "Zeki, our village is called *Little Bite of Bread*. Soon I will live in a *Big Bite of Bread*."

"Ah, ah, but not a big *House of Bread!*" I taunt him, to keep him humble.

He grins and pokes me on the shoulder with his fist. "Pay me respect, runt, or there'll be none of my bread for you!"

I poke him back on the shoulder. We both jump up, and I run. He chases me but cannot catch me, maybe because he is laughing so hard.

In my earliest years, my mother helped me learn the *aleph-bet*. She does not know how to read or write, but she knows the sounds for most letters well enough. She can inscribe the letter for the Most High with a fingernail in wet clay and is also able to write the names of each member of our family and those of her parents—may the Lord give their souls blessed rest—and her brother the priest. He is the learned one. My father is less so, and yet he can read aloud from scrolls of the Torah when the men pray together. My father is not educated, yet he is wise.

In my eleventh year, he taught me to read. It is not as difficult as people say. When you make the sound of a letter with your lips and your throat, you must then make the sound of the letter beside it, and the next, and the next. Then in your mind, you say them one after another, making them flow like water, and you get a word. You do that with enough words, and together they make a thought. You speak the thought, if you wish, or you muse on it. Thoughts connect to other thoughts and you get a story.

My brothers can spell their names, but they do not read or write at length. They are doing-men, not so much thinking-men. But they know many things, are constantly trading stories with each other, composing new ones, exchanging information about weather and dangers and the way to make useful tools with their hands. They are always learning through observation. And at times they will speak wise words.

Words are powerful. Think of *YHWH*. In the Torah, the holiest part is the Ten Commandments. In the Ten Commandments, the holiest word of all is the name of God. We may not even say his name aloud, so holy is it. You may write it but never speak it. If you write it on your doorpost with the blood of a lamb, as everyone does in our village once a year at Passover, it must never be erased. Most important, his holy name must never be erased from your heart.

Words become present in the world and do a task that we cannot see. We must take care not to impede their work.

Above all, we must never misuse them and, most important, never misuse the name of the Most High.

When I am given permission, always on a Sabbath day, I quietly read to myself from the scrolls that my father fashioned from cured lambskin, scripted with ink made of ground charcoal mixed with bitumen he found on the edge of the Sea of Salt. He owns three scrolls, copies he made from those belonging to Uncle Joash. The first contains the laws of Moses. The second contains the strongest prophecies of Isaiah. The third is about King David, whom my father loves with great devotion. He reads to his sons the story of David's life at least once a year. It is full of marvels and tells us much about the Most High. We have learned many of the king-psalms as well.

When trouble comes upon us, my father will pace about the house, his head covered with his shawl, whispering the words of little David facing Goliath, "The battle is the Lord's!" Whenever troubles come too swift and numerous upon our family, he will cry these words loudly as he strides around the house and sheep pen and up and down the pastures.

"The battle is the Lord's! The battle is the Lord's! The battle is the Lord's!"

Troubles always go away—swiftly or slowly, they go.

Words are powerful. Names are more powerful still.

One day, sitting beside my little pool in the pasture, I write the Holy Name on a flat stone with the charred end of a stick—יהוה—*YHWH*. With other stones, I make a small altar, no bigger than my hand. I put the flat stone on top of it. Now the word gazes up at the heavens and speaks in its own way. Maybe the Most High will see it and know that our family honors him. Without intending to do it, my thoughts are suddenly soaring high on the wind, and I open my mouth to make the shapes of his seven names: *YHWH, El, Eloah, Elohim, Shaddai, Ehyeh, Tzevaot*—O Most High, O God Almighty, O Lord of Hosts, O you who are *I Am!*

I breathe these words not knowing what will come next from my mouth. Then more words burble up inside me, like a spring that becomes a trickle that becomes a brook that becomes a mighty river that becomes a sea pouring forth from me. I do not understand the meanings of these words. Where do they come from? Where are they going?

My arms lift to the heavens, and tears run from my eyes. I know not why.

Our family walks to Jerusalem for this year's Passover. I am told by my parents that I cannot bring my sling and beloved Jordan stones with me, and I feel a little naked without them. Even so, my mother has sewn a fine robe for me with the white linen my father purchased in Jericho some years ago. The roll of fabric is now used up, most of it fashioned into Asher's wedding garment and a pillow stuffed with sweet herbs for his wife. There was enough left over for this robe, which mother says makes me look like a prince.

"A prince of sheep," I say to her with a smile and a kiss.

"It is time," says Father. "It is time to present you to the Lord as a man, as we did when you were a baby."

"The runt has grown tall and mighty," says Iosif, who is ambling along the road beside us, he and his wife and their three little children.

"How old are you now?" asks his wife, Myriam, a kindly person.

I hold out my right hand and spread my fingers and thumb. Two times I proudly lift it high in the air and a third time with three fingers.

"Thirteen!" declares my brother Isaac. "See how swift is

the passage of time, a bird on the wing. I held you in my hands, Yehezh, when *I* was thirteen."

"I am glad you did not drop me."

He laughs. "There be moments when I am sorry I did not."

Oh, my breath ceases and my heart pounds as we come up over a rise and behold Jerusalem before us, floating between heaven and earth. Oh, the mighty city, so vast and so beauteous!

We enter the southern gate in a crowd. The din of talking voices and braying animals is terrible. Each street and alley within the city walls is packed with endlessly shuffling feet and a Babel of languages. Many are the tribes and nations that have converged for the Passover. My mother holds my father's hand, my brothers carry their children in their arms, their wives the babies on their breasts in carry-slings. We take care not to be swept away and lost to each other. We are all gaping and overwhelmed. Asher and his bride are very moved, clinging to each other with moist eyes, for this is the first time they have come here as man and wife.

Above us on the heights I see the immense Temple, shining with gold, built by Solomon—Solomon the great king who was the son of a least-son like me. I cannot take my eyes from it.

We now arrive at the door of Uncle Joash's house in the lower region of the old City of David. Uncle, his wife, Sarah, and their son, Levi, greet us and bid us enter their home. They have prepared a meal for us all—it is extremely generous, and my parents thank them profusely. The talk around their table is convivial. After the roast lamb and herbs and unleavened bread, Sarah brings to the table a fat loaf of leavened bread. It is baked with fine wheat, honey, and bits of chopped fig, its crust running with melted butter. I eat too much of this.

After the meal, my brothers talk with Levi in their usual humorous manner, but my cousin does not respond in kind. It seems that he has become a very serious young man, with the headscarf of a newly ordained priest. Because Uncle Joash's role at the Temple is a minor one, because he is just one of hundreds like himself, his son is also of lowly position. Levi is not intolerant of us. He has welcomed us in his quiet way, with his usual smile and murmurs. He often played with us when he was a boy, and he once had a good sense of humor, but now I sense that he is filled with his new importance. He is devout and intensely dedicated to the Law and the service of the Temple rites. My brothers are devout men, too, but they also know how to have fun. They now try to draw Levi into their banter, as the older generation looks on, my parents and Aunt Sarah smiling, Uncle not.

Levi cuts off my brothers abruptly.

"The Passover is near!" he says with a reproachful look that silences them. "Do you not understand? Do you not know that the peoples in the world are beyond numbering? The holiest among these are the people of Israel. The holiest of the people of Israel is the tribe of Levi. Of the tribe of Levi, the holiest are the priests. Among the priests, the holiest is the High Priest."

"You are not yet the High Priest, Levi," says my brother Iosif with a large grin, to show that he speaks in goodwill.

Sudden silence falls on the room. Levi fixes Iosif with a cold look and turns away. Clearly he is offended, though he has no reason to be. I wonder why he is behaving this way. Though I once admired him and love him as one of my own, I now begin to wonder what has brought about this change in him. It cannot be the priesthood alone. Has he become proud and arrogant? Does he look down on us as uneducated country people?

Without warning, all the married women in the room begin chattering about diverse subjects.

"Play the flute for us, Yezekiel," my mother asks me with a smile. From my carry-bag I remove the flute and begin fingering a joyful piece composed by King David.

The tension passes, everyone relaxes.

My father and uncle sing the words in their deep voices, for they know every line of the king-psalms. Soon, other voices join in. Levi sits down on a bench at the back of the room and broods. Iosif goes and sits beside him. They are the same age, about thirty years. They have been friends since childhood. Iosif puts his arm about our cousin's shoulders. Levi returns the gesture, nodding and nodding. Nothing is said between them, though I can see by their gestures that the peace is restored. Even as my flute sings, I am thinking that Levi is not really proud or arrogant but is merely very serious about his new duties and is sorrowing that the world does not love the Lord Most High as he does.

That night, Uncle Joash and his wife sleep on a couch in Uncle's small library, their son on a pallet in the main room. A narrow staircase made of bricks leads to the second and third floors, where our family is apportioned spaces for our blankets and pallets. My parents and married brothers and their wives will have little privacy, but that does not matter, as we have all slept close to each other throughout our lives. I understand why young married people need a special kind of privacy, but I try not to think about that. I, the youngest, am instructed to sleep on the roof. A ladder leads up through a hole onto this flat open area that caps the house. Brick walls as high as my waist gird the four sides. The hard clay surface beneath my feet slightly tilts toward holes in a wall, for draining rainwater onto an alley beside the house.

I undo my sandal straps and wiggle my toes pleasurably. I unroll my thick wool blanket and lie down on it, putting my hands behind my head. I stretch my body, sighing with relief, looking forward to a good sleep. It has been a long day's walk from Little Bite of Bread. I gaze at the sky, expecting to see stars. There are stars enough, but they seem fainter here in the city. Maybe they are dimmed by the competing bright lights on Mount Zion, coming from the Temple. All around me are the upper floors of larger houses, a few with lamplight flickering in their windows. It is an unusual feeling to sense so many people nearby. From time to time, I hear hushed murmuring from behind the curtains in the closest houses. With the slightest effort I could toss a pebble across the gap and into a neighbor's room.

Though I am sliding toward sleep, I am curious by nature —I am always curious—and even when I am tired I cannot rest satisfactorily until this or that puzzle is investigated. I sit up again and crawl to the roof wall. I want to see if I can reach over and touch the wall of the next house, just to test how close it is. Kneeling now, I put forth my arm as far as it will go, and my fingers touch nothing. I bend at the waist and stretch farther. Still nothing but air.

There is a soft amber light coming from somewhere, allowing me to see the merest hint of the brick wall facing me. I look down into the shadows of the alley below. Nothing but darkness. Then I look right to the faintest glow from the street. I look left, and there, not six feet away, is an open window. Lamplight from the room's interior surrounds and illuminates a figure by the window—a young woman standing sideways. She is unclothed and is bathing her body with a wet sponge. Paralyzed for an instant, I cannot think, can hear no sounds other than the sudden pounding of my heart. Quickly, before I can be seen, I sprawl backward onto the roof. Gasping for breath, I sit with my back to the wall, my face in my hands. It is burning hot. The loud drumming in my heart shakes my chest.

Oh, Oh, what have I just seen! It is seared in my mind, a picture so vivid it seems I am still seeing it with my eyes. Slowly, slowly, my heart slows its drumming, and my face, though still hot, is no longer burning. Insane thoughts are raging in my mind: Jump into the air and fly to her! Climb over the wall next to her window and drop into her room. No, throw yourself off the roof into the darkness below. No, go down to the street and bang on the door of the house in which she lives. Beg her to marry you. Now. Now!

But I do none of these. It is all impossibility and madness. I am thirteen years old, after all. Her very great beauty would burn up my mind and then my body. For the moment, I am a plaything or prey of this passion that I know is what drives the rams and bulls and all manner of male things in this world, but have never before experienced with such power over me. Wave after wave washes through my body. Finally, it eases a little, and I am left shaken and alone in the cool of the evening under the stars.

I lift my face from my hands and gaze in every direction. Nothing has changed. The city sleeps, but I do not sleep. I get up and drag my blanket to the wall farthest from the beauteous young woman. I roll myself into it and try to escape into dreams. And strangely, strangely, I do begin to drift into the silence of the mind. It is caused by the exhaustion of the day's journey, no doubt, but there is also a feeling of coolness on my forehead. A small breeze has begun winnowing across the roof perhaps. Like a gentle hand upon my brow.

In the morning, I am awakened by a cock's crow and the cooing of mourning doves. The east is pale grey with a hint of pink spreading along the horizon. I feel poorly rested. My stomach is growling for food. I go down to the kitchen. The young woman's image remains in my mind, delicious and making me yearn to dwell on it, but I am no longer its prey. With some effort I can turn my thoughts elsewhere, fill up my mind with other things.

My aunt has left a platter of bread, a bowl of curds, and a basket of fruit on the kitchen table, along with jars of water and milk. Everyone in the house is still sleeping. I sit down on a bench and eat alone.

When I was a child, once a year my father would read aloud to us from his scroll of the life of King David. Always, he would pause as he began reciting the section where David is standing on the roof of his palace and sees a beautiful woman bathing. My father would condense the king's actual sins—lust, adultery, lying, and the murder of Uriah —into a general summation, saying only, with a glance in my direction, "David's grave mistakes." He skipped over a good deal of what followed until the battles and revolts resumed. Every year as I listened, my eyes wide with the excitement of the adventures of David, I kept silent as I sat on the floor beside the bread oven, taking it all in. Year after year, the part about Bathsheba and Uriah made no sense to me. Though I enjoyed the story of Nathan the prophet cleverly confronting the king with a parable, I was uncertain about what he meant exactly and confused by all the upset and bloodshed that followed. I felt much anger against Absalom his son and strained my mind to find reasons why the prince had committed such evil against his father. Just as confusing were David's anguished laments when Absalom died.

I grew ever more curious about what David's "grave mistakes" had been.

After I learned to read—actually it was the same summer when lions came from the south—I found myself alone in our house one day, and, overcome with curiosity, I took my father's box of scrolls from the shelf above his bed, and painstakingly, with my forefinger slowly tracing each word across the unrolled scroll, I read the whole story in detail. It was shocking. It was horrible. The great and noble man whom I had admired throughout my young life lay in ruins in my heart. I wept.

Now, I think I understand him a little better. Last night on the roof, I too gazed at a woman of great beauty, unclothed, unaware of my attention. I did not do what David had done, and yet I now know that his sins are as seeds within me.

It is a help that the greatest thing of all will fill my thoughts today, for we will climb Mount Zion to visit Solomon's Temple.

Our family, led by my cousin Levi, makes its way through a maze of streets upward to the heights on which the Temple stands. We have chosen the hour just after dawn, as it is cooler then. The sky is cloudless, promising a day of oppressive heat.

As we approach the gate that leads into the Temple's Outer Court, the streets become so congested with people that we can only shuffle along step by step, elbow to elbow with a multitude of strangers. There is even some pushing and shoving, which saddens me, for are we not all of us here for a holy purpose? Finally the crowd becomes a narrower column and enters the gate, with hundreds of people ahead of us, hundreds behind and more converging every moment. Inside the courtyard, paved with white stones, thousands are milling about, many standing silently with heads covered, bowing toward a wide stairway and a gate that leads deeper into the Temple Court. Most of those around us are crying out prayers, a few talking about mundane subjects such as the cost of the sacrificial animals and birds they carry in their arms, the rate of coin exchange, and suchlike.

Levi raises his voice, trying to be heard above the noise of the crowd:

"On the Day of Atonement, when the High Priest enters the Holy of Holies, he and he alone may speak the name of the Most High. That hour is sacred and awesome beyond measure."

"This we all know, Levi," declares my brother Isaac. "Do you think we are ignorant because we tend sheep and do not live in the city?"

Levi ignores him.

"That hour," he solemnly continues, "that hour is the moment of greatest peril for the High Priest, for if he keeps any evil thought in his mind, he will die. He will surely die at the hands of the Lord. And Israel, too, would be destroyed, and along with us the entire world would perish. Such is the weight upon his shoulders."

I protest, "But why would all Israel be destroyed—and the whole world—for the sins of one man?"

Levi wheels and faces me, his eyes blazing over my ignorance.

"God's world is great and holy," he declares, pointing to the sky with a forefinger. "The holiest land in the world is Israel. In Israel the holiest city is Jerusalem. In Jerusalem the holiest place is the Temple, and in the Temple the holiest place is the *Kodesh haKodashim*, the Holy of Holies. If the man who represents the people before God is defiled, then the whole world is defiled and unworthy of redemption. It must then be destroyed."

"What must be destroyed?" I ask.

"Israel. And the world itself."

I cannot stop myself from gasping, "All of it, *everyone*?"

My father catches my eye with a look that tells me to be quiet.

"Lead us onward, Levi," he says.

It is impossible for all the pilgrims to find space within the inner court. Though it is open to the sky and surrounds the great Temple, it is not as large as the outermost court. Many people are being turned back by the gate guards. But Levi in his priestly robe convinces a guard to let our family in.

Oh, the wonder of what I behold when we enter this space! Here, too, the crowd is so thick it is difficult to move, but above the heads of the milling pilgrims the Temple building rises before us. Levi informs us that it is thirty cubits high and stands on the highest point of land. The position of the morning sun is such that our eyes are dazzled by the reflection from its gold walls. The Temple is a little sun come down to earth, illuminating the world.

I can see the great bronze basin in the court's southeast corner where priests immerse themselves to purify their bodies in preparation for rituals. Levi says it is five cubits high and sits upon twelve bronze oxen, facing outward. I cannot see the oxen because of all the people standing in the way, but the basin rises high over all heads. Five cubits! That is the height of a man and a half. It must hold a huge amount of water—a little sea. Indeed, it is called the "molten sea".

Before the entrance to the Temple building is an altar on a platform higher than the courtyard, and smoke is continually rising from it. It is the Altar of Burnt Offerings.

Earlier this morning, my father purchased a newborn lamb in the marketplace. He has carried it in his arms all the way up Mount Zion. Now, to my very great surprise, he turns to me and says, "Yezekiel will present it to the priest."

He places the lamb into my arms, where it nuzzles its nose into the crook of my elbow, docile. I stroke its head.

I am confused, for the tradition is for the father of a family to present a sacrifice to a priest.

"Abba, I do not understand," I say. "I do not know what to do with the lamb."

"Just give it to the priest when you come to the altar steps," he says. "Go forward, Yezekiel."

As I move hesitantly away from my kin, I overhear my eldest brother Iosif say to cousin Levi, "It is right. Yezekiel is the purest of us all."

Instantly, the image of the beautiful woman I saw last night is in my mind. I push all thoughts of her away and gaze instead at the lamb. Trembling, feeling sorry for this small creature in my arms, so trusting, so gentle and weak, I join the line that is approaching the altar. There are thirty or forty people ahead of me. I think of Abraham and Isaac. What did Isaac feel when his father bound him and laid him on the altar? I can now smell blood in the air. Can the lamb smell the blood? It begins to bleat and I stroke its head. Tears are in my eyes. Why is this so? I have seen lambs and sheep slaughtered all my life and have helped with it, too.

Step by step I move forward, following the people in the line ahead of me. When one after another approaches the lowest step of the altar of sacrifice, a priest takes each animal or bird in his hands, all the while murmuring prayers. His voice is unceasing, and he does it rapidly and without feeling. The people who bring the sacrifice also say prayers, though more fervently, a few seconds only, and then they must turn away to make room for the next person. It seems hurried to me, though I can understand why it must be, with so many of us waiting to bring our sacrifices. Another priest carries the lamb or dove up the steps to the altar, where it is quickly killed with a knife. The blood drains into a large basin. The body is washed in one of the smaller lavers by the molten sea. After that, the sacrifice is laid onto the fire. The smell of burning fur and feathers nearly makes me gag. Smoke rises unceasingly, so thick that it blocks my view of the Temple doors.

There are three people ahead of me now. The lamb is bleating pitifully. My soothing words and stroking no longer calm it. It is struggling, and I am forced to hold it tightly.

Then I am in a panic because I do not know the ritual words for offering. Why did my father not tell me what to say?

Now the priest stands before me, his face a mask, his mouth still murmuring prayers.

"O lamb of God," I whisper. Then the priest reaches forward, impatient, and takes the lamb's legs in both hands and pulls it from my arms. He passes it to another priest who climbs the stairs to the altar. The lamb is now crying loudly. I turn away, blinded, whispering, "Have mercy upon me, a sinner, O Lord Most High, have mercy upon your people Israel."

Back I go to my family, who stand waiting for me, my father and my brothers nodding in approval. Levi has covered his head with his prayer shawl and appears to be praying.

"Abba," I stammer, "Abba, I did not say the proper prayer, because I did not know it. Will the Most High accept the lamb?"

"He will accept the offering," says my father. "Did you pray to him?"

I repeat for him the prayer I made while giving up the lamb.

"It is good," says my father.

"It is not correct," says Levi looking dubious.

"It is from the boy's heart."

I am still sad, sorrowing over the lamb that had trusted me and now is dead or dying. And sorrowing that I am such a fool that I had not thought to ask for the correct words to pray. The family loses interest in me as they raise their arms toward the billows of smoke on the platform above us. I step back, and hidden from their eyes I drop to my knees on the hard paving stones and cover my face with my hands.

The little spring within me begins to burble, and words arise—though they are not exactly words but meanings mixed with feelings. All sound fades from my ears. The spring becomes a trickle, then swiftly swells into a river that flows from my heart into my mouth as music that is soundless. And though the sorrowing is strong within it, there is a stronger joy, drawing me upward as if it would lift me above the court and into the sky.

But no. The river soon declines into a stream, then a trickle, then ceases altogether. Once more I am kneeling on hard stone, and my knees are hurting. I hear the crowd around me again. I hear my family reciting the *Shema* prayer in unison, "Hear, O Israel, the Lord our God, the Lord is One!"

I open my eyes. The first thing I see is an older man

standing a few paces from me, gazing at me with great still-
ness. Clearly, this is one of the poor. He is barefoot, his
thin body covered by threadbare weave. He is grey-haired,
long-bearded, his face is brown and wrinkled. He is shorter
than I am. So insignificant is this man that I doubt anyone
else has noticed him. He is the sort one looks away from.
Yet his eyes are unlike any I have known until now. They
are human in all ways, and yet I sense that those eyes look at
things and understand them. They are far-seeing eyes. His
face is without discernible expression, though I can feel he
is pondering me. I reach into my carry-bag and pull from it
the only coin I have, the smallest in the realm. I offer it to
him. Alms cover a multitude of sins.

The old man smiles and gestures that I should put away
my coin, he will not accept it.

I cannot turn my gaze from him. I am curious about him
—nay, more than curious. My soul is stirred by his soul,
for though I cannot see the inner life of this man, I feel it.
He does not command me to look at him. I merely look
because he looks at me in a way no other ever has.

He steps forward and raises both of his hands over my
head, though he does not touch my hair.

He says: "The Most High exalts speaks to the Most High
strengthens."

This utterance makes no sense to me. And then I remember that my name Yezekiel means *YHWH strengthens*. And
there is the name *Yirimiahu*, Jeremiah, which means *YHWH
will exalt*.

I stare at him, my mouth open in perplexity.

"You are a child of the desolation," he says. "When you
are of age, you shall be captive in chains, yet your soul shall
be free. He will strengthen you."

I rise to my feet, astonished now. Who is this man that

he speaks with such authority? And who is the *he* that he refers to?

The old man turns away and disappears into the crowd.

"Abba, Abba," I say, tugging at my father's sleeve. I tell him about the old man and what he said. My brothers and Levi remove their head scarves and turn to me, listening.

"Pay no heed, Yezekiel," says Levi with a toss of his head and a dismissive wave. "The courts of the Lord are infested with madmen."

3

The Servant

I T IS A LAMENTABLE FACT that I have not become as tall as I had hoped for. After the burst of growth some years ago, my body slowed its ascent and then stopped. I am still the shortest of all my brothers. I am an average man. My mother alone tells me that I am comely of face. Other members of the family tease me for being homely. No matter.

I have lived here in Jerusalem for the past three months. The city can be very exciting at times, and it is always interesting. Not a day passes that I fail to see numerous curious sights. The colors, the smells, the constant noise sometimes make my head spin. I have witnessed a riot against the heavy new taxes imposed by the king, though I stood at the edge of it, astonished and full of pity for those people who let themselves become so angry. Daily I see beautiful things, such as the faces of children, the tenderness of mothers carrying babies in their arms, the kindness of many toward the old people who hobble here and there, sometimes mumbling to themselves, sometimes lost.

The number of merchants selling fabulous wares is another astonishment. It seems that almost every street has dozens of awnings beneath which one finds not only the usual bread, fruit, and vegetables, but also jewelry from Africa and Persia, exotic foods, spices from the Orient, and cloth dyed in colors that I have never seen before in fabrics:

indigo and saffron, pale rose and deep purple. I have no money to speak of, so I cannot buy anything of value, but it is pleasurable to admire these things.

I go exploring whenever I am free from my Temple duties and my tasks at the house of studies, which I share with forty young men, age eighteen to twenty-four. Those who are older live in a house higher up the hill. Like us, they are training to be priests and will be anointed when they are thirty years of age. If I persist, that holy day will come for me ten years from now.

Uncle Joash and Aunt Sarah could have permitted me to live with their family, as a few students do who have kin in the city. But Uncle insisted it would be better for me to mingle with my own kind, day and night. Aunt Sarah pleaded with him to let me stay in their home. Levi was not against it; he was sympathetic to me but guarded his opinion in deference to his father. Uncle stood firm, and so here I am.

Like the other students, I wear a dark brown robe provided by the Temple authorities. It is a work-tunic, the hem touching the base of my knees. My waist is bound by a black cincture made of braided cloth. My sandals are my own, and not doing well, as they have given years of service. I must buy new ones soon, when I can see my father again and ask for money. My loins are girded with an old cloth that is none too clean, and I am grateful that no one else can see this. Though priests must wash several times a day, we young ones may wash our bodies and clothes only once a week in the stone bath in the enclosed courtyard behind our house, on the day before the Sabbath. This is somewhat perplexing to me, as the reputation of the Temple is known widely as one of ritual purity, the purest in the world. We students are not bound by rituals in this regard, yet it seems to me that once a week is not enough ablution. We are usually more pungent than I would prefer. Of course, whenever I wish, I may wash my face, hands, and feet in a bucket, especially before going to the Temple, and again when I return to the house as the sun is setting.

Mornings are spent here in our house, studying the Torah under a priest-instructor, and also the later books written after Moses' time. I am deeply absorbed in them, and often find myself moved in my heart as I learn more and more about our people's past, the great judges and kings who led us, and those through whom the Most High spoke to us, that is, the prophets. I am coming to believe that it is a perilous thing to be a king. It is a glorious and beautiful thing to be a prophet, though it must be admitted that these men suffered hardship at times.

After study comes the midday meal, and then we are off to the Temple. Throughout the afternoon, my duty is to carry charcoal staves from a cache in one of the storehouses attached to the Temple complex and to feed the fires on the sacrifice altar. Even with so many of us serving, we scurry back and forth, hour after hour, with only short pauses for a drink of water and a brief evening meal, which is taken in a wooden hall attached to the wall that separates the Temple compound from the king's palace. We are well-fed, mainly with lentil stews, vegetables, bread both leavened and plain. Smoked fish is an occasional treat, but rarely do we taste meat. Priests, of course, are permitted to save a portion of the sacrifice meats for their own consumption. The priests eat elsewhere, on the second floor of a finer brick building that is backed by a wall of the inner court.

From time to time, Levi will come to the house of studies to visit with me personally, asking after my welfare and taking me for a short walk. When this first happened, he brought me a piece of cooked sheep's meat wrapped in oiled cloth.

"I thank you, Levi," I said with true gratitude. "Where did you obtain it?"

"It is the son-portion of my father's portion from the Altar of Sacrifice."

"This greatly helps me," I said, opening the wrap. "Little meat do we eat, though I am glad of fish. Always I have eaten mutton and have missed it extremely since coming to Jerusalem."

"Save it for later or eat it now, as you wish", said Levi with a smile.

I bit into the meat and chewed it avidly. It was lamb, very tender.

"Does your father know?" I asked between bites.

He paused before answering. Then said in a quiet voice, "No."

I pondered this as I finished eating.

"I will bring you more when I can," he said.

And so he did. And so he does.

We the servants are divided into teams that eat at different hours, lest the fire go out. We all smell of smoke and sweat. I am not used to being so dirty. I miss my little spring very much. Its water was cool in summer, cold in winter, but always sweet. Sometimes as I lie awake in the sleep-room, listening to the snores and muttered dreams of my fellows, I yearn for the flock, their soothing voices, the healing green of the slopes, the colors of the open sky from dawn until dusk. I long for my flute, for the freedom to play it whenever the spirit of music moves me. In the dark I sometimes lift my right arm, bent at the elbow, and swing my remembered sling in circles and hurl my invisible twelve stones.

The Servant

I lament that I cannot practice, and then my mind asserts itself, assuring me that such a weapon is not needed in this city, surrounded as it is by the mightiest ramparts in the world. I do not need the weapons of my youth, for my life is now without predators and is set in a new direction.

It is what I have chosen. I wanted it. I begged my parents' permission to pursue it, even though they desired me to remain at home and work with the flock and our land. Nor did Uncle Joash desire me to come to him. I was unsuited to Temple service, he told my father; I was not intelligent or holy or blessed with any other quality than the ability to ward off wolves.

During my last years at home, I had felt from time to time a hint of the mysterious sense that came to me during my childhood. I am speaking of several things here, feelings and moods, but mainly the awareness I had when dreaming of the man-of-light and my memory of his infrequent presence during my hours awake, his hand upon my brow, bringing with it peace. Above every other consideration, it informed me that this is the way my life must go, here in Jerusalem, the holy city. With the slightest effort, I could have resisted it, but I did not. Little by little, I abandoned myself like a child playing in the wind, and I let it carry me.

To be plain about the matter, despite all objections from my family, the Temple authorities need servants, and the numbers who want such a position are not many, as the work is arduous and there is only a token payment, a few small coins per week from the Treasury, hardly enough to buy a new set of sandals. Of course, food and shelter are provided. I believe that all of us remain in service because of the promise of an exalted future after long years of labor and study.

Did I say *all* of us? I would like to think so. And yet

among the students there are some who flout the rules of the house, who use their coins to purchase wine and will drink to excess after stealing out at night to prowl through the city. It is a shameful thing. I do not speak of it to the house elder, for I hope that these young men will become more steady on their feet and in their souls. It is not my task to judge them.

Those who study here are all Levites in origin, and, while it is true that among my fellows there are those inspired by a yearning for the beauty of the Lord's house and the glorification of his Holy Name, many came here because they are poor. The gate opened before them, and they ran through it. It was a means to live and survive, a portal into a future brighter than what was offered in their homes. A minority are from wealthier families, and I suspect they were sent here in hopes of correcting their unruly temperaments.

Most are from the towns around Jerusalem, a few from the north in Galilee, and others from the lower Jordan, mainly Jericho, and there is even a faithful young man from Idumea. I am sorry to say that some of my fellows despise him, as he is cruder than the rest of us, coming as he does from the rugged and less fruitful lands south of Judea. Moreover, as an Idumean, or Edomite, he is of mixed race, for his ancestor Esau married a pagan Hittite. Though I am a son of Jacob, so to speak, and he is a son of Esau, I have read in the Sacred Scripture that Israel is forbidden to abhor an Edomite because both Jacob and Esau were the children of Isaac and Rebekah and the grandsons of Abraham and Sarah. He is of the tribe of Levi, without doubt, and surely a descendent of Aaron, otherwise he would not be permitted to serve here. Somewhere during the many past centuries, there must have been a re-splicing of the tribal weaves through marriage. Even so, the blood of Esau still flows in his veins.

His name is Issachar ben Ephraim, and I like him. We are the same age, and we both love sling-skill, and both of us miss the opportunity to practice it. Sometimes, after a day's labor with the charcoal, we walk back to the house of studies together and pick up small pebbles kicked to the side of the street. We both grin at each other, and, without saying a word, we throw by hand our little shots down the cobbles, to see whose goes farther. We can do this rarely, only when a street is empty of people, which does not happen often.

Though he is an extremely silent person, now and then we will talk with each other. He is from a village near Seir, in the mountainous regions southeast of Moab and the Sea of Salt. When he was a youth, he tells me, he liked to hunt —rather, he needed to hunt, for his family had many children and barely enough soil on which to grow their barley. Though his father is a priest, the man toiled as the lowest laborer in the fields of others, near and far. A few coins and a portion of the grain were his wages, never enough to feed his family.

I think of our family's forty ewes, our plentiful meat, and the hillside ringing with the bleating at lambing season. Beside them in my mind, I place his family's three milking goats, which were the waters of life for his brothers and sisters.

Though Issa is the shortest of all the students and rather thin, there must have been enough to eat during his growing years, for he is muscled in arm and thigh. Due to a lifetime spent under a broiling sun, his hair is not black like mine; it is light brown streaked with dark gold. He wears it long like mine. While he is good with the sling, when he was younger he mainly used bow and arrow, which he made with his own hands. This is a craft I have never learned, for my people are farmers and shepherds.

"What did you hunt when you lived in your homeland?" I ask him.

"Quail and hare. Now and then I was blessed to slay a deer or a wild goat," he says. Then bowing his head with troubled eyes, he adds, "We are forbidden by the holy Law to consume animals or birds that eat carrion, and yet I once brought down a fox and ate it from very great hunger."

This is a remarkable admission, a mark of his trust in me.

"Do you think the Lord will condemn me for it?" he asks.

"Of the judgments of God I have little understanding, Issa, but do not the prophets tell us that he is greatly merciful to his children?"

"This I hope," he says, looking up to meet my eyes, his shame beginning to leave him, though he is still uncertain.

"And remember David eating the showbread when he and his followers were starving. It, too, was forbidden."

"This is so," he says, nodding, yearning to believe me.

"Surely you could have hunted stray sheep and lambs," I add.

"Never," he says, drawing back his head in surprise. "Even a lost sheep roaming alone in the hills belongs to someone. I will not touch it."

"But what if its owner cannot be found?"

"It may yet find its way home. Is its life not hard enough?"

"True," I say. And it comes to me that Issa, though small and poor in appearance, is great and noble in his soul. He studies most earnestly and is probably among the most learned among us, yet he does not push himself forward. He never reacts to the contemptuous words that fellow students torment him with—they call him "red stew", "pottage face", "furry" and "bad twin". He is none of these, of course, but surely he must feel such taunts, though they are occasioned by one man's sin many ages ago. He does not laugh them off, and neither does he retaliate. He merely grows silent, suffering within himself. He seems to accept humbly his status as an alien among us.

"Two nations are in your womb," the Lord said to Rebekah. "And two peoples from within you will be separated; one people will be stronger than the other, and the older will serve the younger."

It is a hard saying, and it sorrows me. Even so, the Lord did not *make* Esau give up his birthright; it was Esau himself who made that choice because he was a godless man and did not hold his birthright of any value.

But Issa is not like his remote ancestor. He is very much more like his recent ancestor Aaron.

Oh, so many questions intrigue me. For example, how many thousands of forebears are in each one of us? How does the Lord sift the goodness and badness in each of us? Are good and evil passed down through the blood, or are they learned as we grow up from birth to manhood? There is a saying among the common folk, "The father has eaten sour grapes, and his children's teeth are set on edge." I like this for its wittiness, but at the same time I feel uneasy about it because it shifts the blame for wrongdoing onto our ancestors. Is not each person responsible before God for his own deeds?

Why does cruelty spring forth from some of my fellow students? I do not understand them. Nor do I understand why there is so much pain and folly in our past? I think of Cain slaying the righteous Abel from sheer jealousy. And there is Ishmael, Abraham's natural son, who was banished to the desert with his mother and whose descendants have brought many troubles upon Israel. I think especially of Iosif and his coat of many colors, sold by his own brothers into slavery in Egypt. What is this evil in the human heart? Where does it come from?

Am I without sin? No, I am like all other men. During the first week when I came to live in Jerusalem, I was eager to know if the beautiful young woman, whom I had seen naked for an instant, still lived beside my uncle's house.

I thought I might learn more about her from Levi. We were standing in the street before his front door.

"The houses crowd close to each other," I began, affecting a casual tone of voice, looking all around me. "Do you know your neighbors well?"

"Some yes, some no," he said with a shrug.

I pointed my finger to the next door building, the one in which the beautiful young woman lived.

"For example, this house," I said.

"A merchant's family."

"Are they friends to your family?"

He pursed his lips, considering. "A little."

"Do they have children?"

I knew they had at least one child, but I wanted to ease the conversation toward the precious question.

"Four children."

"Ah, boys and girls?"

Now Levi gazed at me with a pondering expression, his eyes suddenly amused.

"She is betrothed, Yezekiel, and soon to fly far beyond your reach."

"What? Who?" I exclaimed, pretending innocence, but I could feel my face growing hot.

Levi laughed and slapped me on the shoulder. He said no more about it, which was an act of kindness on his part.

So there it is. Not sin as such, though my heart's attraction is strong. Not an outright lie, but surely an exercise in guile.

During the days following that revelation, I was much distracted with settling into the house of studies and the endless city fascinations. This helped me turn my thoughts in more wholesome directions. Above all, the Holy Name protected me. I whispered it often, and in the darkness of the sleep-room I breathed it continually. Before long, the naked image faded into a remote portion of my mind and my face no longer burned. I cried a little with the sadness of loss but recovered quickly. My eyes, my mind, my heart belong to the Lord, and this I must never forget. For an image of sin can lead to actual sin. Then the sin can lead on to another sin, and then to worse sins.

My consolation is the Temple. It is the site of my arduous labors, the source of my aching muscles and grimy flesh, but it is also the place of my greatest joy. There are moments when the steady stream of sacrifices grows thin, the fire is banked high, and I may rest for a few moments. I turn toward the steps leading from the altar up to the elevated level on which the Temple stands. It is the center of the world; it is the measureless, invisible light of the Most High shining upon the whole earth. It is the house of glory. Whenever I gaze at its open entrance, so high, so dazzling to the eye with its gold facing, and the deeper, richer gold of the *Hekal*, the main chamber within, my heart pounds and my breath escapes me. I yearn to fall on my face and worship the Presence within it. I did this once when I was a boy, when the crazed old man spoke to me.

It is too far and too high for me to see the entrance to the Holy of Holies, which I have heard is hidden by a veil of blue, purple, and crimson linen. Beyond this veil is the dwelling place of the Name of God. There, too, resides the Ark of the Covenant, guarded by two mighty olive-wood carvings of seraphim. In our generation, only the High Priest has ever seen it, but there are accounts from the past that describe it. I can only barely imagine what the seraphim look like. It is said that their wood is overlaid with gold. They are a type of human form, with wings so large that their outspread span touches the walls. Considering the size of the Temple, they must be immense. They are at least ten cubits high, Levi tells me. He has never seen them, nor has his father, but Scripture informs us about what they are like.

I love the Ark with a love that surpasses all human passion, and though I cannot see it with my eyes, it burns ever brightly in my imagination. It contains our history; it is a memorial of our exodus from slavery into freedom in the Promised Land. It is vastly greater than Joshua's twelve stones at Gilead. It carries the Ten Commandments written by the finger of the Most High on two tablets of stone. Above all, it is the Mercy Seat where God comes down to earth and is present to his people.

Whenever I have a few moments to pause from my duties, I turn to face the Temple, and I breathe the Holy Name —I breathe it because it is unlawful to speak it aloud. Then, for an instant, I am within the innermost place where the Name resides, and I am at one with it. I feel the fire that does not give pain; my body, too, is all sweet fire; and yet so stern and mighty is this flash of the Holy Presence that I drop to my knees on more than one occasion. Sometimes I fall prone on my face. This has brought upon me mild rebukes from the altar priest or his assistants, but I cannot help myself. When I am scolded thus, the fire fades in my breast and I stagger to my feet and resume my tasks, even as

The Servant

tears continue to stream from my eyes. I am an overflowing cistern.

The Master of our house of studies has rebuked me at times, saying that my labor is to carry charcoal, not to pretend to be a High Priest.

"Do not be a foolish boy," he says in a worried tone. "Devotion in the young is a fine thing, but it is a shallow stream that runs fast and then runs dry."

He may be right. I do not understand myself. It is better to obey.

A year passes. And another and another. Our routine never varies, yet I am content. Rare are the times when I may see my family; they come up to Jerusalem for the Passover or the Day of Atonement. They bring me gifts of dried fruit, smoked lamb strips, a pot of spiced lentils, and a loaf of my mother's best bread. We rejoice in each other's embraces, exclaim over the bits of news from Little Bite of Bread, the coming of a new baby, the little children becoming big children, the betrothals of the young. We sorrow together over the deaths of the village's elderly, remembering them and telling good stories about them. We share a single meal, which is permitted only once a year. Our time as a reunited family is always too short.

This year during our visit, I ask my father to send me animal skins from home, that I might cut and sew new sandals by my own hand. Neither he nor I have enough money to purchase a pair from a city craftsman. Though I save my pitiful coins for many months, they never amount to enough. Besides, there are times when I see a beggar wailing by the Temple gate with hand outstretched. Into a diseased or skeletal palm I place what I have saved. My heart grows warm with pity, but my feet grow ever more sore.

By the Rivers of Babylon

My father, Buzi, sends me goat and sheep hides through my brothers Iosif and Isaac, who come to the city once in a while to sell their little wooden boxes. All their profits must go to feeding their families. My father is unable to obtain a thick hide of oxen, which is needed for the sole of a shoe. I cut the goat and sheep skins with the copper knife he purchased for me when I was a child and wrap layers around my feet, securing them with thongs. It is sufficient for a little protection, but my heels and toes quickly wear through them.

Long months stretch between visits with family members, and yet I never feel alone. There are consolations in prayer and new understandings that come to me in quiet moments at night, and always I may drink from the clear waters of Scripture, and daily I may raise my eyes to the light of the Temple, even as I serve it in the lowliest tasks.

Even so, from time to time I see things that worry me, for it seems to me that certain conduct among the priests is unsuitable to the holiness of the Temple. I hear them laughing loudly over their meals in their house attached to the Temple building, uttering mocking phrases and sneers. More than once I have seen sacrifice priests stagger under the influence of wine as they leave their meal-hall and head toward the altar. Out on the pavement in the altar courtyard, I see expressions on their faces that are contemptuous of the people who bring offerings. They despise the poor with their sparrows and meager coins. I have more than once seen a sacrifice priest receive a bag heavy with coins from a wealthy pilgrim, stuff it beneath his robe, and then lead him to the head of the line. I have seen certain priests eyeing the beautiful maidens in the crowd and murmuring lustful remarks to each other, subtly smirking and pointing. I say nothing. All men are sinners. I, too, am a sinner. Lord, have mercy upon me, a sinner!

Still, it grieves me, because this mountain—the Mountain of the Lord—is the holiest place in all the world. Do these priests not believe in what they profess? While they are fastidious in their ritual duties, have they given themselves permission to be inwardly rotten? Surely they understand that God desires the inner life of a man to conform to his outer conduct. It seems to me that if they know this and yet do not reform their ways, they are in secret revolt against the Most High God. Is it possible to revolt against him while still believing in him? It may be that they remain in their role only for the fine foods and prestige that come with it.

There is lamentable news. Issa has been informed by the superior of our house that he must leave. These instructions have come from higher on the mountain, from officials in the Temple itself.

When I learn of these sad tidings, I make haste to find him in the little courtyard behind the house. He is seated on the cobbles, cross-legged, intently focused on some work with his hands.

I am shocked by his appearance. He has put on sackcloth and has shaved his head with a sharp knife. There are red nicks all over his skull. This is dress for extreme penance. Why has he done it?

"Issa, I have heard! Why do they send you away?"

He looks up and says nothing. He has not shaved his sparse beard. I, too, have a struggling beard, but my skull hair is thick and long; it has not been cut since my childhood. Many of the students cut their hair short above the shoulders and bind their foreheads with bands of cloth. It is cooler in summer and much easier to keep clean. They do not scratch their pates as often as I do. My custom is to braid my hair in a single rope down my back and fasten its tail with a cord.

"Why are you dressed penitentially?" I ask Issa in consternation. "And why have you made such a savage affair of your head?"

He gives no answer and merely resumes sewing a thick piece of leather, affixing heel strap and toe strap to the foot-base of a sandal. Its completed mate is by his feet.

I sit down on the ground and watch him finish the task.

"Why do they send you away?" I repeat my question more urgently.

"I do not know," he murmurs.

"You wear a sackcloth robe. Have you done wrong?"

"I have done no wrong before God and man," he says. Though his tone is without bitterness, there is sorrow in his eyes. His love of the Temple, the Presence of the Lord, is very deep.

He completes the sandals and sets them side by side on the ground. They are remarkably fine ones, the soles thick, the binding straps wide, the supple thongs tapered for ease in tying. They are large size, certainly larger than his own small feet.

"These sandals are for you, Yezekiel," he says.

I am stunned. When I can find my voice, I say, "Forgive me if I speak boldly. You have so little and yet you offer me this treasure, these finest of fine-wrought shoes."

He nods but gives no explanation. It is true we are friends, but such a gift is too much. I stare at the sandals, not wanting to touch them.

"Now I return to my family and my own country," he says. "I will think of you, for you have been as a brother to me, though I am a wayfarer in a strange land."

"The mountain of the Lord is as much yours as it is mine, Issa, and I think it is more yours than for many who reside here."

He does not respond to this.

I go on: "Ah, Issa, Issa, perhaps the better part has come to you. The realm is far from holy, and it seems to me that a sickness festers in the Temple itself."

His eyes cloud over. "I agree with you," he says in a broken voice.

"Is that why you cut off your hair and wear sackcloth— as penance for others?"

"Yes," he admits with some reluctance. "Only the Most High can save it now."

I wonder what he means by *it*. The situation of lax observance? The Temple? Israel?

"Oh, how can one stand firm in such times as these?" I ask, shaking my head in dismay.

He ponders this, gazing at me steadily, this man of swift glances and usually lowered eyes.

"Yezekiel, think of the arrow that slays the deer," he says. "Where does it come from?"

"Where does it come from, you ask? Issa, arrows are made everywhere in the world, and they are all from wood."

"This is so. But where does wood come from?"

"Forests, groves, the thickets along river banks."

"Yes, numberless generations of trees and bushes rise and fall, making the soil rich. From this soil grow fresh bushes and willows, saplings and mighty trees. Yet one cannot make an arrow from a full-grown tree, no matter how hard and straight the trunk is. One cannot make an arrow from bushes and willows, which twist and turn, always bending this way and that."

"An arrow is made from a straight branch or a newborn sapling, is it not?"

"Straight branches are few, and saplings are soft because they are young. They have countless small branches that make knots, which are weak spots in the shaft."

"How, then, do you find a right arrow shaft?"

"From time to time, a sapling will arise that is supple yet stronger than the rest. It is straight, and it has few branches. From such a sapling I cut an arrow length, and then I dry it and temper it over fire."

"Over fire? Is that not a risk?"

"One must know the character of the wood. As it dries, one senses how much fire it can endure without setting it aflame. Heat and cold, heat and cold, again and again, make it ever stronger."

"A long process."

He looks directly into my eyes, which is not his usual habit.

"You are that sapling," he abruptly says, and then pauses. "Though you do not yet know it."

What is he saying? Does he think I am like a sapling or an arrow? If so, why? He takes a breath and sits straighter.

"And that is why I give you these new sandals, Yezekiel."

I receive them into my hands and thank him.

"Put them on," he commands me with a smile.

I put them on and savor the feel of the new-cut leather and hardy straps. I stand and walk about the courtyard, smiling broadly at such a gift, at the ease with which my feet move inside them, with no loss of security. They grip my foot shape firmly and yet bestow freedom.

"A king's sandals!" I exclaim.

"No," he answers. "A king is a mighty tree. You are small, Yezekiel . . . but straight and true."

Later I walk with Issa to the city's south gate. I wear his gift on my feet. He strides along beside me in his straw footgear, bound with scraps of leather cording. Arriving at the gate, I take my dust scarf from around my neck. It is the one of lamb's wool my mother wove for me when I was thirteen years old. It is ivory colored with black stripes. I place it about his neck. I reach out my right hand and gesture that he must open the palm of his right hand. Into it I place the arrowhead I unearthed from the soil beside my spring, many years past.

"It is a sign between us, Issa, and a memorial of our friendship. You are the hunter. Many ages have passed since this arrowhead flew. May you make it soar again."

He nods and places it carefully into his carry-satchel. No more is said between us—that is, no more is said with spoken words. Presence is a kind of language, and he knows this. We exchange one last look, and then he turns away, shouldering his meager possessions. He walks with determination but without haste toward the lands he came from— beyond Judea, not as far as the desert, but on the edge of the barrens nonetheless. I watch him until he passes over a rise in the road and is gone. I am surprised by the overwhelming sorrow I feel.

Returning to the house of studies, my thoughts are a tumble of uncertainties. He has said that I am an arrow made from a sapling. Or perhaps he meant I am a sapling that might become an arrow. But if I am to be an arrow, what is my purpose, for I am neither hunter nor warrior. I am a person of peace and prayer.

The next day, after the Sabbath meal, I ask the Master of our house if I may speak with him privately. He grunts and leads me to the study room.

"Master, why has Issachar ben Ephraim been sent from us?"

The man shrugs.

"I do not understand why he was dismissed," I say, careful to keep my head bowed respectfully.

"He is an Edomite," says the Master, using the older term for Idumeans. "He never belonged with us."

"But he is Hebrew and a Levite like us. He is devout and more studious than many of my fellows."

A cold eye is now turned on me. The Master makes a dismissive gesture of his hand.

"He is a fanatic. He is inflexible."

"But—"

"You, too, are devout and studious, Yezekiel ben Buzi. Beware that you do not become an inflexible fanatic. Do not question decisions made by your superiors, lest you, too, be cast out."

I bow my head lower and say nothing.

He points to the shelf of scrolls, and in a harsh voice he says, "Do not ever question me again in this way. Now take the scroll of Judges and read from beginning to end. In it, you will learn true devotion to the Most High."

He leaves in a swirl of robes. Night is falling, so I find a wax taper and kindle it from the oil lamp that is kept ever aflame on a ledge beneath the letters for the Lord's name יהוה cut into a white wall stone. With the taper, I light three little oil lamps and set them on the study table. I sit down on a bench and begin to read. The scroll is a long one. I have read sections of it several times—the tales of our people's greatness and follies. Now in obedience, I read it entirely. The Master has set me this task as punishment for my questioning him, for what he perceived as my insolence. Yet the punishment is a pleasure to me, for it is full of stories that stimulate both thought and fervor. I do not notice the passage of hours. When I have completed reading, I offer a thanksgiving prayer and return the scroll to its slot in the library shelves.

My hand brushes the scroll beside it, and for a reason I cannot explain, I pick it up. Returning to the table, I open it and see that it is the book of Isaiah. My eyes alight on a passage somewhere in the middle. It is an oracle against Babylon, given by the prophet a hundred years ago, describing its destruction and the smashing of all its idols. This has not yet come to pass, since Babylon remains a very great city that thrives far to the east. After the oracle on Babylon comes the oracle on Edom. Unlike Isaiah's several other oracles, which describe the destruction of Israel's foes, this one is short and very mysterious:

> *They call to me from Seir, "Watchman, how much longer the night? Watchman, how much longer the night?"*
> *The watchman replies, "Morning has come, and again night. If you will ask, ask. Come back again."*

I think of Issa. He is from the mountains of Seir. The night is now far gone. I extinguish the lamps and make my way up the stairs to the sleep-room, where I lie down and take my rest.

4

The Walls

THIS PAST YEAR I WAS MOVED up the hill to the house of higher studies, where I now live with the senior students. We are sixteen in number, ages twenty-five to thirty. I am the youngest. I sleep in a room with three men who are closer to ordination to priesthood than I am. Many of those with whom I lived in the lower house of studies have departed for their homes or occupations elsewhere, a few of the poorest ones and most of those from wealthier families. Behavior among my fellows has improved over the years, though it must be admitted that in my old house there is always a new crop of personalities much like I lived with, the devout and the rebellious mixed together.

The food is of higher quality now, with meat once a week, fine wheat loaves, and a cup of wine with each meal. I do not take the wine, remembering Samson and others in the past who were consecrated as *nazirites* and were adjured by the Lord to abstain from strong drink. The few times when I took a cup during the first months, I felt the glow of a natural gladness, like warm sunshine in my heart, but my head always ached afterward and my mood fell low. It is common knowledge that wine will do this to you, but most of my fellows are willing to pay the price for the brief happiness it brings. It is very unlike the burst of joy I feel whenever I have an opportunity to turn and face the doors of the Temple and worship the unseen Presence within.

The Walls

We study morning and night, and in the afternoons we assist with carrying sacrifice offerings to the laver bowls where sacrifices are skinned and washed. From there we take them to the Altar of Burnt Offerings. No longer the charcoal for me. I look with sympathy at the servants with blackened hands and smudged faces, seeing my younger self in them. They are always thirsty, and whenever I see a new boy from the lower house of studies stagger under the heat, I take a small bronze basin and fill it from the trickle of water that feeds the molten sea. I bring the water to the parched, and they drink from it gratefully. None of the priests or acolytes rebuke me for this, but they grimace over my indulgence. Now and then they warn me not to dirty my new linen robe by contact with the unwashed. As always, I am obedient, and I take care to avoid any ritual uncleanliness, but my soul has its own laws, which I must obey.

I often see my cousin Levi entering the Temple itself, first through the vestibule and then through the towering doors opening into the *Hekal*, the great chamber within, and then he is lost to my sight. Of course, he would never enter the Holy of Holies at the far end of the chamber, as that is reserved for the High Priest only. When he is engaged in ceremonial duties, Levi wears a long white robe with a purple sash. I see the High Priest very rarely, mainly during celebrations for religious feast days. He is unmistakable in a crowd of priests, for he alone wears a crimson robe with miter cap, upon which is a gold plate engraved with the name of the Most High. I tend to be invisible during major events, as my tawny robe and black sash are indistinguishable from those of the other acolytes.

Now and then I am invited to eat a meal with my uncle and aunt and Levi. Uncle's chilling manners have eased somewhat, now that he has seen my years of perseverance and heard of my repute as a dedicated acolyte. He is cordial and slightly more pleasant in manner, although he maintains the distance imposed by his higher status. He is one of hundreds of priests attached to the Temple complex. A few days a month, he serves within the great chamber, but his duties are mainly as a teacher of those in the final year before ordination. I am still five years away from that.

One Sabbath evening, after I have enjoyed a meal with the family, Levi walks me back up the hill to the senior house of studies. He is married now. He and his wife, Deborah, and their two-year-old daughter, Michal, live on the top floor of Uncle Joash's house. Tonight Levi is carrying his daughter on his shoulders, her legs dangling down his chest, her hands slapping his forehead to make her ride go faster. She is giggling and babbling all the way.

I ask Levi what it is like inside the Temple. He tells me much that I already know, yet it is a pleasure to hear it described by one who has seen it firsthand. The *Hekal* is forty cubits in length. The floor is paved with tiles of thick gold. The walls are lined with cedar, on which figures of cherubim, palm trees, and open flowers are carved, overlaid with gold, just as the ancient book of our kings describes it. At the far end of this largest chamber, gold chains separate it from the Holy of Holies. The doors of the Holy of Holies are made of olive wood, with carved images of cherubim, flowers, and palm trees, all overlaid with gold.

"Have you ever seen the Ark of the Covenant?" I ask.

He stares at me in consternation. "No, certainly not! Nor has my father."

"Yet the High Priest opens the doors to the Holy of Holies once a year and enters, as you once told me. Can you not catch a glimpse of what is within?"

"We lesser priests are nowhere near the doors, and a veil hides what is within."

"I long to see it," I say with a sigh.

"Well, I encourage you to live another half a century, Yezekiel, and then perhaps you will become High Priest." He chuckles. "After me, of course."

"When you are within the *Hekal*, Levi, do you feel the fire of the Presence?"

"The what?" he says, turning to me with a wrinkled brow.

"The glory of the Lord coming from the Holy of Holies. Surely it cannot be imprisoned within a room."

"Ah, I see your meaning. No, I cannot say it is like that for me. One senses something like a spirit in the air, which is the holiness of the Ark and the Name. I do not feel the holiness strongly, yet I believe in it . . . strongly."

"What are your duties in there?" I persist.

"In the *Hekal* are the Altar of Incense and the table of the showbread. Both tables are fashioned of gold, as are the candle holders, basins, fire pans, and the many sacred objects. I and other priests tend the altar fire, ensuring there is a steady supply of charcoal for the burning, and we ceaselessly sprinkle the incense. We pray as we work."

"You pray for Israel?"

"For Israel," he nods.

"I smell the smoke of incense sometimes when I am outside at the Altar of Burnt Offerings. It is wondrously beautiful!"

"Yes, it is wondrous indeed. Your smoke is bitter to the nose and eyes and sometimes makes the stomach turn with the smell of burning flesh. Our smoke is pure, made from precious resins bled from our own trees and then combined with lumps of resin brought by traders from distant lands, frankincense, myrrh, spices, and oils of floral perfumes. The oils are used to saturate the hard components, and the mixture is pounded to a quality of sand in the fingers. We sprinkle it copiously over the glowing charcoal embers in the burner."

"Then it is transformed by fire and rises like prayer."

"That is its meaning. It is worship and supplication combined."

"I have noticed that you always smell very fine, Levi."

He smiles. "Incense smoke penetrates clothing, skin, hair, everything."

"Do I smell poorly?"

"Yes, you do. You should wash more."

"Morning, midday, and night I wash. I am sorry it is not pleasant to be near me."

He glances at me sympathetically.

"It is no offense to me," he says. "I, too, once smelled as you do. Twelve more years, Yezekiel, and then you will be further purified. You will be where I am now."

That is the ordinary path: ordination at age thirty, then seven years assisting with ritual sacrifice outside in the Temple courtyard, and after that one may enter service within the Temple itself. The thought of ordination thrills me. I have more than once asked myself if it is the status of the priesthood I desire, but in the end I conclude that this is not my motive. It is yearning to offer prayers for my people and country in an anointed role. Above all, it is my longing to be closer to the Presence.

I often ponder the question of what is purification? Of course, it is to become without sin, in one's external acts and within the hidden interior of one's thoughts. From time to time, I am troubled by the memory of the naked woman I saw many years ago. The image does not enslave me, but it remains a provocation. When I pass by beautiful women in the streets of the city, and occasionally in the Outer Court where women are permitted, I turn my eyes away from them as swiftly as possible and banish from my mind any thought of them. Oh, I pray that there will come a time when I am no longer afflicted by such desires!

Nevertheless, I continue to weigh the matter this way and that: Is purity of soul a state in which one is without any temptation whatsoever? In which one feels nothing? Are the pure like desert dwellers who in their solitude see no objects to entice their eyes? Are they like a man walled all around by stone? Or surrounded by exalted seraphim? Or protected by the unseen angels who stand vigilant beside every soul? Coming to no clear understanding on these questions, I continue to ask for help from the Most High, and while it is true that I have not fallen in this regard, I am still strongly drawn to love for women.

I know full well that the Most High created us with these desires, so that man and woman would unite to bring forth new souls into the world, and new generations one after another. The desire is beautiful and good, but it must be mastered in oneself. Without this self-discipline, desire becomes lust, which degrades us to the level of beasts. Even so, it is a struggle. Is it possible that the Most High permits us to feel the yearnings of the flesh in order that we might never forget our vulnerability to the beguilements of sin and, thus, continue to call upon his aid? By the same measure, does he allow us to remain without understanding, knowing little about our very selves, so that we may progress farther and farther on the path of obedience? Such was the path of our forefather Abraham, whose obedience was counted as righteousness, though he did not understand. It seems to me that this is the way that leads to more complete trust in the Lord. Thus, I will choose to trust him, now and always, no matter how hard the struggles ahead. No matter the loneliness I feel.

Still, there is the joy that he pours out upon me from time to time. It is a matter of puzzlement to me—and wonder—this question of consolations from the Most High. I cannot make sense of why they come at certain times and then do not come for long periods. I cannot make them happen, and thus I conclude that they are a product of neither my will nor my emotions. Likewise, pondering the wonders of the Lord does not produce supernatural peace or ecstasy. These consolations are given very rarely, and always—always—by surprise. By this, I have come to believe that my Creator wishes to remind me from time to time that he sees my life and guides it.

In words beyond all language, he is saying, *I am here, I am here.*

Few are the times when I see the king come to the Temple. His palace is attached to the Temple complex, with a shared wall between them. There is a gate in the wall, connecting the royal courtyard to the high platform by the Altar of Burnt Offerings. The gate is blocked by weighty bronze doors and is always watched by palace guards. They are dressed in costly garments of purple cloth, with bronze helmets and iron-tipped spears. Each has a bow and quiver strapped upon his back. Cinctured at their waists are long swords. Their faces are set in severity, as if their entire beings are ever ready to sacrifice their lives for the king. Four of these men continuously stand watch by the gates, and whenever the doors are opened and the king walks through with his courtiers, forty more guards accompany them.

King Jehoiachim seems a man weighed down with grave

concerns. In years, he is only in his late-thirties, yet in appearance he looks older, for his hair is streaked with grey, his face deeply lined, his brow permanently scored with worry. His every expression bespeaks age and wisdom. He walks in a dignified manner, as if in procession, and all in the Temple Court bow their heads before him as he passes.

Each year he presides over the royal sacrifice, standing to the side of the Altar as the High Priest and the chief priests slaughter seven bulls and seventy sheep. The king in his golden robes lifts both his arms each time an animal is killed—like Moses at the battle with the Amalekites when Aaron and Hur held up his arms lest he drop them from exhaustion. Also, it is interesting that a servant standing behind Jehoiachim carries an old wooden harp in his arms, but does not play it. Perhaps its strings are so decayed that only discordant notes now come from it. Levi tells me that this is David's harp, preserved throughout these many ages past.

Rarely do I see the prince who will inherit the throne, young Jehoiachin, for he appears only when he accompanies his father on major feasts or for the king-sacrifice, offered for the nation. Like his father, he is pale-skinned, as if he has spent little of his life under the sun. He would be handsome if he were not so puffy-cheeked with pouting lips. Dressed in splendid royal garments, which lack only a gold band on his forehead, he stands a few paces behind the king, looking distracted, as if he would pay a cartload of silver to be anywhere else than here. He is seventeen years old, Levi tells me, and he has several wives.

On occasion I have seen the other prince, Mattaniah, who will not inherit the throne, though he, like King Jehoiachim, is a son of the righteous King Josiah. The throne must go by right of succession to Jehoiachim's son Jehoiachin.

Mattaniah is twenty-one years of age, three years older than his nephew but just as immature—perhaps more so. When he is compelled by duty to accompany the king to sacrifices, Mattaniah slouches behind the retinue in a posture of silly insolence or twitches and makes faces as if irritated by an unruly spirit. On one occasion, I saw him burst out laughing during the most solemn moment, like a witless child.

"Those boys are not young Solomon," Levi once murmured to himself in an unguarded moment as we watched the royal party return through the gate to the palace.

"Yet Josiah was their foresire," I said. "This, too, is in their blood."

"Ah, well," Levi sighed, "perhaps they will grow up some day."

The princes are not respected in private. Of course, in public, all honors are accorded to them by everyone. I do not wish to be unkind, but I think that these two privileged young men are the sort of persons who care for nothing but their own desires and needs. I would never allow them to watch over my sheep for a day, or even for an hour, let alone entrust an entire kingdom to one or the other.

At the house of higher studies, my fellow students are careful not to say anything loudly about the princes, but I do hear them murmuring bits of gossip over their wine. Against my will, I learn shocking things.

One day while I am washing my clothing in the courtyard pool, a few steps from an open window, I overhear the Master of the house conversing in a low voice with another priest. He says that King Jehoiachim has done evil in the sight of the Lord, for he has permitted the return of the idolatry that once infested Jerusalem and was banished by Josiah. Moreover, the king has filled the city with innocent blood.

The Walls

Innocent blood? I have no idea what is meant by this. As quickly as possible, I wring out my clothes and walk to the other side of the courtyard, but the echoing stone walls carry their words to me. The princes also come under the lash of their tongues. The priests refer to Jehoiachin as Jeconiah and, more familiarly, in tones of disgust, Coniah and Coney. They have worse names for Mattaniah. Jehoiachin is a young fool, they say, but his uncle Mattaniah is a wicked fool. He will do evil, much as his brother Jehoiachim did when he was young, and continues to do, and neither of them are like their father, Josiah. The older prince is willful, insatiably passionate for wanton women and strong drink; the younger is docile, spoiled by doting women of the royal household and by rich foods. He is lazy and growing fat.

I am stunned by these accusations, for until now I have heard nothing of this. I stop my ears with my fingers, wanting to hear no more.

When I tell Levi what I have heard, hoping that he will refute it, I am sorely disillusioned. He is a close friend of a scribe in the palace, who has told him much the same things.

One day, not long after, Levi and I are strolling side by side around the walls of the outer court. I ask my reliable and discreet cousin about the situation in the kingdom.

"Levi, my heart and soul tell me that the people of Jerusalem grow ever more quarrelsome with each other. Each year there are fewer smiles, and the sound of laughter wanes in the streets. Are they angry about something that I am unaware of?"

"They are afraid," he says with a scowl, then lowers his head and rubs his face with the palms of his hands.

"Of what are they afraid?"

"Yezekiel, you are no ignoramus. Surely you know the fragility of the nation."

"I know little, if anything, about that."

"Are you so innocent and blind?"

"I am blind but not innocent."

Levi snorts and shakes his head over me. He brings us to a halt not far from the main gate to the lower city. The pilgrims are few in numbers today. There are none nearby to catch our words. Even so, he lowers his voice.

"A lesson for you then, my naïve kinsman. A lesson in history and power."

I lean closer, waiting.

"Israel is not free," he begins. "Under Jehoiachim we paid tribute to the Egyptians for some years. Then, after Pharaoh Necho was defeated by the Babylonians at Karkemish, we began paying tribute to Babylon. We continue to be a vassal state. If we fail to send our annual ransom, there will be retribution."

"This I know, Levi, and it is unfortunate. Yet I feel certain that in time there will be a restoration, as there was under David and Hezekiah and Josiah."

"Do you feel so certain? Look at David's reign, fraught with contention. Even Solomon the Wise fell into grave evils. Hezekiah brought reform, and then he wavered, making alliances with alien nations instead of relying on God. And Josiah? Josiah gave us Jehoiachim! And Jehoiachim gives us corrupt judges and idolatry, along with ill-considered alliances. External follies and internal evils spread like pestilence among our people."

"Peace will fully reign again."

"Yezekiel, are you a child! The kingdom's life has never enjoyed more than brief respites of peace. We are at war.

Always we are at war, either declared or undeclared. This war will continue until the end of all ages."

"It seems so, Levi," I nod in agreement. "Yes, I believe you are correct in one sense. And yet when the people repent and live as the Most High commands us, the invaders fall back. Again and again they are defeated by the hand of the Lord."

"In part you say rightly. But only in part. For you must understand that our leaders, generation after generation, believe that cunning and shrewd negotiations are essential components of the Lord's will."

I reply doubtfully, "But without repentance, cunning and shrewdness will avail us little."

"We seem to be arguing in circles. But on this we are agreed. Cunning and shrewdness only delay the inevitable retribution. It is like feeding a little bit of your body to a lion so that it will not eat you whole."

I bow my head, trying to collect my thoughts, growing more confused over what Levi is trying to say.

For the moment, all I can offer is, "I do not understand the affairs of state."

Levi throws up his arms in frustration. "Yezekiel, you fail to see the proportion of things. Do you think that Israel and Judah are represented by these tens of thousands who stream in and out of the Temple courts? The reality is that the greater number of the people live in sin, heedless of the lessons of old and ignoring the prophets' warnings. High and low, rich and poor, they are riddled with infidelity. Always, always, they forget the Most High and mimic the customs of the nations around us. They succumb to the lure of idols, for they think those demon-gods will ensure a better harvest or prevent illness or fill their purses with gold."

"Are you saying that they wish to have *both* God and Mammon? But that is impossible."

"Indeed. Now you see it."

My mood lowering, bordering on the disconsolate, I murmur, "We need another Isaiah in our times."

"And where in all this unhappy land would we find another Isaiah?" He stares at me long, shaking his head. "Even more do we need another Samuel the truth-sayer," he adds. "Or Elijah, the wonder-worker."

"And Elisha who received a double portion?" I offer.

As if he is only half listening, Levi shakes his head again, focused on his inner thoughts.

"Levi, I have often heard about a man who speaks warnings in the Temple precincts, Jeremiah by name. Perhaps, in our own times, he is the one sent to us by the Lord."

"Jeremiah? No, no, no! Calamities pour from that man's mouth. He proclaims that Babylon will take all Israel into captivity, and we know that such a thing is impossible."

"But, Levi," I argue, "did not Isaiah prophesy the same? He wrote that 'Your own sons shall be eunuchs in the palace of the king of Babylon'."

"Yes, he wrote that. But a few sons is not an entire nation."

"He said that Israel's treasure will be taken to Babylon."

"You inflate the small into the large, Yezekiel. Jerusalem may be invaded at some point in the future and our treasury may be plundered, but what does that mean precisely?"

With a look of fraternal or paternal pity, he bids me farewell, striding swiftly away toward the gate to the inner court, for he must return to his duties in the *Hekal*. I must return to mine by the Altar of Sacrifice.

Walking across the paving stones of the outer court in the direction of the steps leading up to the altar, I am trying to make sense of our discussion, which seems to have been at cross purposes. In part we agree, yet we are not fully of mutual understanding, which is caused, I feel sure, by my ignorance. The entire exchange has left me deeply disturbed.

The crowds are thin today, only a few hundred. As I pass a cluster of thirty or forty pilgrims, some bowing toward the Temple, some just gazing in awe at its soaring majesty, a man steps forth from their midst and blocks my passage. One of the poor, I see, and while I respect all pilgrims, I have tasks that beckon me. When I swerve to avoid him, he steps sideways and blocks me again, his face intently peering at me as if he wishes to ask a question or implore me to intercede for him to the Lord Most High.

"Hear me," he says in a voice both gentle and full of authority. Startled, I halt and incline my head toward him. He is, after all, an old man and thus deserving of courtesy.

He says: "Hear me, O spring of clear water, O man small in your own eyes, hear me."

"Who are you?" I blurt in surprise.

Then recognition dawns. When I was a boy, I saw this very person standing in the Temple court when my family brought a lamb for the altar. He said mysterious things to me then. He looked at me as no other had ever before looked at me. And now he turns his gaze upon me again—upon me and within me.

"I do not know your name," I mumble uneasily.

"Truly, the Most High will exalt," he answers. "I am Jeremiah."

Jeremiah! The very name I have so frequently heard spoken of by the priests or on the city streets. A few of them quietly believe he is a prophet, but most think him a madman. Yet now as I pause to look at him, I know in the depths of my soul that his are not the eyes of the insane. These are far-seeing eyes.

"Hear me then, O spring of clear water, hear me. Be not dismayed by all that is to come to pass. Let not your knees quake or your heart falter, for you shall speak words of consolation in the land of captivity."

"How do you know this?" I ask, my heart beating harder, my tongue barely able to shape the words.

"Fear nothing," he says, and then turns and walks away. I stare after him until he has melted into the crowd.

When my day's work is finished, I wait for Levi to complete his duties in the *Hekal*. I catch him in the courtyard just as the sun is dipping below the palace wall.

"Yezekiel, why are you not long gone to your supper?" he asks.

"My heart is sore troubled, cousin."

"Ah, too many dark thoughts I spoke to you earlier today."

"That is not the cause, Levi."

I recount to him my meeting with Jeremiah.

"Jeremiah!" exclaims Levi. "Have you been listening to that man? Why did you not heed me?"

"He spoke to me once before, when I was thirteen. You were with our family that day. Do you not remember?"

"No," Levi answers, looking doubtful. "Not a week goes by that some deranged soul or other does not fail to shout his delusions in the outer court or the inner court. The guards are sometimes hard pressed to keep them out."

I tell Levi that the old man merely advised me to have no fear, to not let my knees tremble or my heart falter, for I would bring consolation to captives.

"Well, even madmen may babble a true thing now and then," says Levi frowning, staring at the paving stones beneath his feet. "About consolation and captives, I do not know. But you must surely never let your heart falter."

"But why would it falter?"

He takes some moments to think before responding, staring at the ground, casting about in his mind for a proper reply to my question.

"The kingdom is ill, perhaps sick unto death," he murmurs. "You know of what I speak."

He looks up and probes my eyes.

I shake my head. "I do not know of what you speak."

"Only hours ago I told you about the nation's corruption, and now it seems I wasted my breath. You have lived how many years on this mountain and have seen nothing?"

"Do you mean the poor behavior of . . . ?"

I do not finish, for it disturbs me greatly to think of the faults of our priests. I know that all souls are as if climbing a mountain of the Lord, everyone bearing faults and sins. Who but the Lord Most High can judge their progress, their interior conditions?

Levi seems to read my thoughts. He says,

"I mean the *evil* behavior of our most exalted ones, here on the Mountain of the Lord, in both palace and Temple. Isaiah stripped the whited garments from their wickedness, telling how priests and prophets reeled with strong drink, stumbling as they proclaimed their visions, staggering when pronouncing judgment."

"But that was long ago."

"It continues, though now it is hidden cunningly from our eyes."

"I have seen none of this."

"Are you blind, Yezekiel?"

I pause to consider a little. "Well, I admit there is too much wine in the priests' house at times, and they play free with unkindly chatter."

"You are not permitted by them, nor is anyone permitted, to see the extent of their corruption. There is worse and worse. As Isaiah said, *They sell their daughters to pay for their wine, they sell a boy for a harlot.* This, too, continues."

"How can you be sure of such a thing?"

"I have spoken with their victims, who came to me with broken souls, seeking counsel or restitution."

Almost, I am about to ask him why anyone would want to bring a secret shame to light. Then I recall that Levi is considered to be a priest of surpassing righteousness, though without the bearing of haughty condemnation that is so evident in many officials on the mountain. While he is unrelievedly solemn, there is an air of kindliness about him. Now I understand that he could very well be the sort in whom the distressed would confide.

He goes on: "I have also spoken with a few among the violators who repented. Surely you know that now and then a priest will leave the Temple service and go as far away from here as he can?"

I nod. Yes, this is common knowledge. Departures from Temple service are rare, but they do occur.

"Such a one goes of his own will, haunted by guilt and self-horror, resolved to do penance until the end of his days. However, the majority of offenders remain in place and continue with their vile activities."

"Are you able to bring consolation to those who have been hurt?"

"I listen, I offer sympathy, words of encouragement, any practical help I can give them. Full restitution I have no means to give."

He clenches his fists, as if he would strike the despoilers but is powerless to do so.

"Can you not stop the evil-doers?" I ask.

"And how do you suggest I stop them?"

"I . . . I do not know. Can you not protest to the High Priest?"

"The High Priest is infirm and wants no trouble. More-over, he listens to advisors who tell him that all is well. They would deny every accusation, dismissing any proof, any wit-ness I might bring before them, and swiftly they would cast me out."

"Then speak to your friend in the palace, that he might inform the king."

"The situation is just as bad in the palace."

"If all that you tell me is true, Levi—"

"All that I tell you *is* true!" he replies with raised voice and flashing eyes.

His tone borders on insulting, but I take no offense. I now see that Levi is tormented by his beliefs or discoveries. Horrible as the implications are, I wonder if he is imagin-ing some of it, turning suspicions into facts in his mind, or else exaggerating the particles of truth into something larger than it is.

I say nothing, noting his angry eyes, his flexing fists, his mouth set in a ferocious line. Clearly, the source of his anger is the crimes committed by some priests. But he is also an-gry because he feels alone in the midst of a dilemma, and his profound fear of the evils infesting the House of God cannot find any outlet other than frustrated rage.

"Sometimes you infuriate me, cousin," he mutters.

Now I feel my own anger awaken.

"Why do you speak to me this way?" I ask him with a firmness that is unusual for me.

"What way?" he snaps in return, examining my face more closely.

"Your manner is very like that of the haughty ones who rule in the Temple—the ones you find so offensive."

He blinks rapidly, uncurls the palms of his hands, and stares at me with some surprise.

"More and more you speak to me in tones of superiority

and contempt for my lack of complicity with you," I continue calmly but with no hint of retreat. "You have called me naïve and simple and mild; you have called me a child and blind and infuriating. Though not in so many words, you have called me a coward for not equaling you in your rage."

"No, no, it is not that," he says, his face falling.

"You presume that I should have all knowledge and secret information and that I must believe your every word without question."

"Forgive me," he mumbles. "Forgive me."

"I forgive you," I reply with no great warmth.

With that, we both take some deep breaths and let the tension between us ease to a degree.

He gazes at me with a sober expression, and then, to my surprise, a smile slowly spreads across his face.

"This is good to see," he says with a chuckle.

"What is good to see?"

"You resisting me. There is iron inside your gentle ways."

Abruptly, he turns away and begins pacing back and forth in front of me, his smile gone.

"Try to understand, Yezekiel," he says in a contrite tone. "The law courts are infested with corrupt judges who make false rulings. Good men go to prison or are executed for the gain of others—including the gain of the king. In the groves and high places on the surrounding hills, the altars to pagan idols multiply, with hideous sacrifices offered."

"I have heard rumors about those altars. But what do you mean by hideous sacrifices?"

His face contorts. He will not answer.

Now the anger that has been rising within me breaks the surface. It is no longer an instinctive response to his sharp words, his irritation about my caution in believing him, but a reaction to the situation he describes.

"This is an abomination come upon Israel!" I cry.

"Indeed, an abomination," he murmurs, ceasing his pacing, turning to me with a probing look.

I turn away from him and close my eyes. My heart flies upward to the Holy of Holies, sobbing inwardly, though there are no visible tears.

I am sorry, O Most High, I am sorry, I am sorry. I am sorry we are this way.

"Come," says Levi, casting grave looks over his shoulders, taking me by the arm and leading me toward the gate. "Let us speak no more of this. We have had enough for one day."

Several months pass. I carry within me a burden of anguish that prompts me to increase my prayers for all the people, for this holy city, for this holy Temple. I find it difficult to look at the face of each and every priest and not wonder if he is faithful in his heart as well as in his role, or if he is a secret betrayer. I am distressed by this new habit of suspicion that is growing in me. So much easier it would be to ignore the problem. I ponder and grieve, yet I am unable to do anything about it. The feeling of helplessness is perhaps the worst part of my struggle. I feel like a man bound with ropes as brigands pillage his home. When I mention this to Levi, his face sours and he says in a bitter tone, "It is more like a bridegroom tied to a pillar and forced to watch the raping of his bride in the midst of the wedding feast."

O horror, O misery! And yet I can see no solid evidence before my eyes. What am I then to do?

I continue with my duties, and now with my whole heart and soul I plead with the Lord for the purification and strengthening of his household.

We will need much strength. Levi informs me that the king has refused to pay the annual tribute to the king of Babylon,

Nebuchadnezzar by name. My cousin has learned through his friend in the palace that Jehoiachim is keeping back the tribute because he is sore pressed for money to pay for his armies and the upkeep of the royal estates. The king is wagering that our armies are strong enough to dissuade the Babylonians if they should entertain any thought of invading us. Throughout the land we have hundreds of thousands of men —farmers and tradesmen for the most part—fit and able to take up sword and spear if the need should arise. We also have ten thousand bowmen and thousands of chariots and horsemen, most of them stationed at Megiddo in Solomon's stables and in other chariot cities, including the stable in Jerusalem below the Temple Mount. There are additional small forts in all quarters, staffed mainly by swordsmen and bowmen.

To the east we are protected by the deep Jordan Valley rift and by the vast desert beyond it. To the south are rugged mountains, the Sea of Salt, and the wilderness of Moab. To the west are more hills and the great sea beyond Samaria. If trouble comes, it will be from the north.

There is much discussion among my fellows at the house of studies and among the Temple priests. All are worried, yet all seek to minimize the danger. They tell each other that the Babylonian empire, though it is very great in size and wealth and doubtless has an army larger than ours, is so far away that it would be forced to overcome vast distances and numerous obstacles to reach us. Their troops would be exhausted by the journey.

Levi and I are walking in the cool of the evening, on the ramparts of David's Wall surrounding the Old City. The newer walls of the modern city are far mightier, with formidable gates, and they encircle the whole. I have not seen Babylon or the capital of Egypt or the cities of the Hellas lands very far to the north, though their repute as fortresses is the highest. Yet I am told that Jerusalem's walls surpass them all for height and thickness. And, of course, our city is crowned by the Temple of the one true God.

O Lord, may we be worthy of you! Then my heart sinks. *O Lord, forgive us that we are not worthy of you!*

Levi's convictions seem to be changing from one day to the next. He now weighs the possibility that an invasion is not far off.

He says: "The pride of the Babylonian king and the size of his empire demands that no revolt by a vassal state may be tolerated, regardless of how small and distant. If he were to forgive one such kingdom, others would rise in revolt against him. Thus, Yezekiel, an invasion may be soon, though it is uncertain whether it would crush us brutally or merely inflict a token punishment."

"How soon?" I ask my cousin, who seems always to know far more about the world than I do.

"How soon, you ask?" says Levi as we lean over the ancient wall, looking down on the streets below with their countless houses built after David's reign. We listen to voices raised in argument, the barking of dogs, the cries of mothers beckoning children home for their evening meals. All appears to be normal.

"The tribute to Babylon has been overdue these past two years," Levi begins. "Three months ago, emissaries from Nebuchadnezzar rode into the city and met with Jehoiachim and his chief advisors in the throne room. Debates and loud wrangling went on for days. The emissaries were treated royally, given costly gifts; they dined and slept in the House of the Forest of Lebanon, attached to the Pillar Hall and the Throne Room."

"I have never seen those places," I say.

"No, you would not have."

"Are they very beautiful?"

"They are wondrous beautiful." He points. "Do you see those golden roofs above the wall of the palace court?"

Yes, I can see them catching the last glow from the sky, where the sun has fallen off the edge of the world.

"They are glorious settings for acts of betrayal," he says.

"Do you know the outcome of the wrangling, Levi?"

"It did not end well. The emissaries set off for home in grim demeanor. Traveling on swift horses, it would take them a month to reach Babylon. There, a certain amount of discussion and further wrangling would take place in the court of Nebuchadnezzar. He would want to know our military strength. He would inquire about many aspects of the situation that the emissaries and their spies brought back to him. But above all other considerations would be his offended pride. I think the matter of war would be decided within days, perhaps hours."

"Then an invasion may be near."

"Yes, but how near is still in question. To move a vast host from Babylon is no small task. They will have to travel north alongside the Euphrates for many weeks in order to avoid the death of their forces in the great desert. They will be slowed by their dependence on supply caravans carrying much food and hauling battle engines for the possibility of a siege. Arriving at Karkemish, they will leave the river behind and head west into Syria. A week or two at the most, and then they will turn southward. Passing between Damascus and Tyre, they will enter Galilee not long after, and from there they will proceed with speed and ferocity into Judah."

The Walls

There is no more discussion after that. We gaze to the east and watch a large red star slowly rise.

We wait and wait.

Frequently I see Jeremiah in the Outer Court when I am passing through it and, on occasion, in the Temple Court. Though he never speaks to me again, he continually cries out warnings against the kings and priests and all the people, who have chased after—he calls it *lusted after*—alien gods. They are like camels in heat, twin sisters, by which it is plain that he means the Kingdom of Israel and the Kingdom of Judah. For her great wickedness, the northern kingdom was wiped out nearly a hundred years ago, but Judah remains, and her crowning glory, Jerusalem, is as wicked as her sister. So says Jeremiah, claiming that he speaks the word of the Lord.

Pilgrims either listen intently, anxiously, or they jeer and try to shout him down. He has been thrashed by Temple gate guards and thrown out into the street, yet he always returns. Palace guards, too, have maltreated him at the main palace gate, and still he returns.

Again and again I stand at the edge of such scenes and try to assess his authenticity. My heart and soul tell me the man is true. Yet my thoughts are uncertain, for my duty before the Law of God is to give my life for the Holy Name, which is in the Temple, and to labor in such a way that what Jeremiah foretells need not come to pass.

I remind myself that the Holy Name and the Presence cannot be contained within a temple. He is everywhere and all-powerful, and those who would make war against him are condemned to unavoidable defeat.

I frequently ask myself, Who, really, is this old man Jeremiah?

He speaks of the almond tree, which is called the watching tree, and he proclaims that the Lord is watching to ensure that his words will come to pass. He declares that a pot is boiling over and that fury and great evil shall come from the north, breaking upon all the inhabitants of the land, and that Jerusalem's walls will be surrounded and breached.

Bystanders scoff at him, saying "No peril will come from the north, as the nations there are weak and great Babylon is far to the east."

Today, I hear him crying out in the Temple Court, just before he is grabbed by guards and expelled:

"My people have committed two evils. They have abandoned me, the fountain of living waters, and have hewed out cisterns for themselves, broken cisterns that can hold no water."

"Who is this man Jeremiah?" I ask the Master at my house of studies.

"Which Jeremiah?" he retorts.

"The one who day and night cries out in the Temple Court."

The Master's answer is a long vilification, a highly articulate stream of contempt.

I ask my Uncle Joash. He answers with more of the same, but guarded. He is holding to the official policy, but I can see that he is of two minds.

"Jeremiah, son of Hilkiah!" he replies irritably. "Oh, yes, I have known of this man since my youth, for we are nearly the same age. He is from a priestly family, like ours. When I was in the house of studies, he came up to the city from Anathoth, a Levite town in the land of Benjamin. From his earliest years, he has bleated the same message."

"Do you believe the message, Uncle?" I ask. He turns furious eyes upon me, his lips locked. I hasten away.

In a private moment, I ask the same question of Levi. He answers cautiously. I press him for a clear reply. His face contorts in pain.

"I say it with difficulty, Yezekiel, but I say it after a long weighing of thought. I have come to think that he may be a prophet such as we had in elder days."

"Yet few heed him."

"The palace and Temple and all manner of the wealthy and powerful listen, but they do not *hear*. They listen only in order to use his words against him, for they loathe his troubling of their conscience. They listen in order to debate him, that they might thereby seek to quiet the fears of the common people."

"I have seen him humiliated but witnessed no debate."

Levi sighs. "From time to time, a clever priest or a palace advisor will confront him with Levitical and political arguments committed to memory. Always, Jeremiah confounds them. At times he is only silent and raises his arms toward the Temple. One day, I feel certain, they will try to silence him forever."

"But if he is a true prophet, then to negate his message is to defy the Lord Most High."

"Yes," says Levi in an aggrieved voice. "That is the core of the matter, but they do not see it. With learned voices and great dignity of office they justify their every rejection of the truth."

"Perhaps they will reconsider. It may be that the faith of the people will make them change their minds."

"The faith of the people? Yezekiel, Yezekiel, you see your own goodness reflected as if in a mirror. You still do not grasp the extent of the evil, from Temple top to marketplace. In the groves on the high places, children are now being sacrificed, slaughtered, and burned by their own parents —by our own people!"

"May the Lord stop this abomination!" I groan.

"It is no longer a few who commit such mad acts. Observe from the city walls at night, and you will see hundreds of fires. More and more every day, and neither palace nor Temple put a stop to it. So, too, in the Temple's most hidden chambers, in the darkest hours of the night, pagan idols are secretly worshipped by apostates of the priestly class, which means that they bring demons into the holiest place in the world."

"But how could you know such a secret thing?"

"My father was invited to join them. He attended their ritual once, at first not knowing its nature. For all his faults, he is not an idolater. He refused to be initiated and told me about it because he wanted to warn me, fearing they might invite me, also."

"It cannot be, it cannot be," I choke out. "Will your father try to stop them?"

Levi's face flushes. "He will not. He is afraid of them."

"Then you must stop them! I will help you!"

"I do not know who they are, or where in the Temple complex they commit their evils, or when. My father will not tell me."

Then his composure entirely collapses. He bends over and hides his face in his trembling hands.

"I thought I could hold it back," he sobs. "I thought I could stand in the breach."

Now added to my previous shocks, I am stunned with the realization that if my strong and learned cousin is so cast down, our future is dark, indeed.

The Master of our house is in a fit of rage. Throughout the Sabbath day, I hear his feet stomping on the floorboards above, shaking down showers of dust, and loudly venting against this "cracked pot" named Jeremiah. Fleeing to the studies room or to our wash-court, I find no refuge, for his voice penetrates to every room and, doubtless, into the streets as well. Short of plugging my fingers into my ears for hours on end, it is impossible to avoid learning the cause of his upset.

Until now, I have had the impression that Jeremiah is so poor in aspect and influence that he is of small import to the authorities. They considered him an irritant, perhaps, or an insignificant disturber of the peace, but no real threat. However, Jeremiah continues each day to appear in the Temple courts or at its outer gates whenever he is spotted by guards and prohibited entry. Perpetually barred from the palace, he nevertheless is often at its gate, crying out that the kingdom relied vainly on help from Egypt and now retribution is coming; relying on man rather than on God was doomed to failure. The city will be overthrown by the king of Babylon, he says, and Jehoiachim will be vanquished.

But the rulers and the multitudes pay Jeremiah little heed. Even so, he has sufficiently disturbed a number of palace officials and the city's wealthy class for charges are to be brought against him. He is hauled before a court with the intent of condemning him altogether and, by the same stroke, inhibiting any imitation of his behavior. Yet certain elders of the Temple plead with the king to let Jeremiah go, arguing that the old man was merely repeating what prophets of the past have foretold, and in those days the kings had listened and honored the prophets. Though Jeremiah's defenders are a small minority among the priestly class, a few are of such high repute for learnedness that the king and judges relent, hesitating to offend the Temple. They let the old man go.

Then Jeremiah writes down all his prophecies in a book, through the hand of his scribe, a man named Baruch. When

Jeremiah reads the book aloud in the Outer Court, a great throng gathers around to listen. Hearing about what is happening, palace officials hasten to the scene, seize the book from Jeremiah's hands, and bring it to Jehoiachim. This much is known by the general populace.

Through Levi and his palace friend, I learn that the king commanded that the contents of the book be read to him, but when he heard what it contained, he grew exceedingly angry and tore it apart, then threw it into a fire. He gave orders for Jeremiah's arrest and punishment, but the old man and his scribe were by then in hiding in the city, thus escaping the king's wrath.

"Do you understand at last?" Levi asks me. "Our rulers speak one thing with their lips, declaring that Israel's strength is from the Lord Most High. Yet their acts say otherwise, revealing that they believe the nation's strength is in their own cunning and might of arms."

"That is a contrary message, Levi. It seems to me that such can only come from a divided heart."

"From a forked tongue, Yezekiel," he corrects me with ferocity. "A serpent's tongue."

My brothers Iosif and Isaac have come up to Jerusalem for three days, seeking to sell their wares, to buy food, to hear any news that may be adrift in the streets. To my surprise and pleasure, Asher has come with them.

I am very glad to see these good and godly men who are my blood-kin and also my bosom friends. They have brought gifts of bread and dried lamb strips and a new head scarf woven for me by my mother, Naomi. They find me in the Temple Court after much searching, for the Temple heights are more congested than ever. Driven by rumors, people from outlying districts have moved into the city, and more are flooding in every day. Makeshift tents have been erected in all streets. Because of the overcrowding, my brothers and I eat a midday meal together on the edge of a sloping road that skirts the Temple Mount. It is noisy with passersby, but we can converse frankly without much danger of being overheard. They want to learn anything I can tell them.

"A prophet says that Babylon will invade us," I say. "It is coming very soon."

At the word *prophet*, they are instantly respectful. Attentive, they absorb every word I can remember of Jeremiah's messages. When I have told them all I know, they are sobered but not frightened.

"The king's chariots are on the main roads in large numbers," says Iosif. "Coming up to Jerusalem from Little Bite of Bread, we met lines of foot soldiers with spear and sword on every road, wide and narrow. Our army is large."

"Levi says that our army is small compared to Babylon's and that we have grown slack and ill-trained. The prophet says that the kingdom will fall."

"It cannot be, Yezekiel. Look at this city so mighty, its walls so high, the gates so heavy with iron and timber that nothing can break through. The invaders might make havoc among the landed people and smaller towns, but they will not enter here. I will convince father to bring the family inside the walls. Uncle Joash will give us shelter."

"I fear not, Iosif, for his house is even now crammed with country people related to Aunt Sarah."

"We will be content with a little space."

"There is no more space, for already I begged his hospitality on the chance of your coming. He refuses."

"Then we will bring our tents."

"We will camp in the streets," Isaac adds. "For generations our forefathers dwelt in tents."

"Yes, but the city will fall," I argue.

"The word of a prophet should be respected," Iosif counters, "yet prophecy may be changed by repentance."

"The rulers and the people will not repent," I say. "Look all about you. How many of these people passing by us wear pagan amulets around their necks or clutch in their hands little Baals carved from wood and bone?"

My brothers gaze at passersby, and within a minute they have seen more than they wanted to see. Their heads droop in disgust.

"*Gillulim*," murmurs Isaac. He has used the word for idols that conveys uncleanness, and, in crude speech, implying excrement.

"It is worse on the mountain," I say, pointing up the slope to the Temple and palace.

Taken aback by this, they struggle to disbelieve such an evil accusation.

"But it is the *Hekal*, it is *qodesh*, the holy!" Iosif protests.

"The presence of the Lord is ever holy," I say, "but those who serve him are not always so. Indeed, few are those who now revere his glory with whole heart, soul, and might."

"What, then, would you have us do, Zeki?" Asher asks. This is the first time he has entered the discussion, as he has been listening keenly until now, my sweet-tempered brother who throughout our lives has always been full of laughter and causing laughter in his wake. Now his eyes are red with worry. It strikes me that, of the three, he is the most ready to believe what I have told them.

"I am unsure, Asher. I do not wish to live your lives for you, but I would advise you to convince our father and mother and all our kin to take the sheep and move south for some months, perhaps for a year. I think the invasion will not last long—at least in terms of unleashed war. All Judea will be occupied by Babylon, but in time life will resume, and then you can return to your home."

"But where would we go?"

How it comes to me, I do not know, but the way suddenly opens in my mind. As if a cloud of smoke is dispersed by a clean wind, standing before the eyes of my soul is my friend Issa.

"Go to Idumea," I say.

"It is inhospitable country," says Isaac with a frown. "The mountains are sharp-edged and the pastures few. The sun bakes hotly there."

"It is not desert. You can survive."

"Moses and all the people survived in the desert for forty years," Iosif muses, using his deepest tone of voice, the one he employs when he is emphasizing his position as first-born.

"In those days, the hand of the Lord was mighty to save," Isaac points out.

"Is he no longer mighty?" Asher reproves him with a look.

"No, no, I do not say that." He groans. "But Idumea! The Edomites have ever been hostile to us. Their cities are vainglorious, and they rejoiced over the fall of Israel."

"Not all of Edom," I say, shaking my head. "Is not goodness to be found unawares, even in the midst of ill-intentioned peoples?"

My brothers look at me dubiously.

"Go to Idumea," I say again. "Search among the humblest dwellings by the mountains of Seir, and you will find a village—I do not know its name—and among its people is a man named Issa, son of a priest named Ephraim. It is a poor place, I think, yet the people are rich in heart."

"But what about you, Yezekiel? Will you come with us?" Iosif asks.

How I know the answer, I cannot say, but it is as sure as a letter carved in stone.

"My task is here. And here I will remain."

5

The Refuge

WATCHMEN FROM OUR NORTHERN BORDERS ride into the city in great haste. Their horses are frothing and spent, weary unto death.

"They come like a plague of locusts!" the riders cry, unable to contain the news as they jog on foot from the gates and up the mountain to the palace.

The alarm spreads rapidly. Wails and tears fountain to the skies; the city roars with dismay. Captains ride outward to all forts. Armed camps are pitched on the surrounding hills. The chariot cities have been warned and are making ready for main resistance; the infantry battalions merge into a sizeable force that will meet the invader on the northern roads. Smaller groups of fighters are dispersed in the heavily forested Judean mountains to engage the enemy if he should penetrate farther south than the Jezreel Valley and Mount Gilboa. In the event that the Babylonian army seizes mastery of the roads, these last will constantly harry it from the heights. Thus, we are protected to a degree, and yet if the invading forces are too large, they could overwhelm all opposition.

In the Temple and royal precincts, voices are subdued. Advisors to the king are counseling surrender and payment of tribute, pleading that no Israelite blood be spilled. He refuses.

"Prepare for siege!" Jehoiachim shouts to the people

from a battlement overlooking the city rooftops. "None can breach our walls. Our storehouses are full of grain and fodder. Our cisterns beneath this mountain are deep and overflowing. That vast host will starve from lack of food and drop from thirst."

The king's words are shouted again and again by heralds in every square and on every street corner. They are ideal exhortations meant to stir the people's resolve. But they are not the whole story, and anyone with good sense knows it. Though there be some truth in what the king says, the enemy's hosts will have at their disposal the wells that are everywhere in the land and the lakes in the north. Moreover, the River Jordan is only a long day's march from Jerusalem, if the invader's forces divide and the main body comes down the river valley from Kinneret. The country people are scurrying from all quarters to bring their animals and foodstuffs into the city, true, yet the enemy will scour all lands they pass through, and their wagons will also be full-laden with food to feed the army for a long endurance.

Our scouts have returned at great speed to the city, further alarming the populace with their latest reports. The Babylonians have swarmed into the land, with clouds of dust and columns of fire in their wake. They have taken Jezreel with only small resistance and occupied Mount Gilboa, where they now command the heights overlooking the valley and the three main routes leading to Jerusalem: the Jordan in the east, the wide swing westward around the mountains and into the coastal plain, and the rougher but more central highway through the mountains. Their army is dividing into three branches, each one larger than our entire forces. Our chariots engaged them in Jezreel but were quickly overwhelmed; a remnant retreated hastily toward Megiddo. It is likely that even now they are encircled and trapped there. Destruction of our most elite warriors will surely follow.

The Refuge

At the Temple, slaughter of offerings increases. The smoke continuously billows upward. The Outer Court is crammed with tents and is loud with raucous din, the constant human cries of supplication, and the bellowing of animals scenting the blood. The number of students has dwindled in my house, for many have abandoned their duties to hide or flee—fleeing to who knows where. Thus, my studies are put aside for the sake of additional Temple duties. I now spend hours each day doing what I thought I had left behind forever: carrying charcoal and freshly hewn wood to meet the Altar's demand. There are fewer priests in the Temple precincts. Many of them have fled. And so I must also help with the ritual slaughter, years before my ordination, alongside my task of carrying fuel. I am seldom free to wash myself of soot and blood, but no one seems to notice. Night and day I labor at both tasks, stealing only a few hours of sleep between midnight and dawn.

Even in dedication to my duties, my heart feels the leaden temptation to futility. The Lord desired from his people the sacrifice of total fidelity, and now the consequences of our disobedience cannot be placated by merely increasing the volume of offerings. He is no pagan idol that must be sated by blood until its belly is full and gore spills from its maw. Even as I toss and turn in fitful dreams, the sacrifices continue.

We pray for deliverance. Again and again we pray for deliverance, but the Babylonians press ever closer.

In the night, an hour or two before daybreak, I am in service at the Altar of Sacrifice. Animal sacrifices have dwindled to next to nothing, but the rule is that the flame must not go out. Sunrise is not far off, and the immolation of birds and grains will then resume. I am feeling nearly spent, pushing my limbs and my dazed mind beyond the limits of endurance. Into my exhausted thoughts comes the memory of King Saul's death on Mount Gilboa, defeated in battle with the Philistines because of his sins against the Most High, his disobedience to the prophet, his consulting a witch, relying not on the Lord who could truly save. Is this to be Israel's fate in our times?

I have just silently asked this question when I look up from the altar fire toward the closed doors of the *Hekal* and behold an argument on the outside steps. A group of priests are gathered before the doors, arguing with each other furiously. One of the king's chief advisors, also raising his voice, is with them, accompanied by three or four palace guards. There are about the same number of Temple guards standing nearby.

I hear feet racing up the Altar steps behind me and turn to find Levi, out of breath and panting with acute emotion. Another man has run up the steps and stands beside him. Seeing his face by the light of the fire, I recognize Jeremiah's young scribe, Baruch.

"Yezekiel, the time has come," says Levi. "The weight of the balance is tipping."

"What do you mean?"

"I mean, does Israel believe in strategies or does Israel believe its prophets?"

I do not understand what he is telling me. He points in explanation to the argument still underway before the Temple doors.

Among the thirty or forty men gathered there, a small figure stands like an immovable pillar, saying nothing. It is Jeremiah.

Baruch explains:

"My master has received a revelation from the Most High. He is commanded to take the Ark of the Covenant and the

Tabernacle of Meeting from the Temple and bring them for
safekeeping into the mountains beyond the Jordan.''

I am stunned. Stunned most of all by the fact that the Ark
has never been visible to anyone but High Priests throughout these past centuries. Will I see it at last?

"Come," says Levi to me.

When he and I and Baruch arrive at the pavement before
the doors leading into the *Hekal*, I see that the argument has
sputtered into ashes. The king's servant and his soldiers are
hastening toward the palace gate. Of the hundreds of priests
attached to the Temple, only a dozen or so are present. Of
these I recognize certain elders who have defended Jeremiah
during his recent conflicts with the palace. The son of the
High Priest is also present, a man who will soon inherit the
High Priesthood, for the present High Priest, Jehozedak, is
very aged and ailing in health. This "Priest-Son", as he is
informally called, seems to be foremost in authority here.
He says a word to the Temple guards, and they open the
doors to the *Hekal*.

Uncertain if I am allowed to enter, I stand outside while
all the others go in with bowed heads. Levi comes back,
takes me by the arm and pulls me inside with him. My
mind is shocked into emptiness. As we proceed down the
long chamber, my eyes note in passing the countless candles
and oil lamps, the gold floor, the gold walls, and the gold
tables. Only the three priests on night duty are inside the
Hekal, waiting beside the incense altar, from which a thin
vapor is rising. Now the group kneels and bends before the
Holy of Holies. None excepted, we put our faces to the
floor. Jeremiah is lying prone, off to the side, looking insignificant as always, though he is the main agent of what is
about to happen. He is the last of us to rise to his feet. The
Priest-Son stands and beckons to two other priests to help

him. These three old men, along with the night-duty priests, slowly open the doors wide. These doors are many cubits in height and very heavy in weight. Their hinges squeal as the pins revolve, and then before my eyes is the high and wide curtain of many colors. Without further delay, the six priests pull the veil aside, and, behold, there is the Ark and its seraphim!

There are two seraphim, very great in height, which immediately seize the eye. Ten cubits high, three times the height of a tall man, these giants date from the building of Solomon's Temple. Each has an outstretched wing that touches the wall of the Holy of Holies, with the other wing extended over the Ark and touching the wingtip of its companion seraph. They stand upon their own feet, facing us.

More ancient is the smaller set of cherubim, which are made of solid gold. They are fused to the lid of the Ark, called the "Mercy Seat", dating from their original creation in the desert, at the command of Moses, who was obeying the precise instructions from the Lord regarding its details and workmanship. These cherubim are facing each other with their wings outstretched above the Ark.

The Ark itself is also radiant gold. The artisanship in its making is exceedingly skilled and refined. Attached to both its sides are gilded poles on rings, the very ones used by our ancestors to carry it through the desert, across the divided sea, the mountains, the Jordan, and into the Promised Land.

I drop again to my knees, gasping for breath, my heart pounding in awe.

Beckoning to the assembled, the Priest-Son selects twelve men to take up the poles, six to a side, who will carry the Ark out into the *Hekal*. I can see that these men, some priests, some Temple guards, are young and strong, but all are filled with fear, approaching the Ark with anxious faces and trembling knees. Nevertheless, they obey.

The Priest-Son begins to pray aloud, and his fellow priests join in. I am praying, too, pleading wordlessly for the mercy of the Lord Most High to come to our aid and for the glory of the Lord to remain in the Temple undiminished, that the light will not go out of the world.

Slowly, bearing its great weight with strain, the porters bring the Ark through the *Hekal* toward the outer doors. I follow last of all. No, not last, because I now notice Jeremiah a few steps behind me.

The east is glowing with the rose light of dawn. Two guards lead the procession with torches held high. Down the steps we go, and then past the Altar of Sacrifice, and then slowly, step by step, we progress through the Temple Court and, finally, through the Outer Court. Here, the refuge people are still asleep within their tents, all unheeding what is passing through their midst. Ahead of us, the Temple guards open the great gates leading into the lower city. Out on the streets, there are no pilgrims or passersby to be seen in any direction. Jerusalem seems calm and at peace, despite the threat looming ever closer from the north. Cocks are crowing. A dog barks and sets off other barking dogs nearby.

Outside the main gates, two carts are waiting, each drawn by a pair of horses. Onto one cart the Ark is carefully lifted and then covered by a cloth. Onto the other is placed a very large rolled tent, Moses' "Tabernacle of Meeting", which once housed the Ark during its long journey across the desert. Its sheets of fine linen are woven from purple, violet, and scarlet thread, with cherubim embroidered upon them. The colors are somewhat faded, perhaps by age, perhaps by long years under the sun during the exodus. The same colors are in the veil of the Holy of Holies, but richer, brighter. Beside the tent is placed the golden altar of incense, now bereft of fire and smoke. Again, the whole is covered by a large cloth and secured by ropes.

Jeremiah is helped up onto the back of a donkey. Looking very frail, he sits there with his hands firm on its neck strap. Baruch takes the creature's halter rope and leads it forward. As it clips and clops away on the cobblestones, Jeremiah casts a final look back at the Temple, and then he faces forward with resolve.

The carts and their drivers follow. Most of the younger priests and a few old ones, accompanied by Temple guards, fall in behind.

Levi and I keep pace. At first I feel only my awe, but it soon gives way to a new worry. What will happen to the Ark? Will it be safe? And what will happen to Jerusalem, indeed, to all Israel—the kingdom so hard-won by our beloved King David, and so hard-preserved by the shed blood of its people?

Now we are at the main city gate, the one for the road leading downward through the hills to Jericho and Gilgal and the river. The Priest-Son is speaking with the chief of the gate guards, while watchmen on the battlements observe us from above. I cannot hear what is said, but the discussion is brief—and thus I conclude that the palace has given permission for the Ark's departure, or else the spirit of the Most High has moved these soldiers' hearts to let us pass.

I am about to walk through the open gates when I feel Levi's hand restrain me by the arm.

"Let us go with them," I say to him.

"With my whole desire I would go with them, Yezekiel. Yet duty calls me to inform my father about what has happened. If I go away without telling him, he would take it as a double betrayal."

"Surely he knows."

"No, he does not. I am ashamed to say that he holds fast to the greater body of priests who reject Jeremiah and adhere to palace policies for fear of falling into disfavor. Their reputations and incomes carry great weight in their deliberations."

"More than the will of the Lord?"

"They believe that the will of the Lord is served by preserving their privileged positions."

I say nothing, not wanting to reinforce my cousin's grief over his father and his disgust at the majority of his fellows. Not wanting, moreover, to slide into bitterness and judgment.

"Where is the Ark being taken?" I ask.

"Baruch tells me that Jeremiah will bring the Ark to the mountain that Moses climbed to see God's inheritance, the place where he gazed out over the Promised Land but was not himself to enter."

"Mount Nebo?"

"Yes, and there he hopes to find a suitable cave in which to hide the Tent, the Ark, and the altar of incense. He believes that angels will guide his steps to the right place. He will block up the entrance so that none may find it."

"None? God-willing, it will be found again, after the war has passed over us."

"Do not forget the prophecies, Yezekiel. In time, the war will indeed pass over us, or rather through us. As Jeremiah said, great trials will follow."

"Then we must pray that the cave of the Ark never fades out of memory."

Levi nods.

"Let us pray for that. Even so, I fear for the Ark. Moses' body is buried on that mountain, and after so many generations there are none now living who know the place."

"I must go with the Ark!" I exclaim.

"Go, if you will, Yezekiel. But understand the risk, for time is short before the storm breaks upon us. You might not be able to return to the city if it is besieged."

Now my heart is divided in two: I yearn to follow Jeremiah, yet I know that my duty is here, even if it means death.

Levi and I watch the dust rising from the road where the carts and those accompanying them are making progress toward the lip of the land. Finally, when the road slopes downward, they are lost to view.

We turn away, feeling a chasm of emptiness opening within us. Saying nothing, we head back up the mountain. The guards close the city gate, and the sun rises.

I have resumed my station by the Altar of Sacrifice. Offerings are meager, a few sparrows, pigeons, and sheafs of humble grain; no fine wheat. It may be that people are holding onto their animals and other provisions, preserving them for the siege to come when hunger might become our chief enemy.

There are only two priests engaged in ritual slaughter. I alone am carrying the offerings up the stairs and throwing them onto the fire. The fire is also feeble, as only three youths from the lower house of studies are fetching the fuel. By noon, the sacrifices decline to nothing, and we are all left idle. The two priests wander away. The three youths quench their thirst with water from the molten sea, which is now overflowing from disuse. Then they, too, depart.

The Refuge

Levi comes running up the steps from the courtyard below. He is winded, his face red from exertion.

"I am leaving the city, Yezekiel," he says when he can speak at last.

"Where are you going, Levi?" I ask.

"Perhaps to Egypt, for they are no friends of Babylon. My plan is to convince my parents to leave with me at once. We must move swiftly and go far. Only hours or minutes remain until the enemy's host falls upon us."

"Hours, minutes?"

"Immense clouds of dust arise from the north, and another from the road to the western sea. There are no tidings yet from the Jordan, but it will not be long. Come with us, Yezekiel."

"No. I will remain with the Temple."

Anxious and perplexed, he examines my eyes, realizing I mean what I say.

Then, for the first time in our lives, my cousin shows me human warmth. He places his hands on my shoulders and kisses my forehead. Surprised by this, and equally by the tears in his eyes, I do not know how to respond. Such a kiss is a rare thing, for use on solemn occasions or for expressing deep emotion. Through my mind there passes an image of the prophet Samuel anointing young David with oil and kissing his forehead in portent of his future sufferings.

"I saw you, Yezekiel, in the times to come," Levi says with a shaken voice.

"You saw me?" I ask uncertainly.

"It was a picture in my mind for a fleeting moment. In a stormy wind sent from heaven, you saw something and fell into the dust, full-shocked by a . . . it was . . . it was . . ." Levi shakes his head. "There are no words for it."

"Perhaps it was the mind's fancy, swift passing and without consequence."

Again he shakes his head. "Fare well, Yezekiel," he murmurs. "Fare you well in the approaching trials. Long will be the days of our purification."

"If the days be short or long, Levi, may you be safe, and may you and Deborah and your little Michal prosper."

"The times of prospering are over," he says despondently.

I put my hands on his shoulders and gently shake him. "Think of what Jeremiah tells us, and also what Isaiah told us. Tribulations will increase, but in the end a root of Jesse, a shoot of the House of David, will arise and bring healing and justice to the nations."

"Yes," he says, but his stricken countenance reveals that his belief in those prophecies is paling before the onslaught of fear.

Taking hold of his emotions, he steps back.

"Do not lose heart, Levi. Do not be captured by the eyes of the serpent, which paralyzes the mouse with terror."

"Mouse?" He smiles for the first time in ages—a sad smile, but still a smile. "Am I a mouse? Or do you mean Nebuchadnezzar coiling about tiny Israel?"

"No, that is not my meaning. Nor do I mean death."

"By *serpent* you mean the ancient enemy of mankind."

I nod in affirmation. "The serpent would flood our minds with fear, seeking to convince us that he has won and thereby dishearten us so completely that he might more easily devour us."

Levi bows his head and wipes his eyes on his sleeve.

"I must go now."

With no more to be said, we clasp hands. He abruptly turns on his heels and hastens away down the cobbles. I walk back to the Temple, where I climb the steps to the

Altar of Sacrifice. No servants or priests are on duty there; they have abandoned their stations; they have all run away. A few embers are still glowing on the altar. I walk to the shed behind the Temple precincts where the altar wood is stored. I find a few pieces of green acacia and the last of the charcoal staves. I carry them back to the altar and lay them over the coals. With the breath of my mouth I make the red embers become tongues of fire, igniting the fuel. As I watch the flames rise, I wonder over Levi's mysterious words about a storm wind sent from heaven.

There are no animals, birds, or grain offerings to throw upon the fire. I stand beside the altar praying, facing upward to the Temple and the open doors of the *Hekal*. The Ark is gone, yet the Name and the glory of the Lord Most High remains.

I offer myself to him. It is not much, but it is all that I have to give.

In the hour before dawn, I wake to find myself curled up on the paving stones beside the Altar, my body shivering. There is no more fuel; the fire has burned down to ashes. Coming fully awake, I hear alarmed cries from beyond the open gates of the courts, voices shouting the news that advance troops of Nebuchadnezzar's army have encircled the city during the night. From three directions, greater numbers continue to arrive, swelling their ranks beyond our worst imaginings.

I run hastily down through the streets to David's walls and climb a stone staircase to the top of the ancient battlement. From there I can see the hills beyond the newer city walls. Countless campfires and peaks of tents are visible, and as I strain my eyes, I perceive a vast swarm of soldiers settled on all the land.

Along the walkway, a few scattered men gaze intently over

the rooftops toward the modern city's main gate. Hungry for information, I approach a man whom I recognize as an official of some kind, for in the past I have seen him coming and going through the palace gate.

"How stands Jerusalem's defense?" I ask him.

He turns an imperious face toward me, examines my Temple robe, and decides to answer:

"Their forces have encamped beyond bowshot," he replies with a scowl. "But there is no need for it. There will be neither battle nor siege, as the king has changed his mind."

A younger man, a companion of the first, further explains:

"The outer gates have been thrown open as an earnest of good will, and Jehoiachim is sending an embassy to plead for the Babylonian's mercy. He will pay the tribute in hope that they will go away without doing damage to Jerusalem."

"Will the Babylonians accept it?"

Both men look at me as if I am witless. The younger one shrugs.

"Yes, if their intent is merely subjugation," he says. "No, if they are set on plunder and ruinous punishment."

As the sun rises, I hasten down the steps and make my way quickly through the newer streets toward the outermost battlements. There, as I approach the city gate that leads to the Jericho road, I see that the doors are open wide. I climb the closest stairs and arrive on the walkway, which is crowded with ranks of archers and spearmen standing at the ready. I am just in time to see three of our chariots rolling forward toward the enemy lines. There are no warriors accompanying them on foot or horse, so I presume that they are bearing palace negotiators and interpreters. Is King Jehoiachim among them?

Though I am at some distance, I can see that the embassy has come to a halt in a flat, open place halfway between the gate and the enemy lines. They are waiting. We all wait. The sun climbs higher.

At midmorning a vanguard of mounted men rides slowly forth from the Babylonian line, passing through an opening in their pickets. Beyond that gap, the peaks of high tents can be seen, many of them red or blue, a few shining with the semblance of gold. The vanguard of horsemen is about forty strong. The riders appear to be ceremonial, though they are followed by two columns of foot soldiers with spears and swords held high. The enemy's trumpeters flank the horsemen, blaring a proclamation of their arrival.

As if to deflect them, I say, "The battle is the Lord's!"

But no one can hear me, for the trumpets drown all other noise.

I raise my voice louder, crying out as my father used to do when I was a child:

"The battle is the Lord's! The battle is the Lord's! The battle is the Lord's!"

Finally, through the picket gap comes a gilded chariot with a canopy above it, drawn by four black horses. Three men stand within it, a driver, a ceremonial guard lifting high a plumed lance, and a man wearing a costly golden robe and blood-red turban. He wears no armor. Is he the Babylonian king, or is he the king's ambassador? Perhaps he is a very high commander, the highest of all Babylon's invasion forces. It is difficult to tell, as these people are widely known for their love of lavish dress.

I think it is not Nebuchadnezzar himself, because the place of parley is within bowshot of the city wall, and no king would dare expose himself to such a risk.

The Babylonian chariot halts. One of our chariots drives forward to meet it. I cannot hear what is being said. I can hardly see who is speaking. The meeting does not last long.

Both embassies wheel their chariots around and proceed back to their own ground. Our three chariots enter the city gates, and as I gaze down upon the people riding within them, I see that all are finely robed, royal counselors and high captains of the palace guard. The king is not among them.

When the chariots enter the city, one of the palace captains leaps off and runs headway to the stairs and up to the battlements. I overhear him telling his wall lieutenants that the gate must remain open and that word is to be passed to all the city's defenders that the Babylonians have offered terms of a peaceful settlement. They promise that no one will be harmed and the city will be left undamaged if the tribute is paid and the Israelite soldiers lay aside their arms. The invader's chief ambassador will arrive later in the day and will speak to King Jehoiachim himself, to formalize the agreement. The lieutenants run off along the walkway in opposite directions, spreading the news.

In the afternoon, the Babylonians' grand chariot enters through the city gates. The man I had seen at a distance, golden-robed and turbaned in red cloth, is seated on a cushioned chair within. I catch a glimpse of his face as he passes by below—it is pompous, confident, yet betraying no emotion. He is neither young nor old; his cheeks look rouged; his eyes unnaturally enlarged by black kohl, his long beard intricately braided. Marching on each side of the chariot are six Babylonian soldiers with swords sheathed and as many ceremonial guards bearing lances topped by red pennants. At a leisurely pace they proceed from the gate square onto the main street leading up the side of the mountain to the palace.

A hundred Babylonian soldiers quietly enter through the gate and station themselves in the gate yard, their manner by no means menacing, though their faces are grim and their weapons are at the ready.

A larger unit of Babylonian soldiers stands outside, filling the road and the hills on either side. The gates remain open. Our watchmen on the battlements are nervous and our warriors anxious as they lay their bows and spears in piles in obedience to their commanders. Murmuring one to another, they wait to hear about the outcome of the conference between our king and the Babylonian envoy. We all wait.

I look down at the alien troops and listen to their harsh guttural voices as they converse with each other. They are not as tall a people as we are; their bodies are stocky, their faces sunbaked and hard. They wear bronze breastplates, with leather skirting to mid-thigh, beneath which is a knee-length tunic of rough brown weave. Their sandals are heavy leather and strapping, their calves bound in bands of cloth. Their conical helmets are copper, a light metal, which I presume makes for ease of wearing. This vast horde, this many-faced beast, bristles with spears and swords. I see no bowmen among them, which I have heard is typical of Babylonian troops, for unlike the Assyrians, Persians, and Egyptians, they rarely launch a barrage of missiles at a distance or attack with cavalry, preferring instead to overwhelm opposition with a mass of agile foot troops fighting at close quarters. Clearly, their strategy has won them an empire.

Shortly after—too short a time for a royal conference—I hear the Babylonian chariot returning, the clattering of wheels and the clopping of its four horses descending the hill, along with shouts coming from farther up. Now with the contingent of his guards, the Babylonian envoy enters the gate square as his herald blows three trumpet blasts. Immediately the hundred come to attention and spread around the square. From outside the gate I hear the sudden roar of a multitude of men giving a battle cry. They pour in through the gaping doors and make a mass that fills the square, leaving only a circle of empty space in the middle.

Now I see that a man is being dragged along behind the envoy's chariot. The chariot halts by the empty place, and the man falls down. His hands are bound at the wrists, and a drag rope is about his neck. He is barefooted, dressed only in a blood-soiled undergarment.

It is King Jehoiachim!

Babylonian officers kick him repeatedly and strike him with rods, while other military commanders stand around, mocking the dishonored king in words unintelligible, like the grunting of swine and braying of donkeys.

Realizing what is happening below, witnesses watching from rooftops and on the battlement raise an uproar of shocked protest, men shouting and women wailing.

"It is the king, the king! They are killing the king!"

"Alarm! Alarm!" our soldiers yell above the clamor. But it is too late.

Now the red-turbaned envoy stands and makes a gesture with his right arm, like a sword-thrust. A chief of the Babylonian troops steps forward and plunges a sword into the king's breast. A pool of blood spreads from his motionless body.

Soldiers grab the king's body by the ankles and drag it outside the walls, where they throw it onto a heap of trash and offal. In obedience to roaring commands, the mass of troops in the gate court are mobilized to action as an unceasing flood pours through the gaping doors behind them.

As I watch all of this, I am too shocked to think, to move, to do anything but stand in paralyzed fear as I observe the most horrible thing I have seen in my life. Then, my mind clears, and I realize what I must do. I must return to the Temple. I must protect it. But the streets are now too crowded with screaming people scattering in all directions before the rushing onslaught of invading soldiers. So far, they do not appear to be harming Jerusalemites, nor are they doing much damage to property. I see them overturning or robbing the tables of market vendors, but only in passing. They are fanning out onto all streets, generally heading in the direction of the mountain. A few dozen are rapidly climbing the battlement steps nearest to me, followed by more and more. Townspeople, priests, and other officials scatter as the enemy reaches the walkway. Our soldiers, who until now have been stunned with confusion, are scrambling for their weapons. The Babylonians quickly disarm them, and those few who persist in showing resistance are hurled from the battlement to shatter on the pavement below.

I look no more, for I am intent on reaching another staircase farther along the wall. It leads down to a street on the northern side of the city, a fair distance from the main gate. I leap into action and run. The walkway, narrow as it is, offers me a roadway close to the sky, and as I race along it, I pass countless rooftops on my left and, on my right, a plague of milling Babylonians, pressing forward to enter Jerusalem by any entrance they find. The walls curve and curve ahead of me, the sun coming into view, blinding me without warning. I keep stumbling onward, until at last I am in the mountain's shadow. With my breath tearing in and out of my pounding chest, I stop for an instant to look up at the Temple above me on the heights.

The north staircase is near, with panicking people going down it—in haste to get off the walls and into their houses, where they hope to bar their doors and let the storm pass by.

There is pushing, and some people fall off the stairs with a cry. Down the staircase I go, taking the steps carefully, resisting those who shove me from behind, and then I am safely on the street and running with the hem of my robe gathered up in my fists. I have progressed through four or five blocks before I begin to hear roaring voices and clanging armor increasing on every side. Now I am at the edge of the mount on which the Temple stands. There is no road here, but I know a path that leads upward. I begin to climb. The way is steep and rocky, ending at a small doorway in a wall of the Temple complex. It is nearly invisible because it is shielded by bushes.

I push open the wooden door, and once inside I close it behind me, finding myself in a chamber that holds cleaning tools and other items of Temple maintenance. I push open the door on the far side of the room, and, bounding through, I enter the inner court. Despite the Babylonian promise to do no harm—a promise now revealed as a ruse to let them into the city—the Temple guards have closed the gate doors between the inner and outer courts. They have also barred the high doors leading into the palace compound. Most importantly, they have closed the mighty doors of the *Hekal*. It is my hope that these especially have been sealed from within. There is no other entrance to the Holy of Holies.

Quickly I climb the steps to the fireless Altar of Sacrifice. There are no servants or priests to be seen anywhere, so perhaps they are inside the *Hekal*. A few guards stand by all the gates, looking uncertain about what will happen, though they have readied their spears and exposed their swords. A handful of bowmen stand by the king's gate.

I do not know what to do. I have no weapons, no sling or staff. I am no arrow in the bow of the Lord, but a man who prays. I have no embers to rekindle the altar fire, and yet I know that prayer is not dependent on fire or sacrifice. I turn and face the doors of the *Hekal* and drop to my knees, begging the Lord for his mercy on the nation. Even as I pray, the prophecies of Jeremiah course through my mind.

I now feel certain that I will die here. This I accept; this I offer to the Most High.

I put my face to the stone pavement and pray unceasingly. I hear loud booms, the sound of the gates into the inner court being hammered by a great force or weight. With a crash, the gates swing open, and now I am surrounded by the stamping of rough-shod feet and the growls of Babylonians. Still I do not lift my face from the ground and continue to invoke the Holy Name.

I hear the hoof-beats of horses and donkeys entering the inner court. Looking up, I see the bodies of Temple guards and king's bowmen, all lying in their blood. A few Babylonians have fallen with them, arrows protruding from their corpses. I am the only Israelite left alive, and I do not know why I have been spared. I remain kneeling, stunned, gaping at the mayhem around me.

Numerous carts are being drawn into the inner Temple Court, some pulled by donkey teams, some by horses. Soldiers begin battering the bronze doors of the Treasury building with a wooden ram. When at last the doors are shattered, the plunderers run inside. Within minutes they are hauling out sacks of coins, chests full of gold and silver, and various furnishings such as candelabra and jars of priceless oil, incense urns, thrones dating from past reigns, and gilded musical instruments—all of which they commence packing onto the carts.

Other carts are being drawn close to the steps leading up to the Temple itself. Twenty Babylonians are mounting the steps carrying a heavy log with an iron head in the shape of a horned bull. When I realize that their intention is to break the doors and enter the *Hekal*, I jump to my feet and race after them, hoping to stop the desecration.

I reach the base of the Temple steps only to be barred by two soldiers, who hit my legs with the butts of their spears, collapsing me to the ground. They kick me in the ribs and buffet my head with blows, and then they pull me up onto my feet. The two grab my arms and a third seizes my hair, and together they drag me out of the Temple Court and through the Outer Court. When we reach the street, I am thrown down onto the cobbles among a cluster of bleeding priests and a few palace officials. My vision is blurred, for my eyes are swollen, my nose is running blood.

After a time, I can see more clearly, and the bleeding stops. The carts are constantly rattling past us, laden with Temple plunder. Hordes of Babylonian troops now fill the surrounding streets. They are breaking down the doors of the wealthy homes, pillaging them, and dragging forth the owners. Now and then another terrified soul is thrown onto the ground beside us, usually a beautiful maiden or a strong young man or an older figure of stature, many of them in costly garments. Their jewelry is torn from their necks and ears, and their hands are forced open to expose what they may be hiding. And all the while, the crowds of common folk and the tent-dwellers who had come into Jerusalem for safety are milling about, confused and frightened by the invaders brandishing spear and sword in menacing gestures, shouting in a language that few if any of us can understand. I see no more killing, but panic now rules our people. They flee in all directions, though there is no place left where the enemy has not penetrated.

An older soldier in bronze body armor and a feathered helmet struts about those of us who are penned together.

He is laughing contemptuously, pointing at us and trading comments with others of his rank. Ringing us are numerous soldiers, with lances pointing toward us like a stockade of lions' teeth.

"Your king, your mighty king, is no more," the Babylonian bellows. Keeping pace with him is one of our own, a palace interpreter, looking wretched and subservient, translating the Babylonian's words into Hebrew.

"His body lies on your offal pile, where it rots beneath the sun, food for dogs and vultures. Anyone who tries to bury him will be instantly slain."

The afternoon is waning, yet the sound of tumult never ceases. With barked commands, we prisoners are told to stand. We are driven downward off the mountain at spearpoint.

Prodded along by blows and jabs, we pass through the city gate and onto the road to Jericho. As we emerge from the shadows of the great bronze doors, I look to my left and see a flock of crows at the top of a dung heap. The birds are in a riot of cawing and pecking at a naked human body, which must be the king's. Small boys stand several paces away, hurling stones at the birds, which rise and circle and then settle again. The Babylonians do not drive the boys off, perhaps because they think these lawless young wretches are mocking the corpse.

I turn away and plod onward, whispering the *Shema* prayer.

I do not know where we are being driven or why. It seems to me that the angel of death approaches, that the enemy will kill us all.

We have not walked very far before I notice more bodies discarded beside the road, several dozens, perhaps a hundred. Judging by their dress and armor, I realize that these are people of rank in the city, alongside high commanders of our Judean forces. They have not fallen in combat; there are no battle wounds upon them. They have been decapitated.

A few steps farther along and we arrive at a field of beaten grass, where our guards command us to sit down. We obey, wondering what will come next. My fellow prisoners are weeping and murmuring. Some among us, crazed with fear, jump up and begin screaming. They are knocked back down by the guards, who stomp on them with their boots until the screams become muted whimpers. Youths leap to their feet and shake their fists, shouting, "Betrayal, betrayal!" They, too, are knocked down by staves and fists. Even so, no one is killed.

Night falls. We huddle together, trying to keep warm. Few, if any, can sleep. Cries and prayers arise from time to time. No one attempts to flee, for twice as many Babylonians are encamped around us. They keep vigilant watch. I smell the food they are cooking on their campfires. Their raucous boasts, their laughter, and their guttural chants make sleep impossible. I pray until the sky pales in the east.

Just before sunrise, we are roused by more barking commands. A donkey cart comes to a halt beside us. It is carrying large cane baskets and a clay water urn. A servant of the enemy, a Hebrew like us—whether slave or hireling I do not know—dips a jug into the urn's open top, and with it he fills a cup. Desperately thirsty, we file forward one at a time, prodded by guards, and we drink. When all have had their fill, another servant throws disks of poor-man's bread at us.

We are commanded to sit down. We sit down and eat the bread.

From time to time, other groups like ours are driven past on shuffling feet, heads bowed, dejected. None of them seem greatly harmed in body. I see Temple priests and rich merchants and even palace officials, their insignia and ornaments stripped from their robes.

Are we all being herded toward some distant pit where we will be executed?

And still I pray, begging the Most High to give me strength to face what lies ahead, that even in my last moments of life I will not betray the Covenant.

6

The Road

T HROUGHOUT THE DAY I am a cracked cistern, though I hide my tears from my people, lest I add to their burden of despair. My face is calm, a mask of patient endurance; my soul is a tempest.

We are herded onto a road that circles Jerusalem and near the north gate joins the route leading up and over the Judean hills. Hour after hour we walk, with no explanation of where we are going. When the sun dips below the western ridges, with Samaria somewhere beyond them, we camp again by the side of the road.

I roll my body into the sackcloth the enemy has distributed among us. When we were driven out of the city, there was no time for me to fetch my meager belongings from the house of studies—indeed, the thought did not cross my mind, for I had expected to die. I now possess only my working robe, dusty and stained, and the head scarf my mother recently wove for me from lamb's wool. I kiss it, as if to bring her closer, and cover my head with it. As the darkness deepens around me, I try to pray, wordless prayer, silently watered with tears.

And then I feel him with me—a brief touch, a breath— my soul a parched land drinking unexpected rain. Is this the presence that watched over me when I was a boy among the flocks, the old companion of my childhood solitudes?

I do not know. It may be the unseen guardian of the kingdom roaming among the people to give reassurance to the anguished as they seek sleep. Or it may be the Most High himself who travels with us, suffering with us, even though he has now, at last, permitted chastisement to fall.

In the morning, the people are wakened by the shouting soldiers and their trusties, the translators and betrayers. We rise and eat dry bread and drink our water portion, and then we put one foot after another as we go onward toward an unknown end.

We are many hundreds of captives, not the full populace of Jerusalem, but the wealthy and powerful, king's advisors from the royal court, important priests, figures of noble lineage, battle champions who were captured, and the greatest artisans, along with a selection of the city's maidens and young men in the flower of youth. Among us on the dusty road is a river of carts and pack horses carrying gold and silver from the Temple treasury and the abundance of Jerusalem's palaces.

Arriving at Ramah, we join numerous groups of people winnowed out of Jerusalem and gathered in the valley for a purpose that no amount of terrifying rumors can explain. There we are encamped by force outside the town walls. Ramah is Rachel's town, and now with a skip of my heartbeat I remember words I heard Jeremiah crying out in the Temple court: "A voice is heard in Ramah, mourning and great weeping, Rachel weeping for her children and refusing to be comforted, because they are no more."

All around me, a constant wailing of women's voices arises from the crowd of prisoners and the local inhabitants alike. Is this the place where the Babylonians will destroy us?

But no, after a short rest, the mass of captives are herded onto the northbound road. On the fourth day, we are passing through the valley of Jezreel, its fields of blue flax flowers now burned, a harvest of ashes. There I speak with one of the king's advisors, who is lagging behind, a man in ankle chains. He walks with a veil wrapped tightly across his eyes, and a boy is leading him by the hand. I identify myself as one of the Temple attendants. His mouth becomes bitter, as if to say, why does one so lowly speak with me, I who once was great in the palace? Even so, we stop for a moment as the crowd surges about us.

"Why do we travel north?" I ask him. Until now I have held onto the hope that, despite all prophecies, we are being moved to a lesser city or town in Israel. There, we will know servitude but not exile.

"We go north because we are being taken to Babylon," says the king's advisor. "All of us would perish if we were to go by the eastern route."

Now, at last, I know the truth of the matter. And with it the answer to my question. We must go north as far as Syria in order to circle the tip of the Arabian desert. When we reach Syria, we will turn east and, in time, will arrive at the River Euphrates. At that point, we will have covered barely half the distance. Then we will turn south onto the great road that leads to the city of Babylon. If the people do not succumb during the march, we will come to the city in a hundred days.

The king's advisor snaps angrily at the boy, telling him to leave us. The boy goes.

Unwrapping his eyes, the king's advisor stares at me from hollow sockets, still bleeding.

"Kill me," he says.

I am stunned, unable to reply.

"With your hands," he says. "Do it! Do it now!"

"I will not kill you by any means," I tell him. "Take heart and be a man."

"You with two eyes, *you* be the man. I am no more. The kingdom is no more."

"Do you not heed the prophets?" I remonstrate. "Though we are now chastened most severely, yet shall we be restored."

"Prophets!" he scorns. "They are fools who listen to voices in their dreaming minds. They have ruined us, for they dispirited the people."

"They can hardly have dispirited us, for none took heed of their warnings save a few."

But my words have no effect. An hour later, he staggers away from the road and begins to run with his chains clinking, not knowing where he is going, tripping over rocks, crawling, rising, stumbling onward toward a refuge that he cannot see, that does not exist. A laughing soldier follows him, his long strides more than a match for the old blind man. Tiring of this play, he plunges his spear into the escapee's back, pinning him to the ground.

Here, then, is the heart of the matter: The people did not listen to the prophets, who showed us what the Lord may do in the face of invaders if only we would keep faith. In ages past, the Canaanites and Egyptians and Philistines were thrown back, ofttimes when we were greatly outnumbered. Yet the Babylonians have pressed forward and seized us as a bird of prey grips the hare in its talons. And this was because of our sins. Deaf and blind, we go down into bondage in a foreign land, for deaf and blind we have been.

The guards are ferocious, long lines of them walking alongside us, carrying wooden staves with bronze spikes to prod us if we falter in our steps or to strike us if we drift from the road in the direction of the trees. Now and then a man of higher rank in full armor and plumed helmet rides past on a horse, inspecting the guards and the captives. Such captains wear sheathed daggers and swords, rarely used, for the people are exhausted and, most deadly of all, dismayed. The captains are always accompanied by two other riders, lieutenants with bows slung over their shoulders and long black quivers at their waists, packed with arrows.

Though the taunts against us have declined in number, the enemy's malice is still fresh, for our captors lost comrades during the invasion. Now and then, one of our young men, filled with the thoughtless rage of the young—a toothless lion roaring—will shout recriminations or pick up a rock and hurl it at the guards. He is pulled from the crowd and beaten. Perhaps blinded, sometimes killed. Or if one of these youths sprints into the bushes, hoping for freedom, the lieutenants on horseback will converge and give chase, and the fugitive will be felled by an arrow. For the most part, the people have become docile. The constant sobs and pleadings to the Most High have fallen silent. We merely walk.

In my thoughts I repeat again and again the song of David when he was seized by the Philistines in Gath, and I often whisper the words:

"*My enemies trample upon me all day long, for many fight against me proudly. When I am afraid, I put my trust in You.*"

Galilee's forests have appeared on the heights. There are no sheep in the lower pastures. From time to time, I see vultures clustering in burned fields, feasting upon human bodies left unburied, unclean, a reproach and a silent witness. Whole villages are empty. The kingdom's forts are in ruins.

Traveling in our group is an older man, a merchant of

Jerusalem. He has trouble walking long distances, and so from time to time I take his arm or help him to his feet when he stumbles. His name is Jotham. He has little energy to talk during the day, yet he sleeps beside me at night, and then we speak with each other. This conversation helps me, since I feel less alone whenever we converse. I learn many things from him about the country to which we are being taken. He was a trader of textiles, journeying each year to Babylonia, Media, and Persia to sell his wares and bring back rare spices for Jerusalem's markets. He stayed long periods in the city of Babylon and knows their language.

Jotham will on occasion translate things the guards say or sing. He also describes the city, which, if his memory is reliable, is one of wondrous beauty. It is situated on the bank of the great river and surrounded by tributaries and canals that are ever expanded for irrigating grainfields and orchards that extend from horizon to horizon. It is so large in size that those who dwell in it number a thousand times a thousand, it would seem. Its walls are mighty and lavishly decorated. Its buildings are unlike any others in the world, with palaces crowned by gardens on rooftops and terraces. Its main temple soars to the sky.

"Higher than our Temple?" I exclaim in astonishment.

"The land is flat, and thus their temple does not stand on a mountain like ours. Even so, it is higher in construction. These are the people who built Nimrod's tower."

"Size does not mean holiness."

"You say rightly, Yezekiel. Though my eyes are old, never have I seen holiness in Babylon."

I weigh his answer with some thought, wondering if lack of holiness in a man condemns him to be entirely evil. And if the same holds true for cities and nations.

"Is it an evil land?" I ask Jotham one night when my heart is cast down. "It seems to me that only an evil land could breed such men as our captors."

"Yes, there is evil there," he replies in a musing voice. "Yet there is also evil in Jerusalem, is there not?"

Reluctantly, I have to agree.

"And did our forefather Abraham not come from Ur of the Chaldees?"

"This is true," I admit.

"And are not the Chaldeans neighbor and kin to Babylonians, more than any other peoples in alliance with them? Large numbers of Chaldean troops accompanied them when they invaded."

"They all looked alike to me."

"They are mingled and bonded, and you would have to live among them to read the differences."

"I have heard that some of the Babylonian kings were Chaldeans."

"It is true. Nebuchadnezzar himself is a Chaldean."

"Is he?" I say, surprised.

"You ask if it is an evil land, Yezekiel. But recall that Abraham and Sarah were Chaldeans. When they passed over the Euphrates and came into Canaan, they were strangers in *our* land. Yet Abraham is the father of us all."

In the dark, I bow my head and say no more.

The thoughts of the mind can deceive us, and the movements of the heart even more so. Anguish recedes a little and then returns as a flood. At night I weep. It may be that Abraham, too, wept in the night, in exile from his homeland, not knowing what the Lord would do through his obedience.

Before the eyes of my heart I keep the memories of a blessed time. I see again the faces of my family. I remember the water of my spring on the pastures of Little Bite of Bread. I think of the sky and birds and colors. There are times in the deepest dark of night when I raise my right arm and hurl my boyhood sling. At other times when no one can see me, I wave my hands in front of me, feeling the invisible waters of the air. And when a cooling wind is blowing, I thank the Most High for sending me this reminder of his presence.

There is no music now. Only the drunken bellowing of lust-songs by the soldiers encamped along beside us. Or their eerie hymns to their gods, chief among them an evil idol named Marduk and a lesser one named Ishtar. Whenever this poison begins to fill my ears, I quietly hum, or sing in a whisper, the king-psalms of David.

The dust raised by countless feet is hard to endure. Many of us are racked by dry coughing. We have been permitted to keep our head scarves, I presume because the Babyloni-ans realize that we would not survive the dust and burning sun without them. Some of the captives have brought their cloaks with which to wrap themselves for warmth at night. I regret that I do not have mine, for the nights are cool and promise to become more so at higher elevations.

Every night I remove the sandals that Issa gave me and set them neatly by my side. To my dismay, one morning three weeks into the journey I wake to find that they have disappeared. Without doubt, someone has stolen them, pos-sibly one of our guards but more likely one of my fellow captives. Throughout the following few days I watch all the feet beside me and ahead of me, hoping to pick out the thief. But never again do I see my sandals. Fighting anger in my heart, I walk barefoot from then on, enduring the small punctures in my feet, the cracked soles and blisters. My feet were leathery when I was younger and with the flock. After too many years of city life, they have grown soft. This walking will toughen them, I hope. Still sorrowing, I accept this new trial and try to let go of my resentment, day by day, step by step.

We are constantly hungry, though we are not starving. The distribution of bread is regular. There is ample water.

Farther north into Syria we go, nearing Damascus, whose walls and towers I can see in the distance. We do not enter the city, I suppose because it would present opportunities for captives to scatter and escape into its myriad streets. As we trudge onward week after week, I estimate by the position of the sun that the road is turning degree by degree toward the east. The hills to the left and right of the road become steadily lower in height. We pass through a series of connecting valleys that are green with farming.

Jotham tells me that Karkemish is not far by donkey or camel, but at the pace we are going, we still have four or five days of travel before we reach it.

Troops and captives alike are visibly tiring; the cavalcade goes ever slower. Since passing into Syria, the soldiers have discarded their heavier metal shields, shaped like the sun, and even the lighter ones made of leather and studded with bronze, piling them on military transport carts. For them, there is no more danger.

I walk without much thought or feeling. I do not allow myself to dwell on my body's fatigue and its aches. My mind is fatigued as well, though it is refreshed a little by night prayer and small discussions with Jotham.

He likes very much to inform others, doubtless from kindness, wanting to prepare us for what is ahead. There is another aspect to the man, I think, a quiet satisfaction he takes in being the learned one, the knower, the experienced; and in this way he feels elevated a little above the destruction of his former life. I do not fault him for it, as he delivers his small dissertations without a hint of pride.

"There be times when you mention the Babylonian language," I say to him one evening as we drift toward sleep. "At other times you refer to the Chaldean tongue. When you listen to our guards, which of the two is being spoken by them, which do you translate for us?"

"Ah, these names can be confusing, Yezekiel. You see, 'Chaldean' is a term interchangeable with the broader term 'Babylonian'. In ages past, the whole of the lands between the rivers, from the sea in the south to the mountains in the north, spoke Akkadian. And after that came Aramaic, which along with other influences gradually merged, creating this new tongue now known throughout the empire. There are dialects, of course."

Though I am too tired for a linguist's lesson, I do not interrupt. As he goes on, I remain only a little less confused as his mind roves wide and deep across time and the complex histories of the peoples and nations east of Judah. He speaks of the very distant past, the kingdoms arising out of Sumer especially, from which so much language, religion, and arts have come, spreading throughout the lands their numerous gods and cults. He digresses at length on the origins of written language and Chaldean science and their roles in the present Babylonian attainment of power.

Noticing that I have said nothing during his discourse, he changes the subject.

"I overheard a captain informing a troop leader that the number of captives from Jerusalem is three thousand."

"What will they do with us?" I ask.

"We are young and old," Jotham answers. "Those who are strong of body will most likely be put to manual labor in fields or building projects. The artisans will doubtless be placed in shops where their various skills will be used. A person like myself will probably be employed in their counting houses. Perhaps I will be used as an assessor of textiles." He pauses. "These people are rich in knowledge. Among their highest classes are men who know marvels about the stars in the heavens, and many are exceedingly clever in the mastery of numbers. Their libraries are filled with books of clay, far more than all Israel's scrolls combined. If they wished, they could erect an entire city with their tablets, for they are unceasing keepers of records. The merchants of the middle caste are so wealthy that their palaces put our own to shame. But Babylonian skill in making cloth is low, which is why they rely on trade for the better sort of fabrics."

Now Jotham warms to the subject of his main area of knowledge; I can see the rising enthusiasm in his eyes.

"Did you know, Yezekiel, that the weave of cloth in that land is sixty threads to a thumb-length, about the same as ours in Israel. In Egypt, however, the looms and the skills are so refined that their cloth is more than two hundred threads per thumb-length. So you see why they may need people like me, to help oversee imports."

"Will they employ you for wages, do you think?"

Jotham looks at me with pity. "We are *slaves*, Yezekiel. There will be food and shelter, no doubt, but we will be valued as little more than beasts of burden."

Another day or two, and finally we pass through a long valley that opens onto a wide green flatland. I behold in the distance a city shining in the sun, capped by a fortress of immense size, far higher than the city's walls. Beyond it is a line of blue water.

In the past, Karkemish was an independent city-state. Then it was conquered in turns by the Assyrians and Egyptians, and now it is ruled by the Babylonians, who fought a great battle here only a few years ago, seizing the city and its lands for their empire. It is a major crossing point on the Euphrates, ringed by stone battlements and earthworks, containing a great number of houses and what looks to be a temple rising several tiers above the rooftops. The whole is surmounted by the fortress on a hill that commands a view of the river at its feet. Spreading in all directions are vast grainfields, growing tall on these fertile floodplains, ready for harvest.

We are ordered to sit down in a harvested field by the road. An interpreter tells us that here we will remain for three days, because troops and captives need rest if we are to proceed farther without total collapse. We are given our usual bread and water, and for the first time in weeks fresh fruit is distributed. The laborers in nearby fields stare at us with contempt or curiosity, but none of them hurl abuse. The guards seem to have eased their vigilance somewhat, though not enough for any of us to take flight.

We rest or sleep. Throughout that day and the next, more groups of captives arrive and are forced to sit down in our field. Now crowded with weary, dejected people, there is room enough, however, to permit standing and stretching and wandering around within the confines of the pickets. Invariably, each group of guards divides, and half of them march off to the city, where I suspect they will search for taverns. We are still surrounded by sufficient troops to keep any of us from going astray, but brutality has all but disappeared. Indeed, we are permitted to light small cooking fires. At first I wonder what, if anything, there is to cook, until I see Babylonian servants bearing baskets full of freshly caught river fish and distributing them among our people. They also bring brass vessels on chains, containing glowing embers, with which the people make numerous small fires from wheat-chaff and the twigs of bushes lining the road.

Knowing how tired he is, I bring Jotham a slice of broiled fish on a platter of flatbread, along with a handful of ripe plums and figs. I find him lying on the ground. He looks at the food but waves it away.

"My heart is sore weary unto death," he says in a tone of lamentation, almost a chant. "The light goes from my eyes. I once believed I would die in my own land, on my bed of fine linens, with my wife and children to keep me company on my passage into the hands of the Most High." He sighs. "Now I am alone."

I place a hand on his shoulder.

"You are not alone, Jotham," I say.

A light returns briefly to his eyes. "Yezekiel, good companion, where have you come from?"

"From Jerusalem, like you."

"I mean where in the mysteries of the Lord have you come from, that you would be for me a mercy at the last and stand in good stead for my sons."

"We are all in his hands, Jotham. If I am a mercy for you, you are equally a mercy and comfort for me. Rest now, and it may be that the Lord will grant you many more days. And then you will see Babylon again."

"It is Jerusalem the golden that I wish to see with my eyes."

"God grant it be so. Even now you may see it within your heart."

He closes his eyes, and soon I know by the sound of his breathing that he is asleep.

We are traveling again. The road is wider than the one that brought us up out of the south, and it is smoother underfoot. Though there are other roads on the eastern side of the river, we were not ferried across at Karkemish, and thus I conclude that we are on the main route to Babylon, on the western bank.

We pass numerous villages and two sizeable towns during the first three days. The traffic of carts heading north and south is constant. The carts belonging to our cavalcade bear our bread, which is distributed in the morning before we begin the march and again at nightfall when we encamp.

The span of the blue Euphrates is greater than any river I have seen before, three or four times wider than the Jordan, faster and much deeper, I think. The Jordan is brown and shallow, at least the portion of it that I saw at Gilgal when I was a boy. Here, there are large rowing ships and barges on the water, perhaps for carrying grain southward to the cities of Babylonia. Fertile fields extend in all directions.

Jotham has not done well during the past few days. I must now keep an arm around him at all times, helping to bear him up and moving forward. His breathing is labored. When we are encamped on the fourth night out of Karkemish, he dies.

Through an interpreter, I ask the guards' permission to bury the old man's body.

"Throw it beside the road," says one, pointing.

I beg him to let me bury it in soil. I will dig with my hands, I plead.

The guards make jokes and laugh. The interpreter tells me that I have permission to make a hole and throw the body into it.

"We will plant a pomegranate on top of it," scoffs one of the guards. "Pomegranates now line the road all the way back to Jerusalem, and more will we plant before we reach home."

"In years to come, we will eat the fruit of your people's flesh," says another.

They will not give me any tool to dig a burial pit. The interpreter refuses to help me dig. Nearby us, four youths are sitting with heads bowed, covered by their shawls. I go to them and interrupt their prayers, asking them to help me bury a body.

They stand and listen to my request respectfully, but at first they hesitate. They do not want to touch the body because that would be unclean according to Mosaic law. Nevertheless, they quietly observe the situation—the corpse, my aloneness, the lack of tools.

"We will help you," says one of the boys at last.

I would carry the body myself, but Jotham was no small man to begin with, and years of prosperity have added to his weight. The boys take ankles and wrists, and, accompanied by two guards and a torch-bearer, we carry the body outside the encampment and lay it down on the grass. Dropping to our knees, we dig into the sod with our fingers and begin pulling it up. By the time the roots are exposed and plain soil appears, our fingernails are broken and bleeding. Still we work on, until finally we have exposed a shallow pit about three feet deep.

To our silent indignation, the guards strip the body. Averting our eyes to respect its dignity, we lay it in the pit, and, scooping with our hands, we cover it with soil.

"A cook-pot for jackals," exclaims a guard, making his companions guffaw with laughter. "They like to dig."

Another splits a pomegranate in two, clamps his large white teeth into one half and sucks the juice from it. He pushes the uneaten half into the soil.

They gather up Jotham's clothing, and, gesturing with their spears, they direct us back to the encampment.

"Sit with us," says one of the youths when we are again among our own people.

I sit down with them, the five of us in a ring facing each other. The youngest brings a rag and bowl of water, and with a look of deep sympathy he washes my hands. I am overwhelmed by this act of kindness. When he is done, I cover my head with my scarf and put my face into my hands. I pray for Jotham's soul, murmuring the *Kaddish* and the *Shema*.

I hear the boys joining in with their quiet voices—half deep—they are no longer children but not quite men.

"The man we buried, is he your father?" asks one of the boys after we remove our scarves.

"No, Jotham is a man I met on the road."

"May he rest with Abraham."

By the light of their little cookfire, I observe their faces, which are kindly and virtuous in mien. Despite their young years, strength of character is also evident. There is the particular mark of learnedness, too. Moreover, they appear to be unblemished and very good-looking.

"Were you taken from Jerusalem?" I ask.

All four of them nod sadly.

"I am Mishael," says the oldest of the four. "These are my friends Azariah, Hananiah, and Daniel. We attend school together, and our families are kin to each other. We live close to the Temple." He blinks away tears. "We *once* lived close to the Temple."

"I am Yezekiel ben Buzi," I tell them. "I am from a village in the direction of Hebron."

"We know your face," says the one named Hananiah. "We have seen you serving at the Altar of Sacrifice, where we often went to pray."

I do not recall having seen them before. But now I

understand the quality of fineness about them. If they lived close to the Temple, they must be from families connected to the royal house or belong to another rank of nobility.

After some persistent probing on my part, I learn that they are all of the tribe of Judah. Moreover, they are related through diverse marriages to the family of Mattaniah, brother to the king. This they tell me with diffidence; they display no pride regarding their high estate. In fact, I sense in them a certain shyness on the matter, which may be due to Mattaniah's bad reputation. They quickly turn the topic to me and my origins. I tell them a little. They are interested in my life as a shepherd boy, my encounters with wolves and lions. They have heard about my cousin Levi, whom they admire, but know next to nothing about his father, my uncle.

When we have exchanged our simple accounts, I ask them, "Are you afraid?"

They fall silent, their eyes growing thoughtful.

The youth named Daniel—the one who washed my hands—has not spoken until now. He says, "We are afraid, as Joseph was afraid when his coat of many colors was taken from him and he was sold into slavery."

A keen insight is embedded in this reply.

"If I catch your meaning aright, Daniel, you wish to say that no one can foresee all ends. The Most High permits adversity, even the most terrible, so that a great good may come from it, beyond the horizon of our sight and understanding."

Emphatically, all four boys nod in agreement.

Daniel is the youngest of his fellows by a year or two. He is not their leader—indeed, there is no leader among them, which is unusual with groups of boys. Yet he appears to be foremost in thought, perhaps wisdom, for the others listen with particular attention to what he says.

Azariah says, "Behold, here comes this man of dreams."

The other three smile. He has made a reference to a line from the book of Genesis, the passage describing how Joseph's brothers looked at their youngest brother with envy and resentment, conspiring to kill him.

"In part it is so," says Mishael, and all of them except Daniel nod.

"How do you mean *in part it is so*?" I ask.

"Like Joseph, our friend Daniel has dreams."

"We all have dreams in the night," Daniel replies, looking embarrassed.

"Not like yours," says Mishael.

I peer more closely at Daniel. He has grown very still in body and has lowered his eyes.

Azariah turns to me and says, "He has told us only a little: A man of light came to him in a dream and spoke words of reassurance. We will suffer many trials, he said. Ahead of us lie many roads, many waters, and we will know muddy ditches and palace banquets."

"A man of light?" I murmur, my heart quickening, for that is the very expression I once used to describe the figure who came to me in a dream when I was a boy.

Daniel looks up at me, wondering, I think, what my reaction will be.

Now, I close my eyes, and no one says any more.

I see again my childhood dream in which a dreadful peril came upon me, when before my eyes a great gate arose, as high and wide as a palace, all made of shining blue tiles, and upon it were living monsters, roaring lions and dragons intent on devouring me. I was preparing to die when a man radiating light bent over me and placed his hand upon my brow, and all fear fled from my heart.

"The man of light tells you not to be afraid," I say. "It is in our nature to fear, and there is no wrong in this. Even so, after fear must come trust. Overcome fear by choosing to rely on the Most High alone, and then nothing can vanquish you. They may kill the body but not your soul."

The four youths murmur in agreement. Daniel's eyes are now shining. How long he and I contemplate each other, I do not know. This moment is beyond measuring by time.

Day after day we travel onward. Though we have been accompanied by mosquitoes and flies all the way from Judea, they assault us now in force. The lowlands breed them in greater numbers, vexing us during daylight hours and making it difficult to sleep at night. I wrap my head and hands tightly in the sackcloth, but to no avail, for these insects and other biting-stinging things creep in through the loose weave. My ankles are bloody from their attacks. Thus, constant fatigue is becoming near-exhaustion.

There are compensations, however, such as more fish and fruit to eat. Also, the soles of my feet have become tough as hide, no longer tormenting me. The nights are warm; the days are becoming ever hotter. Captives and guards alike stop frequently to go down to the river to soak their head cloths. There, we also plunge our faces into the shallows and fill our bellies with water, for the occasional cups from the carts' barrels are no longer sufficient.

Now and then, other carts move alongside us and slowly forge ahead. I see some of our older people borne upon them as well as a few younger ones who are lame, perhaps, or of exalted status, valuable to the Babylonians in one way or another. And most shocking of all, the High Priest, Jehozedak, and his son. I do not see Prince Jehoiachin, the son of King Jehoiachim, or the king's brother Mattaniah, which makes me wonder if the entire royal family has been slain. If this is the case, it would spell the last of King David's line. But of course we know nothing. They may be farther ahead or behind on the road.

The four young men who helped me bury Jotham stay close to me. Or is it I who stay close to them? There is a bond between us now, though I doubt if any of us could define it. From time to time, I see these boys beg permission of the guards to bury people who have fallen by the wayside. Sometimes it is allowed, sometimes not; it depends on the capriciousness or malice of individual guards. A few are better than most. They stand by, leaning on their spears, observing the burial with apparent indifference, and yet one can see that there is curiosity and even a hint of sympathy. It is difficult to know what goes on inside those cruel faces, for they can be indulgent one moment and kill someone the next.

"Are you a priest?" Mishael asks me one evening as we eat our bread together.

"No, I am in studies for the priesthood."

"We are far from the Temple. Can you become a priest without the Temple?"

"I do not know whether this is now possible for me, so long a way from Jerusalem. Yet those who are consecrated to the priesthood remain always priests. I have seen Jehozedak on the road with us, and it may be that other Temple priests are captive."

Hananiah intervenes to give further instruction:

"The Law of Moses is certain on the matter, Mishael. It is written that it is an *everlasting* priesthood."

Azariah takes up the instruction: "Long before Levi and Aaron, Melchizedech was a priest of the Most High God. He passed his priesthood to Abraham, and from Abraham to Isaac and Jacob; then it was inherited by Jacob's son Levi, and down through his generations to Aaron."

Daniel now speaks: "In the chronicle of the exodus from Egypt, it is written that the Most High says, 'There at the altar I will meet the Israelites; hence it will be made sacred to my glory. Thus I will consecrate the meeting tent and the altar, just as I also consecrate Aaron and his sons to be my priests. I will dwell in the midst of the Israelites and be their God.'"

"And thus all priests are of Aaron's line of the Levite tribe," Mishael adds. "And yet I return to my first question: Can a priest serve without the Temple?"

Daniel replies, "The priests of old served the Most High in the desert. There, the Lord commanded Moses to make an anointing oil to consecrate Aaron and his sons as his priests."

"Therefore, the priesthood is a matter of the anointing, not of the place?" asks Mishael.

"Yes, though without ceasing we will long for the Temple in Jerusalem."

Moved by such reverent discussion among these young prisoners, I now raise my voice and sing from a song of David:

One thing I ask of the Lord
this I seek:
to dwell in the house of the Lord
all the days of my life,
that I may gaze on the loveliness of the Lord
and contemplate his temple.

For a time we all fall into silence. By the light of our fitful campfire, I regard their dusty torn robes, their dirty bruised feet, and their hands with broken fingernails and blood-scabs.

Most of all, I contemplate their faces. I see sadness, worry, grief, and yet there is also faith of uncommon strength.

"Daily we go farther and farther from Jerusalem," laments Hananiah in a burdened voice.

Daniel replies with a hand on his friend's shoulder. "Thus, within our own hearts we will dwell in the house of the Lord, and with our souls we will gaze upon his loveliness."

Azariah looks at me directly. "And in Babylon there may be some of our own priests. If so, they will make the anointing oil for you, Yezekiel."

"This I hope," I say, though I am troubled by doubts, surrounded as we are by perilous uncertainties.

Within three days we are passing through a growing number of villages and towns, closer and closer together, separated from each other by grainfields and cultivated fruit orchards. Scattered everywhere are date palms swaying in the hot wind. Intermingled with the constant agriculture is extensive industry: the clanking of hammers on metal, tall furnaces belching fire, the thwacking of weaving looms in open-fronted roadside shops, and hundreds of cookfires sending up columns of smoke beside houses made of yellow-brown brick. As our rabble of captives shuffle past each habitation, children run out to the roadside, staring in amazement or yelling gleefully, throwing pebbles at us. The Babylonian troops, flanking us in long lines, are marching in better order now, strutting before their own people to make an impression of conquerors returned.

On the southern horizon a mountain rises above the plain. When the road bends to follow close by the winding Euphrates, I note that the mountain is in fact two mountains, one slightly larger than the other. By the end of the day, I

can see that it is undoubtedly a man-made structure, a city—
the city—divided in half by the river. An amber haze hangs
over it, and as we make our final camp in the setting sun,
the cloud turns blood red.

All around us, the drove of captives sits or lies down with
relief. We are now a mixture of three or four groups, numbering more than a thousand perhaps. Even this multitude
is but a third of the deportees, so it would seem that many
people follow behind us on the road. Though I hear some
weeping, the main mood is one of quickened expectation
or anxiety, evidenced in intense discussions as our people
speculate on what lies ahead. Heads turn frequently toward
the dual mountain, which is near, glowing with the light of
countless torches. Music comes to us from there, faint but
frantic in nature. Our own guards are rejoicing by their fires,
yelling and singing under the influence of strong drink.

My four companions and I sit together and try not to let
the revelry consume our thoughts. We share our bread and
sing king-psalms and pray.

Hananiah says, "You eat little, Daniel, and your eyes are
unusually heavy. Last night I heard you groaning in your
sleep. Were you troubled by darksome dreams?"

"The man of God, like an angel of light, came to me
again in a dream," Daniel slowly answers. "He bore ill tidings of trials to come."

"Are you sure it was the very man of light who came
to you before? Could it have been merely a tale of worries
produced by your mind as you slept?"

Before Daniel can reply, I say, "There is no mistaking a
visitation from the Most High when he comes in dreams.
Or when he sends a messenger. When I was younger, when
I was your age, a man of light came to me in a dream, too.
And though I have forgotten dreams more numerous than

the stars of the heavens, dreams beyond recall, I remember this one as clear and certain."

Daniel gazes at me intently, surprised, perhaps, or reassured that his own experience is not a strange aberration.

He murmurs, "There were wild animals roaring all about me, but they were held back by an unseen hand and could not kill me. In that same dream, I saw you, Hananiah, Mishael, and Azariah, surrounded by flames, but you were unharmed."

"Were you not with us, Daniel?" asks Mishael.

"No, I was not there. I do not know why."

We sleep only a few hours before we are roused by bellowing guards and the clamor of their army making ready to march. The morning bread ration is distributed; we are herded down to the river to drink and then back to the road again.

For two more hours, we captives trudge along in no great eagerness to arrive at our destination. The Babylonian troops behave as they did the day before, marching in good formation, stamping their feet in rhythm, chins held high, chests thrust out. Now, however, they have all donned their best dress, exchanging their brown, knee-length marching tunics for embroidered ankle-length robes, orange-colored or white and black in checkered patterns, ornamental slippers of sturdy cloth, and every brow bound with a yellow band. The horsed captains and their lieutenants are garbed more splendidly than an Israelite king. All swords are in hand, and a forest of spears is held upright. More and more townspeople gather along the way as we approach a gate into the half of the city on this side of the river. The growing crowds are cheering their troops, and whenever there is a gap in the guard lines, they spit at us or hurl small stones.

The walls are close now, very high, extending toward the river to the east and far into the west where there are fields and outcroppings of dwellings, as if many villages have been drifted by the wind against the outer walls or the city itself is growing new limbs.

Before us is a high, wide gate, surmounted by guard towers. The battlements we have seen so far are not made of stone blocks, as is the case in Jerusalem, but rather of carefully constructed masses of clay brick. Through the open passage we are driven onto a street paved with brick. Everywhere we see a maze of three-story dwellings with flowering bushes and latticed vines growing on flat rooftops. On every high building, people are watching the procession from their roofs or leaning out of windows, cheering their own. They are also throwing fruit pits, stinking slops, or bits of broken crockery that fall upon us captives like a merciless rain. Though some of us are cut or bruised by it, none of our wounds are serious. On we go, street after street, until we arrive at a wide avenue—so wide that three or four chariots could race along it side-by-side. Though stationed at every corner is a single chariot and foot soldiers, mainly the way is kept clear by our guards.

We turn left onto the wide avenue, which runs straight in the direction of a bridge over the Euphrates. The bridge is walled waist-high, the river running swiftly below. Boats under sail move up and down on it. Reaching the other side of the river, we come to another wide avenue, an extension of the first, leading toward a brick gate that is higher and more heavily constructed. Two stone lions guard it, one to a side, both about ten cubits in height.

Now we are entering the eastern half of the city, its buildings higher and more densely packed together than those of the section we have just passed through. Here, too, there

are wider avenues and courtyards, all thronged by countless Babylonians selling or buying food and wares or merely
gawking. It comes to me that in this land there must be a
dearth of stone for construction, as without exception all
the buildings are made of red, brown, or yellow brick—
and marvelously clever are they made, with precise dimensions and straight streets, very unlike the winding streets
of Jerusalem. To our right is the most imposing building I
have seen so far, vast in breadth and many-tiered, its roofs
luxuriant with gardens, indeed a forest of wild and domestic trees and flowering shrubs. Guards in purple tunics and
bronze armor stand watch at a golden-gated entrance—a
palace, I think, perhaps Nebuchadnezzar's very own. Standing on the lowest battlement wall above the entrance, dozens
of gaily robed men and women are watching our arrival.
Many of our guards turn toward this audience and bow
at the waist, before straightening swiftly and moving us onward. Here, too, all Babylonian captains dismount and kneel
briefly, touching their foreheads to the pavement before rising to resume their duties.

Opposite on our left is an enormous edifice that is larger
at its base than the palace. Like a mountain upon a mountain, it is a rectangular, stepped tower, soaring high above all
others. Remembering what Jotham told me about Babylon,
I presume that this must be the temple dedicated to their
supreme god, Marduk.

Here, at last, we are brought to a halt in a vast square in
front of the temple. We are commanded to kneel, facing
the tower.

Trumpeters pace back and forth before us, while between
every trumpet blast a chorus of heralds cry out an acclamation in the Babylonian tongue, followed by its equivalent in
Hebrew: "The Foundation Stone of Heaven and Earth!"

Upon completion of the third acclamation, we are given the order to sit down. With sighs of relief, we comply. There are now more than a thousand captives in our group, three times as many troops guarding us. I estimate that the Israelites on the road behind us will arrive during the coming days and weeks. What will the Babylonians do with us all?

For a time that becomes nearly unendurable, we wait beneath the beating sun, cowering under our head scarves, sweating and fighting off feelings of despair. When the sun begins its descent after the midday hour and the shadows of buildings lengthen, the captains begin calling orders to their lieutenants.

Lines of troops now move into our midst, dividing the captive throng equally in two, and then again dividing each half, making blocks of about two hundred and fifty of us in each quarter.

Those penned with me in our quarter are now divided by guards into groups of fifty. Officials in linen robes and golden sashes walk the aisles between the smaller groups, pointing this way and that with bronze batons. These soft-looking Babylonians are further adorned with brilliant red sandals on their feet and jewelry about their necks or hung from their ears. Now and then, one of our young people is pulled from a group and told to stand with others likewise chosen in a separate cluster apart from the main body of captives. Though they are dirty and threadbare, their natural beauty is evident. Mainly boys and youths but also a smaller segregation of girls and maidens who huddle together fearfully, not knowing the purpose of this treatment.

There cannot be a single youth or man among us who lacks the courage to race forward to stand as a wall of protection between these young women and our captors. As a body, we rise to our feet and are about to do just that when we are intercepted. Knowing men's nature, the Babylonians have quickly rushed three ranks of soldiers into position, blocking us. Anguished and enraged, we stand powerless, with limbs shaking and fists clenched. Our utter frustration is eased only when we notice an armada of litters borne by servants come to a halt nearby. After disembarking, a swarm of Babylonian matrons surround our girls and young women. With the assistance of their own armed servants, each of these richly dressed persons takes charge of one or two girls and leads them away.

A few of our men throw themselves at the blockade of soldiers and are struck down by swords. The guards begin roaring again, commanding all captives to sit or be slain.

One of our own interpreters, a ragged captive like us, tries to calm our rage, crying out loudly, "Fear not, fear not! Those painted sows are wealthy dowagers in need of maids."

Whether this is the truth of the matter or mere speculation, we do not know. Yet we cling desperately to the thread of hope that the daughters of Israel will remain unharmed. We all sit down.

A splendidly attired Babylonian now walks through a portal in the walls of the palace compound, entering the square with measured steps. Purple-robed, with artfully curled hair, braided grey beard, and dyed crimson lips, this man appears to be of higher rank. He strolls leisurely among the seated crowd, aisle after aisle, holding a long baton atop of which is a gold lion head. He pauses from time to time as if in deep thought, then with the baton he taps a young captive on the chest, for no reason that I can apprehend.

I overhear our interpreter murmur in a tone of dread, "The chief eunuch from the palace."

Finally, the chief eunuch draws near the group where

my young companions and I are sitting. The accompanying guards make gestures that we are to stand. We comply and wait uneasily before the eunuch. Slowly, he examines each of us with his piercing eyes—our faces, our bodies. Now and then he uses his staff to lift the hem of an older boy's robe, inspecting what is hidden beneath. This shaming, this being treated like cattle, might otherwise have ignited fiery reactions from us, but the threatening gestures of the guards reduce us all to paralyzed silence. The eunuch glances at one of his servants, who steps forward carrying a brass pot and tiny ladle. With the ladle he tips drops of red dye onto the breasts of eight youths. My four companions are thus marked. I am not.

"How privileged you will be, my fine young fellows," the eunuch says in Hebrew to the selected ones. His silken voice enunciates the words accurately, though with a vile accent. There is an official court translator standing beside him, but the eunuch apparently wishes to speak in our own tongue, perhaps to demonstrate his power over us, as if to say that he is master of our language, our nation, of our very lives.

He continues, "Rich foods, costly robes, sweet perfumes, the glory of the house of Nebuchadnezzar surrounding you night and day. You will be taught our language and the wisdom of the ages known to our people alone, for Nebuchadnezzar the Great desires that the cream of all nations be tutored in our ways. You will now become eunuchs in the court of the King of Kings."

At the word *eunuchs*, the eight youths look alarmed and step backward uneasily.

With a sly look, the splendid eunuch fingers the hilt of a dagger sheathed at his waist.

"What is the pleasure of women compared to such an honor?" he asks with an insinuating smile.

The youths cast their eyes down and give him no answer.

With a gloating chuckle, the eunuch walks away, followed by the servant with the dye pot.

The court translator lingers a moment. He carries a small bronze baton tipped by an ivory dragon head—I presume a symbol of his minor authority. I can discern from his countenance and accent that he is fully a Hebrew like us. He must be one of the small number of Israelites sent by Jehoiachim to Babylon in recent years as a token of fealty. His face is repulsive, for upon it is the contemptuous expression of one who considers himself to be superior even as he festers with inner guilt. His skin is garish with cosmetics, and his beard is oiled and braided according to the custom of the Babylonians.

"Tremble not, young stags," he says with a smirk. "In the palace there is a class of high servants called eunuch by name, and though some have been gelded, some are not."

He, too, laughs and walks away.

With shaken hearts we all sit down again.

"They will separate us soon," observes Hananiah.

"Each to his station of slavery," Mishael adds with gloom.

"Our time together nears its end," says Azariah with a sorrowful expression.

"Yezekiel, our friend," says Daniel, "we are well met upon the road of sorrows. All honor and glory to the Most High for bringing us together. You have strengthened us."

"As you have strengthened me, Daniel."

"I do not know if we five shall meet again, but it would be a happiness if this be the Lord's will."

"For me also. Let us pray for each other always."

The four youths nod. "We will," they say, each in turn, and I know in my soul that they will be faithful to this bond, beyond all distance and sight.

Guards are barking orders, translators repeating the commands in Hebrew. The splendid eunuch is with them, overseeing the selection with imperious self-satisfaction.

"Trust in the Lord with all your hearts, and do not rely on your own understanding," I tell my young companions as my final word. "Acknowledge him in all your ways, and he will make straight your paths."

Daniel bows to me and says, "If our trust is great, then his generosity is without limits."

Growling, the guards grab the youths who have been marked by dye and pull them to their feet, using their spear points to push them into a huddled group. My four companions rise of their own will and go to join them.

I am left with the remaining captives, all of us wondering about our fate to come.

7

The River

OUR NUMBERS HAVE BEEN REDUCED by the separation of the very beautiful from the majority of exiles. There is a further division of the remainder into groups of a hundred and two hundred, and a single party of around four hundred. I am in this latter. The smaller lots are led away en masse to side streets opening off the square—north and south. Ours is herded onto the main avenue leading to the east.

We shuffle along the avenue toward a great gate, which rises at some distance from the temple square. After passing under its high arch, we are on a road beyond the city walls. Here, too, a basalt lion sculpture stands guard, facing outward to greet visitors or attackers. It is larger than life-size, and it differs from the others I saw in that its four claws pin the figure of a prone man to the earth.

Through my mind flow words from one of David's songs, when he was hiding in the cave from Saul, who was seeking to destroy him:

I lie in the midst of lions that greedily devour the sons of men; their teeth are spears and arrows, their tongues sharp swords.

The monstrous statue is one of the very few pieces of stone I have seen in the Babylonian capital, so it would seem that it is a rare material in these regions, used only for their art and idolatry. Metalwork such as weaponry and kitchen implements are everywhere, however, and thus I presume that metals for such items are brought fully forged from other lands or raw ores are brought down by boat from the mountains of northern Assyria.

The road strikes eastward straight and true, still cobbled and bordered by spreading villages that look like accretions to the outer wall. Soon, we pass over a dug moat on a wooden bridge that is narrower than the one by which we entered the city. The moat appears to encircle the entire city, as it curves in both directions until it is out of sight. Doubtless, it has its inflow and its mouth on the Euphrates and is likely matched by another half circle of water on the west side of the river. Yes, now I recall passing over a bridge on that side, just like the one we are crossing.

The moat may be deeper than it looks, but the water is brown and seems to flow sluggishly, bordered by banks of reeds on the shores. The boats on it are small, flat-bottomed, each of them poled by one or two men.

Proceeding through the outermost fringe of dwellings, I look back over my shoulder and catch my breath in wonder. Now I can see that the city is surely one of the greatest in the world—indeed, far larger than Jerusalem. I estimate that it would demand at least a day to accomplish a brisk walk on foot around its entire circumference.

Within the hour, the guards direct us onto a dirt road to our right. It cannot be far from the winding river because now I see the peaks of sails gliding beyond a long row of date palms extending southward as far as the eye can see.

We captives are mainly young and middle-aged men, though a quarter of our number are women of middle to old age. A few younger are among them, not many. What will the Babylonians do with us all? Where are we going? Our single Hebrew interpreter knows nothing. The guards will tell us nothing. They are more relaxed and less punitive than they were when accompanying us from Israel. Though they carry their spears at the ready, they wear only their tunics now, bearing their battle gear in backpacks. They let us move along at our own pace, and they ensure that we are fed and watered throughout the day. At nightfall we camp on an open meadow, at no great distance from the palm trees. A light breeze is swaying their fronds and stirring the branches of lesser trees that crowd the river's edge. I sit down on the ground, wrap my arms around my knees, and bow my head, seeking to hide within my innermost self.

A light breeze rustles the countless flags of leaves and bulrushes. I look up, for tonight it seems there is no escape from the world around me, no refuge within. A mist rises in the direction of the river, but above us the first stars appear, very bright. Hearing the sound of bleating goats, I gaze curiously at the sparks of lamplight from villages on the nearby low hills. I wrap myself in my sackcloth and lie down beside my fellow captives, all of us weary and, I think, relieved that no great harm was done to us today. What awaits us upon our arrival at the unknown destination, none can tell.

As the air cools, dew falls, the first I have felt since leaving our homeland. For the moment, the air is thick with humidity and sweet aromas. This twining of alien scents is a consolation after the passage we have made through semi-arid routes and the grainlands of Babylon, days of endless dry plodding, during which I longed for the perfumes of wild plants created by the Lord's generous hand—flowers, leaves, bark, sap, fruits. Their smell now revives the memory of the lush vegetation I encountered as a boy on the banks of the Jordan near Gilgal.

I roll onto my back and gaze at the stars.

As long as there are stars, I reassure myself, *as long as there are stars so high beyond the reach of human evil, all will be well in the end.*

Then without me knowing why, my throat-flute is singing the words of a king-psalm:

"O Most High, when I begin to fear, in you I will trust."

I sing in a low voice, with bass notes, repeating this refrain again and again, and to my surprise other voices quietly join in. I feel hope slowly returning. Before long, we are all asleep.

We left the Euphrates behind us a day ago, the road veering steadily away from the mighty river. Increasingly, the land has given way to more variety. Grainfields continue as before but occasionally swell into hillocks, near and far from the road. Villages and small towns are built on their heights, though some are lower, close by the road. Herds of goats browse on profuse copses of wild bushes bordering every stream or canal, and now flocks of grazing sheep have also appeared on the slopes. I often see in the fields a heavy beast like an ox. The grunting and squealing of swine can be heard behind fences made of mud and wicker. There are the usual donkeys and camels passing by us, going in both directions, carrying wares and bundles of firewood, sometimes with an old man or woman sitting atop the enormous loads. They stare at us with angry or curious eyes. We suffer no more insults.

Long rows of vineyards surround the towns. Date palms are beyond counting, and there are manicured orchards aplenty, bowing under the weight of a variety of fruits. I recognize figs and pomegranates, but a species of tree that droops with yellow orbs is new to me. Olives are also cultivated here.

This land seems to be blessed with an extraordinary abun-

dance of waters. I am told that there is another river as great
as the Euphrates at a not very far distance to the east, in the
direction of the land of the Persians. It, too, is a possession
of Babylonia. Its name is Tigris. Thus, so lavishly irrigated,
this empire has become not only very wealthy but also very
powerful. As I walk along, I think longingly of Israel and
ponder how mysterious it is that our homeland is not so
blessed, though we are the people chosen by the Lord Most
High as his own. I weigh the matter this way and that. I
remind myself that the rain falls on the just and the unjust
alike, but I cannot help wondering why it is so. Perhaps the
Lord foresaw that hardships train us in a way that soft living
cannot. If *we* had been given this land between the rivers,
we might have become a people as cruel and proud as our
captors. And did not God call Abraham to *leave* Chaldea, to
make of him a small tribe, the weakest among the peoples,
that we might be formed into a nation of heaven's offspring,
as numerous as the stars, and more readily fashioned in the
ways of obedience to his holy will.

How is it, then, that we have now fallen so low?

After two more days of journeying, we arrive at a town
that is larger than the habitations we have passed until now.
I cannot pronounce its name in full, but in Hebrew it means
Kebar-Handmaid-of-the-Great-Water. It is situated on the
bank of a lesser river, the Kebar, which feeds the Euphrates
far to the west and from which the town derives its name.
I would guess that mainly Chaldeans live here, for we are
now passing into the ancient realm of the Chaldees. Ur, I
am told, is yet many days farther south of this place.

Now, a hundred men and women are separated from the
four hundred, and I am among the smaller group. Our translator, a fellow captive named Gad, tells us that we will remain here, and the other, larger group will be taken farther

along the river to a city called Tel-abib. Gad informs us that to reach that place would demand another day or so of steady walking. For me, the arduous journey has come to an end.

Our Babylonian guards no longer outnumber us. We are, after all, docile strangers in a strange land. When the larger group of exiles goes onward, a smaller number of guards guide those of us who remain down to the river to drink. I say *guide*, not drive at sword or spear point. Their behavior is not in any way threatening. It seems they are now confident that none of us will try to escape. Looking nearly as fatigued as we Israelites, I think they are glad for the end of their long trek to Judea and back.

After we have quenched our thirst, we are commanded to sit by the bank of the river and to wait for further instructions. Before long, a party of local men passes out through the town gates and descends to meet us. They are smiling, gazing at the disheveled band of foreigners with fond approval. Though they are dignitaries of some kind, they are not gaudy like the Babylonian officials we have seen until now. Their robes and sandals appear to be simpler but of good quality, and their hair and beards are neatly dressed. They wear rings on their fingers, none on their earlobes, and their faces are unadorned by cosmetics. They are, perhaps, merchants, landowners, or minor local authorities. Now they converse with the chief of our guards. Clay cylinders are exchanged. Low bowing is made on both sides.

That done, the foremost man among the townsfolk approaches us and spreads his arms wide. So, too, does he spread his smile. He makes a long declaration in his own language, nothing of which can we understand. When finished, an interpreter steps forth from his retinue and loudly declaims in crudely accented Hebrew what his master has said. Our own interpreter, Gad, seated beside me, murmurs, "Yes, he has the meaning right, some words wrong, but in the main he is making sense."

Through the town's interpreter, the principal man tells us this:

"Well do you come, O Israelites, to Kebar the Handmaid of Mighty Euphrates. We the people of this city give you our greetings."

Gad whispers to me, "They call this place a *city*—a grand name in their tongue—when in fact it is just a town, two thousand people or less, I think."

I whisper back, "Its walls are high, and there looks to be something like a temple and also a fort."

He shrugs. "Kebar may be an administration center for a province or—"

But we are unable to continue, as the headman has more to say:

"The Great Nebuchadnezzar has commanded that you will labor among our people for the good of yourselves and for us who have dwelled here since the time of Hammurabi, as ordained by Anu the most high god and creator of the universe, who is father of Marduk. You may worship your own gods, but you must never forget that all the heavens and all the gods must bow down before Marduk the All-seeing."

Disgust seizes my heart at the utterance of this ignorant blasphemy against the one true God. I sense my fellow Hebrews squirming all around me. Heads are lowered, several of us cover our faces with our scarves and begin praying in silence.

The principal man continues:

"This portion of the land is rich in harvest and flowing with many waters. Here you will know plenty in all ways, if you accept the laws of our land. You may build houses and grow your own gardens. You may trade and buy and sell. You may husband your own animals and weave and sew and make music as it pleases you. Truly, in time you will prosper, if you work with all your strength. No wages will be given to you, for it is right and just that Nebuchadnezzar, who has conquered you, deserves your service.

"Even so, does Nebuchadnezzar the Merciful desire that you live in bounteous health and gladness. You may marry and raise families. You will suffer no harm at the hands of Babylonians, save if you break our laws or seek to cast off our authority over you or try to flee. You know the length of days you have traveled, its arduous ways, its hunger and thirst, and the merciless arid paths. Remain, then, in this fruitful land, and you will regret nothing.

"This day you will cross the ford of the River Kebar and make camp on the far side of the river, facing our city. There you will build your houses. Until you have made sufficient clay bricks for your dwellings, tents will be provided for you. Wheat, barley, oil, and other foodstuffs will be given to you without cost, until the time when your own harvests prove sufficient for your needs."

This part of the man's speech is spoken mildly, in the most warm and cordial tone, as if welcoming guests or respected employees. Now, however, his smile contorts into a grimace and his voice becomes a growl.

"Six days a week will you labor in our fields, to plow, to plant, and to harvest; and you will maintain our canals and irrigation ditches, doing all manner of diverse tasks that your overseers demand of you. You will not waver in any task, hide yourself from such works, claim recompense, give insult to your masters, revolt and do any harm to our people, lest the doom of the sword and axe fall upon you. You cannot wander away to other cities. And again I say to you, do not set off in return to your homeland, which would be punished by your death. Swift is justice in our kingdom, hard will fall Marduk's divine punishment should you abuse our generosity."

The smile returns. He and his retinue turn away and re-enter their town gates.

Now, our band of exiles is guided along a riverside path to a place at the eastern end of the town where the bank slopes down to the water's edge. The ford is only wide enough for two or three people to walk abreast. The water is warm, rising to my shins in midstream. A long line of us wades across without mishap, and in due course we are passing through a border of water reeds and then climbing the far bank.

Our guards are few; I estimate no more than a dozen. They do not bellow at us, merely grunt their instructions and point the way we must go. Now we pass through a dense thicket of willow bushes and finally arrive at a meadow of beaten grass and patches of damp mud. Swarms of mosquitos and stinging gnats rise up to greet us. We cluster together, gazing all about. Beyond are fields and more groves of trees, including towering date palms. I see three oxen standing at a distance, harnessed to high-staved carts, and local men loading baskets of produce onto them. Melons, garlic, and onions, it looks like.

At the edge of the meadow is a long, single-floor brick building, roofed with layers of bulrush and capped with clay. Its several windows and single door indicate that it is not a barn for sheltering animals but, rather, is a residence for numerous people. Indeed, it must be so, for beside it are two large bread ovens shaped like cones, one on each side of the building, with eight women tending them. Goats are tethered nearby. The women and the goats alike stop to examine us with curiosity.

The town interpreter arrives, and, after calling our attention, he announces in a loud voice that this plot of land is our new home. The building is where our guards will live temporarily, until we have shed any foolish thoughts of flight. There is another garrison in a fort across the Kebar; more soldiers can be here within minutes if there is any disturbance.

"Will you make trouble?" he asks of the crowd.

Among us, heads are shaken. No, we will not make trouble.

"From one full moon to the next, you are exempt from work, as you build your dwellings and turn soil for your gardens. At the end of these days, you will be assigned your tasks in service of Babylon."

Murmuring arises from among us. A handful of weeks to build a village, a town? Impossible!

The interpreter silences the protest with a scowl.

"Will you make trouble?" he growls.

Again, heads are shaken. No, we will not make trouble. Satisfied, he leaves.

Unsure of what we are to do next, many of us lower ourselves to the turf and wait. Others wander around, eyeing the building where our guards have sat down with their backs to the wall and their spears laid aside. Our conquerors look like peasant youths in military costume, no longer posturing with ferocity but merely grateful for the end of their journey. They take off their copper helmets, open pouches, and remove from them square wooden boards and pebbles, set them up, and commence playing games of chance. Ignoring their captives, they drink from wine skins and share jokes with each other. I next stroll to the ovens, where I nod to the old women, who, amazingly, return my nods with little bows. They point to the ovens with large grins, where the intoxicating aroma of baking bread promises a delicious reward for our compliance, as if to say, it will not be long, soon you will eat. I smile in appreciation. It is the first smile I have ever given to a Babylonian.

I had expected haughty contempt from them. Though they are Gentiles, idolatrous pagans, it must be that some root of humanity yet lives in them. I have much to think about in this regard. In the book of origins, it is written that God created man in his own image and likeness—yes, even this people. Are we not all the children of Adam? Are we not all the children of Noah, all survivors of the great flood?

The situation seems very strange to me. We are prisoners, but for the moment it appears that we will be permitted to live as ordinary village folk. I hope this will last. I stroll back to the river, and no one stops me. I sit down among the willows at the water's edge and observe a train of carts being pulled across the ford by donkeys and drivers. They are laden with staves, rolls of tent cloth, and numerous wicker baskets brimming with fruit and grain.

I close my eyes. The river burbles as it passes. The willow leaves rustle in a breath of wind, giving shade and perfume. The color green is healing to the parched soul. Though this part of the world is exceedingly hot, it is not sun-burned. The land all about appears to be amply irrigated. We may survive here. Our lot will not be one of unmitigated suffering. This is Abraham's birth-land. The Lord Most High is everywhere.

By nightfall, we have completed erection of our temporary shelters. The Babylonians brought tent ropes to distribute, but we had to cut our own pegs. To our great surprise, this was made possible by the dozen iron knives the guards handed out at random, after carefully counting them. As the sun began to set, they collected and counted them again. There must be thirty or forty tents now standing in no great order around the muddy meadow. I have been busy all day, putting up tents for the women among us who have no husbands or sons to care for them—a small number, distracted with grief and bearing signs of disorientation or near-crippling despair.

As I have done for the past three months, I sleep rolled up in my head scarf and sackcloth. I have also managed to scavenge a piece of left-over tent cloth which I drape over my body. Though this provides some protection from the swarms of insects, I am sweating profusely and cannot sleep. With only my eyes exposed, I watch the stars in the sky and a waxing quarter moon. With the days remaining until the full moon, added to the twenty-seven days until the next, we have between five and six weeks of illusory freedoms before hard servitude begins in earnest. To make this place habitable and our lives endurable, we will need every moment of it.

At dawn, the women from Kebar arrive to bake the daily bread ration. Stored in the long building are numerous large clay grain jars, from which the bakers scoop the day's allotment of flour. Our temporary guards dwell in the building, too, so there is no opportunity for theft, should anyone be impulsive enough to try. Most of the encampment is awake now, and hungry, but it will take an hour or more before enough bread is ready. Some people have saved fragments of yesterday's meal, and they now devour them in the open, heedless of those who are watching. I have little doubt that there are also hoarders who eat secretly. No one would force them to give up their excess, but, still, it is generally held to be a matter of honor that we must share what we have, and such people think only of themselves. I try not to judge them in my innermost thoughts, but I do see emerging patterns that range between selfless generosity and heartless greed.

Most of the exiles have seated themselves around the ovens, waiting, yearning. An old man raises his voice among them:

"Today we must begin making bricks," he declares. "*Thousands* of bricks!"

"None of us know how to make bricks!" arises the protest from several mouths.

"Will the Babylonians teach us how to make them?" ask others.

A young man rises to his feet, short but burly of arm and leg.

"I know how to make them," he says. "It was my labor in Sechem before I was captured."

Sechem. The former capital in the northern kingdom of Israel, a land of Ephraimites mingled with Samaritans. Is he trustworthy? Or has our common enslavement unified all captives?

"Good, good," many voices clamor. "You will make our bricks!"

"I cannot make everyone's bricks. If we want a town of our own, we must all work together."

This is met with some murmuring among the crowd. Clearly many of these people are not accustomed to manual labor.

"What is your name?" I ask him.

"I am Tzvi ben Saadya," he answers, turning to me, thumping his chest with his fist. He laughs: "I leap like a deer but I am very jolly!"

He has made a joke about the meaning of his names. I smile in acknowledgment.

"You will be our teacher," I say.

"Yes, yes, I will teach you all," he eagerly replies. "It is not hard. Some of you must bring clay-mud from the riverbank, others must knead it and put it into molds, others will lay them out in rows where the sun can harden it."

This is greeted by groans from a number of listeners. Otherwise, silence.

"Tzvi," I say, "do you remember the travails of our people in Egypt? They were forced to make bricks for Pharaoh."

"I remember my schooling." He raps the side of his head with his knuckles and grins. "I am a *rabbi*!"

This is so obviously a ridiculous claim that chuckles erupt all around.

"A rabbi of mud," he clarifies. Now everyone laughs. The spirit of the gathering is lightening.

"Do you use straw?" I ask.

"Ah, ah, how could I forget the straw!" he exclaims, slapping his forehead. "Yes, everyone from baby to codger must cut straw to mix with the mud. It makes the mud bind together and helps the brick dry evenly. It is then three times stronger than plain mud brick."

"But we have no tools!"

"That is so. Yes, this is a problem. We need sharp implements to cut straw. We need buckets for carrying mud. We need wooden molds."

"Surely the Kebarites know this," says the old man who launched the discussion.

"Apparently they do not," says another old man bitterly. "Or, if they know, they want to see how we will deal with the problem."

"We must ask them for tools," I say, raising my voice to be heard above the harsh discordance of opinions that now are offered on all sides.

"That is what they are waiting for," argues the bitter one.

"It is their game of amusement. They want to shame us and make us beg."

"Do not poison the air with your ill temper, Naphtali," says the calmer old man.

"Ha! I am clearing the air with truth, Shimeon!" the bitter one shouts back.

"I will ask them," I say. "I will beg."

At this point, our little gang of guards wade into the group, shouting incomprehensible commands in angry voices.

"They tell us to make bricks," explains Gad. "'Make bricks! Make bricks!' they say."

Confusion spreads among us. Most people just stare blankly at the guards or wander about, some picking grass with their bare hands, hoping it proves they are working.

I ask Gad to inform the guards that a few of us wish to cross the river and plead for tools from the town officials. Our keepers have no objection. Tzvi and I, Gad and Shimeon head directly to the path down to the water. We wade across, accompanied by two suspicious guards, who come along to ensure we will make no "trouble".

We are told to wait by the main gate of Kebar while one of the guards goes in to request a meeting with the town's chief man or any such official. For an hour, we stand in the sun with a subservient demeanor. Finally a retinue appears, about ten armed soldiers from the town's fort and three well-robed men of authority. Their expressions are as haughty as ever, but in their eyes is evidence of mirth, and their mouths are buckled in sly amusement.

"What do you want?" asks the one in charge. "Why aren't you making bricks?"

Gad and I step forward to explain.

A guard hits the back of our knees with the butt of his stave.

"Kneel, kneel," whispers Gad.

We kneel.

Shimeon, being the oldest, now negotiates with the elders of Kebar. He asks for shovels, buckets, mattocks, a plow, an axe, scythe and sickles, explaining why we need each one. I point out that we also need squared wood for making brick molds.

I conclude with: "These, sir, will help establish us firmly here and make us better workers in the service of Kebar."

"In the service of all Babylon," the headman corrects.

"In the service of all Babylon."

"A tool can be used as a weapon," says the headman with a threatening look, his mouth twisting, as if to say that he is well acquainted with the subterfuges of slaves. The captain of the guard, standing with crossed arms beside him, scowls at us and growls at length in their language. Gad translates:

"He warns us that any incident in which a tool is used against his people will bring swift punishment down upon us. If a Chaldean is wounded by an Israelite, three slaves will be wounded in kind, and each will also lose one eye. If a Chaldean is killed, three slaves will be executed."

"Is this understood?" demands the headman. "Will you announce it to all of your people?"

All four of us nod in agreement. Shimeon as our formal spokesman replies:

"It is understood. We will announce it to our people."

The headman and captain dismiss us with abrupt arm gestures.

We bow humbly, rise to our feet and turn toward the river, heads lowered, shoulders slumped. But with our backs now turned to the Kebarites, we are smiling in triumph, for we have obtained a promise of tools. As we approach the ford, a donkey cart rattles into the water before us. It is filled with every tool we requested. So soon? How is it possible? Then we realize that they had anticipated our needs and merely enjoyed inflicting some additional humiliation.

Much of my time during the following three or four days is spent carrying buckets of mud up the river bank to the brick-making yard we have made at the edge of the village, an open spot exposed to the full force of the sun. I also spend an hour or two in the evenings, helping gather chaff in the fields nearby, but soon discontinue the practice, as there are many of our people too old or weak to carry the loaded buckets, and anyone can cut straw. The bricks are now our main concern.

Of course, river mud is probably good enough for our purposes, but on the third day a seam of pure clay is found at some distance along the shore upstream. The division of opinion regarding whether to use mud or clay is full of long, sober examinations of every fact and conjecture, and sometimes there is rancor, but in the end the general consensus is that we need to build quickly. Fetching the distant clay would prolong the time needed for construction of adequate housing. We do not know what kind of weather dominates this part of the world. Will there be a rainy season? And if so, how soon will it come? Would the tents be sufficient cover for those without houses?

Because we lack leadership, people are divided into those who are pro-mud and those who are pro-clay. Angry arguments sometimes erupt into pushing and shoving, and even a single fistfight between two young men. Shimeon stops them by stepping into the battle and receiving a few blows before the combatants realize what they have done and uncurl their fists, astonished and shamefaced. Both bow their heads before him and mumble apologies, begging his pardon.

"Let us hold no grudge about today's affair," he says in

his calming voice. "Yet let us learn from it. See how the enemy—and our fears—would have us tearing each other to pieces."

The two antagonists wipe their cut lips and bleeding noses —and repentant tears from their eyes. They are essentially good young men, but frustrated and impatient.

"Come now, no more of this," Shimeon says to them. "We will all work together, each as he sees fit. Some will port mud to the brick yard, others clay, if they prefer. If we entrust our village to the Lord's providence, we will have shelter enough."

The two young men, looking thoroughly repentant, head off in different directions, one to the nearby shore, the other along the path leading upriver.

The Chaldean cooks have been watching the conflict, giggling and making sly comments. Our guards have been enjoying it, too, chuckling and joking among themselves. Soberly, we Israelites turn away and go about our tasks.

Tzvi now steps up and brings resolution to the simmering conflict. He tells us that mud is sufficient for a good brick as long as enough straw is kneaded into it. We have a limitless supply of mud only a few steps away from the village. Pure clay is less abundant and takes longer to fetch. Yet pure clay does not need straw, he says. The most productive method, he emphasizes, is to mix clay into mud, with a little straw as insurance. Within hours, mounds of both clay and mud are rising like giant anthills in the brickyard. Some people carry, others scoop and knead, others mix with straw, and everyone at one time or other is busy packing the mixture into molds.

Day after day, the fiery sun bakes our bricks, hundreds soon mounting upon hundreds. Though "Tzvi the rabbi" works as hard as any man, he frequently leaves off his own labors to wander around the brickyard with furrowed brow, inspecting the manner in which the mud-clay mixture is kneaded with straw and packed into the molds. He is not above dumping a freshly packed mold and scattering the contents with his foot, demanding more straw. He further requires that three holes must be poked into every brick. People want an explanation.

"When these bricks are laid one atop another," explains Tzvi, "we will use mortar, just as our ancestors in Egypt did. The mortar will fill the holes and harden. This is how the bricks are kept from sliding off each other and knocking you on the head in your sleep. A bad dream from which you would not wake up."

People smile nervously, remembering the ground tremors of Israel, and perhaps the oldest ones recalling a major earthquake in times past.

"Our mortar will be clay and sand, like thick soup, when we lay it," Tzvi continues. "I don't know if there is pitch or bitumen around here, the kind I collected near the Sea of Salt, but I will beg lime from the Kebarites, if they have it."

Even in his newfound officiousness, Tzvi can be humorous, saying ridiculous things with comic facial gestures. "I am Nebuchadnezzar the Great and Merciful!" he declares, mimicking the grandiloquent speeches we heard from the Kebarites on the first day. "If you build this little toe of Babylon aright, you will be happy, happy, happy!" Thus, no one takes offense at his gruff instructions. Clearly he loves his position, but I do not think anyone faults him for it, as his abruptness and quibbles are never personal.

In fact, he is a very effective foreman, and within weeks there are thousands of bricks stacked here and there around the yard. About midway into our month of grace, Tzvi begins to perform experiments. Taking a brick, he will try to crumble it with his strong fingers, or he will strike it hard with a stick. If it passes that test, he will drop it from his waist onto hard ground to see if it will shatter. If all is still well with the brick, he directs his helpers to add it to a stack. The ever-increasing number of stacks are separated by a few feet. Tzvi makes a charcoal mark on each, denoting what day the bricks were first molded. Throughout all this time, he has selected about a dozen men to be his "servants", as he calls them, sharing in the physical tasks and receiving preliminary verbal lore about durable bricklaying. He has further taken upon himself the role of overseeing all construction, adamantly refusing to let anyone build prematurely with unseasoned bricks. He is insistent that the bricks must be thoroughly dried. "Soon, soon," he promises. "Do you want your house to fall on you at the first rain?"

By the third week, anxiety increases because time is running out. Too swiftly, the moon is swelling toward its fullness. We have a week, possibly a few days more, to complete our impossible project, and still no houses have been built. Nevertheless, people are working with better efficiency and have also developed the excellent habit of coordinating many of the tasks. There are at least sixty men capable of hard labor, and the rest contribute in any way they are able. There is a good balance of productivity between cutters and carters of straw, between the porters of clay and mud, and between the molders and stackers, and so forth. There is also a general improvement in attitude. There have been no more fights and only mild quarrels.

Finally, Tzvi declares that the earliest-made bricks are ready, construction may begin. Tyrannically, and wisely, he supervises the use of the first few stacks. That same day a donkey cart full of ground lime is brought across the ford by a Kebarite workman. Tzvi's men have prepared a deep wooden trough in which to mix the lime, mud, sand, and water. The lime, we now learn, comes from a large deposit near the River Tigris. Mixing is an arduous effort that requires not only muscle strength but the right timing; otherwise the mortar will dry too quickly.

Under his watchful eye, Tzvi's "servants" begin laying foundations on harder packed soil on a rise that borders our encampment. They first pace off eight foot-lengths by ten foot-lengths. We do not have any measuring rods for the standard long-cubit—the length of a big man's forearm—but that is no privation because in practice the use of the foot is easier. We are building rough habitations, not the Temple in Jerusalem.

Of course most people want their own house to be among the first built. A scramble of grabbing and running might have occurred were it not for the unofficial authority of Shimeon and Tzvi—as well as Tzvi's minions. A few of his men guard the brick stacks, while the rest of them, along with additional helpers, set to work.

They plan six small houses for widows with children and the very old who have no family here to help with the building. I must admit my astonishment at seeing the rise of twelve residences within the space of the week. Wisely, Tzvi has designed the buildings in such a way that each house shares a wall with the next, thus reducing the number of bricks needed. Other workers have cut saplings from the nearby poplar woods for use as roof beams, and still others, warming to the communal event, cut thick palm branches to lay atop the beams.

I am learning the trade of brick-laying. Learning many things actually. In Little Bite of Bread, we made our houses of rough field stones, the flattest we could find; their irregularity of shape and weight held it all together, but not always with evenness or perfect balance. From time to time, there were accidents, such as a portion of a wall slipping, a few upper stones toppling inward or outward. This was a rare occurrence, but a worry.

Tzvi has concocted an ingenious device for laying bricks straight and true: a long string of wool, at the end of which he has tied a little stone. When suspended from the peak of three staves bound together, it hangs straight down to the earth, pulled by that mysterious force we all live with daily but cannot remotely understand. With this as a guide, we lay the bricks carefully one on top of the other, slapping a thick layer of mortar between each layer. Such a flimsy thing, this string, but as is the case with so many small things in life, it has the power to prevent catastrophes.

A growing number of hands are soon involved in construction, people glad for relief from the tedium of gathering mud and clay or kneading it all day long. Eager for solid shelter and driven by worry over the shortness of time, they are quickly learning the various skills. During part of each day, therefore, I return to the unwelcome tasks they have left aside, carrying mud, mixing straw with it, and packing it into molds to feed our limitless need for more bricks.

Each evening as the sun dips below the horizon, I walk to a secluded screen of reeds upriver and bathe myself, standing knee-deep in the water, washing off the dried mud on my hands and arms, legs, and face, and scrubbing my flesh to remove the offensive accretions of sweat. How remote to me is the ritual purity of the Temple. I also seem to have no fat left anywhere on my body, though my muscles have thickened and hardened. After returning to my scrap of tent cloth, I pray the king-psalms from memory and offer to the

Lord Most High other words from my heart, beseeching him to help us keep our bond as his people and to speed the erection of the village. Then, with my eyes unable to stay open any longer, I roll myself in my head scarf and sackcloth and pull the tent cloth over it all.

At sunrise I rise and pray again. How many days of freedom—small freedom, I correct myself—how many days are left to us? I count the houses and note that there are now close to thirty, almost all of them with thatched roofs completed. Several house dwellers have moved their scanty belongings inside, and many have used their tents to cover the thatch, providing additional protection from sun and rain.

The brick-making continues, but at a slower rate, for with all interest now focused on construction, the number of people willing to do the most menial tasks is dwindling still further. I ask myself, *What is needed here? How can I best contribute?* Seeing clearly that the demand for materials will soon exceed the supply, I bow my head and set myself to the most unwelcome tasks. Even so, on the night when the moon is a hair from being full, Tzvi finds me rolled up in my tent cloth and shakes my shoulder vigorously to wake me.

"Yezekiel, Yezekiel, open your eyes. I must speak with you."

I open my eyes, groaning, for he has pulled me from a sweet dream of my little spring back home. I sit up and regard him groggily.

"I need you to lay mortar," he says.

"Now?"

"No, tomorrow."

"I am making brick," I object. "Few are making brick, and soon we will run out."

"Yes, yes, but anyone can make brick. I saw the skill of your hand and eye when you laid mortar one day. I need the best men to do this job. I beg you."

"I will serve you, *rabbi*, as you wish."

He laughs, slaps me on the shoulder, and goes away, leaving me to return peacefully to my beloved spring.

It may be a miracle of providence, or it may be my imagination, but the moon seems to hover in full for longer than normal. For three more days, I labor from dawn until dusk laying brick and mortar, paying close attention to Tzvi's string all the while. I stop only to eat a swift meal of the flatbread the old ladies of Kebar keep baking for us and to drink from waterskins. Then, back to work. It is slow, painstaking work, and yet the walls appear to rise of their own accord. It is the mystery of time, of course, which can stretch long or short according to how fixed one's attention is on the immediate task, *this* brick, *this* scoop of mortar, *this* scraping away of excess. Moreover, the worthier the objective, the more swiftly time goes—even disappears altogether.

On the winds of time, which is now a gentle breeze and at other moments a tempest, the mind muses. Especially does it muse when the air is calm.

I am carefully fitting corner bricks to overlap with bricks of the adjoining wall. *Ah, if only I could mold a whole wall in an instant*, go my thoughts. *I could carry it here on my shoulders. I could put four walls together and make a house in the blink of an eye.*

Then I smile at the notion. *Life is like this*, I remind myself. *You cannot move a whole wall on your shoulders. You move the wall brick by brick. This is how God has built Israel, little by little, step by step.*

8

The Sweat of Our Brow

THE REPRIEVE IS OVER, the moon reaches its fullness. On the morning after it begins to wane, a hundred soldiers from the fort wade across the river, bellowing as if to speed the sunrise. They and our temporary guards surround the village to keep anyone from taking flight, which is unnecessary, as we are all emerging half-awake from houses and tents and standing submissively as we await what is to come next.

As the sun becomes a red oval struggling to escape the treetops, a major overseer is carried across the ford on a chair, his servants panting under the weight. He is set down ceremoniously in the village's central open space. He wears a linen robe with a silver lion pendant on his breast. Standing, waving a bronze baton, he strolls about imperiously, selecting us one by one and directing us into three separate clusters, presumably according to our strength and usefulness for particular tasks. He is assisted by the soldiers and Kebar's crude interpreter, with Gad contributing some explanations. Of the hundred exiles, around sixty are segregated into an uneasy group composed of robust men, I among them. I presume we will be put to work at field labor and maintenance of irrigation canals. The next largest group is composed of men and women who appear to be of lesser physical value. They will do lighter work such as menial chores in a pottery factory, feeding animals in nearby farms, picking fruit in the orchards, housecleaning in Kebar's homes, and anything else our overseers find for them to do. The third group is the smallest, the handful of souls left over. There are two mothers with five small children and a baby, as well as the very old and feeble—or those who have become feeble-minded because of the ordeal of walking from Israel. Gad, interpreting, informs them that they must be productive, engaged in small tasks such as learning to weave willow baskets if they do not already know how, grinding barley, gathering firewood sticks in the nearby copses, and watching over the village's fires lest they go out.

Each group will have its own overseer and armed enforcers who will keep watch on us throughout every day, ensuring that we go to our appointed duties and perform them diligently. As this is being explained to us, our captors flick their leather whips, a demonstration of what will be laid across our backs if we resist. The swords sheathed at their waists underline the message.

Nevertheless, this does not prevent five or six older Israelite men from a final frustrated outburst. "I was a judge in Israel!" protests one, his face flaming red. "I owned a hundred trade camels!" blusters another. "I am important in the royal palace!" declares the bitter Naphtali, who is among the ones who cannot yet accept that their former life is over.

Snarling like mad dogs, the guards leap upon them to slap their faces and kick them to their knees. After a few strokes of the lash on their bent quaking backs, the once-powerful old men are then commanded to get up and join the others. Silence now reigning, the two larger groups are herded toward the river.

We wade across the ford and come to the road that runs

along the town side of the river. There, the overseers and guards divide our group still further, and then I with thirty others are commanded to walk in the direction that I recall leads to the city of Tel-abib, how far from here I do not know. Is that where we will be working?

Accompanied by ten armed guards, we turn and shuffle forward, putting one foot after another as the day grows warmer and our bellies begin to complain, for we have not yet eaten. A donkey cart follows us, driven by an old man in a loincloth, his hair white, his wrinkled skin as brown as an African's. Along the way, he sings monotonously in a high-pitched voice, and though I do not know any of their language I do hear names of their gods such as Anu and Tiamit, our now familiar Marduk, and Osiris, Khnemu, and Neper. I shudder at their very mention and try to keep from choking on the road dust.

Gad walks beside me, looking downcast.

"Give no attention to the wretched singing," I say to him, "for that old Babylonian is invoking their gods."

"He is not a Babylonian," Gad replies. "He is a slave, one who has lived here a long time, with plenty of rebuke upon him. See his one eye. He is Egyptian, and some of the gods he praises are of his own land, a god of death, a ram god that controls the river flood, and a god of grain."

"How do you know this?"

"A trader's son learns much of the world. In addition to Babylonian, which is oft called Chaldean, I know Egyptian, Assyrian, and even a little Persian."

"That poor slave mixes his gods with those of this land."

"Yes, it seems so," Gad replies despondently. "I wonder, is he what we will become?"

"It need not be so."

We soon notice that the Kebar has countless channels, no

more than ditches, striking off into the distance on both sides of the river. Clearly they have been made by human hand, as they are evenly spaced and very straight, and, wherever one of them meets the river, a low weir-dam of logs regulates the flow of water into these side canals. The river water reaches each dam by passing beneath a narrow bridge that permits further traffic along the road. Between every two ditches, a field of grain is growing tall, ready for harvest. It looks to me that barley, millet, and emmer wheat are grown here.

Gad has been listening to the guards' conversations along the way.

"They say there are two main harvests every year," he explains to me. "Sometimes three if the weather conditions are unusually good. We are now late in the first growing season. I expect we will be put to the task of cutting and gathering sheaves."

But no. The sun has climbed a quarter way up to midday when we are shouted to a halt. We have left the last ditch about three hundred paces behind. There appear to be no more green fields ahead of us. Beside us now is an expanse of parched earth populated by struggling weeds, extending toward the southern and eastern horizons. Dizzy with heat and hunger, we lower ourselves to the ground. Oddly, the guards do not beat us for it, but instead, distribute a disk of barley flatbread to each man and then let us stagger down to the river to fall flat on our bellies to drink.

Our respite is not long, only enough to permit us to revive. In the meantime, three non-military Babylonians have arrived by horseback. All three are carrying a bundle of straight rods affixed with small red flags. Two of the men dismount. The third gallops off across the dry barrens in the direction of a distant hillock. He travels at right angles to the road on a track that appears to be parallel to the last ditch we left behind.

Our guards command us to get up and get our tools from the donkey cart. The Egyptian slave grins toothlessly and croons as he watches us from the seat of the cart. The tools are mattocks and a kind of shovel, plus two dozen wooden buckets shaped like deep scoops with girding bands and metal lips.

The men with red-flagged rods now set to work. The first plants a rod by the side of the road, the second walks inland with his rods, aiming by eyesight for the distant slope, where the third has planted his rod. The middle man is walking toward it with great care, dragging a shallow line behind him with the base of his rod. Every so often, he plants another rod. Now I understand that they are delineating a new field. And it takes little guesswork to conclude that the new field will need a new irrigation trench.

So we are to dig. Following shouted orders, the thirty of us set to work. The trench or ditch must be four feet deep and eight feet wide. It must follow the line marked in the dust by the pole men. It must never deviate from this line or there will be punishment. The soil removed from the trench must be scattered across the field so that we do not build a trench wall, for when the canal is in operation, it must overflow smoothly, flooding the field. And so we dig and dig and dig. And carry and scatter. Then back to the endless digging. Only the surface is hard baked and is broken up by mattock without too much difficulty. Beneath the crust is looser soil. Even so, it is unthinkable that we will be able to accomplish a hundred-foot length, so deep and wide, in a single day. After an hour passes, we are soaked in sweat and our skin is so chafed by our wet, cumbersome robes that we want to discard them and continue in loincloths and head-scarves. But the guards will not allow it, explaining that too much exposure to the burning sun would kill us. Onward we work, and soon our hands are blistered and screaming for relief, our tongues leathery with thirst, our faces and legs beginning to burn. But any unwarranted ceasing of labor invites swift retribution with the lash.

However, the guards are not madmen; indeed, they know that even animals like us need water, else we will become useless to them. Thus, every two hours we are given a short break to drink water. The one-eyed slave and his donkey cart are parked beside us. In the cart stands a clay water jar with a big copper cup. Everyone drinks until bellies are swollen, and then it is back to work. At the third break, we are given another barley disk, this time soaked in rancid olive oil.

The sun courses across the sky, and as it begins its downward descent, I wonder how long the workday will last, how we can possibly endure it to the end. During one of the breaks, I see that the trench is now about forty to fifty feet long. The overseer with his measuring rods nods approval over the depth and width. We are making progress.

My body cries out for rest. It threatens to collapse under me. I pray for physical strength and for the moral strength that can, at times, overcome the body's limitations. Somehow, the answer to this prayer provides just enough fortitude for me to continue: this shovel full, this bucket full, this plodding across the field to scatter the results, then a scurrying return to the trench as quickly as I can, for my back is already striped with whip marks. Most other Hebrew backs are likewise marked, and yet we do not give up. No one has so far collapsed, though we go slower and slower. Perhaps the guards and the overseer are weary, too, in their own way, for the lashings are fewer, even as we work less efficiently.

Seventy foot-lengths, eighty. Eighty-one, eighty-two . . . Now a few men are dropping face down in the dry earth, groaning, trying to rise on hands and knees under the lash, but collapsing again. The guards and overseers leave them where they lie.

The sun sets. Eighty-three and -four. We are laboring half blindly now, staggering around, unable to make more than a semblance of work. The overseer and guards consult with each other. The chief guard calls out that the day's work is over. I cannot remember the dreary plodding back to our village. I cannot remember if I eat anything at all upon arriving there. Despite my sunburn and blisters, my hunger and exhaustion, I stumble to the bit of tent cloth I left rolled against a wall. I curl up inside it and instantly fall asleep.

Gad shakes my shoulder before sunrise.

"Wake up, Yezekiel, wake up. I hear voices calling in the fort. Soon they will come to fetch us."

Unwillingly, I rise from sleep, groggy, wondering where I am.

"Eat now, Yezekiel," urges Gad. "You will need strength." He gives me bread, grapes, a handful of dried dates, a cup of water. I have just completed consuming it all ravenously when the overseers and guards arrive in the village with their usual bellowing. Another day begins.

The trench lengthens. On our second day of work, we complete the first hundred feet and begin another, accomplishing ninety more feet before the light departs. It is a solid accomplishment. No one collapses during the day, probably because all of us took care to eat before dawn. Day after day, we become a little stronger, though toward the end of that week three of our number—among the oldest—suffer heart attacks and are carried away on the donkey cart. Two of them die, and one is permanently weakened. For those who remain, our skin is browning, feels less burning, with patches of dead skin peeling from our faces, arms, and legs. Now on our sixth day, though we are fewer in number, we have completed before sunset our assigned portion of a hundred feet.

Six days we have labored on the ditch, six brutal days of blistered hands, aching muscles, and numerous stings from biting insects. We are told by the overseer that tomorrow we will have a day of rest. This news is greeted with exhausted rejoicing, for the truth be told, even we the strongest might not be able to push ourselves one more day. I wonder if this seventh day will be the same as our Hebrew Sabbath. I have lost track of days.

That night, I am with several men around Shimeon's fire. His station of labor is the pottery factory in Kebar, his duties to stoke its kiln, stack dried pots, and carry buckets of finer clay to the men at the wheels. Even in this less grueling place, the lash is still in use. Slowness in tasks will earn you three lashes. Dropping a fired pot and shattering it will give you ten.

He assures us that tomorrow is indeed our Sabbath day, as he has carefully marked the days all during the journey from Israel and during the past month. Nebuchadnezzar, he says, grants to all peoples who have made their home in Babylon the right to practice their religions.

"How do you come by this, Shimeon?" I ask.

The old man lowers his gaze and puts the palm of his hand over his right eye, which I now notice by firelight is swollen and bruised. There is a red welt across his forehead and cheekbones.

"Someone has struck you," I say.

"When our overseer announced that there will soon be a day of rest for us, within the month perhaps, I begged for a meeting with the town officials. It was a difficult meeting. I pleaded that tomorrow should be our day of rest, even though it is not the Babylonians' rest day. In the end, I convinced them that of all their subject peoples, only we Hebrews would willingly offer our bare breasts to the sword rather than disobey our God."

"You took these blows upon yourself for our sake, Shimeon."

"Foremost for the Lord's sake, and then for ours," Shimeon continues. "In truth, I deem that even here in this desolate place, half of us would go to the sword in an instant before dishonoring the Most High. I told them this. Indeed, I think they respect us for it."

"Half?" snorts Naphtali. "I say a tithe, or less than that. And what is this nonsense you say about *respecting* us?"

"The king and his counsellors understand that our faith is more precious to us than life. Thus, he grants a concession so that we may settle here more peaceably and serve him well. The local administrator promises that every seventh day we will have our day of worship."

This is greeted by murmurs of approval, though some among us are silently disdaining the king's motives.

We are reclining on the ground, our muscles aching, longing for sleep but entranced by the fat carp Shimeon is roasting on a spit. He caught it in a basket trap that he had woven from willow wands and sunk in the river, tied to a tree by the shore. Returning in the evening from work, he was overjoyed to find that his trap had captured a prize. When the fish is done, we all sit up and lean closer while Shimeon divides the steaming flesh with a wooden knife he secretly fashioned. He rolls the pieces in flatbread drenched with olive oil. There is not enough to fill every guest's stomach with fish alone, but there is a hefty bite for each, like a banquet to us. We are feeling very grateful to him.

"The Babylonians are not so terrible," someone mutters in an undertone, wiping his mouth and licking his fingers. "See, they still give us bread and oil."

"Give?" another retorts. "You call it *give* as if they were generous benefactors?"

"I do not say that. Even so, we are not starving."

"Ha! They do not want their mules to die."

"We are less than mules. We work like slaves for them."

"We *are* slaves."

The grumbling continues for a time, and when all the food is consumed to the last crumb and flake of flesh, we linger a while, staring at the fire.

"I believe we need a name for our village," says Shimeon.

"Why do we need a name?" Naphtali argues. "This is not our home."

"It is our home in exile," Shimeon counters. "We must make of this hard place a home for our community so that we may strengthen the spirit of Israel among us."

"If you must name it, call it Zerubbabel, for that is what we are, *strangers in Babylon, scattered by confusion.*"

I speak up. "By nature, you are a fighter, Naphtali. Your angry words come from a heart that sees no way to fight and thus sinks too easily into sour resentments."

"And who are you to judge me, Yezekiel ben Buzi, shepherd boy and charcoal bearer?"

He has told us that he once was a wealthy shop-owner in the City of David and that his son was a scribe in the palace. He does not know what has become of his son. This is his main sorrow, his main love, and it is torturing him. I do not counter with an assertion that I am a Temple attendant and priest in training. No, that would be a capitulation to his effort to assert his position in a hierarchy that no longer exists. Furthermore, in my heart of hearts, I *am* a shepherd boy.

"I do not judge you," I say. "Yet I see that it is your very self against which you struggle. Turn your strength against the real foe, which is the evil spirit of despair. Fight and struggle, yes, which is your way, but use it to build up and not tear down."

Naphtali stares at me but can think of no reply.

Shimeon clears his throat and says, "Why not call our village Zebadiah?"

"A man's name?" asks one of the others dubiously.

"A great name from the past, but one that means *a portion of the Lord* and *the Lord is my portion.*"

Silence reigns as the suggestion is absorbed. But it does not sound quite right to me. Perhaps I am thinking of my own small portion, my village, Little Bite of Bread. But I can hardly dare suggest such a name—consoling to me, but redolent of our several deprivations, such as our too-small bites of bread.

"Do you mean to say, Shimeon, that we are still the Lord's portion, here in exile?" I ask.

"Yes, we are still the Lord's portion, though brought low for a time."

"We will not be here long," says Naphtali. "A year or two and the kingdom will recover and rise again. Or else Egypt will defeat Babylon and we can go home—home to Jerusalem."

I do not know what makes me say it, but I cannot contain the words burning in my heart:

"We may be here for untold years," I say in a lowered voice.

"What mad talk! How can you think that!"

"Our captivity may be so long that few of us now living will return."

One by one, the others get up and leave, shaking their heads, leaving me alone with Shimeon. He gazes at me, saying nothing, perhaps wondering if I am an inspired messenger of unwelcome news or am playing at being a prophet —a false prophet. Finally he sighs and says:

"You are very weary, Yezekiel. Hard labors you have endured these past days. Now you must sleep."

The quality of Shimeon's character draws others to him. He is never angry, always a peacemaker, but in no way a timid one. He leads by an undefinable authority. More and more, whenever he speaks, people listen, though I cannot explain why this is so. I, too, pay close attention to what he says. Is it a purely natural effect, prompted by his physical height, a voice deeper than most men's, the way he carries himself with quiet dignity? That may be part of it, but I think it is due more to his way of never raising his voice in order to be heard, to his natural intelligence, and, more significantly, to the wisdom in what he says—usually simply expressed. Above all, I think it is something in the man's spirit.

He is not a priest, nor was he wealthy in Israel. Indeed, his former occupation was lowly, for he was a small-scale fisherman on the Jordan, smoke-curing whatever he caught and selling his catches in Jericho.

"Have you ever been to Gilgal?" I ask him.

His eyes light up. "Yes, for I lived an hour's walk upriver from it. I often went there to pray."

"Do you remember Joshua's memorial stones?"

"Always," he answers with a smile. "And I see that *you* remember them, too. Have you visited the stones?"

"Once when I was a small boy. I can never forget it."

"It is an unforgettable sight. Yet it is the lesson the Lord wrote with those stones that we must not forget."

I nod in agreement, flooded with gratitude that even here in this wretched place there are godly men like Shimeon.

"Our help is in the name of the Lord," I say, little more than a breath. "He can do the impossible if he wishes."

"He may part a river or a sea that we may go forward, as all created things obey him, except for man. The hardest barrier is in our hearts, Yezekiel, for we are often divided wrongly within ourselves—good and evil struggle there, our will and his will wrestle like Jacob and the angel of the Lord."

"Aye, it is so," I groan with sadness.

Shimeon says nothing for a time, gazing thoughtfully into the dying fire. He throws a few bits of wood onto the embers and watches as they flare.

"Such grief in your voice," he says at last. "For what do you grieve?"

"That we so often fail, that we let evil gain the upper hand inside ourselves. That the present condition of our people is due precisely to sin in human nature."

"Sin is a grief, to be sure," says Shimeon in a musing tone. "Yet has not the Lord Most High made us this way?"

"Made us evil?" I protest. "That cannot be!"

"He did not make us evil. He made us for freedom, that we might always choose what is good."

"He has *permitted* evil but never wills it, you mean?"

"He permits it, yet he is ever working to correct us and lead us to the light, without destroying our inner freedom."

"He leads us, *if* we attend to his voice."

"If we attend. He never forces."

"He never forces," I nod in agreement. "Yet he does rebuke us."

"He allows chastisement in order to awaken our memory."

"Day by day, our people more and more forget who they are, Shimeon." My voice falters, then chokes. Tears are not far away. "In this exile we are diminished, in this present darkness, this falling into the pit of Sheol, the fires of Gehenna."

"Ah, ah, Yezekiel, be not so cast down. It is true that we are the children of the desolation, yet we are not condemned to slavery of mind and soul, if only we would look up!"

I cover my eyes with the palms of my hands.

Shimeon says, "We left Israel behind months ago. How little we have prayed since then."

"How little we have prayed," I murmur, brokenhearted, feeling that we exiles are on the brink of being lost altogether, hidden forever from the eyes of the Lord.

"Though many pray in the secret places of their hearts," the old man goes on, "the Most High has chosen us *as a people*. I am coming to think that we must gather together to pray for his help—for his light in this dark place."

After drying my eyes on my sleeve, I say, "Shimeon, you are respected. Would you lift up your voice over the village and call us to prayer?"

He lowers his face and closes his eyes. After a time he looks up at me directly.

"It is one way. It is a good way. There is another way, which may be more effective over the course of time."

"How so?"

"You and I should pray together now. Then, when we have established the custom, we will invite others to join us, one by one."

"It is a slow method," I reply doubtfully.

"But more sure."

Every night from then on, I go to Shimeon's door, and seated by his cookfire, he and I recite verses from the king-psalms. A measure of peace returns to me. I feel the presence of something beyond human emotion—so mild, so gentle, so faint, as if it were a scent on the breeze. Little by little, as day follows day, the onerous labors and the lashes become easier to bear.

We are seeing other improvements in our treatment— small adjustments and survival methods. Though my Jerusalem robe is becoming tattered and thin, I treasure it. I now save it for wearing on the Sabbath only. For daily use, I have fashioned a crude garment from a piece of castoff sackcloth, tearing a hole in the middle for my neck and binding my waist with a braided belt of bulrushes. The belts do not last long, but the materials for replacing them are plentiful.

On our third Sabbath, Shimeon and I, Tzvi, and three other men gather to pray together. Until today, we have only recited king-psalms, but now we begin to sing them. This return of singing is a good sign, I think, for through it the heart is lifted even as it laments, and lifted higher still when we sing praise for the hand of the Almighty in his wondrous creations and deeds. We also retell the stories of how the Lord has rescued our people in the past. Because I am the most learned among them, I speak aloud passages from the holy books, what I can remember. The more I speak, the more I remember. My sleep is increasingly restorative, I find, and my dreams less troubled.

By our fourth Sabbath, more than twelve have joined us for our nightly prayer. There is a kind of sifting going on among our people. Most say they are too tired or too busy to attend shared prayer. Perhaps, also, they make their choice based on an unspoken assumption that prayer is of no practical use. They might not think this in so many words, but in their under-thoughts it is what they believe. It is wrong, but understandable, for until now our major preoccupation has been an unceasing struggle for survival. If the majority of our people are giving little thought to the living God, I hope at least they have left behind, or abandoned on the road, their amulets and household idols.

The high overseer has announced that soon the people of Kebar will no longer supply us with food. We are granted an extensive field behind the village and instructed to plow the soil and plant grain for our own consumption. A plow is supplied, but no horse or donkey to pull it. Men must strain under the traces to drag it through the sun-beaten soil. The soil is good but very dry, and thus, in the short fragments of time when we are not engaged in slave labor, many of us begin the task of making our own irrigation ditches. Although it is an additional burden, it is somehow a lighter task, because it is for our own benefit. When our first weir-dams are opened and the waters of the Kebar flow into the two great arms encompassing our field, cries of gladness arise from villagers who have come to watch. As the ditches overflow and flood the field, there is greater rejoicing. The dams are closed. The flood water sinks deep into the fields. Planting begins.

Behind most of our houses private vegetable plots have been dug and planted. Many fish traps have been woven, and as a result our diet is improving. Dates are free for anyone to pick. In addition, an abandoned olive grove has been allotted to us, its trees poorly tended for years, their branches unpruned, their fruit stunted. Among us there are a handful of men who know how to bring the trees back to greater productivity, and they are determined to do what they can. But the grove is far from the river and from irrigation ditches on our side of the river, so carrying water in buckets under starlight or moonlight becomes a nightly task, nearly futile considering our fatigue, the distance, and the olives' unslakable thirst. Before long, it strikes the tree shepherds that another irrigation ditch might be dug. It takes several weeks to make this trench and its branches that thread between the trees. But in the end, the water flows, and thus our olive trees are reviving, their fruit swelling. Ofttimes, when I help with branching the trench, I whisper the words of King David:

> Blessed is the man who follows not the counsel of the wicked
> Nor walks in the way of sinners, nor sits in the company of the insolent,
> But delights in the law of the Lord and meditates on his law day and night.
> He is like a tree planted near running water,
> that yields its fruit in due season, and whose leaves never fade.
> In all that he does, he prospers.

I cannot see that I *prosper*, but I am alive, and though I feel exhausted most of the time, my strength now appears to be enough to meet the demands of my new life. Perhaps this is due to the invisible water that I have reflected upon since I made the little spring in the pastures of home. Yes, it appears to be present, usually without motion, sometimes merely seeping, and on occasion flowing.

Water is the lifeblood of the world. Day after day, Sabbath unto Sabbath, the sky above us remains clear blue. Not once since our arrival in Babylonia has it rained. Yet the river flows unceasingly. God made rivers, God made mountains and hills that give birth to the rivers, God made the clouds that rise up far beyond our horizons to pour forth their abundance on the heights, flowing downward to water the earth.

As I said, a great sifting has been underway regarding the matter of prayer. Winnowing would be a better word for this mysterious process. We are now about eighteen who regularly meet to pray at night, and six more have joined us on the Sabbath. The number is better than Naphtali's dour prediction of a "tithe", though nowhere close to Shimeon's hopeful half of our population. The reason is, of course, that deep in the soul of every person there is a foundational placing of trust in either God or in oneself. And this basic law in our nature, this choice, is made more difficult by our circumstances. Our work amounts to nearly double what would have been the lot of even the most servile laborers back in Israel. There is no adequate free time, save what we steal from sleep. And though many undertake village work on the Sabbath day, I cannot bring myself to do this. We need real rest, but most importantly, we must keep the laws of the seventh day if we hope to rely totally on the saving hand of the Lord.

Only a minority see this truth or are willing to abide by it. Not only do we strive to build a self-sustaining life for the village, there is no slackening of our duties under the overseers. The majority among us plough the Babylonians' fields east and west, north and south of Kebar, and we also harvest their grain, porting it in heavy sheaves on our shoulders, loading it onto carts. Some of us are put to work on the threshing floors, which is very hot work and bad for the lungs. Every night I hear racking coughs coming from our houses.

Mainly I continue to dig new ditches with my crew, though not infrequently we are taken from this chore and put to dredging the older irrigation canals that have grown shallower with silt. Up to our thighs in brown water, we are relieved to find it cooler work, but it is hard to scoop the heavy mud from the canal's bottom. Moreover, leeches are a constant problem, sucking on our flesh and robbing our blood. It is impossible to pull them off; they can be removed from the skin only during breaks when we touch the parasites with a tiny glowing coal on the tip of a smoldering twig, making them fall off of their own accord. I am grateful that our overseers keep fires going beside the canals, probably for their own protection, because they know the smoke holds the mosquitoes and swarms of stinging gnats at bay. For the most part, they turn a blind eye to our war against the leeches, though some of the guards take amusement in watching our struggle.

We have been here three months now. How is it possible that so much has been accomplished? Our village grainfield is soaring green with copious heads of barley, more abundant than anything I ever saw in Israel. The rows of beans and peas planted on the borders of the field are flowering lavishly, some already growing pods. In the same manner, the private village gardens are swiftly ripening with melons, leeks, cucumbers, and onions, not yet ready to eat but promising a better future. No house lacks such a plot, as the desperate fear of hunger and the desire for more strengthening kind of food drive us all. I, too, have my plot on the edge of the village, though I am wanting in time to water it adequately—a few beans and pea plants twining up sticks. I supplement my usual stark fare with a handful of wheat or barley now and then, which I glean from the fields whenever I am put to harvesting. This scavenging amounts to little, and it was becoming still less because of rats and mice, which forced me to make three clay pots with lids, skill-lessly shaping them by hand and baking them in the embers of a cookfire. They are crude pieces, but they seem to have stopped the constant theft by predators. Moreover, town cats have somehow crossed the river, or have come out of the wilds, and are constantly chasing the rodents night and day.

The officials of Kebar have now granted us an hour of sunlight each day, as evenfall approaches, to work on our own village projects. I doubt that this enormous boon is pure benevolence on their part, as I suspect they merely wish to see us settled and closer to self-sufficiency. Even so, I have no free time to build a more permanent shelter for myself. I am the only one in the village who still sleeps in a tent—rather, my scrap of tent cloth. There are a few bricks left, but not enough for a shelter, and no one is making more. I have little time or energy for it—seldom at night and definitely not on the Sabbath. Someday, perhaps. Though most of the dwellings already have two or three people living under a single roof, a few men have invited me to share their tiny homes, impelled by kindness or pity. I have declined their offers, knowing that this would impose great discomfort on them, as the houses have barely enough room as it is.

I continue to work on the Kebar side of the river, digging more new canals and sometimes dredging older ones. Other days I am harvesting grain, sickle in hand, bending from morning until close to sunset, when the guards give the command that we must now return to the village—where more labors await us. On such days, the muscles in my back become a torment. There are moments when I pause to wonder why I do not die under this unceasing demand on my body. I try to praise the Most High silently throughout each day, and this, I believe, is the reason I am able to carry on. Now recalling the three men who suffered heart attacks during our first week of digging, I am disconcerted by my lack of consideration of their fate. Two died that day, and the third has proven to be so damaged—though he is not very old, less than forty years—that he is only able to shuffle about the village and scour the nearby woods for branches to donate to the Kebarite women who make our bread. From time to time, I help him in his small tasks.

During one such venture, we sit down on the ground side by side, for he is short of breath. He confides in me that he wants to die but cannot bring himself to take his own life.

"The Lord forbids it!" I reprove him.

"Yes, yes, I know," he says, shamefaced. "Yet I cannot help my feelings. Life has no purpose for me. I am useless and a burden."

"You are not a burden, Eli."

"Oh, I am indeed a burden. Others feed me in exchange for what? For what? To gather twigs when once I was a stonemason in Israel, mighty of arm and thigh, my eye clear and true. Now I must lie down on the ground to rest after the slightest task." He points to the center of his chest. "And all day a spear stabs at my heart, again and again."

"You must rest more. You do not need to prove your worth."

"I must give what I can. Even so, I pray that soon the spear will give a final thrust, and my body will be thrown into the valley of bones, where I can take my rest at last."

"The valley of bones?"

He gestures beyond our village field to a swelling on the horizon. "On the far side of those hills. It is where the two who died were taken."

I remember that day—the groans and agitations that

followed when we learned that the guards would not let us bury the bodies. The one-eyed man on his donkey cart had carried them away somewhere.

Now I am ashamed. How little thought I have given to the matter since then. How little feeling.

"Eli, Eli," I say, with my hand on his quaking shoulder, "your worth is in the eyes of the Lord, not in your mind's own weigh-scales."

He mumbles disconsolately.

"Your name means *the offering* and *the lifting up*," I say. "Could it be that the Most High desires you to live so that your sufferings may be offered to him as a sacrifice of praise?"

Now he looks directly at me, absorbing what I have said, weighing it rightly, I hope.

I go on. "In this desolate place where we no longer offer burnt sacrifices of lambs and doves, so far from the Temple, cannot another kind of sacrifice be offered?"

Mutely he tilts his head, considering.

"It may be that you, Eli, do the greatest work of all."

He frowns, uncertain.

"Do not abandon us," I say urgently. "Do not abandon us!"

Startled, with his eyes blinking rapidly, he nods.

"Help me up," he says.

I take his arms and pull him to his feet. Saying no more, we continue to gather fallen branches. We walk slowly back to the village, a large bundle on my shoulders, a few twigs in his hands.

But I can see that even this child's task is too much for him. The skin of his face is grey, his chest heaving with the effort to take in more air.

"I will bring you to your dwelling now," I say firmly. "You will rest and then rise up on a better day."

"Nay, I am finished."

I take his arm with my right hand. "In which house do you live?"

"I have no house," he says, and nods in the direction of a terebinth at the edge of the village. "I live under the shade of that tree. There I will die."

I pull him onward, and though he resists at first, he reluctantly follows. The terebinth is exceedingly rich in leaves and smells strongly of resin. Clusters of small red fruit hang from its branches. A cracked copper cup and a heap of rags by the trunk appear to be the sum of Eli's possessions. I help him down to the ground, and he sighs, a little color returning to his cheeks.

"Leave me," he whispers. "I must die now."

"I will not leave you," I say. "I will build you a shelter. Though this shade be good, rain will come before the year is out."

"I will not live to see the rain."

"Even so, I will build you a shelter."

The sun is low in the west, its fiery glow now invading the space beneath the tree and bringing with it waves of heat. I have little time to accomplish what I promised, so I hasten to the poplar woods and find four fallen saplings. Back at the tree I erect the poles in a cone and bind the apex with a strip of sackcloth torn from the hem of my robe. Then I run to my own squalid tent—if tent it can be called —and tear it into two equal parts. One I take back to the tree and drape it over the sapling poles.

"Your house," I tell Eli. "It is no palace, but please do me the honor of taking up residence in it."

He meets my eye and manages to produce a feeble smile. He crawls under the shelter and lies down. I take his copper cup and run with it to the river. By the time I return to his tent, carrying the cup carefully lest the water spill, the light is fading in deepening dusk, and he is sleeping. I leave the cup near his feet, where he will find it upon waking.

For three days I do not see Eli at his pitiful labors around the village. I check each evening to see if he has died, but his frail flesh perseveres. He sleeps and sleeps. And on the fourth day when I go to see him, the shelter is empty. I search in the nearby woods and find him moving slowly about, gathering twigs. I hear him whispering praises to the Most High, intermingled with "This I offer, this I offer."

On a day not long after, at the hour when all laborers have dragged themselves back to the village, the last of the resident guards depart. They leave with grimaces and guttural sounds of disgust, slapping their heels as if to rid them of the dust of our presence. From now on, they will only return in the mornings, to ensure that we go obediently to our work across the river and to deal with any disturbances that may arise.

A cart arrives from Kebar, full of old and dented copper pots and a few iron vessels, which are tossed in a heap on the village commons. The baker women of Kebar step forward and, speaking through our interpreter, Gad, call us together to make an announcement. They declare that they are no longer needed as cooks. We can gather our own food and make our own bread. The empty barracks are full of wheat and barley jars, they say, a supply that should last until our own harvest is in. Next, they inform us enthusiastically that commerce between the "city" and "Slavetown" will continue. We can buy, sell, and trade as we wish.

"With what?" someone shouts. "With what would we buy, sell, and trade?"

Without warning, the Babylonian women, young and middle-aged and old alike, open their robes to display their naked bodies to us, giggling and posturing lasciviously. Shocked, open-mouthed with astonishment, the crowd of Israelites is for the moment paralyzed. Then most of us turn away, sickened.

Gad shamefacedly informs us that they have offered themselves as concubines to any Israelite man. The Babylonian women depart with final declarations called out with unseemly glee.

I take Gad aside and ask him for a translation of their parting words. He tells me:

"These women say, 'Come to us across the river, we will make you happy. Let us mingle our two peoples'."

I scowl in reply, "Surely some of them are married."

"Surely, most of them are, maybe all. But that is no matter to them, for it is their way. They call themselves *the daughters of Ishtar*. It is said that in the city of Babylon is a great temple dedicated to Ishtar, their goddess of fertility, where every mature woman must go and offer herself as a prostitute. Once she has thus known a man—any man—she may return to her home as a sacred, consecrated daughter of Ishtar."

"This is disgusting!" I blurt.

"Aye, it is disgusting, Yezekiel, but are we not too many men without wives here?"

I look at him with surprise.

"We are not animals in heat, Gad. The Babylonians consider us beasts of burden. Let us not degenerate still further."

"Yes, yes, you are right," he says with a rueful shake of his head. "Still, where will we find wives?"

"Do you yearn for a wife merely to satisfy your lust?"

Gad examines the dust at his feet, shifting from foot to foot uncomfortably. He mumbles, "To gratify my belly, too, for I do not know how to make bread. There are eighty men here and about twenty married women—or soon to be married."

"Then you can learn to make your own bread. And while you study the art of bread, you can practice waiting upon the Lord. It may be that in good time, if you pray for a spouse to cherish and honor and protect, the Most High will send you one."

Gad sighs and casts a glance across the river.

I fear for him and pity him as well. Even so, I do not count myself immune to the power that draws all men toward consummation. Yet I know why I have no desire to accept those women's offers. Their wantonness is repugnant, their idolatry horrifying. Moreover, it must never be forgotten that Israel's chastisement has come about chiefly because of mingling with the alien nations and their ways. Even Solomon the Wise succumbed and thus brought havoc upon his people.

Not long after the aforesaid incident, there occurs an event that further puts us to the test. Resting beneath the stars after a day's labor under a merciless sun, most of us sit wearily in our dooryards or quietly converse around dying cookfires. We hear laughter and raucous song coming from the direction of the river. Within minutes, a rabble of drunken Babylonians, mostly youths but among them a few mature men, stumble into the village commons, weaving from drink and bellowing words that sound vile enough without translation. A few are naked; the rest wear flimsy groin covers. Inflamed with lust or possibly sheer riotousness, they make sexual gestures that are clearly designed to entice.

"They are demanding that we give them our women," explains Gad. On hearing this, we Israelites rise quickly to our feet and advance on the intruders, greatly outnumbering them and making a wall that blocks them.

This does little to ease the provocation. Indeed, it only makes the intruders worse, for they now discard all their clothing and prance about in a lewd dance. Several of our men step forward, picking up reeds with which they had been weaving baskets. They proceed to give the Babylonians a lashing, laying welts upon their backsides. None of the Kebarites are badly hurt, but they scream and race away toward the river.

Nevertheless, it is not the end of the matter. In the weeks that follow, we field hands receive more than the regular lashings, usually on the flimsiest of excuses. We bear it without fighting back, which would invite worse treatment. Thus, our anger is driven deeper into our hearts with each stroke, hardening our resolve to resist these depraved overseers, regardless of the cost. However, the naked invasion that precipitated the conflict is not repeated.

I am often awake with worry half the night, sitting alone in the dark, trying to pray, feeling nothing. More than once I have seen shadows flitting from houses and disappearing into the deeper darkness by the river. I fail to see any of them return before morning and frequently find myself working side by side during the day with men who are bleary-eyed from lack of sleep. It does not take long for me to conclude that some of our men are secretly crossing the river to meet with women of Kebar. Moreover, it soon becomes a nightly occurrence, and though I am relieved that the numbers engaging in this kind of commerce are a minority among us, they amount to a considerable portion.

One night I cannot contain my grief and indignation. Spotting a figure darting from his house and heading toward the willows, I rise to my feet and bound after him, catching up to him just as his feet splash into the ford.

"What are you doing to yourself?" I cry.

"It is not your affair!" he shouts back.

"You are a son of Israel. Remember the laws of Moses. Do not forget the commandments of the Most High."

This gives him pause.

"Who are you?" he spits. "Who are you to tell me what to do?"

"I am your brother."

"You are not my brother."

"Remember the courage of Joseph, who fled from Potiphar's wife."

"Who is Potiphar?" he snaps.

"Do you not know the Sacred Scriptures? Do you not know our people's past?"

"That was long ago. Now we have a new life, a new world."

"It is not new. It is as old as our captivity in Egypt."

"This is Kebar, not Egypt. And Kebar is teeming with beautiful women who yearn for me."

"They do not yearn for *you*; they crave attention and pleasure from anything male."

"And here I am, very male."

"But not a man," I sternly argue. "Not yet a true man. Gird up your loins and return to the village."

"See to your own loins!" he growls, pushing me away. I fall into the water, and he sloshes onward to the other shore.

The next day is the Sabbath. Fully a quarter of our people have gathered by a fire in Shimeon's dooryard. After prayer and song and recitation of Scripture, we fall silent.

"They call our village *Slavetown*," laments someone out in the shadows.

This is met with murmuring and groans.

Shimeon raises his voice in answer. "Regardless of what they call us, the Lord is our portion, and therefore we must trust in him."

"*Us* and *we*. Even donkeys in a field think of themselves that way. We need a good name."

"You recall that we discussed this before, Naphtali, and could not settle the matter."

"Why not *Zerubbabel*, as I suggested? It is better than *Slavetown*."

"Worse," Gad interjects.

I am glad to see him here; he has turned toward prayer at last, and hopefully his whole life will follow.

"Why worse?" Shimeon asks.

"*Zeru Babel* in their language means *seed of Babel* and also implies the *seed of Baal*."

Baal, the name of horror from our past. The demon-god that devours human sacrifice even as it devours human souls.

I clear my throat and enter the discussion. "We are not the seed of demons. As Shimeon has said, we are the Lord's portion."

There is nodding around the fire. Shimeon regards me

thoughtfully, saying nothing, but with a gesture of his hand he encourages me to continue.

"We are his little portion here in exile," I say. "Very little and without power, but we are his." Then, remembering how sweet, how beloved to me is the name of my own home village, I press onward. "Names have power. This power is not only an influence on the mind and emotions, it affects our souls as well. I think we should call ourselves the *hakheleq haqatann*, the small portion."

The ensuing discussion swings back and forth for a time, until as the fire collapses into embers a concord is reached, even a peaceful harmony. It is agreed that we will call ourselves *Hakheleq*, the Portion. We will use this name, and only this name, whenever we speak of the village. If we are persistent in this, gradually the rest of our fellow exiles will come to accept the name and take pride in it.

"The Kebarites will not like it," someone objects.

"We need not explain everything to them," says Shimeon. "Yet whenever we think or say the name of our village *Hakheleq*, we will silently add 'We are the Lord's little portion just as he is our portion, and therefore we will trust in him'."

9

The Yehudim

S EVEN FULL MOONS HAVE I SEEN since leaving Jerusalem. The eighth is near.

Rain showers fell off and on for a few days—Babylonian winter. Eli has lived to see it. He continues on as usual and is looking a little better, week by week. Of an evening I will sit with him under his tree, and we will eat our bread together. Usually I have nothing much to say, as I am always very tired. More and more he fills the silence with small observations.

"The terebinth is the most beautiful tree in the world," he says.

"The cedars of Lebanon, I hear, are also most beautiful," I reply.

"Aye, and the olive is beautiful in its fruits."

"So, too, the Babylonian palm."

"Ah, yes, the palm date. And let us not forget the fig."

"So sweet, so sweet."

On and on we go, naming all the trees that we know, comparing their diverse merits, and discussing how this great richness of life tells us something about our Creator.

"Did you know, Yezekiel, that beneath the terebinth, which as I say is the most beautiful tree in the world, many people in Israel offered prayers to their idols?"

"I heard of it. And they offered horrible sacrifices as well."

"Do you think they chose the terebinth as the place for such evil because it was like a little temple, so shapely in form, with its wondrous smell so much like incense?"

"That may be so, Eli."

"And do you think that this most beautiful tree is like unto the tree in the garden of Eden?"

"I had not thought of that," I say. "Perhaps you are right. Ever does the serpent beguile Adam's children to repeat the first sin. He craves us to worship him, and what better place for such blasphemous rites than in a temple of great beauty."

Eli nods in agreement.

"But the terebinth is not evil, is it?" he says, puzzling over the thought.

"No, not evil in itself."

"Then we may make of our own terebinth a temple to the true Lord. We will praise him here—here in lands east of Eden."

His insight moves me.

"I am grateful that you did not die, Eli. You teach me."

"Ah, ah, how can a fool teach a wise man?"

"I am not wise. And if there be a fool beneath this terebinth, it is not you."

He laughs. Until now I have seen but one smile from him and never a laugh. It is like water in the desert, a sound that gives me joy, for I see that Eli's heart and soul have grown stronger.

"Then let us now praise the one true God," I say.

I sing a king-song that exalts the Lord, and he joins in, stumbling but fervent.

The days are cooler now, but not as cold as our winters in Israel, where there was sometimes a delightful sprinkling of snow, covering the earth with a robe of purity, though swiftly melted. Here, snow and frost are unknown. The rain must be falling more heavily in the highlands and mountains far to the north and the east, for the river Kebar is beginning to rise, swollen by the abundance of waters flowing down from their sources.

All the grain harvest is now stored and dry. The time has come for plowing the fields, and for weeks I am busy with this task, sometimes with a donkey pulling the plow, at other times with two men bound in the traces with a third at the handles. The fields are vast. But finally, all cultivated lands within a day's journey of the town are plowed, and then comes the flooding of fields by means of canals and ditches, soaking the soil deeply in advance of the next planting. At this point, our daily labors are eased for a short time, with an additional half-day granted for completion of village tasks.

The sun returns. It is growing warm again. The fields are still damp, and when they are just about firm underfoot, the sowing of seed begins.

Hardly any of us Israelites are good at the task. After all, most of us were taken from Jerusalem, where few are knowledgeable in the skills of husbanding the earth. I know more than most city people, as I recall the way I once helped with our small plots in Little Bite of Bread, but I am no farmer. Despite our ignorance, all able-bodied men are forced to engage in the sowing, helped along by overseers' bellows and the abiding lash. Under their watchful eyes, day after day we learn the best way for scattering seeds so that none are wasted. Bread is life—for them and for us.

One late afternoon, in the eighth month after my departure from Jerusalem, I am at work near the road, about an hour's walk from the town. Under a guard's direction, I and a crew of four others are repairing a weakened weir-dam, laying new poles across the top. Behind me I hear the muffled roar of what sounds like an army on the march or a herd of camels in motion. I look up and see a cloud of dust rising above a large number of people plodding along the road in our direction.

The guard lashes me once across the middle of my back, and I look down and continue my work. Soon enough, however, from the corner of my eye I see that the people walking past are sore-footed with slumping shoulders, many carrying satchels and rolled blankets. Their robes are soiled, and their faces strained with fatigue—men, women, youths, and children. Lines of soldiers accompany them. In my estimation, about fifteen hundred people trod by.

At completion of the day's work, a guard leads our crew back to the town. As we wade across the ford, we hear a commotion of disparate voices ahead in the village. And there on our arrival, we come upon a crowd of strangers, about two hundred people or more, seated on the grass in the village commons, looking bewildered. It is the travelers. Overseers are shouting at them, but for the present there appears to be no interpreter. Where is Gad?

Using my best surmise, I wave my arms to attract the newcomers' attention.

"People, where are you from?" I call.

"Jerusalem, Ramah, Bethlehem," a few voices reply. "What is this place? Who are you?"

"I am an Israelite like you, as are all those who dwell in this village. We, too, are captives, but arrived here some months ago. Do not be afraid!"

But my words fall short of the intended effect, for what I tell the newcomers fails to reassure them. They erupt with wails and loud demands for further explanations.

I try to reassure them once again and add what else I know, but it is obvious that it will take time for them to understand fully what has befallen them, that this is the final station of their journey, that their former life is over.

As the sun sets, we are interrupted by donkey carts arriving from the ford, loaded with tents and baskets of crude bread. The drivers toss their loads onto the ground, promptly turn their carts around, and head back to the river. Children scramble for the bread, followed by mothers and a few younger people who dust off the hard disks and break them into smaller pieces so the children can eat. The Babylonians' message is clear: You are animals; you are *our* animals.

Guards and overseers stride around, yelling instructions that no one can understand.

Gad is suddenly nearby. He shouts, "They say you must put up tents!"

Most of the new arrivals remain sitting or lying, gaping at the jumble or hanging their heads.

I approach a man who is staring at the pile, as if wondering where to begin.

"Where are you from?" I ask him.

"Jerusalem," he replies. He spreads an arm. "All of us are from the city or nearby towns."

"Why so many of you?" I ask him.

"Nebuchadnezzar has deceived us not once but twice," he says morosely. "Two kings has he destroyed, and two bands of slaves has he captured. We are lost!"

People lying nearby sit up and raise a chorus, "We are lost! We are lost!"

"You are not lost!" I cry above the din. "You will work hard here, but you will be fed and sheltered."

This is greeted with a few looks of half-hearted hope, but mainly with subdued crying.

"They treat you harshly now to show you who is master," I explain. "It was the same for us when we arrived in the first deportation. Your situation will improve, little by little, if you work diligently for them and do not lose heart. See, we the first-comers are not destroyed."

The man shakes his head and sits down, looking away from me. In his fear, he is withdrawing into solitude.

Regardless, I ask him, "Tell me where are the others."

"What others?"

"You were a great crowd on the road, and here I see only about two hundred."

"The headman of that town says two hundred stay here; the rest go onward to a place called Tel-abib and other cities. Maybe Ur. Maybe Nippur. We do not know."

These people are disoriented and weary, and now they merely roll themselves in their blankets, singly or in family groups, guarding their baggage close by them. Despite the lack of pegs, I and some of our men manage to put up a few tents before the darkness of night makes further effort impossible. By torchlight we go through the crowd, gathering women and children and leading them to shelter.

It seems that the Babylonians are not given to imagination. Indeed, it appears they follow a set plan and schedule for the incorporation of masses of slaves into their empire, as the pattern that emerged during my own arrival is now repeated stage by stage. When we first arrived, and throughout the next two months, our condition felt crushing, impossible to survive. Thoughts of a swift, merciful death had played about the edges of my mind, and perhaps in the minds of many others, and had invaded deeper into the hearts of more than a few. Exhaustion and the specter of a hopeless future breeds despondency and can lead in the end to despair. One must resist stumbling down this slope with all one's inner might.

Now there are three times more Israelites in the Portion, bringing with them needs far greater than ours were in the beginning. Again we are faced with an overwhelming amount of houses to build and too many people to feed with our minimal resources. Even so, the brutal habits of our guards and overseers diminish more quickly than was the case for us who first arrived. While their behavior is still very strict, ensuring obedience in hard labors, they seem equally concerned with exacting a concerted effort to enlarge the village in order to establish a permanent habitation for all our people.

Since the second wave of captives from Jerusalem arrived, the Kebarites have supplied us with abundant bricks of their own making, cartload after cartload every day. These Babylonian bricks are cleanly crafted and are swiftly made in great numbers, for the town of Kebar has several large kilns used solely for baking their bricks. The making of our own sun-dried bricks is a longer, slower method, and the bricks are poorer, too easily chipped or crumbling at the edges. Clearly our overlords across the water are not aiding us from sheer kindness. No, they want to see the new arrivals quickly rooted here, so that the captives' energies will thereafter be fully engaged in serving them.

We of the first wave of exiles are now well-experienced in house building, and so it is our lot to do most of the labor, hoping that the newcomers will learn from our example and our instructions about how it should be done. Many are eager enough, and just as many are uncertain or lazy, standing off to the side with dangling arms or sitting on the ground gossiping and fretting as they watch us. Before long, these ease-takers are compelled by Babylonian spearpoint to carry bricks to the building sites or to mix mortar under Tzvi's direction, which suits us fine. Thus, the construction of the village is moving forward. Moreover, it is generally improving our people's spirits. To have a home of one's own is no small thing, for it is a need written in the hearts of all human beings. The greatly increased need for food has also been considered, as every day a cartload of milled grain arrives, and twelve of our women have been appointed permanent bakers.

Day after day, week after week, moon unto moon, the village expands in uneven rings around our original commons. For lack of spare time and energy, I have not yet built a house for myself, though I manage to elicit Eli's permission to build him one beside his beloved terebinth. It is very small, but I think well made. Out of concern for my well-being, he pleads with me to take the new dwelling for my own, or at least to move in with him, but this is wishful thinking on his part, for it has only enough space for one person, and his need is greater than mine.

His happiness is boundless. On the evening of the day his house is completed, we sit together beneath the terebinth, admiring the "little palace", as he calls it. Again and again, he raises his arms and lifts his eyes to the heavens, uttering praise to the Giver of All Good Things and thanking him for his servants, who are the instruments of his mercy.

We sing together for a time and then fall silent.

Looking up, Eli points to the clusters of red terebinth seeds.

"Have you noticed, Yezekiel, that they look like droplets of blood?"

"I had not noticed until now, Eli, but yes, they are like droplets of blood."

"Innocent blood," he whispers with a forlorn look.

I imagine he is thinking of the countless children sacrificed on altars under the terebinths of Israel. I wonder how he can love this tree so much, why he is not repelled by its evil history.

"Does it trouble you?" I ask.

"It reminds me to pray," he replies.

More silence. He now seems to be gazing at a far distant place, beyond or above.

He says, "Lovely was the terebinth created by the Lord Most High, and if some men have defiled it, other men may restore it."

I nod in agreement, intrigued by his curious mood.

"Not by the blood of children," he adds in a voice of one who is seeing a living dream. "Not by the blood of children," he says again, "but by the blood of the lamb."

I ask him, "Do you intend to sacrifice a lamb by way of reparation for the evils committed in our homeland?"

His gaze slowly returns to me, and he shakes himself.

"I do not know what I mean," he says as if waking from the dream.

I still live under a tent that is just sufficient for covering my body at night. I have, as well, a grain jar that I managed to procure in exchange for extra labors for a Kebarite. The lid fits tightly; it keeps the mice and river rats from plundering my own plunderings, my meager gleanings. My poor handmade jars do their duty as well. Our people—those of the first wave who know me—have given me gifts such as dried fruit, a small flagon of olive oil, sometimes a disk of bread that is a most welcome supplement to the daily allotment due all laborers.

I do not ask any payment for services such as helping to build houses, carrying buckets of clay for roofing, or performing repellent tasks such as gathering dung for the middens beyond the village. Several other men perform such tasks without charge. We know that the weaker and the older among us can barely provide for themselves, and if our people are to survive here, we cannot live as we once did in Israel —that is, basing our economy on silver and gold and copper coins. Our main currency for the time being is generosity, and I truly hope this will last. The situation has brought the added blessing of increased confidence in each other, for both the first and second wave of exiles are beginning to mingle well. Of course, the spectrum of human personalities is much the same with both. There are holy people and sinful, wise and foolish, intelligent and simple, noisy and quiet, generous and greedy—yes, as is ever the case, there are some who strive only to ensure that their own desires are fulfilled. Driven by fear or by habitual selfishness, they refuse to share what they have, clinging tightly to it as if it were their means of salvation.

There is no salvation here, save in working hard and not losing heart, in prayer and sacrifice for each other. Above all, if we are to be saved, it will be through our trust in the Lord, despite the fact that there is little in our new world on which to base our trust. Though we do not know what the future will bring, we may still live as children of the Most High. If we forget this, we will become slaves not only in body but in our very souls.

Several newcomers, men young and old, have joined us for nightly prayer. An even greater number, though still a minority, are with us for Sabbath prayers. Women are coming, too, sitting in a group at the edge of firelight.

Around sixty of us gather together one Sabbath evening. Those who know the words are singing a king-song, the others are raptly listening, mouthing the words, or attempting to sing along with us. Afterward, when head cloths have been removed, the perpetual discussion about our situation breaks out. It has been repeated countless times over and looks to be without end. Naturally, the newcomers want to know more about details of life here in exile, what they can expect, how dangerous are the guards, how plentiful the food supply, why some people have their houses built first and others must wait, and all manner of other topics. Resentful quibbles jostle with genuine curiosity.

Tonight Shimeon brings up the subject of the village name, hoping that the newcomers will adopt it as we have. He describes the process by which we arrived at *Hakheleq*, and as is usually the case whenever he speaks, people fall silent and listen attentively. Just as usual, anything said must be countered by objections. In the end, however, after long listening on our parts, and calm explanations, the murmuring and head-nodding indicate that most of the newcomers agree it is good to have a name and that this name, the Portion, which is also a secret prayer, works well enough. Though their response could not be called enthusiasm, the general agreement is a victory of sorts. Our identity is slowly being strengthened by the mortar of prayer and patient leadership.

Then contention again erupts.

"So, we have a name. But who decided on this name, and why were we not asked?" exclaims one of the most vocal grumblers. I look at his facial expression, his sour mouth, his suspicious eyes, very much like the expression of a few others in the gathering. Inwardly I sigh. Why are some people like this? Why must they snarl and object to everything, as if by asserting their voice they acquire substantiality or influence or simply give vent to their frustration with our lot. Or is it that they exist at the center of the very universe, and all other human beings are an irritant to their independence, all decisions save their own are less worthy of consideration? For such people, no answer will ever suffice.

"A name is not enough. We need elders to lead us," says an old greybeard wearing a once-fine robe. Clearly he is unaccustomed to manual labor and, I suspect, would like to see himself appointed to a less strenuous role.

"Do we not have enough overseers?" shouts a young man, the kind who would prefer himself to lead, no doubt by brawn and bravado.

"Elders would not be overseers to use the lash on us," Shimeon replies in his imperturbable voice, trying to soothe the rising emotions all around. "They would guide us and judge matters of disagreement among us."

"We must pray!" declares Eli in his feeble voice. "We must praise the Lord Most High!"

But none of the newcomers pay him any attention.

"Our brother Eli is right," I put forth with strength. "We must pray to the Lord for guidance in our new life, to help us find order according to his holy will."

The murmuring grows in volume, along with a few scowls, belligerent outthrust chins, and raised voices interrupting each other. Shimeon is old and tired, and I can see he is sorely taxed by these shallow men.

"This is not Jerusalem!" someone calls out.

"You say rightly," I reply, rising to my feet and addressing the crowd. "This is not Jerusalem, and that is why we need elders to hold us together, lest we dissolve into factions or, worse, fall into the evils of our captors' guile."

Murmurs and various opinions follow, with much shaking of heads and small arguments left and right. I can see that there is no real unity among us.

"If only we had a king to rule us," laments a mournful voice.

"Nay, Jehoiachim is dead," says another.

"And look where *he* led us."

"Do you wish to end like the generation that clamored for Saul?" I point out. "Think of the evils Saul brought upon Israel."

"Yes, but after Saul came David," a man protests.

"Now David's line is dead. The kingdom is no more," another argues.

I raise my voice again, saying, "In the book of origins, Moses wrote that the scepter shall never depart from Judah."

"But it *has* departed!"

"Nay, nay, nay," says another. "They did not kill the princes. The son, Jehoiachin, they left as vassal king in Jerusalem, for he was soft and spineless by nature. Yet after three months, Nebuchadnezzar changed his mind and sent his troops back to the city to seize Jehoiachin. He must have feared that even such a puppet would harbor anger over the execution of his father and in time would rise up in rebellion. The boy has been taken in bondage with his royal household to somewhere in Babylon, along with ten thousand more captives from the city—ourselves among them, as you see."

"Woe unto woe! Three thousand in the first deportation, ten thousand eight hundred in the second. Where will it end!"

"Alas, alas, there is now no king over Israel!"

Another newcomer supplies more information.

"Not so, not so. In the boy's place, Nebuchadnezzar established his uncle Mattaniah as vassal king."

"Mattaniah?" several voices groan. "That evil wanton, that corrupted and corrupting one!"

"The very one. Nebuchadnezzar has changed Mattaniah's name to Zedekiah. He renames him as if to prove further ownership over him."

I break into the discussion. "Is the kingdom made of such bloodlines only? Remember that Isaiah foretold a king of kings who would arise from the stock of Jesse, and he shall rule over all the Gentiles. In *this* way, the scepter has not departed."

"Phagh! Where is this stock, where is this king of kings?"

"He will come, if we do not lose heart and betray the nation by apostasy."

"What are you saying? How can *we* preserve the nation?"

"Here in the Portion, we must do as our forefathers did before the age of Israel's kings, when our people were ruled by wise judges."

"Ha! Where are the wise but in their graves?" scoffs a man. "Do you see any wise among us?"

"I see no farther than the morrow. Yet I know that a dead tree may shoot forth a rootstock, which in time becomes a living tree. Can we not hope for this? Can we not work together for this? And as we labor side by side to build an island of Israel in exile, surely we will need to preserve order among us."

Silence greets this as my point is absorbed. But before too many more minutes pass, the wrangling resumes.

"Do we not have enough *order* imposed by our captors?"

"Though much of their order is odious, still the matters of our own law need proper administration. What if there is adultery or theft among us? What if there be unjust violence —even murder?"

"Hand over the culprits to the Babylonians for justice!"

"Justice?" I ask. "Tell me what form of justice can we expect from them. Think of the bodies littering the road all the way back to Jerusalem."

"We will kill the Babylonians!"

"That would be madness. Ten of our own would be executed in retaliation for one Babylonian killed."

A momentary silence greets this.

Someone shouts: "Then *we* will kill our bad ones, like Moses did in the desert!"

I raise my voice again. "Kill our own people? And who will justly judge their guilt or innocence?"

More silence.

The meeting breaks up shortly after with little resolved. But we have a name, and that is a beginning.

The newly arrived Israelite women have involved themselves in bread making, pounding grain and even dried legumes with wooden mortars and pestles. Some are skilled in making special breads. They harvest the huge clumps of ripe dates hanging from palm trees and cut them finely into the batter, sweetening the sour dough and helping its rising. The oldest, a widow called Chaya-Ayala, more than eighty years old, is learned in food and drink. The children like to hang around her cook pots, begging for a bit of dough to eat, chanting her name in sing-song because it rhymes so well.

"My old bones still have plenty of life, but I won't be leaping around the way I once did," she says, making a joke of her names—*life* and *gazelle*.

She instructs the younger women:

"Red dates do well enough. Grapes from a vineyard are best, when they are covered with the white dust, but wild grapes and other berries will also suffice, as long as they have the dust."

A young women asks, "Why is the white dust necessary?"

"It is fallen from the air, where the leaven lives. When it finds a sweet thing, it clings to it and feeds upon the sweetness inside. If you cut grape or berry, exposing its juices, the leaven will grow even more swiftly upon it. When it is added to the bread dough, it grows still further and makes bubbles that expand the loaf. This, when baked, makes a bread that is soft and sweet on the tongue."

Another sweet thing, recently discovered, is wild honey. In old dead trees, bees make their hives in cracks and hollows. Some very brave souls dare to harvest the golden syrup and the white combs, willing to suffer much for their love of it. Others know that when a burning branch of green wood is waved around the hives, the bees will be pacified by the thick cloud of smoke. The swarms will still cover the harvesters' hands and heads but will not sting.

Commerce is also underway. Some of our men have crafted clever square baskets with lids, hinged with wicker loops—the Babylonians have only round baskets and marvel over the innovation. Our women have been selling their loaves to the women of Kebar, who know only how to make tough, poorly risen loaves, halfway between flat and leavened. In payment, they receive coins of the realm, trinkets, kitchen tools, and much-desired spices, especially cumin and fennel, and even a powder made from the ground bark of cinnamon which is imported from Persia.

Other women have dried the hard seeds of a plant I do not recognize and dyed them in a variety of colors. The dyes they concoct from herbs they find in the nearby fields and woods. They pierce the seeds with a needle and string them to make necklaces and wristlets. Though the Babylonian women have plenty of jewelry of their own, and often much finer, they are eager for the novelty.

Our livestock is increasing as well. With the coinage trickling into the village, enough is pooled to purchase five goats, three of them giving copious milk, two heavy with kid. In addition, by trading their smuggled bits of gold or costly gemstones, some families have managed to purchase ewe sheep and a young ram. Between the families, there number perhaps twenty to twenty-five sheep. Predictably, these people claim private ownership, but it is to their merit that they seek ways to distribute the small amount of milk. Seven of our Hebrew women are pregnant and have the greatest need for adequate nourishment. The combined goat and ewe milk is proving to be enough. Children are coming. The children who are our future. May they live to see Jerusalem the golden with their own eyes!

For the time being, people are being generous, as most of them have gained some sense that survival depends on helping each other without counting the cost. Needless to say, there are some very selfish characters in this second wave of exiles, a small minority, who tend to go off by themselves to hoard what they possess. They have smuggled a surprising amount of gold and silver coins on their persons and will pay a large fee to anyone willing to build them houses ahead of due time. Only a few workmen accept to do so, despite the strong allure of money. Tzvi sighs over the shamefulness of it, but he can no longer control the comings and goings at the brick stacks, which the Kebarites keep constantly supplied. No one else pays the greedy ones any attention; indeed, no one really wants to have much to do with them. They are exclusively the former wealthy of Jerusalem, suffering from the loss of their pathetic comforts and fearful of the rest of us. It is saddening to see this kind of behavior, yet the greater part of those who once knew plenty in our homeland are adjusting well, looking for ways to strengthen us as a group, sharing a measure of what they have, and caring for widows and orphans especially. Yes, here we are. We, the children of the great choosing by the Lord Most High, we who are, at the same time, the full spectrum of Adam's children.

Clinging to the rim of a gully upstream from the village, a solitary Arabic gum tree fights for space with alder and poplar. The local people call the poplar "woman's tongue", because the countless small leaves of this species create near-constant chatter in the breeze. They think this a great joke, the women laughing harder than their men.

A cluster of Kebarite women with their household servants watch as Gad and I and two of our young men chop down the poplars to give greater breathing space for the gum. For this exercise we have been given honed iron implements like giant knives, and equally for this exercise four guards from the fort have been sent to watch over us, lest we become dangerous with such tools. When a poplar falls, we drag it away, assessing each sapling and larger bole for their potential usefulness as roof beams, and every branch is saved for later use as firewood. We waste nothing. Even as the light increases around the gum tree, servants are making incisions in the bark in order to tap the golden syrup that begins to ooze slowly from it.

I am puzzled that these prosperous women are here, for they are robed in fine, brightly colored cloth, wear many rings on their fingers and earlobes, and have tried to make their faces beautiful with kohl and rouge. Why would they be interested in watching four slaves, sweating and dusty, chop away at tree trunks? Surely it is a poor sort of entertainment.

During a break for a drink from a waterskin, I say to Gad, "The ladies of Kebar are persistent. How dull their lives must be if this captures their interest."

Gad says, "They are enjoying observing us and saying admiring things about our bodies. Especially the two younger brothers and you."

"Me? I am a scrawny wretch."

"Not as scrawny as you once were, Yezekiel. In truth, you have become handsome in recent months. One of them greatly favors the 'Yehudah brothel boy', as she calls you."

"What!" I exclaim.

"She speaks of this and that detail of your appearance, especially your—"

"I do not want to hear it," I murmur angrily.

"If you say so," he shrugs.

"I am not a boy and I am not a harlot!"

"No need to tell me. Tell them. All the world is a brothel to those people."

I try not to let my anger overwhelm me. Yet I cannot help noticing from the corner of my eyes that the rich woman who watches me titters frequently and whispers to her friends as she points in my direction. When she smirks and begins making willowy body movements, I keep my eyes, even the corners, fixed upon the tasks at hand. I am painfully aware that I am protected only by my loincloth, the bands tight about my lower waist and groin and upper thighs. Though this minimal dress is suitable for hot work, I now feel nearly naked, wishing I could be hidden from those probing eyes, wishing I had worn my sackcloth work-robe, which covers me from shoulders to knees.

The Kebar women sit down on portable stools their servants have brought. They are fanned with palms by these same servants. They drink from flagons and nibble at sweetmeats, the scent of which wafts toward us. I grow almost dizzy with the smell, yearning for the merest bite. When we four slaves pause to drink from our waterskins, I keep my back turned to our observers.

A guard barks. Gad and I and the two young ones finish our break and begin piling larger poles, and after that we cut branches into suitable lengths for firewood. When this is done, we straighten and bow our heads to the guards, as Gad asks permission for us to begin carrying the poles back to the village. One of the guards grunts a refusal. The other guards take our tools from us. The women rise and leave with their servants, heading in the direction of the river. The guards then surround us and point with their spears that we should follow after the women.

"*Anaw-khaw, anaw-khaw,*" Gad breathes, his word for a groaning sigh, as we shuffle barefooted in the dust, heading downriver on a path that leads to the ford. "O *anaw-khaw,* the dogs are barking overmuch today."

"Why is it so?" I ask.

"They seek to impress the women, I think. These are women of high estate in the town."

Arriving at the ford, we slaves are commanded to halt as the servants carry the women across to the other side, two men to a woman, making a chair with their arms, the women uttering playful screams, raising their legs high to keep their robes from getting wet.

Next, we and the guards wade across. On the other side, we are led through the town gates and along street after street until we come to a high-walled courtyard, which we enter through a red-painted metal doorway. The courtyard surrounds a soaring building of five floors and numerous windows.

The women climb up an exterior brick staircase that leads to the roof.

One of the guards now points to a giant clay pot in which grows a beautiful shrub, a small tree in fact, covered in pink blossoms. Speaking no longer in dog utterance, he gives instructions in a low rumble. We slaves are commissioned to move the pot onto two thick wooden planks and with these to carry it up the staircase.

The Yehudim

We bend and carefully tilt-and-walk the pot onto the planks. Then, straining with all our might, we raise the planks, a man at the end of each one. Step by arduous step, we carry it to the base of the staircase and begin to climb. I am at the bottom end, struggling to keep the planks level. One slip and the pot will topple to the courtyard, and then who can tell what punishment these Kebarites would inflict on us!

The ascent of this little mountain seems endless, and I do not know how we do it, but in time, with all our muscles strained to the limit and our hearts hammering painfully, we arrive at last on the top level. There we are commanded to ease our burden down onto the flat roof. Aching, we straighten our bodies and wait. This wide-open terrace is fully half the dimensions of the building, the other half an apartment with a single doorway and windows from which indigo curtains are billowing slowly in a breeze. The breeze is very welcome to me because I am sweating profusely, my loincloth soaked with it, my chest heaving for air. The women are talking with the guards, conferring about where the pot should be placed. They point here and there, discussing and discussing while we slaves stand waiting under the burning sun. I notice that the terrace is walled waist-high and furnished with costly tables and chairs, shaded in places by warm-colored awnings.

Finally, it is decided where the beautiful tree will find its permanent home, in the corner where two walls meet. Dutifully, we walk the pot to its final position. That done, we presume that we will now be taken back to the village. I am yearning to leave, to return to the poplar poles, a field, a ditch, the leeches, anything to get away from these people.

But no. The woman who had examined me by the gum tree now sways toward me with a mischievous look on her face, her eyes playing seductively, her lips pouting in a sensual smile. As she nears me, I see that she is about forty years old, her age artfully reduced by paints. She circles me, dragging her fingers lightly over my upper body, stopping to stroke my cheek and look deeply into my eyes, then resuming the stroking while her friends grin with appreciation of her performance. Shuddering with revulsion inside my heart and soul, I retain my servile mask, standing motionless with my arms at my sides, my hands pressed to my thighs. I stare straight ahead, as if I have been carved from stone.

The woman murmurs something I do not understand. She says it again insistently with a lift of her chin and a commanding look in her eyes.

Gad whispers to me, "She wants you to lie with her."

I say nothing, neither accepting the offer nor rejecting. I am a stone without emotions.

Again come the whispered enticements, which Gad fails to translate, though their meaning is clear. I am thinking of Joseph in Egypt. Unlike poor Joseph's predicament, there are plenty of witnesses here today.

Haughty now and slowly raking her fingernails across my chest, not breaking into my flesh, but leaving red trails on my skin, the woman snarls. It is a horrible sound, an animal sound, and I see a black fire of hatred flare in her eyes. Abruptly she scowls, tosses her head, and saunters away. My eyes follow her. She enters the doorway to the apartment, shouldering aside a grey-bearded man who has been standing there watching. A person of substance and authority, he is robed in fine white cloth with a golden cincture and shod with red sandals. Jeweled ornaments glitter on his neck and fingers. He now beckons to the guards and gives them some kind of instruction. They bow to him and swiftly stride to me and Gad. Taking our arms, they bring us into the apartment.

Thanks be to the Most High, the woman is not there. Only the grey-bearded man, and another who is younger and less opulent, bending over a table, reading a clay tablet beside a stack of similar documents. He looks up and observes us with disapproval.

Gad and I stand before the older man, our hands by our thighs, our heads bowed respectfully.

"You are the interpreter?" he demands of Gad in an irritated tone. "I am told you speak our language."

"Yes, lord."

"And this filthy one beside you, does he speak Chaldean?"

"No, lord."

"Then you will translate."

"As you wish, lord."

"Yes, I wish," he says, with his eyes becoming cold slits. With a lash of his arm he commands, "Translate for the dirty one."

Gad translates, telling me that the man appears to want a conversation. Through ongoing interpretation, the discussion continues.

"Lift your face. Look at me."

I do as bidden.

"Explain to me why you give insult to my wife."

Astonished, blank of mind, I cannot think of a reply.

"Answer!" says the man. The other Babylonian, apparently of lesser office, steps forward and snaps at me, "Answer the Lord Governor."

So this is the governor . . . of Kebar town, of Kebar region? He is not the headman we met when we first arrived many months past.

"I do not know how to answer, lord, for I meant no discourtesy to your wife."

Unblinking he holds my gaze, looks away, and begins pacing around the room.

"I saw you," he says accusingly. "I saw your behavior with her."

My behavior to the woman was in no way incorrect, so I remain silent, fearing to give offense by an honest explanation.

Turning back to us, the governor murmurs something at length and gestures to Gad to interpret.

"Yezekiel, the governor says that in this land, it is a great insult to a noble woman, one of the *Awilu*, to spurn her offer. You should know that *Awilu* is the very highest class; only the king himself is higher."

"I heard no offer and spurned her not," I reply.

The governor snorts: "You spurned her. She is furious. She wants me to burn you alive."

I swallow with sudden fear.

"Ah, but," he says with an amused, accommodating air, "many of you *Wardu* spurn nothing, many of you are eager for such offers."

Gad explains, "*Wardu* is their term for slaves."

"You who are lord over Kebar," I say with deference, "may not know that in our land and in our religion we are under the law of our God to respect the marriage bond, never to dishonor another man by sleeping with his wife or to dishonor the woman. Or to engage in carnal relations with any outside of marriage."

"Is it so?" he asks with a frown. "Yes, I think I have heard mention of that. You are a strange people."

I bow my head respectfully, mentally praying to the Lord.

The governor smirks. "Your God's law has not stopped your men from slithering across the river at night or hopping like frogs in heat." He mimics frog noises and hissing sounds, which makes his assistant and the guards laugh outright.

"In all religions, lord," I reply, "there will be a few who flout their gods' laws."

"Well, I shall not burn you," says the governor with a sour laugh. "You interest me, you *Y'hudi*. Tell me more about your customs."

Taking my life in my hands, I say:

"Among your many subject peoples, lord, there may be those who would arise against you in anger if their women were violated. Yet they would do so only with sword or bow in hand. We Israelites would defend our women without weapons of any kind, with our bare breasts, if needed."

"Or with reeds," he says with a snigger. "Yes, yes, I have heard accounts of how you drove off our drunkards."

Growing convinced that I will be executed momentarily, I resolve to leave this world with words of truth on my lips:

"Willingly, lord, would we go to our deaths to defend our mothers and wives and daughters. Would this not be a great loss for Kebar and for Babylonia?"

He flicks an angry look at me. "Are you making threats?"

"I am informing you, lord."

He purses his lips, pondering. At last, coming to some conclusion he says:

"Rest assured, *Y'hudi*, no harm will come to your women at our hands. We will respect your customs. The Great Nebuchadnezzar wants all his foreign peoples to be at home here, to live in prosperity and peace."

"I am very glad of it, lord."

"We honor the kingdom of Judah, though you are in service to us."

Such honor, I think to myself.

With a magnanimous expression, the governor continues, "You should know that never would we destroy a nation as great as yours. While it is true that Jehoiachin no longer reigns, his uncle Zedekiah is now king in Jerusalem."

Mattaniah-Zedekiah, the wanton corrupter, the puppet king dancing at the end of Nebuchadnezzar's strings.

Abruptly changing the subject, the governor says, "I hear that you call your dwellings *Hakheleq.*"

My heart skips a beat.

"Answer me. Is it not so?"

"Yes, we do so call the village," I say with my eyes cast down subserviently. "In our tongue it means a small piece."

He paces back and forth, smiling all the while, amused by something beyond my reckoning. Through my mind there flows the hidden meaning:

We are the Lord's little portion just as he is our portion, and therefore we will trust in him.

"Well, that is intelligent," the governor says at last, turning to me. "You are small, small indeed, a little piece of the Kebar province—and of the empire."

Thanks be to the Most High, it seems he has heard nothing about our silent practice of turning every mention of Hakheleq into a prayer. This bodes well, for it indicates that spies have not unearthed it nor have Hebrew informers betrayed it—if there be any such creatures.

Suddenly he scowls and jabs a forefinger at me and then at Gad.

"But you are no less our servants. Never forget this, *Y'hudi.*"

Gad and I bow before him.

With a flip of his hand, he dismisses us.

Unaccompanied by guards for the first time, we wade across the ford toward Hakheleq, feeling elevated in spirits. We have not been beaten, we have not been burned, we have not betrayed God with Potiphar's wife.

Gad shakes his head, his smile of relief turning to a frown.

"He called us *Y'hudi*. What an ignorant man. We are *Yehudim*, Judahites, the people of the Kingdom of Judah."

"Yes, we are Yehudim, but above all we are Hebrews of Israel."

"They like to change the names of their vassals, it seems. They think it tells us they possess us, and the new names are a chain that binds our hearts and souls."

"They cannot bind our hearts and souls unless we let them. Within ourselves we are no less Judahites, Hebrews, Israelites, and forever the chosen children of the Most High."

Gad's frown relaxes into a smile. "But did you note that at the end he called us *servants*, Yezekiel? We are no longer *wardu*, no longer slaves."

"Let us not deceive ourselves, Gad. We are still slaves, wearing a new name that can be blown away with a breath."

Ten months have passed since I first arrived in this place. By hindsight, the time seems to have gone quickly, though there were untold days when each hour seemed eternal. Now, however, our situation continues to improve. There are more of us capable of working, and among us there is a broader range of skills and ideas. There are fewer beatings. The Babylonians seem pleased with our progress, more confident that we are now firmly rooted here and are compliant to their will. I have not heard of anyone running away. There have been no revolts, no executions, though perhaps ten of our three hundred or more have died from various ailments or diseases, their bodies carted off by the Egyptian to the unknown place beyond the hills.

A majority of the newcomers are now living within solid walls beneath weatherproof roofs. Our overseers keep a sharp eye on all our doings, and as soon as anyone moves into a house, he is thereafter pressed into servile tasks for Babylon. Seeing the pattern of things, some people delay their removal to better shelter, but most prefer to be housed as soon as possible. Though it means they must thereafter work at hard labor, to have a home to call one's own is worth the price.

There are some feeble-bodied souls, and a few lazy ones, still sleeping in tents, but even they must work at less arduous village tasks. No one save the truly crippled is exempt from porting bricks to building sites. Even young children must carry a single brick, though I am relieved to see that the overseers refrain from striking any of our little ones if they stumble under the burden or burst into tears or shatter a brick by accident. The overseers and guards will yell rebukes but inflict no physical hurt. Ignorant as they are, they sense instinctively that to harm any of our children would incite a total revolt. Should an adult or adolescent make the same mistakes, however, he will not fail to receive a cuff to the back of the head, a kick to the rear, or a lash to the legs.

Despite the continuing humiliations, a pattern is emerging, little by little, of increased flexibility. On their own free time, our people can wander back and forth to Kebar without guards, as long as they are engaged in buying or selling or trading. Small industries are encouraged, such as weaving and pottery. Some of our skillful ones have made looms and pottery wheels. A few older people have been appointed shepherds to watch over the Portion's growing flock of sheep and goats, and still others are exempt from the more brutal kinds of service as long as they work all day on the village's expanding fields of grain and vegetables.

There is a crude intelligence behind the program of our assimilation into the empire. They want to retain the assets of slave labor but at the same time would have us settle here happily, forgetting our homeland as if it were a fading dream. Happy slaves are productive slaves, they think. Happy? How could we ever be content with the stark contradictions in our new way of life? Such blindness on the part of our masters reveals how poorly they understand us.

10

Mother and Child

A MONG THOSE NEWCOMERS who have been granted ex-
emption from heavy labor, there is a mother in her
late-middle years and her young adolescent son, whom I
first notice one day near sunset as I wade the ford on my
return to the Portion. I see them sitting waist deep in the
water at river's edge, fully dressed, their ragged robes flowing around them in the current. They are not washing themselves; the mother is packing wet mud onto the boy's head
and neck. I conclude that they are doing what many of us
do, applying a repellent to stinging insects. Poor souls. I give
them no more thought.

Not long after, on my appointed half-day for assisting
with building houses, I return to the village after midday
bread and prepare myself to begin mortaring bricks. As I
cross the village commons toward the most recent construction site, a young lad stumbles a few feet from me, giving
a yelp of pain as he falls, spilling four bricks from his arms.
One of them shatters. I glance quickly all around, hoping
no overseer or guard has seen the mishap. Thanks be to the
Most High, none are in our immediate environs. I hasten
to the boy and help him to his feet, but he can hardly keep
upright. I recognize him as the one who sat in the river with
his mother.

"Your ankle is twisted," I say. "Let us go to your dwelling
and find cloth to bind it."

"The bricks," he sobs in a high voice. "They will beat me."

"No one will beat you. I will help with the bricks. Even the broken one can be mortared into a wall and none the wiser. But we must move swiftly lest any unkind eyes turn in our direction."

I gather up the bricks.

"Take my arm," I tell him, and he complies, his trembling hand gripping my elbow.

"Where should I bring you?" I ask.

"There," he says in a quavering voice, pointing with his free hand to the edge of the village where the offal pile rises between the last houses and the fields. Slowly, we hobble in that direction. As we go along, I feel sadness for this poor soul, nearly as tall as a man, close to fourteen years old, I expect, but in his distress speaking with the unbroken voice of a child. He is a dirty-footed, dusty-robed boy, not strong, but striving to work nonetheless. A good spirit, it seems, within a pitifully frail vessel. Now I notice that the tears he shed and wiped with his sleeve have washed off some of the grime on his face, revealing tawny skin beneath. Looking closely, I see that under his eyes are dark purple smudges and that red spots densely cover his face and forearms, very much like a virulent pox. His spindly neck and close-shaved scalp are also covered with marks of the disease. How can this boy possibly survive!

In time we come to a sort of shelter, a weather-beaten square of cloth suspended over a cone of branches—hardly enough space for two people, not much larger than my own. The boy tells me that here he lives with his mother. I help him sit down on the grass and then I examine his leg. The ankle is swelling and livid—and riddled with the red spots. Worrying that I may be exposing myself to a pox, I collect myself and shove the thought aside. I remove my head scarf and wrap it firmly around the ankle.

"No," says the boy, "no, no, you must not use your fine scarf."

"Long ago it ceased to be fine. I will find another."

I finish binding the ankle and secure it with a strip of cloth I tear from the hem of my sackcloth robe.

"Where is your mother?" I ask.

"In the Kebarite fields across the river," he says, struggling to rise to his feet. "I must return to my work now."

I push him gently back down.

"I must work, I must work!" he protests.

"You will not be able to carry bricks until your leg is strong again. If you force yourself to do so, you may damage your ankle beyond healing, and what good would you be to your mother if you were lame?"

"Then I will go to the fields and help her."

"How will you cross the river, and how will you find her?"

"Would you carry me?"

"Nay, I will not carry you."

He hides his face in his hands.

"What is your name, lad?"

He shakes his head and will not answer.

"Listen to me," I say with the voice of authority. "Get inside your tent and lie down. Rest your ankle. Take a little ease now, two days, three days, and the investment will repay you greatly."

"The overseers will beat me when they notice I am not at work."

Perhaps, I think to myself. *Perhaps. But I doubt that anyone will notice, for this boy and his mother are the lowest of the low.*

"No one will beat you," I tell him without a shadow of doubt in my voice, though there is some in my heart.

He crawls into the tent and lies down on his back. Doubtless it is as hot as an oven in there, but at least it is out of the sun.

Straightway, I go to find Tzvi. I come upon him striding about a half-built dwelling, checking the angle of a rising wall, giving instructions to his bricklayers and mortar men.

"You are here at last," he grunts when he sees me. "Why so late?"

"Tzvi, I need your patience," I say. "Among the newcomers there is an old woman with a sickly son. They are weak and sorely in need of better shelter than the scrap of tent in which they live. Hot wind has been blowing harder from the south, even as the sun beats down without mercy."

"Who are they?" he asks.

I describe them to him, as I point to the far side of the village.

"Ah, I know who they are. The gleaners."

"Yes, the gleaners. And a pitiful gleaning do they accomplish. They need our help."

He muses. "There are so many more houses to build, and the clamorous press me continuously."

"The woman is a widow, I think."

He falls silent.

"Widows and orphans must not be neglected," he says with a sage tone, nodding up and down. "But I have too many houses yet to build. Will you build it for them?"

"I will."

"All right, Yezekiel, I let you go. And I will tell my men to give you all the bricks you need."

"Thank you, rabbi."

He grins at the old joke. It is understood that he has no actual authority over what I do, but by mutual agreement, I and all the other workmen behave as if he does. This has made for more efficient construction in the past and fewer conflicts among our people, and thus the unsigned covenant continues.

For the rest of the afternoon, I carry bricks and stack them beside the gleaners' tent. The boy sleeps through much of it. Once or twice he rises on an elbow and observes me, then falls back down and drifts away.

At sunset, the mother returns, carrying two small satchels. She looks overheated and exhausted from long hours of bending as she picked the offcast barley and wheat, seed by seed, from the ground.

She stares at me uncomprehending, then at the stacks of bricks.

"Where is my child?" she asks.

I explain what has happened. She wails and crawls inside the tent.

"I must go now, lady," I call after her. "Tomorrow I will return and begin building you a house." But she does not seem to hear me.

I am myself overheated and exhausted, but when the sun has set and a cooler breeze blows down the river valley, my tent waffles a little and I slip quickly into sleep.

At the end of the following day, after a grueling trial of endurance dredging a sluggish canal, I return to the Portion, wash myself in the river, and eat a bit of bread that some generous person left by my tent flap. There is a short delay while I pray with Shimeon in the dooryard of his new home, a little brick hut where he lives alone. He gives me a sizeable chunk of smoked dried fish. I eat it with a kind of desperation, feeling new strength invading my body. After prayers of thanksgiving, I set off to find my gleaners.

They are sitting in front of their tent, quietly talking in the cool of the evening. They look up and gaze at me wonderingly, as if I am an apparition.

"No one has bothered you? No one has beaten you?" I ask the boy.

"No one has noticed my absence," he replies.

"I thank you, sir, for helping my child," says the mother.

"I will do what I can," I say. "First, will you tell me where you wish your home to be built?"

Tears fill their eyes. They do not reply.

"I think you do not want to live beside a dung heap," I say. "May I suggest that we lay the foundation a good many paces away from here?" I point to a spot that looks ideal. "Would it be acceptable to you if I build there, between the field and the village edge?"

Mother and son hesitantly nod their heads, as if they hardly dare believe in my offer.

And so it begins.

Mainly I spend the next two hours porting bricks to the place where I plan to build. The mother and son both try to help with this, but I insist that they simply rest. I also lay out a foundation. At first I make it the usual size, but then, moved by sorrow over their plight, in the dusk I make it somewhat larger. There are bricks aplenty now, courtesy of our captors. I lay my last brick in total darkness, going by the feel of my hands.

Returning to their tent I cannot see their faces.

"I will return tomorrow," I tell them. "An hour or two a day can I give you. But soon I will have a half-day to labor in the light."

"I thank you, sir, for helping us," says the woman, "and indeed you are the saving of us, here at the end of all hope."

"There is no end to hope," I say. "The greater the darkness, the more complete our trust should be."

"In the Most High is our confidence," she says. "You have shown us this."

"He is our hope and our salvation, lady."

"I am Ruth."

"I am Yezekiel."

The boy says nothing. I hear the sound of his suppressed weeping.

I wearily cross the village to my own small habitation and fall into the mercy of sleep.

Day after day, the walls slowly rise. The boy is able to hobble more or less normally beside me now, carrying one or two bricks at a time. I mix our mortar and do all the bucket carrying, for it is heavy, sloppy stuff. When I am laying and mortaring bricks, he continues to port them from the stacks. He is pitifully thin, and his pox neither worsens nor fades away.

He says little or nothing when I ask him questions. He never initiates conversation, but his eyes are now bright with the happy thought that soon he and his mother will have a home. There is also, I think, the human quality of feeling reassured that he is not bearing burdens alone.

I have asked his name once or twice, and invariably he mumbles something, but I do not catch the answer. Ruth herself only refers to him as "my child", as if he were a baby or toddler. I have come to think of him as *Ruth's boy* or *Ruth's son*. Regardless, I need not know these people in any depth. It is enough to give—giving is a reward in itself

—and in this I am finding my own unexpected measure of happiness.

Throughout one of my half-days, the boy and I cut poplar poles in the woods. He helps me carry them to the new house, where we lift them onto the capstones and set them in place. I have made one of the walls lower than the facing wall, to ensure that the roof will slope, allowing rainwater to run off harmlessly—if rain should ever return to this land.

More and more I see a certain strength returning to my assistant, not much, but enough to make my work less demanding. He now walks with barely a limp. Tzvi comes to inspect from time to time, and nods his approval. The mother returns home each evening, anticipating the sight of the day's progress, always bursting into smiles of delight, raising her arms to the heavens, praising the name of the Lord.

By way of thanks, she gives me a small barley loaf, which I try to refuse, considering their meager means and their hunger, but then as she presses it upon me with painful urgency, I understand that by accepting her gift I allow *her* to be the giver. It is good bread, too. She has taken great pains to make it tasty. This additional food is surely increasing my strength, yet I regret that it costs the lady so much in effort. Until now, she has baked her bread in the evening at the village's communal oven, working in the semi-dark. She keeps a pot of sour dough rising within her tent. Now with the roof poles on and the boy away each day at the river cutting reeds, I offer to make her an oven in the yard beside her home. There are more than enough spare bricks for this, and I set to work immediately, despite her objections. When it is done, all objections dissolve in the air, and she bustles about in search of twigs to make the first fire, to beg embers from her neighbors, to check her pot of dough, to raise her hands to the heavens every few minutes. Her joy infects me, and I, too, lift my arms.

The next task is to lay bunches of reeds over the roof poles. After tying the stems together tightly, the boy lifts the bundles up to me, one by one. I drag them higher, securing them to the poles with strips of plaited willow, all the while trying to keep my wits about me lest I make a misstep and fall inside the house. Then commences the chore of hefting buckets upward to spread a layer of clay over all. The sun does the rest, baking this final cap to a smooth finish.

At last comes the day when mother and child have a home of their own—though not yet completed, it is livable. I have made one small window and an open doorway, which I hope to finish one day. They move into the house with wonder, gazing all about its cool interior, scarcely believing it is their own. It does seem spacious. At their request, I cut their old tent into two equal parts to become their sleeping pallets. They bring inside their few little pots and satchels of grain and, finally, the much treasured, reverently handled pot of sour dough.

"Tomorrow, after your work, you must eat with us, Yezekiel," says Ruth. "Will you come?"

Will I come? Never would I decline a meal, and especially not from these eager faces.

"I will be honored, lady, to be a guest in your home."

The woman smiles, the boy bows his head with brimming eyes.

The following day is another canal dredging. I am covered with leeches, the sun blazes mercilessly, and our crew is driven by an unusually brutal overseer. He has no patience for our attempts to burn off the leeches. A quick drink of water and a bite of bread are permitted, but no other free time. I do not think any of us escape lashings on our backs.

The sun is already setting by the time I reach the river and wash myself. In the light of Shimeon's cookfire, I burn off the remaining leeches. My lash marks are hot aches beneath my sackcloth robe. I long for sleep but do not want to disappoint Ruth and her boy—and if truth be told, to disappoint my own belly. So I dress myself in my Jerusalem robe and go to their house, putting on a brave face for them.

Cheerfully, they invite me inside, and there I find a humble feast spread out on a reed mat, lit by a flickering clay lamp. Behold, here is a glistening wheat loaf, a bowl of oil in which to dip the bread, a pot of cheese curds, a tiny pat of honey on a grape leaf, and a whole fish steaming on a charred stick. We three sit down, facing each other, smiling and smiling. We give thanks to the Lord, Giver of All Good Things, and then we eat. I try not to bolt my food, but it is difficult to stop myself, and my hosts clearly enjoy watching me devour the meal. They share in it as well, but more slowly, taking care to let me have the largest portions.

"Milk and honey!" I exclaim with a full mouth.

"And wine," says the boy proudly, handing me an old skin. I drink a little from its spout. It is new wine but of surpassing sweetness. I have not had a drop of wine—or of milk or honey—since leaving Jerusalem nearly a year ago. Oh, the wondrous, wondrous happiness to be with a family and to feast together!

"Such bounty, Ruth," I say, then stop myself blurting any more words, lest I imply that I am amazed that plenteous food comes from these poor people.

"Aye, bounty from the hands of the Lord," she replies, nodding and smiling, but offering no explanation.

"My mother has guarded her secrets well," says the boy

with a grin. "She has labored for weeks to weave wool she begged from both sides of the river. With the scarves and mats she made, she traded in exchange for this meal—our gratitude meal."

"Never will our gratitude to you suffice, Yezekiel," says Ruth. "Never. But he who sees all things will bless you a hundred times over. For this we pray."

"For this we pray," echoes her son.

Now a quiet settles upon us. My body's aches are forgotten; my heart grows warm from the sips of wine, but more from seeing the glow on the faces of these two. I am feeling very great affection for them.

The boy's legs are crossed at the ankles, exposed from the knees downward, with their scabs and red spots. I feel a pang of worry for him, sorrowing over the disease that will not go away.

"O my friends, I thank you for this sumptuous banquet, this most beautiful gift from your hearts—from your labors. May the Lord reward you a hundred times over for it. Yet I wonder if it would have been better to obtain a healing ointment for the boy."

Ruth and her son regard me with an odd look, but make no answer.

"Mother, it is time," says the boy.

Ruth furrows her brow.

"On such a festive night, the first in our new home, we may begin again," he adds.

After a moment's pondering, his mother brightens. "Yes, it is time. Here is a true son of Israel, and we can trust him."

I am completely puzzled by this. The boy rises to his feet and leaves the house. He returns shortly with a bucket of water and a rag.

Sitting down again, he soaks the rag, and with it he rubs

vigorously on one cheek. A spot disappears. He rubs again and more spots are gone from cheeks, forehead, chin, neck. More rubbing, soaking, wringing, rubbing, soaking, wringing, and one by one the horrible red spots disappear. Finally, he wipes beneath his eyes, and little by little the purple shadows dissolve.

"The disease has been cured," says Ruth with a laugh. The boy joins in.

With tilted head, I say, "I do not understand."

Mother and son smile at me.

"I am the ugliest creature on the earth," says the boy. "No man would desire me."

No man would desire him? A very strange thing to say. I look closely at this newborn face. My eyes' perception suddenly shifts, and for the first time I see that Ruth's child is very fine featured, and if he were not a male he would be a person of exceptional beauty.

"Leah, go outside now and wash completely," says Ruth.

Leah?

When we are alone, Ruth turns to me and explains.

"My husband was a dealer in precious gemstones and a fashioner of jewelry in Jerusalem. When the soldiers came, they dragged us from our shop, but not before Hiram was able to gather a few stones into a bag and hide them under his waistband. We were driven to the city gate and out onto a road where we joined crowds of others like us, arrested for no reason we could understand. No explanations were given, only blows. We were forced to walk north, and early along the way the soldiers began plundering the people. When they came to Hiram, they felt the hidden sack of gems in his robe and tried to tear it from him. He resisted, and they killed him there—there on the road. It was at the time we were walking to Ramah with thousands of others. I could not bury him, for no one was allowed to stop.

"At Ramah we were divided into groups. From there we were to be taken by soldiers on to Karkemish, though we did not know our destination at the time."

"It was the same for us in the first expulsion," I tell her.

"When we were encamped at Ramah, terrified and grieving deeply for the loss of my husband, I saw Babylonian soldiers dragging young women from the crowd of our people, and taking them off somewhere to violate them."

Ruth's face grows bitter with the horror of the memory.

"I looked at Leah as she wept for her father, and I knew that of all the daughters of Israel she is one of its finest flowers. In the middle of the night, I told her of her peril, and we agreed that she must wear her hair very short, to take on the semblance of a boy. I had a little iron knife with me, very sharp, which I use for my sewing. And so I cut her hair as close to the skin as I could in the dark, and I am saddened to think how many times the knife nicked her scalp. Then we bound her chest tightly with a head scarf under her robe. I threw dust upon her. In the morning, our group was driven northward on the road, under guard, but from that time forward none looked at her."

"And the disease?"

"On the second day, the scabs on her head set me thinking. Our disguise might work for a time, but if she were covered with a rash or pox, it could deflect interest of any kind, for it would inspire disgust and avoidance."

"You were prudent, Ruth, very wise. But it was surely an ordeal all the way."

"An ordeal, yes. But lighter than one that might have come about. The next day, as I said, the idea of a disease came to me. There is a berry I know that stains the skin and which in the past I had used for dying wool. Whenever I came upon such berries on shrubs growing beside the road, I picked a few without being seen. And during our night encampment, I dabbed the juice onto her face and arms and legs. I kept a sack of them. They have dried now, but can be brought to liquid by mashing in my mouth. We use the red juice mixed with ashes to make the pouches beneath her eyes. She is very ugly and repellant, is she not?"

"She surely is. I mean to say, she surely was."

Ruth smiles. I smile. Then I laugh, shaking my head. "It is very convincing."

"Tomorrow before sunrise, we will resume the disguise, but for these few hours of celebration we will be who we truly are."

"I think you need not worry any longer, Ruth."

"I never let up my vigilance."

"I understand. However, I can assure you that no woman has been violated since our arrival here at Kebar. Though these Babylonians are sick with their lusts, their need to have a compliant force of slave laborers is proving to be of greater importance to them. Their behavior has been harsh but never rapacious. They know, they truly know, that we would not overlook the violation of any Israelite woman. If such were to happen, our people would rise up in revolt. The Babylonians are convinced that we are willing to die to defend our women and children."

"Are you certain?" she asks with a worried tone. "Do you trust them?"

"Indeed, their governor assured me of it. And though I do not wholly trust them in all matters, on this one point I do."

She nods, eyes closed, absorbing it all.

"Also, I will be as a protector to her, if you wish."

Leah returns to the house, fully washed and clothed. Glancing at her loose robe, I can apprehend that she has freed herself from the chest band. She wears it like a shawl over her head. She is now in the shape of a young woman. I am staggered by her beauty. Here in truth is a flower of Israel.

I look away. Unable to say more, I rise and thank them both for this wondrous meal, which, I assure them, has given me new life. I will return, I tell them. I would like to make a door for their dwelling.

During the days and weeks that follow, I observe without comment that Leah now lives as she was meant to live, that is, without wearing an exterior lie. Because the house is mainly completed, we no longer work side by side. Whenever I meet her by chance, I find myself curiously unable to say much, if anything. It is new shyness in me, which matches her own natural modesty. She has told me only that she is a firewood-gatherer and also assists the older women in baking bread for those in the community who cannot do it for themselves. So far, no overseer has commandeered her for slave duties. So far, neither mother nor child has asked me to be her protector.

Still, from time to time, Ruth will send Leah to find me, usually in my decrepit, fast-decaying tent. Always it is an invitation to a supper, usually on my half-day devoted to village construction—Tzvi has pulled me away to other building tasks. Now and then, I discover a barley loaf waiting for me after a wearisome day in the Kebarite fields and canals. Occasionally I am able to arrange an hour or two to finish smaller aspects of Ruth and Leah's house.

"A man must eat by the sweat of his brow," Ruth often declares, assessing with maternal admiration my thickening arms and strong neck. Whenever she says this, in my mind I add an unspoken companion proverb, "A woman must eat by long patience and the skill of her hands."

Now, in addition to her gleaning, she makes a small income by hiring herself out to weave for people who have looms, and by weaving her own creations on a hand loom that she fashioned for herself from saplings strung with a fibrous cord. The people with sheep have allowed her to take home remnants of yarn, and she also begs for wool across the river. She has learned, as well, that flax is grown in fields upriver—a two- or three-hour walk. The owners have agreed to give her a bundle of raw fiber in exchange for spinning an equal weight for them, using their excellent distaffs. For her own use, I have carved a more humble distaff. Her sales and barter increase. She makes a linen dress for Leah and thicker blankets to cover them while they sleep.

Ruth leaves no hour unproductive. If a fragment of spare time presents itself, she will wander here and there on both sides of the river, gathering bits of raw wool rubbed off by the animals on bushes. The resulting lengths of narrow cloth are rough, but she deftly sews them together with yarn, using a fishbone needle. She sells them as rugs or bedding throughout the village and increasingly in recent weeks has bartered with Kebarite women. She also weaves floor mats from the rushes her daughter harvests along the river. Her enterprises are many and quietly accomplished without groaning or complaint. She continues to glean in the nearby fields, begs for oil, and scavenges for wild spices such as coriander and nutmeg seeds and the bark of a struggling cinnamon tree in a ravine an hour's walk south of the village. She uses dates and raisins as the other women do, but there is no bread like hers. This bread, I feel, is so tasty and filling, not only because of her care in handling its ingredients and in the baking, but because of the love she invests in it. Yes, there is love in her eyes, along with a very great goodness, gratitude, and her own generosity, she who has so little.

She loves her daughter, of course, and the daughter loves her, as if the prematurely wizened and suffering woman were a queen. Ruth also bestows love on any person in need who crosses her path. I have seen her go hungry for the sake of giving her daily bread to another widow. Her daughter, it strikes me, is very much of the same character. There are no more than two dozen children among us, but I often see Leah playing with them or teaching them small crafts or games. In the eyes of the Portion, she is now unquestionably a woman, with a graceful form beneath the robe. Her black hair is growing in again, still very short, but lustrous. No longer a weak, ill-favored boy of fourteen years, she has become an inexpressibly beautiful eighteen-year-old woman with large, shining eyes, clear skin, and a quick smile. Doubtless many men here would like to begin the process of betrothal, but I have noticed that the girl always physically withdraws herself when any would-be suitor approaches their house. So, too, does the mother erect an invisible fortress of unwelcome, never rude but always unresponsive. Bewildered, the young men back away.

Leah says little when I am around their house. From time to time, she speaks to me shyly with her eyes, a glance of thanks when I bring an armload of heavier wood chunks for their home oven. I widen their window frame so that light may better enter, removing some bricks, remortaring, bracing the opening with lengths of poplar. There is another glance of appreciation when I hang a cloth over the window, to keep insects out at night. I still plan to make a real door one day to fit in the doorframe, but no flat wood is ever available, and to fashion a single plank would cost a day's labor, which I do not have to spare. I am testing a method for tying a row of very straight saplings together, seeing if they will stand upright well enough to swivel on a doorpost. For now, I have rigged a slender sapling across the top of the entrance, while Ruth labors at sewing together lengths of her weaving, making a blanket that will hang from the rod.

A year has passed since my arrival in this land. As our people proceed with their lives, a strange kind of normality settles upon us. Of course, we continue to feel the pain of being so far from our homeland and families—and for me, there is also the ache of being so far from the Temple. The weight of the physical yoke is no lighter than before, and yet our captors' rule over us is now more like restrictions we have learned to live with rather than cruel subservience. It is still slavery and still difficult to bear at times, though I think that most people live through each day without rage or hatred or despair. Ours is a hard lot, but no more arduous than that of many people in Israel who once lived in poverty and heavy labor before the exile. We have learned well our tasks in field and canal, vineyard and orchard, striving always to do our best. Rarely now do I witness the use of the lash. Commerce steadily increases and, consequently, a certain measure of prosperity. By this I mean that there are strokes of pleasure in people's lives, such as a colorful rug on the floor, an extra delicacy at the evening meal, the happy invention of a new tool, the sound of laughter around a cookfire. Our basic needs are met. We have each other.

Above all, there are signs that most of our people are turning to the Lord with greater attentiveness. More than half the community now gathers to pray together on Sabbath days, and on other days they come together to pray in small and large groups of their own—a good many more than the "tithe" that Naphtali once predicted. I must add that during recent months I have on occasion come across dying bonfires in which the burned remains of metal and bone Baals can be seen. And, as far as I know, there have been no pagan rites committed by our people.

From time to time, Ruth will invite me to a meal in their home, always on the Sabbath. I am very grateful for it, and yet whenever I am with them there is a certain inner tension for me, as I sense my heart drawing ever closer to Leah, without any sign of corresponding feeling on her part. She behaves as a sister to me, and while it moves me that she does so, I feel an unresolved yearning, a sadness that more might have grown between us but has not. I ask myself why I am so drawn. Is it marriage I am wanting? What could a man like me offer to such a woman? I am poor, I am not intelligent in thought or clever in the ways of providing, and I live in the Portion's most abject dwelling. I wear tattered clothing, and doubtless I carry with me the scent of those who sweat much and wash less than is desirable. My life is mainly work and sleep and prayer—and whenever a blessed opportunity arises, an extra meal.

One Sabbath evening, I wash in the river as usual and then, in preparation for the village gathering for prayers, I don my Jerusalem robe. It is deteriorating too quickly, riddled with holes, as moths and mice have got into it, but it is the best thing I own. Later, after the community's prayer and song, Ruth steps forth from the women's group and takes me aside.

"Will you eat with us this night?" she asks.

Instinctively, I grin with thankfulness, then try to cover my too-much eagerness.

"Yes, lady, I would be grateful for time with you and, of course, for your cooking, which is like no other's."

She smiles. "Good, good, for we have prepared something special for you."

The meal itself is indeed special, as always. There are honey-eyed barley cakes, salty curds, strips of smoked fish, leavened bread in oil, and a little wine. Afterward, with conspiring looks, the women unroll a newly made rug, revealing two garments wrapped inside. One is a tightly woven linen robe, dyed dark blue, the hem and neck embroidered with a pattern of purple pomegranate fruit. The other is a rougher garment that appears to be a short work-robe, sturdy and durable by the looks of it. It is wool, but loosely woven so that the cloth can breathe, giving shelter from the sun while not overheating its wearer.

"For you, Yezekiel," says Ruth.

"For you," Leah repeats with a quieter voice and a look.

I am speechless. I swallow and blink. They press the garments into my hands.

I bow to the mother and then to the daughter.

"These are fit for a king," I say at last. "I hardly dare wear them."

"King or no, you had better accept them," says Ruth, "otherwise, you will soon be naked if those tatters you now wear continue to fall to pieces."

"I am sorry for my appearance, Ruth."

"That is no great matter. But I warn you, do not wear the blue robe when you go into the river, for the dye will run, and then you will have a blue body. But the work-robe is safe; it is raw wool without dye."

I press the garments to my face, inhaling their wonderful scents. As I am doing so, Ruth places a narrow roll of linen cloth by my feet.

"For underneath," she says with a shrug, "to wrap yourself."

A new loincloth!

"Enough, dear lady, you shower me with gifts and honors."

Ruth and Leah laugh with pleasure. The mother says, "You showered me and my daughter with a home, and you kindled hope again in our hearts and wellness in our flesh."

"I have done so for others, Ruth."

"And taken nothing in return."

"Nothing do I desire."

"Nothing?"

"Nothing."

"Leah, roll the garments in the rug, so that Yezekiel may carry it all to his house."

They know I have no house. They are speaking this way in order to express respect for me, as if I am a reputable townsman.

Leah rolls up the robes in the rug.

"I will return your rug tomorrow," I say to Ruth.

"Nay, nay, the rug is yours to keep."

It is too much. I am very grateful. But now words fail me entirely.

I rise to my feet, preparing for departure. Leah rises, too.

"I will carry the linen," she says.

Ruth smiles her approval.

So we set off side by side, making our way across the village by the light of dying fires. She says nothing. I say nothing, though my heart is pounding hard.

When we arrive at my tent I thank her.

As she turns to go, I blurt out fervently, "You are the delight of my eyes!"

"You are the delight of my heart," she answers in her gentle way, then runs off to her home.

I cannot sleep that night, and hardly at all the next. On the following half-day of freedom, I begin building a real house for myself. This is necessary because such splendid garments and a royal rug must have a proper home in which to dwell. The hut will be very small, because the Kebarites have stopped carting bricks across for us. I use, instead, the discarded mud bricks I find scattered here and there at the edge of the village, broken or badly chipped. I make my own mortar. Because of the walls' holes and cracks, I coat the exterior with river mud. I cut saplings and reeds. A week passes, and then another week. Both Tzvi and Eli come to inspect.

"At last!" says Eli.

"A mud cave it looks like," says Tzvi. "A poor thing, but it will do."

And all throughout the building and roofing stages, I have thought of nothing other than Leah's last words to me. I do not chase after a repetition of the joy she gave me with those words. What is inside my heart does not fade. There will be time enough for it to grow. If the Lord desires it to grow. If both our hearts are set on its growing. For now, I put my hand to completing the door for their house. When it is finished, I carry it across the village to them, taking care to wear the new work-robe they made for me.

The women's faces light up when they see me.

I install the slab of saplings in the doorway, wishing I had leather hinges upon which it would securely swing. Until I am able to procure thick leather, however, braided reed cords must suffice. They will need frequent replacing. Then I think that this is all to the good, for it means I will have a reason to visit often.

I open and close the door. It creaks but holds fast as it swings in and out. I pound a sharp peg into the opposite doorpost, leaving a finger-length of peg exposed. A bit of rope bound to the door can be looped about the peg to secure it in closed position.

Beaming, Ruth pushes the door until it is open wide.

"The heart is the gate of the soul," she says, turning to me. "For you, Yezekiel, this door is always open."

The Letters

M ANY LAMBS HAVE BEEN BORN to the Portion's flock. Their bleating is a sound that evokes long memories in me, a rejoicing over the purity of new life mingled with longing for the pastures of home. Because of their growing numbers, most of our sheep are now grazed on the uncultivated slopes of the low hills beyond our croplands. Sometimes our shepherds will graze a few on the grass that grows closer to the village, guiding them with staves to keep them out of gardens and fields. I always pause to watch, remembering my own flock, wishing I could be a shepherd again. But no, my strength is needed elsewhere.

Foremost among the tasks before me is the building of a home in which Leah and I will one day live. We are to be married six months from now. We are betrothed, having completed the traditional formal agreement with the correct witnesses. In fact, there was a surfeit of witnesses on that Sabbath day when we stood facing each other in the village commons. There were approving bystanders aplenty, people we hardly know, along with frolicking children and the elderly who smiled and smiled, evoking their own memories or anticipating the joys that will come to the betrothed. My friends Shimeon, Eli, and Gad stood for me as my witnesses, while Ruth and the very ancient bread-maker Chaya-Ayala stood for Leah. I expect that everyone felt the painful awareness that our families were absent. Yet there was joy that day.

By the Rivers of Babylon

And the joy continues. Every evening after work, I set my hand to carting buckets of clay from upriver and spend the remaining time in the waning light to mold a few bricks. I am planning to build a new house beside Ruth and Leah's, one wall shared with theirs. The new construction will be sixteen foot-lengths by twelve foot-lengths, so much bigger than their present dwelling, because . . . because after Leah and I are married, there may be little ones living with us there.

Week after week, the stack of bricks mounts higher, though too slowly for my satisfaction. Whenever my mind races ahead to the coming wedding, I restrain it by recalling the seven years that Jacob labored for his future father-in-law, Laban, who had deceived him into marrying the elder daughter, Leah, followed by the additional seven years Jacob labored in order to marry his true beloved, Rachel. For me there is no cunning Laban, and *my* Leah is as cherished as Jacob's Rachel.

Six months becomes five months, then four. During this period, I have tried without success to obtain Kebarite bricks, so fine, so hard and well dried. I have no money to purchase them, and the will of the Most High has determined that none of the town's kilns will exchange their bricks for my offers of extra labor. Gad and Tzvi often give an hour or two to help me, fatigued though they are. Eli with his damaged heart contributes by sitting on the ground cutting straw to mix with the clay. Sometimes he will sing to us the songs of Zion as he watches us filling molds. He has fashioned a crude harp that he twangs as he sings. The sound is nothing like the Temple harps I remember from my years in Jerusalem, but it has its own humble beauty. His voice, too, is without charm, but it is all from his heart and, thus, moving to hear.

Three months before the wedding, Tzvi assures me that

there are now sufficient bricks and that they are fully dry, as durable as they will ever be. He has obtained a little lime for the mortar. I hope it will be enough. I commence laying the foundation, the beginning of three walls—the fourth being the existing wall of Ruth's house. Then the first line of bricks goes on top of the foundation layer. The next day, a second line. And on the third day, in my eagerness, I work far into the dark until I realize with a start that the flicker of light enabling me to continue is provided by Ruth and Leah, who have been standing behind me unseen, holding up small olive oil lamps. When I realize what they are doing, I laugh, and they join me in the laughter.

"Enough, Yezekiel," says Ruth. "Your zeal, doubtless, will give Leah a magnificent home, but there will be no husband to live in it if you die from lack of rest. Away with you now!"

So I take my leave and cross the village to my mud cave-house, crawl inside, and happily collapse. As I do every night, I drift off to sleep with the thought of the walks Leah and I have taken by the river in the cool of the evening. The touch of her hand. The glance of her eyes into mine. The sound of her voice when she quietly utters a prayer or speaks a thought that contains good wisdom. And always, the sight of her face.

Love is an ocean, fathomless in depth and holy. It drowns the black flames of fear; it silences the hiss of serpents; it is stronger than death. In these waters I dwell almost always now. Yet there are moments at night when my soul is cast down by thoughts of our people's sufferings, when I consider the evils across the river and sense them all around me in this new land, when I am exhausted and uncertain of the future and fears rise up in me. Lying in the dark of my cave, unable to sleep, I wonder if it is wise to marry and bring children into a world such as this.

The eve of the Sabbath. The sun is lowering as I lay the last of the sapling poles over the new roof. I leave all work aside then and go to wash in the river in preparation for the day of the Lord. I am just coming up out of the water as the sun touches the horizon, there in the west where Jerusalem lies. I am drying myself behind a screen of reeds when I hear voices of men crossing the ford. I recognize Shimeon's deep bass and that of another man.

Now dressed in my clean Sabbath robe, I walk down the path to greet them.

Shimeon speaks first, introducing me to a young man in his early twenties, footsore and dusty.

"This is Gemariah ben Hilkiah," he says, with a hand on the other's shoulder. "He was taken recently from Jerusalem with other skilled craftsmen. The dispersion continues, as you see, though the numbers are now very few. He is a gold-smith by trade, and Babylon is sending him under escort to work in Tel-abib."

I bow to the newcomer. "A long road you have traveled," I say with sympathy. "I know this road well."

"Gemariah, this is Yezekiel ben Buzi, who once was a servant in the Temple in preparation for the priesthood."

"No more is that my path," I say. "The Lord Most High has chosen to bring me instead to this land, and I praise his holy will."

"My path, too, has taken new directions," Gemariah replies wearily. "I will serve our captors in my trade, but I beg the Lord that I not be forced to make golden idols."

"May he protect you from it."

"Also, I seek my father, Hilkiah, who was taken in the second captivity after Jehoiachin reigned for three months, at the time when Mattaniah was made king." His face sours. "It is Mattaniah, now called Zedekiah, who sends me to

Babylon, I and a few others of high skill, as a gift to Nebu-chadnezzar.''

"Do you know where your father was sent?"

He shakes his head sorrowfully. "I do not know. It is my hope to find him in Tel-abib or, if he is elsewhere, to learn where he now lives."

Shimeon says, "The escorts are lax. They halt overnight in a Kebar tavern, and Gemariah has permission to take his rest with us. They travel onward tomorrow. Let us go to my house, and we will make a meal. Join us, Yezekiel."

Over the meal of bread, oil, dates, and smoked fish, we three converse about the fragments of knowledge we have been able to gather in our limited ways. Gemariah is the most informative. He tells us that while there are many people missing from the life of Jerusalem, those taken into exile were a small fraction of the general populace. Commerce and some industry have resumed. There are Babylonian officials at court and a contingent of their troops encamped outside the city, but the kingdom appears to be returning to normal.

"And the Temple?" I ask.

"They stripped the Temple of all portable gold and silver but have not touched the inner and outer walls. The treasury is empty. Despite the new poverty, priests are returning. Though the Ark is gone, the Name and the Presence remain, and thus worship must not be neglected. The sacrifices are offered but are small and inconstant. Pilgrims are few."

Throughout his account, Gemariah has kept a hand pressed firmly to his breast.

"Do you know of the man named Jeremiah of Anathoth?" he asks.

Shimeon frowns, straining to recall an elusive memory.

"I think I heard that name before, when I was living on the Jordan near Gilgal."

"I spoke with him twice in my life," I say. "I have heard him teach in the Temple courts, where he proclaimed the words of the Lord in the face of all threats. He is a true prophet, I believe."

"He *is* a true prophet," says Gemariah with an intense look. "Even now does he proclaim the Lord's messages to his people."

He stands, and then, opening the front of his robe, he touches what appears to be a lambskin wrapped about his chest, secured by a cord. He unties the cord and tenderly pulls on the lambskin's edges, easing it out into our view. He hands it to Shimeon, who stretches it full open. It is covered with densely crowded Hebrew script.

"I bring you a letter," says Gemariah. "In fact, three copies of the same letter."

He unrolls two more skins from his body. By the fire-light, I see Hebrew letters written on his bare torso.

Catching my eye, he smiles. "It might be said that I am a fourth copy, for the ink of the innermost layer has impressed itself upon my very flesh."

The letter, we soon learn, is from Jeremiah. Shimeon cannot read and write, so I read it aloud to him. As I go on, I feel my hands trembling and my voice choking with emotion, for the prophet's message contains both woes and consolations:

> From Jeremiah in Jerusalem to the elders of the exiles, and to the priests, the prophets, and all the people whom Nebuchadnezzar has taken into exile from Jerusalem to Babylon.
>
> Thus says the Lord of hosts, the God of Israel, to all the exiles whom I have sent into exile from Jerusalem to Babylon: "Build houses and live in them; plant gardens and

eat their produce. Take wives and have sons and daughters; take wives for your sons, and give your daughters in marriage, that they may bear sons and daughters. Multiply there, and do not decrease. But seek the welfare of the city where I have sent you into exile, and pray to the Lord on its behalf, for in its welfare you will find your welfare." And further says the Lord of hosts, the God of Israel: "Do not be deceived by the prophets and diviners among you, and do not listen to the dreams which they dream, for it is a lie which they are prophesying to you in my name; I did not send them," says the Lord.

For thus says the Lord: "When seventy years are completed for Babylon, I will visit you, and I will fulfill to you my promise and bring you back to this place. For I know the plans I have for you," says the Lord, "plans for welfare and not for disaster, to give you a future full of hope. Then you will call upon me and come and pray to me, and I will hear you. You will seek me and find me; when you seek me with all your heart, I will be found by you," says the Lord, "and I will restore your fortunes and gather you from all the nations and all the places where I have driven you," says the Lord, "and I will bring you back to the place from which I sent you into exile."

When it is finished, Gemariah says, "One copy will I leave in your keeping for the elders of Kebar. The rest I must bring to Tel-abib and other places, wherever I may. Who, then, are your elders that I may deliver this and speak with them of further warnings?"

"We have no elders," Shimeon replies ruefully.

"After all this time, you have no elders? But surely—"

"Shimeon is our elder," I say, and then, seeing the old man's look of consternation, I add, "though he does not know it."

"Nay, nay, nay," Shimeon mumbles, embarrassed.

"Then I will leave the letter with you two, that you may read it to all the Israelite people of this place."

"We will," Shimeon answers and carefully rolls up the lambskin.

"You mentioned additional warnings, Gemariah," I say.

"Yes. As he has written here, you must take no heed of false prophets who will arise among you. They will deceive many, even themselves, with their oracles in the name of the Lord, for their mouths will be full of lies. They will prophesy swift return to the Kingdom of Judah, but it will be a false hope. Furthermore, the Lord of Hosts says, concerning the king who now sits on the throne of David and concerning the people who dwell in Jerusalem who did not go out into exile: he will send upon all of them the sword, famine, and pestilence, and he will make them like vile figs that are so bad they cannot be eaten. He will make them a horror to all the kingdoms of the earth, to be a curse, a terror, and a reproach among every nation where he will drive them, because they did not heed his words, which he persistently sent to them by his servants the true prophets, but they would not listen."

With a deeply troubled look, Shimeon asks, "Jeremiah believes this latest king will be deposed, you say?"

"It is the Lord himself who promises it. Within ten years, Zedekiah will be deposed and destroyed. Do not be dismayed, my brothers. Though it will be the end of the kings of David's line, it will not be the end to the *offspring* of David."

"I can see the fall of a king," says Shimeon, shaking his head. "But it is hard to imagine *all* of Israel taken into captivity."

"Indeed, it will be all, save for a small remnant who will be kept back in the countryside of Judah to till the soil and tend the vine as servants of Babylon."

We are stunned to silence.

"A river of light pours from Jeremiah's mouth, and now from his pen," says Gemariah in conclusion. "Do not let it spill into the dust."

"Fear not," I reassure him. "We will do as you say."

Another month passes, during which Jeremiah's letter is disseminated among the Portion's populace. Needless to say, no rejoicing greets the prophecies, but neither is there widespread despondency. Most people, I think, continue to weigh the message this way and that, reserving judgment. A few are outraged by it, demanding to know who is this Jeremiah and by what authority he spreads such dire predictions. Shimeon and I offer our defenses, but to little avail. People generally believe what they want to believe. Having done what I can, I let the matter go.

Besides, I have other important matters on my mind. Fairest are the moments when I may walk with Leah beside the river, getting to know her better, she coming to know me. The new house is finished, with a door as well, and now Ruth and Leah are making it beautiful inside with a reed mat, a window curtain, and bedding for the future. In addition, I have enlarged their vegetable garden and also spent many days weaving a wicker compound for a little rust hen that Ruth managed to obtain from a Kebarite in exchange for one of her braided rugs. This very beloved hen gives an egg a day, and once a week Ruth boils the carefully saved seven, and we have a feast. Though there is not yet any meat in our diet, we are feeling stronger. Leah's hair is now thick and falling below her shoulders.

One Sabbath day, I walk with her beside the river, discussing how we might find a cockerel, which would ensure fertile eggs, followed by an increase of hens and, in turn, a greater number of eggs. Our conversation wanders musingly on the topic of birds. Like everyone else in the village, we have tried to capture the edible kind, such as the pigeons and doves that have begun to roost in the rafters of house roofs and sheds but are clever at evading human hands. So, too, are the fat little moorhens and quail that scavenge the grainfields. We have no bows and arrows, of course, since this is forbidden by our masters. A young boy did make himself a crude bow and a crooked arrow, but this was spotted quickly by an overseer and confiscated. Others have tried to make fowler's nets with webs of string weighted at the edge with pebbles. Endlessly stalking the ducks and geese that frequent the river's bulrushes, they seldom have any success. I very much miss my boyhood sling. If I can obtain a bit of leather and cord, I will make a new one and then go hunting. In the ford there are water-worn bits of gravel that might provide adequate shot, but they are not as good as the smooth rounded stones I took from the Jordan—my *Joshua-stones*, I called them.

I think my eyes are changing. During the past two years, I have been so weary and preoccupied with survival that I have paid little attention to the strokes of beauty that are everywhere in this land. When I was young in the fields of my faraway home, I was often raptured by the colors of the world, the sky's constant changes, the music in the wind, the distinct behavior of varieties of birds, the house sparrows chirping in the rafters, the swallows' astonishing flight. For too long now I have not observed, have not looked up, have felt no wonder. Now the wonder of my beloved's face is teaching me to see again.

As Leah and I continue to talk, my heart feels such longing to make music for her on the flute I had when I was young, but it is lost to me forever.

We seat ourselves on the riverbank.

"See, Yezekiel, the water has changed from brown to grey. Soon, I hope, it will become blue."

"You love the color blue," I say.

"Yes, it is the color of the sky when the day-star pours out its radiance. It is like a royal robe. If the Creator of heaven and earth has made this color to be the dome over all things, does this not remind us that he is the King Most High?"

"The true King of kings."

"The *only* King of kings."

"The robe your mother made me is very blue. It feels too regal for one such as me."

"It is perfect for one such as you."

"You think too highly of me."

"Can a man see the whole of himself, Yezekiel? Other eyes may see him more truly than he sees himself."

I smile, flushed with gratitude, even as I remind myself that she sees me this way because of her affection.

She says, "There is a stone found only in Persia that the people of that land call *lajevard*, which means 'sky stone' or 'heaven stone'. My father imported it, and very costly it was. He cut it into cubes and beads, making necklaces, rings, and broaches for the wealthy of Jerusalem. It is deepest blue, so intensely blue as to be nearly purple, as if four skies were melted together to multiply their blueness."

"Were I a king, Leah, I would purchase this stone for you, that you would wear it like a queen, for you *are* a queen."

"As you are a king to me, Yezekiel."

I open my hands before her. They are rough-chapped, blistered, scarred.

"There is no gold and silver in these poor hands, but I give you what I have."

She touches my hand with her own. I enfold her hand in

mine. She gazes into my eyes with understanding. Suddenly she looks up with a glow of wonder.

"See, the Lord of heaven and earth sends us *lajevard!*" she cries, pointing to the nearby willows.

At first I see only a scattering of little birds in the branches. One is an emerald-green bee-eater, very pretty but not blue. Then I peer more closely and spot a white-throated bird with a crested head and a long beak like a spear. It is poised to dive into the river. In an instant it shoots like a lightning bolt, leaving in the air behind it a mirage of the bluest blue I have ever seen in my life.

"It is a fisher-king," whispers my bride to be.

Some time ago, shortly after our betrothal, I fell into the habit of contemplating the mysterious nature of love. I called it an ocean. Now I believe that love is more like a spring that swells up through the soil and becomes a pool that spills over and runs into a stream that grows ever larger in its course, becoming a mighty river, which, reaching its consummation, flows at last into the ocean of God.

Time, too, is a river that sweeps us along in its current. And thus, when I have left aside the measuring of its passage, it brings us to the day of our wedding.

Leah and I face each other in the dooryard of our new home. Above us is a linen canopy, held aloft by children lifting it on four poplar poles, a reminder of the Tent of the Covenant. Friends gather around. I promise Leah that I will honor and protect her all the days of my life and without fail to guide her and our children in the ways of the Lord. She promises to love and honor me and to guide our children in the ways of the Lord all the days of her life. I sing a king-song of rejoicing, accompanied by Eli strumming his harp. Shimeon recites aloud from memory what he recalls of

Levitical statutes for marriage. Our guests lift their arms to the Most High and praise him spontaneously for his countless favors, for preserving us until now, for sustaining the people of Israel throughout the ages, for many other blessings small and large. Suffering and bondage are forgotten for a while, and an oil of gladness pours out on every heart, as if the fruit of a heavenly olive grove in Paradise is pressed down, fills the basin, runs over, and submerges us.

Afterward there is a feast of plenteous food provided by Ruth and her friends, dates stuffed with cheese curds, ripe figs and berries, honeyed barley cakes, and even a cupful of wine for each person who attends. A donated sheep has been roasting over a fire pit for hours. The meat is sliced, and all lips become wet with the dripping fat. Laughter mingles with voices exclaiming proverbs and jokes and advice to newlyweds. Hearts are merry as never before.

Then I am dancing, as David danced before the Ark, and with my arms raised to the heavens I sing:

Let the heavens rejoice, let the earth be glad.
Let the sea resound, and all that is in it.
Let the rivers flow with praise, and all within them.
Let the fields be jubilant and everything in them.
Let all trees of the forest sing for joy.
Let all the earth shout with joy unto the Lord,
And worship him with gladness;
For this is the day that he has made;
let us rejoice and be glad in it.

Leah does not mock me for my whirling and leaping, as Michal mocked King David, for she is dancing with me, her arms raised to the heavens and her smile exultant, and all our company is rejoicing with us.

As the sun sets, the wedding draws to its close. Guests

leave for their homes after wishing Leah and me long and blessed years together. My friends depart with shining faces. Ruth's friends go with happy tears. And finally, the lingering children dance around us in a ring, singing in their high voices a few lines that someone must have taught them:

"Beautiful is she, beautiful is he, beautiful is the Lord who made them!"

With a smile of farewell to us, Ruth enters her home and firmly shuts the door. Leah and I look at each other, link our hands, and enter our new home as man and wife.

It is midsummer now and exceedingly hot.

Today demands the usual long hours of labor, but inexplicably they are not arduous. My work team is porting new clay jars from the kilns and loading them onto carts standing by the edge of the pottery works. We move slowly, carefully, fearing to do damage. The overseer does not try to drive us to greater speed. Under his direction, we pack the jars with straw, making a protective pad between each one. He goads us lightly, issues no threats, and, though he carries a whip, he does not use it. I muse on the fact that during the past month I have not seen a single lashing. I surely do not wish to see the practice resumed. Perhaps our masters are finally confident that we have been thoroughly trained in subservience. Not a soul has failed to learn the necessity of unquestioning obedience, for life depends on it.

As the sun eases lower toward the western horizon, my crew mingles with others returning to the Portion. Our workmen compare the day's events, and we learn that every crew has been engaged in tasks lighter than usual. So, too, food distribution at midday and afternoon water breaks have been ample, double portions of bread along with grapes and figs. Moreover, by all reports there has been little barking and snarling on the part of the overseers.

Arriving at the bank of the ford, we pass a single guard, with another on the far side of the river, both of them leaning on their spears. They are observing our passage with some indifference, perhaps boredom. Strangely, as my feet enter the river I hear behind me an eruption of loud wailing coming from the gates and windows of Kebar. By its volume, I estimate that a large number of women are grieving over something, presumably the death of a high official or an especially beloved townsman. I conclude that the matter does not concern us. When we reach the village commons, I am surprised to see numerous reed carpets laid out on the ground, covering almost the entire space. Upon them are baskets and pots full of foods of many kinds, along with flagons of oil and wine. Most astonishing are the steaming stewpots from which the aroma of cooked meat arises. Nearly the entire populace of the Portion gathers around this lavish feast, staring at it with wonder.

"Kebarite servants laid this out an hour ago," I overhear someone tell a neighbor. "Why have they done it?"

"They told us nothing when they left."

"Is it for us? Dare we eat it?"

"Is the meat lawful? Is it swine?"

"I smell goat meat in herbs."

"Is it cooked in milk?"

"No, the broth is clear."

A single overseer shouts in our own language, "Eat!" Then he withdraws.

Three hundred people commence to obey, and are very glad to do so. There is no grabbing or gobbling, as the food is obviously abundant. A mood of cheer mixed with puzzlement predominates among us. Ruth and Leah sit down on the ground beside me. We exchange smiles as we consume the meal together, concentrating on the meat and its broth, dipping our cups into the cauldron again and again. We have not tasted meat since the wedding. I note the welcome feeling that comes when my body is filling with adequate nourishment, my energy and my mood soaring.

The sun sets as we finish eating, and small fires are kindled around the edge of the commons. People do not disperse. Discussions begin as everyone tries to fathom the meaning of all this. The answer soon comes.

From the mouth of the path to the ford, four Babylonians emerge into the light and halt at the edge of the gathering— our main overseer, two guards carrying torches, and a man who is new to us. This person is about my age or perhaps a little older. He carries no weapons. His face is tranquil, without a trace of menace or haughtiness in it. No cosmetics adorn it. Though his good robe and sandals indicate that he is a person of substance, if not authority, his apparel is fairly simple compared to that of high officials. All eyes are upon him. Who is he?

"Hearken, *Y'hudi*!" cries the overseer. "Hearken, hearken!"

This is an unnecessary command, for the people of the Portion are already completely alert, silently waiting and watching.

The well-dressed man steps forward. From his robes, he extracts a clay cylinder and lifts it above shoulder height in his left hand. In his right hand, he holds a bronze tablet, an image of some kind. Lowering both, he sweeps his gaze across the crowd.

"Greetings to you, O people of the Kingdom of Judah,"

he begins. I am startled to hear him speaking in our own language and with very good pronunciation.

"Greetings to you from Nebuchadnezzar the Great King of Kings. He turns his benevolent eyes upon you and sends you this letter, with words for your instruction, that you may know you are welcome here and that he desires your prosperity. He bids you to listen attentively to the voice of Heaven, passed down from Ea the father of Marduk, from Bel who is the god of order and destiny, from Utu the god who rides upon the sun chariot and is the enforcer of divine justice."

Inwardly I groan. What little I know of Babylonian religion is always vile and always confusing. Still, I have no choice but to listen.

"In ages long past did Hammurabi the Great King, revered in memory by many nations, receive from Utu, whom some nations know as Shamash, the laws that guide men's lives in justice. These laws I will now read to you, that you may know the due punishments for each and all crimes committed by man."

He raises the cylinder and proceeds to proclaim the details of this code. We remain seated for nearly two hours, listening attentively, for our lives may depend on how well we absorb the laws of the empire. Clearly the man is reciting from memory, and, most astonishing of all, speaking in concise Hebrew of exceptional quality.

At the end, our people shake themselves from their rapt attention, inhale deeply, sigh, and turn to each other for whispered discussion. Voices around me are saying, "This law is not bad, there is much justice in it. It seems close to our own laws." However, it is plain to see that some are uneasy. I, too, am disturbed, thinking that we are now to be ruled by a justice that has not come from the hands of the Most High, the true and living God, but through the medium of evil idols.

The Babylonian remains silent for a few moments. Then he calls out:

"People of *Hakheleq!*"

His use of our proper name brings all murmurings to an abrupt halt.

"Be grateful," he says, "be grateful that you were not taken in bondage by the Hellas people, those sea-warriors of the north. Beauteous are their cities and valiant their battle champions, but savage are they toward those whom they capture. Harsh would be their use of you, without mercy, without sufficient food, as their islands and mountains are less fertile than our broad lands. Think also of the Egyptians, who in times past treated you brutally and killed your firstborns. You are fortunate to have been taken by Babylon."

This is greeted with stony silence.

"If the code of Hammurabi is unclear to you, raise your questions freely, and I will answer."

None among us responds at first. Finally, Shimeon stands and says, "O lord, you who are the voice of Nebuchadnezzar, I ask if these laws apply equally to the peoples of Babylon and the people brought here from Judah."

The man replies: "It is the will of Nebuchadnezzar that you see the wisdom of our kingdom's laws and thus be content to make your permanent home here. When you have sent down deep roots into this rich soil, like unto a tree planted by many waters, and when you bear fruits for your own well-being and that of this land, you will understand that these laws are the wisest in all the earth, a light from the heavens to protect you. Are you answered?"

"In the main, lord," Shimeon replies with a solemn nod.

"I further ask how judgment and punishment are to be administered."

"Crimes committed against Babylonians by Babylonians and Hebrews alike will be judged by Babylonian courts. Crimes committed by Hebrews against fellow Hebrews will be judged by your own judges."

"We have no judges."

"Then you must appoint from among you a body of men to give rulings on your affairs. There is one exception to this: If a Hebrew *kills* a fellow Hebrew, he not only commits a crime against his victim." The man looks down at the ground momentarily, frowns, and looks up. Speaking with some reluctance, he continues. "You must understand that such a crime would also destroy a property of Babylon. In this case, the one who kills would be taken before a Babylonian court."

Property, I think. *We are still as cattle to them. Or a kind of thinking animal.*

"May I reassure you, however, that a Babylonian who kills one of your people would also be taken to our court."

People are weighing this. We have just been informed that we can expect some protection, that we cannot be slaughtered at will. And that we are, perhaps, living in a very peculiar condition that combines slavery with a degree of self-ruling freedom.

Shimeon speaks again: "Are we free to adhere to the laws of our religion?"

"Yes, this is certain, insofar as they do not conflict with Babylon's laws. Therein lies no real discord, for I know that you reject theft and murder, untruth before judgment seats, the coveting of another's possessions—"

"And of another's wife."

"Be at peace, for no Babylonian will seize your wives and daughters into enforced marriage or concubinage."

This is greeted by murmurs of approval.

I stand up and ask, "Will we be forced to worship your gods?"

"No," the man answers.

"May I ask still further, lord, how you come to know our tongue so well and speak it with such beauty and clarity?"

"I speak many languages. I study much. My life is one of learning, that I may better advise the governors and those who advise the king himself. I have traveled across the entire world, as one of several envoys sent by the king to learn of diverse peoples and histories."

"Have you seen Jerusalem?"

"I have visited Jerusalem six times and spent the greater part of a year living there, reading your texts and conversing with your elders."

Smiles appear on many faces.

"Lord, permit me to ask if you have visited our Temple."

"I have climbed Mount Zion with respect, and I have gazed with awe upon the wonder of the world, Solomon's Temple made of gold."

I now see that this man, though he is ignorant of the full meaning of our Temple, speaks sincerely.

"Do you know of Moses and his law?"

"I have read with deep attention a scroll of the laws of your god, copied from original tablets once held in the Temple."

His reply generates great surprise and also a number of questions raised by other voices. I sit down.

"Did you enter the Temple?" a voice cries out anxiously from the crowd.

"Yes."

"Did you see the Ark of our Covenant?"

"No, the Temple was empty."

Now I am recalling with great relief that Jeremiah and the better priests took the Ark and the Tent to Mount Nebo, so that it would be hidden from the invaders. Apparently, not all our people know this. I sense bewilderment in those seated around me.

The meeting continues for a time, and then, because hours have passed, it comes to an end. People begin to disperse. I rise with Ruth and Leah, and we return to our house. Ruth's cookfire has dwindled into a hint of coals. I breathe on them and add twigs until little tongues of flame arise, onto which I place larger pieces of wood. The women leave me to my own thoughts. With much to ponder, I sit down by the fire and put my chin on my hands.

Not long after, I look up at the approach of two men. I am surprised to see the village overseer and the Babylonian who recited Hammurabi's laws. Hastily I rise to my feet and incline my head to them.

The man dismisses the overseer with a gesture of his hand. To me he says, "May I sit and converse with you?"

His unprecedented manner of courtesy leaves me speechless for a moment.

"Your questions impressed me at the meeting tonight," he says. "I would speak further with you, if you will."

"Certainly," I say.

We sit down facing each other across the fire. He places his clay cylinder onto the ground beside him, followed by the bronze tablet. With a swift glance I see that it is an image of a man on a throne, seated beside a reptilian monster. Is this a depiction of Nebuchadnezzar?

"An image of Marduk and his servant the dragon," my visitor explains, seeing my consternation. "It is insignia, not an object of worship. You need not fear it."

I look away.

"I am Abil-ilishu," he says.

"I am Yezekiel ben Buzi."

"What is the meaning of your name?" he asks.

"It means, 'The Most High will strengthen', or my God will make me strong."

With a curious mix of wryness and sadness, he says, "Your present condition seems in no way strong. In fact, it is very weak."

For a moment I wonder if he intends to convey smug contempt, wishing to shame me and thereby exalting himself. But no, I see much sympathy in his eyes.

"The weakest," I nod in agreement. "And what is the meaning of your name?"

"It means 'a son of his god'."

What is his god, I wonder. But I refrain from asking the question, instinctively drawing back from inquiring any further; my cursory exposure to these vile Babylonian gods has incited ever new vistas of disgust.

"You are a teacher of a kind," I say.

"Mainly I am a teacher, living in Ur for most of my life. *Ur of the Chaldees*, as your Scripture calls it, the land of your forefathers. At this time, however, I am appointed to travel throughout the province of Tel-abib and other regions, to instruct the communities of your people in our laws."

"Your mastery of our language is admirable."

He dips his head in acknowledgment.

"Are you people of Israel suffering much here?" he asks with an inquiring look.

Can I trust him? It may be foolishness on my part, but I answer as candidly as possible:

"There has been great hardship, yet our situation is improving."

"I regret the hardship, though I am pleased to hear of the improvement."

I can think of no response to this. The man puzzles me more than ever. He is the first Babylonian I have met who regrets our lot. Or is he presenting a false face, in order to survey the secret feelings of a captured people?

"To be *wardu*," he says in a regretful tone, "is a terrible burden that could make a man mad or drive him to outbreaks of rage."

"Extreme suffering can destroy, or it can lift up," I carefully reply.

"Lift up? How could that ever be?"

"When he is cast into an abyss of sorrows, each man faces a great test. Will he rebel in rage or slyly betray, thus losing himself in one or the other? Or will he become numb and indifferent to everything, merely pulling the plow or carrying the brick without feeling or hope, and thus losing himself in this way? Or will he submit to the yoke, while at the same time laboring hard to preserve his inner fidelity to truth? If he chooses this path, he becomes more than he thought he was."

"You mean to say that the inner man grows stronger. Yet he may still lose his life under the yoke, might he not?"

"His life is in his character and his soul."

"I see," my visitor says, but I wonder if he really does see.

"Do not your own people have this principle written within them?" I ask.

"My people?" replies Abil-ilishu with a distant look. "My

people seek ever to avoid the test by being always the con-
queror and thereby never failing to supply their needs and
luxuries. Surely it is the same with your people in the Kingdom of Judah."

"It is the same with some individuals, but not with our
whole people. Babylonian minds are very alien to us."

"Babylonian minds?" he answers with a droll look. "Do
you wish to understand my people?"

"Yes."

"That is praiseworthy, but obscure. Why do you wish to
understand us?"

I ponder the question a moment, and then I reply, "To understand the ways of another mind, another people, points
in the direction of deeper truths embedded in our common
human nature. As is the case when two, three, four men
stand at different places on the land and direct their eyes
to a single point in the distance, they may arrive at more
certain measurement and the relationships of spaces."

"Just so," he says with a smile. "You are mathematical."

"I think not, for I can barely count to a thousand, and
of the mysteries of dividing and multiplying I have no real
knowledge. Still less do I grasp your people's measuring of
angles and lengths to obtain mastery of elusive forms."

"We call it geometry."

"Ah."

"The builders of your Temple in Jerusalem had great intelligence in these matters."

"It is so. But the builders were guided by our God, and
they numbered no more than a handful of learned men.
Most Israelites are simple folk. I myself am ordinary in every way."

The man nods, but says nothing.

"But why are all your women weeping and loudly lamenting?" I ask. "Has some dreadful event come to pass?"

Abil-ilishu chuckles quietly. His amusement is beyond my ken.

He explains, "In our rite, the beautiful young shepherd-god Tammuz, consort of Ishtar, dies once a year and is later reborn. He goes down into the underworld at the summer solstice when the fertility of plants, animals, and humans is lowest because of the heat and extreme dryness. Every year at the solstice, the women of Babylonia, and those in neighboring lands, weep the tears of Ishtar, so that her grieving is embodied throughout the entire empire and will ensure the return of the rains. They think they bring Tammuz back from the dead. In this way our fertility is preserved."

And your power, I think.

I say, "Yet it is your cleverness with rivers, canals, and dams that preserves your crops."

"True. All the lands between Ur in the south and Nineveh in the north would be like desert were we to lack control of waterways."

"Yet still you weep, and still you rejoice? It would seem that you believe your gods ensure the fruitfulness of waterways."

"Our people believe it is so. From Sumer of ancient days we inherited the divinities of canals and irrigation."

Recalling his amusement, I dare to ask him:

"Do you believe in the divinities, Abil-ilishu?"

He frowns, and his eyes shift away from me.

"I am a true son of my gods," he says.

Through my mind pass vague, horrifying images of Babylonian magic, most of which I cannot imagine. My cousin Levi once informed me that from age unto age Babylon, and the ancient kingdoms out of which it grew, have exported their mystery cults to the whole world. Their magicians and soothsayers, men of great craftiness, performed illusory marvels as demons clouded the minds of devotees, warping their emotions and imaginations, making them believe they received answers to incantations and blessings from the sacrifice to idols. The Baals that have plagued my own nation had their origins in Babylon. The children burned on the altars outside Jerusalem were slaughtered because of Babylon.

"I am a son of my gods," he says again, as if to convince me. Yet I sense a lack of conviction in his voice.

"Do you practice divinization through omens and portents; do you read signs in sheep livers?" I ask him.

"No, *I* do not."

This surprises me, for if he were a true son of his gods, he would be very much involved in such practices.

"Incantations and other forms of magic?" I press, hoping I do not go beyond the bounds of civility, inviting retribution.

He pauses for a time, examining my eyes with a solemn expression. Glancing at the bronze tablet of Marduk, he reaches over and turns it face-down with an expression of distaste. Its back is entirely covered with the wedge-shaped letters of their language.

"I do not involve myself in the sick madness of magic," he replies at last. In a lowered voice he adds, "I perform the proper external form of worship in the rituals demanded of all citizens, those that honor our major gods, but that is all. Within the secret places of my heart and mind I keep myself aloof."

This is an extraordinary confession—and I think a dangerous one, for here in Babylonia their religion is paramount. This unusual man is entrusting himself to me by an exercise in profound honesty. Why? What does he hope to gain from it?

I push harder:

"How have you come to be so different from your fellow countrymen?"

"Look up," he says, pointing to the starry night. "See the vast serenity, layer upon layer of excellence in the heavens. See also the order in the realm of plants and animals and seasons. They are guided by fixed laws that cannot be penetrated by auguries or controlled by incantations. Still less can the principles that rule our lives be placated by the spilling of human blood in evil sacrifice or by indulgence in frenzied lusts."

He has used the word *evil*!

"You say rightly, sir. In my religion, we believe that engaging in all such evil activities involves commerce with demons."

"I have read that you Hebrews believe so. Your faith intrigues me greatly, which is why I am glad you are willing to speak openly with me on these matters. Seldom in my life is it possible."

"I am also glad."

"Religion, religion," he says with a sigh. "It is as if the mind of man has sunk into a fever swamp of symbol-images and ill spirits. O pity and degradation, how can one find truth in such times as these!"

"We say, keep the heart and mind pure by obedience to the wisdom of the one living God and by praying to him always for the light that leads to truth. And this truth in turn will lead to freedom."

"The *one* living God," he replies with an uncertain shake of his head.

For a time we both fall silent as he absorbs what I have said.

He looks at me with another sigh.

"High are our mathematics and astronomy, Yezekiel ben Buzi. So high that they are the marvel of the world. The empire goes from strength to strength. At the same time, we are like jackals, tearing the meat from living bodies."

He may be referring to Babylonian wars of conquest, or he may be speaking of secret practices in their religious sacrifices. I do not know. I do not wish to know.

Nevertheless, uninvited, he chants in a low voice:

To Erech, the sacred city of Babylon, they were summoned,
the eunuchs and the eunuch singers,
Whose virility Ishtar turned to effeminacy to terrify the
people,
They who bear the dagger, who bear the razor, the sword,
and the stone knife,
They who eat the potency of men to make glad the mood
of Ishtar—

He is interrupted by a renewed burst of heinous wailing from across the river.

With a shudder I ask, "What of your women's role in the rituals of Ishtar? It seems to me that in your religion no woman is safe from men's lusts. Are you married? Do you have daughters?"

"I am married, but I have no daughters, only sons. My wife is exempt from the rituals, as she is from Media, the land beyond Assyria, and has her own gods. In addition, I am given much freedom of action, since I am a valuable servant with unique knowledge of history and travel to foreign lands as well as my proficiency in many languages."

"Then you are one of the noble *Awilu*?"

He raises his eyebrows. "You know this term?"

"I have met *Awilu*," I say neutrally, recalling the governor and his wife.

"I can see by your eyes that it was not a happy occasion. But to answer your question, I was born of the *Mushkenu*, which is the largest class of our people, neither rich nor powerful but free. Now, after long years of study and effort —and usefulness—I might be considered a lower *Awilu*."

"I see by *your* eyes that you are blessed with a rare freedom to think for yourself, as your mind roves far beyond the gates of an empire. Even so, may I ask this: Should not a man's external action be in unity with his internal condition?"

His face darkens with sudden pain.

"Yes, it should. But a man must also feed his family."

I perceive his dilemma and now understand his interest in conversing with one such as me—one who lives beyond the gates.

Finally, he stands and soberly looks me in the eye.

"I must go. May your god strengthen you, Yezekiel."

"May you be a son of the true God, Abil-ilishu."

Strangely, he does something that has not happened to me since leaving Israel. He bows to me. I bow in return. With no more to be said, he turns and leaves.

The fire dies away. I get up and enter our dwelling, where I find Leah still awake. I lie down beside her.

"There is new hope," she whispers so as not to wake her mother on the other side of the wall.

"There is hope, if our captors abide by what they say."

"May the Lord make it so."

"O that we might fly away, my Leah! I would carry you across the desert and mountains to the gentle hill country where I was born, and there we would build our home and raise our little ones in peace."

"Do not forget Jeremiah's warning, Yezekiel."

"I do not forget. But seventy years is a very great length of years, and this land is filled with a poisonous cloud of evil spirits that are ever seeking to twist men's minds."

"We will endure. The Most High asks us to bear children here and prepare them for the future time when we will return."

"Yet I wonder, will the children born in exile desire to live in Israel, which would be as a foreign land to them?"

"They will, if we teach them to keep Israel alive in their hearts." She pauses, takes a breath. "I pray that a child will be given to you and me."

"I pray for this also."

"Perhaps many children."

"More numerous than the stars in the heavens."

With my hand on her face, I can feel her smiling in the dark.

We hold each other closely. As always, she is the delight of my eyes and the joy of my heart, yet I cannot dispel my worry over the unknown that lies ahead of us.

12

Elders and Prophets

NOW IS THE BEGINNING of my fourth year of captivity. I gaze about the Portion, remembering how it looked but a short time ago. It has grown and grown, and increasingly it appears to be little different from any other village or town that I saw during the journey along the Euphrates. A considerable number of our buildings have been reconstructed with flat roofs, as is the case with all the buildings across the river and with so many houses in Jerusalem.

I plastered the inside walls of our house a few months ago and also replaced the roof to make it flat. A ladder allows access to the new floor above, which is open to the sky. Leah and I often climb up to be cooled by a breeze on the hottest of nights, and sometimes we sleep there. Ruth prefers to sleep indoors, finding the ladder too difficult to climb with her weak legs and painful joints. I muse gratefully on the way our home is becoming ever more domestic, step by step.

We are not living in mud-and-reed huts like swamp dwellers; we are here as valued members of the Babylonian empire. Or so we are told. It is true that brutal enforcement of our servitude has all but disappeared, replaced by rewards and enticements. The increase of small freedoms allows us to forget for hours, even days on end, that we are prisoners. Even so, we may not go wherever we want and must remain within the immediate environs of the town and village. Only under the watchful eye of an overseer are we taken to distant fields or canals. We continue to live without the lash as long as certain tasks are fulfilled.

As usual, a majority of us are engaged in heavy labor of one kind or another, some to maintain the needs of the village and others to do the harder work for the Babylonians. If a man is strong and below a certain age—I estimate forty years or so—the overseers ensure that he works for them. But none of us receive wages. It is understood that we are still *wardu*, though the name is no longer used as a sneer against us. We are now "*Y'hudi*" and "resident aliens"—the pretense or presumption is that we are contented immigrants. Some among us do behave as if they are untroubled by enforced exile, and I suspect it is due to the shortness of memory in human nature combined with the small measure of prosperity granted us. To have comforts and the promise of improving one's situation enable some people to endure what would otherwise be unendurable for them.

It is still unlawful to own a weapon of any kind. If a man were to be caught possessing one, he would be brought to court in Kebar, with harsh penalties for the offender. It has not yet happened, though I worry that the younger men from the second wave, who suffered less brutality, might one day try to rebel. The elders' repeated warnings to them are often met with indifferent looks and even resentment against us who are only trying to spare them needless suffering. I can understand their immature ideas and impulses, but at the same time I fail to understand how the Babylonians reconcile the prohibition against weapons with the permission we now have to own tools of all kinds, some of which are every bit as deadly. But then, as I once said to the law-teacher Abil-ilishu, I cannot comprehend the

Babylonian mind. The contradiction is probably due to the fact that a bow, spear, or sword is an instrument of warfare, and tools are not. There is in this, I think, a symbolic aspect.

The Portion now has its own brick kiln, employing eight people full time. As the supply of mud and clay is inexhaustible, this has made it possible to enlarge houses, to build sheep pens and courtyards around homes, and to increase by great numbers the bread ovens owned by individuals and families for their own use. Small shops have opened in the village, selling or trading the usual wares such as textiles, humble jewelry, and special foods made by our enterprising women. Due to the increase of our flocks, there is a butcher shop where pieces of goat and mutton may be bought. There is also a steady production and trade in shoes, as animal hides are in better supply. People are tired of going barefoot, and now many are the proud wearers of a kind of thin boot that reaches the top of the ankles and is tied with thongs. Even Kebarites come to purchase boots, mainly the better ones made with tight stitching and trimmed with colorful embroidery. Ruth makes these and sells two or three pairs a week. With her profits, she buys more hide. She gave Leah a beautiful pair and offered to make a set for me, too. But I told her I prefer to go barefoot, at least until such time as sandals can be made. For now, thick ox hide is impossible to obtain, so the making of solid-sole sandals is beyond our reach.

In addition, a new thing called a "banking house" has been instituted. It specializes in money exchange and the *embankment* or storing of coins for individuals. People who have saved more than a few *geras* or a *shekel* or two tend to be afraid of thieves and do not want to risk leaving their wealth unattended when away from their homes. A person who deposits his money with the "banker" receives a clay tablet receipt for the total, minus a commission that the banker takes for his services. The banker's building is his own house, reinforced by double-brick walls, stout bars on the windows, and a man who stands guard over the hoard night and day, with a sharp-pointed staff by his side. The doors are made of thick wood with iron hinges and locks, obtained by bribery from complicit Kebarites.

If a man wants to buy a sheep or rent his neighbor's labors, he may go to the banker to request a loan. Shamefully, usury is extracted from the borrower, who risks losing everything he owns if he cannot pay back the very high interest. This practice is in direct disobedience to the fifth book of Moses and is condemned by the prophets. While I understand that lending may be helpful to the growth of the Portion, I believe that grave troubles will come from the usury. If loans go into default, will our judges be called upon to administer the banker's rules? Will our judges become enforcers of sin? They have not yet tried a case of anything more complicated than petty theft—though, considering human nature, I suppose worse will come. They will need the wisdom of Solomon.

Most important of all, the people of the Portion have built a house consecrated to the Lord, its portal open wide to the village commons. I helped to lay its bricks, making of each brick a prayer.

It is large by our standards, like four houses together. Inside, inscribed on the wall facing the doorway are the letters יהוה—YWHW. Beneath it, an oil lamp flickers atop a terebinth table. In this place, we exiles, deprived of the Temple, gather for prayer and to recite the parts of Scripture that people remember. There are no book scrolls among us, only the letters of Jeremiah. From time to time, I am called upon to recite from memory. I go there most nights before sleep, and our family always attends on the Sabbath, when a major portion of the community comes together. There is no room for all of us to fit inside the building, but people are content to sit on the ground outdoors. The establishment of the house has given us a greater feeling of solidity, an elusive sense of unity, for though the structure is plain, it recalls us to the glory of Mount Zion. So, too, the sound of the *shofar*, the ram's horn trumpeting on the eve of the Sabbath, evokes myriad emotions, a reminder of the past and a call to keep faith in the present. Its notes proclaim, *Come to me! I am the Lord! You will endure!*

The house of prayer, or the "gathering place" as it is called by some, is also used for meetings of the elders and for judgment of the few conflicts that have occurred among us—contentions over patches of garden, accusations of small thefts, defaults on loans, petitions for divorce—though this last is rare. The power of a community's reproach is considerable and is usually enough deterrent. No one wants to become a pariah. Equally, no one wants to be handed over to a Babylonian court. If our own court judges a man guilty of taking his neighbor's goods, proved by the testimony of two witnesses or by the discovery of the stolen property in his possession, he will be forced to repay it twice over. Depending on the seriousness of the theft, he may also receive a lashing with stiff reeds. Shame, combined with the destruction of his reputation, does the rest.

Of adultery I hardly dare speak. As far as I know, it has not yet occurred among our three hundred people and more, our numbers slowly increasing. I dread to think about the fate of adulterers, though it must be said that I cannot imagine anyone willing to administer the punishment of death by stoning. For one thing, we have no stones. For another, a person caught in adultery could easily wade across the river to seek shelter among the Kebarites, for whom adultery is probably a daily occurrence, at worst a misdemeanor.

Our court, such as it is, came about last year after tortuous discussions that uselessly devoured months of our time. A great number of people attended the meetings each evening, most of them with something urgent to say, especially names to propose for the role of judge. Tempers were hot, which is always the case when human nature is driven by fear. People did not forget the unjust judges who had plagued Judah, and of course they wanted honest men, but they especially wanted men whom they knew would be sympathetic to them if they were ever taken before a court. Hence, the ceaseless agitation and interruptions, with hardly anyone listening to others. It was enough to make me avoid those meetings altogether.

Under the urging of Shimeon and Tzvi, I did attend a later meeting in which negotiations seemed to be nearing a point of decision. It began with unruly arguments but ended well.

By that point, the names of about thirty men had been proposed, and just over half of them were finally accepted as candidates. Not one of them was acceptable to all, but they each had a sizeable number of supporters. They were a mix of characters, some respected for their intelligence, others for their prosperity, a few because they looked strong and eager for the role, but all of them with a reputation for fair dealing with village folk. Among the ones I knew personally were Gad the translator, two brothers named Amos and Abner, who owned the largest sheep flock, Tzvi the builder, who was regarded fondly by all, and Shimeon, who was generally revered as something of a sage.

It was he who brought the meeting to order when he stood up in the middle of the gathering and recited in his

strong voice the words from an ancient text, which I rec-
ognized as the *Devarim*, the fifth book written by Moses:

> You are to appoint judges and officials for your tribes in ev-
> ery town that the Lord your God is giving you. They are
> to judge the people with righteous judgment.
>
> Do not deny justice or show partiality. Do not accept a
> bribe, for a bribe blinds the eyes of the wise and twists the
> words of the righteous.
>
> Pursue justice, and justice alone, so that you may live,
> and you may possess the land that the Lord your God is
> giving you.

Slowly looking all about the circle, appearing to catch every
eye in a group of well over two hundred people, Shimeon
then addressed the gathering as if he were speaking to each
one personally:

"Woe unto us if we choose wrongly. Woe upon woe
if we choose according to friendships and loyalties and the
prospect of benefits. Choose, then, the man who is not only
wise in his counsels but righteous unto the Lord, for the
one who judges will himself be judged by the Court most
high."

This silenced everyone, and faces looked away or at the
ground.

"Consider carefully what you do," he went on, "for you
are not judging for mere mortals but for the Lord." Then,
raising his voice to a roar, he concluded with a final admonition: "May the fear of the Lord our God be upon you!"

With that, he sat down.

For a time, not a word was said, until at length a man
whom I had known since our arrival in the Portion rose to
his feet with groans and creaking bones. It was Naphtali, the
old fellow of bitter looks and endless grumbling. He lashed
out an arm to gain attention and declared in a loud voice:

"Listen, you bad-tempered ones, never satisfied. Have you no eyes, no ears? There are some among us who have wisdom. Not much, but enough to guide us. Shimeon is the best. Then comes Tzvi the builder. Also, you should consider that poor bricklayer named Yezekiel. Slow of thought and dour of countenance is he, yet ofttimes the man will surprise you."

He sat down abruptly, or rather collapsed to the ground with the aid of able-bodied men beside him.

"Aha, aha!" came a volley of retorts. "It's plain to see that *you* want to be a judge, old man."

"Nay," growled Naphtali. "Beg me, if you will, but never would I accept such a thankless task. If you cannot decide, I say that three men should be chosen by the first-comers, and three others chosen by the second-comers, and one agreed upon by all, to make the holy number seven."

An outbreak of debate followed.

When it had subsided, a few voices arose, proposing my name. Shimeon looked at me, waiting for my response. But I knew in my soul that to judge my people was not my task. I firmly declined.

Then Eli the harpist stood, and in his trembling voice he said, "There is one here who once was a judge in Israel. Why not him? He would know the ways of laws and courts."

"Who? Who?"

Eli pointed to an old man sitting at the edge of the crowd. "Ehud the Benjamite."

All eyes turned upon the man named Ehud. He lowered his head and would not look up.

"Will you stand?" Shimeon asked him. "Will you offer yourself for consideration by the people?"

But Ehud refused to answer.

"Please stand and break the impasse," Shimeon pressed him.

Slowly, with great reluctance, Ehud rose to his feet, and shuffled into the open space in the center of the gathering.

He raised his eyes momentarily and then dropped them again.

"You wish me to be a judge over you?" he murmured in a broken voice. "You do not know what you are asking."

Then I remembered him. He was among that group of once-important men who resisted the Babylonians years ago, on the first day we were taken to hard labors. "I was a judge in Israel!" he had shouted in outrage, before being struck to the ground by the guards.

"You do not know what I am!" he now exclaimed.

He threw himself to his knees with tears streaming down his face and into his white beard. He gathered dust in his hands and poured it over his head. "I am not worthy to be a judge!" he cried. "The Lord has brought me low because of my sins. In Israel I made unjust decisions. It is right that I am now a cleaner of streets, a dung-gatherer in Kebar, for donkeys, camels, and dogs are more innocent than I."

Then he lay face down in the dirt and would not move. Astonished, no one said a word.

Shimeon got up and came to him, kneeling down by his side.

"Is there innocent blood on your hands?" he asked in his quiet voice.

"No, no innocent blood," Ehud sobbed. "But tainted gold and silver were in my hands."

It was difficult to think of a reply to such a confession. What answer would suffice? None.

"I beg you to beat me," Ehud cried out once more.

For a time, silence continued to reign. Finally, Shimeon rose to his feet and said, "All right, we will beat you."

He was gone a moment, searching for something at the edge of the crowd, and returned carrying a willow switch. He laid one stroke across Ehud's back, firmly but not hard enough to give real pain.

"Beat me, beat me," the old man pleaded.

Shimeon held out the switch to the crowd. At first no one responded.

"Are there any here who were harmed by false judgments in Israel?" he asked.

One after another, six people got up and approached the prone figure in the dust—a woman, two young men, three older men. With solemn faces they took the switch and struck Ehud's back, though none of them did it with great force. They returned to their seats.

Everyone waited in silence.

Shimeon said, "Are you beaten to your satisfaction, Ehud of Benjamin?"

The reply was a groan.

"Are you answered?"

Another groan.

"Now stand up and face the people."

The old man got up on hands and knees, his face flaming red with sorrow and shame, tears making runnels in his dusty face. He stood and raised his eyes to the people.

"You are chastised," said Shimeon. "And now you will become our judge."

That night, the process of choosing the other judges went swiftly. Three men, Tzvi, Shimeon, and Abner the shepherd were chosen from the first wave, confirmed by raised arms and acclamations. Three were chosen from the second wave,

all elderly men, prudent in thought and speech, the olive or-
chardist, a carpenter, and another shepherd. Ehud the Benjamite made the seventh.

And that is how we came to have a court.

The choosing of elders happened about the same time,
though more peaceably. Shimeon was again acclaimed by
all the gathering of the people, who appointed him with
nary a dissenting voice. Three others, men much like him,
were also affirmed by acclamation. Tzvi, too, was appointed
—it is interesting that Shimeon and Tzvi have the double
role of judge and elder, which testifies to the esteem in
which they are held. Tzvi, who was a jolly joker four years
ago, has matured into a thoughtful man, and perhaps he always was one beneath the surface. Without exception, the
elders are sober personalities, moderate of speech but quick
to understand. They are not given to wrangling, nor are
they easily disturbed by the fractious, who by temperament
or habit like to argue the elders' decisions.

In the main, their decisions are about the affairs of the
prayer house, its upkeep and usage. They also lead during its times of prayer, give teachings on the sacred texts,
and are fastidious about correct celebrations of the Day of
Atonement, the Festival of Booths, and the Passover. They
offer counsel to those who seek it. They will, on occasion,
adjudicate secular disputes that are not within the purview
of our court. In addition, they make judgments about religious matters, judgments not binding as if they were law,
but rather prudent advice for the community as a whole.

This has proven to be a crucial need.

From the beginning of the exile, there have been apostates.
I do not mean the pitiful men who were driven by lust to

cross the river during the night, for theirs was a matter of sin
—breaking God's law, but not repudiating it. No, I refer to
the cowardly who would curry favor with our masters, sup-
posing that by adopting Babylon's religious practices they
would no longer be identified with Israel. This was naïve,
but I suppose there were enough rewards of a secret kind
to keep them from repenting. They continued to live in the
Portion but were avoided by the faithful, and I think they
also suffered from secret shame. Thus, they sought to recruit
others into apostasy in order to feel less alone and to bol-
ster their self-respect. Their covert attempts at the seduction
were not greatly successful, but in time they made sufficient
headway into our community that they were emboldened
to speak out.

I recall a number of meetings, following the election of
the elders, in which individual apostates tried to refute a
teaching or to declare their new loyalties, hoping to draw
others to their side. One such sad and memorable event took
place on a Sabbath night when Shimeon stood among the
people giving an account of the kings of Israel, the few righteous ones and the many who adopted alien gods and fell
into evil practices, thereby corrupting the nation. He had
just begun telling the story of King Manasseh when three
young men rose to their feet, elbow to elbow, and one of
them yelled:

"The reign of El Shaddai does not hold in this land!"

Stunned to silence, the whole crowd looked to Shimeon
for a response.

"Do not blaspheme the name of the Lord Most High,"
he said with great authority, without losing his peace.

"He was god in Judah, but not here," came the shouted
reply. "Each of the gods has his own territory, and none
may infringe on another."

Many in the crowd groaned and flushed, turning their faces away.

"The Lord Most High reigns over all the earth!" Shimeon declared with great strength. "Hear, O Israel, the Lord our God is one! There is no other god but him!"

Linking hands and prancing into the center of the gathering, the disrupters chanted, "Praise be to Marduk! Praise be to Ishtar! Praise be to Tammuz! Praise be to Baal!" Still chanting, they halted face to face with Shimeon as if to challenge him.

"The gods of Babylon would lead you on a dark path that ends in torment!" he said, peering intently into their eyes.

"It is not a path but a wide bridge, a bridge to bliss!" one of them replied haughtily.

"A bridge to eternal fire," Shimeon roared like a holy old lion.

Seated nearby, I felt an impulse to get up and strike the arrogant three, to startle them back to sanity. They seemed to me a wicked parody of the three young men who visited Abraham and Sarah. Intending to rebuke them or at least to push them out of the gathering, I was rising to my feet when Shimeon bellowed:

"Be silent!"

Strangely the three young men closed their mouths and dropped their arms, looking bewildered.

"May the Lord rebuke you!" he continued in a lower voice, but just as forceful. "May the Lord rebuke the spirits that have taken control of you."

Staring at Shimeon with animosity, the three remained mute, as if bound by unseen hands.

"Would you have us adopt the practices of Babylon?" he said. "King Manasseh rebuilt the high places and did according to the abominable practices of the pagan nations. He erected altars to the Baals and worshipped all the gods of the heavens. He built evil altars in the house of the Lord, and on them he burned his sons as offerings. He engaged in soothsaying, augury, and sorcery, consulted mediums and wizards. He seduced Jerusalem and all Judah into his ways, and they did more evil than the nations the Lord destroyed. Then the Lord brought Assyria against him with terrible retribution, until he was captured and repented of all his idolatry."

The three young men wheeled about, waded through the crowd, and disappeared into the darkness beyond.

Some good came from the episode, for after that, the number of people who attended Sabbath prayers increased. One of the three young men came to the house of prayer and knelt before its open door in sackcloth, with ashes on his head, refusing to leave until Shimeon and the other elders came to him. They stood around him and placed their hands on his head and shoulders, praying. He wept and promised to make penance and never again to partake in the evil rituals. In this he proved faithful. The other two took up residence in Kebar and came no more to the Portion.

There were other kinds of disruption that could have led to serious divisions among us, and these were not as easily discerned as was blatant apostasy. Many are the ways that the ancient enemy of mankind seeks to beguile us.

An entirely different group of Israelites lived among us, men who had no patience with apostates. They were apparently devout, adhering to the Mosaic laws, often attending evening prayers, and always there on the Sabbath. They were unnecessarily vocal during prayers, seeking to pray more loudly than others and with more beautiful wording. At other times, they would interject their opinions on fine points of the law while an elder was teaching the people.

They were often right on certain matters, and so the elders humbly accepted the interruptions and listened attentively to what they offered. Yet I felt a growing unease in my soul regarding these men. It seemed to me that while they appeared to accept their position as less than elders, they behaved as if they were the true elders. They could expand on an elder's teaching and at times adjust it without giving the impression that they were correcting him. It was hard to fault them for it, for they were never offensive, yet I worried that there was something unhealthy in this relentless conveying of superior vision and understanding. Many people flocked to them after prayer times, showering them with questions, bowing to them when given a helpful reply. I sorrowed over the way so many now bypassed our elders, who were truly wise, who had Sacred Scriptures in their minds and hearts, and the holy spirit of God in their souls, but were unlettered men.

As the months passed, the community prayers were little by little changed by this small body of self-appointed "elders", five in all, the same number as our true elders. It began with their minor innovations that looked like an exalted form of mystical expression, faces lifted to the roof, arms raised, trembling hands, shaking body, loud groans and sighs. Because it appeared to be a release of profound spiritual emotion or a prompting by the spirit of the Lord, I saw nothing obviously wrong in this. And yet it drew undue attention to them. It seemed humble, and yet, oddly, it did not *feel* humble. As the months went on, the mystical expressions increased in intensity. Now the five were giving utterances of praise in unnatural voices. And then came prophecies. It was the prophecies that prompted me to seek Shimeon's wisdom on the matter. Until now he had let it continue without comment, and I wondered why.

When we were alone by his fire one night, I told him that an uneasiness, a lack of peace, had been growing in me regarding the men who were now prophesying in the name of the Lord, exalting him in ecstatic utterances.

"Whenever they cry out," I said, "my soul flinches away from it and I cannot sing. I feel dead inside when they speak. Why is this?"

"They speak much truth," he said, though I could see that he was weighing the question.

"They always speak truth," I said. "I am sorely troubled that I may be resisting a work of the Lord."

"To be cautious in testing a matter is not the same thing as resisting it," he replied.

"I do not understand myself, Shimeon. What is wrong with me? I know that the spirit of prophecy is a blessing from the Lord."

"Yes, a great blessing. Think of Elisha when he came unto the company of prophets who behaved as these men do in our house of prayer."

"Such a gift is a beautiful thing."

"A beautiful and *rare* thing."

He sighed deeply and said, "I do not know what to do about it. Neither do the other elders. We must keep praying for light."

And so I prayed for light.

On a Sabbath evening not long after, nearly the entire community had filled the house of prayer and spilled out into the yard surrounding it. After our usual prayers, Scripture recitation, and a final singing of a king-song, Amos, one of the elders, stepped from within and stood before the wide entrance, facing outward to the larger portion of people.

A shepherd, a man of few words, and simple-spoken,

he began his teaching, which that night was about the recorded chastisements of Israel. There were many in our past, and thus I knew that a long instruction was about to begin.

Amos had managed to get through only two accounts, when to our surprise, the five aspiring "elders" or "prophets" came out of the house and swept past him. They were dancing with their arms lifted high, faces raised to the heavens, trembling and shouting acclamations in words I could not quite discern. Surprised, Amos fell silent. All of us watched in amazement as the dancers twirled and chanted, almost in a frenzy.

Finally, I could pick out what they were saying:

"Jubilation! Redemption! Return!"

The crowd took up the cry, "Return! Return! Return! Jerusalem! Jerusalem!" and soon were working themselves into a state of wild excitement.

At that moment, Tzvi and Shimeon stepped forth from the prayer house and abruptly halted, observing the display with consternation.

"Listen! Be attentive!" Shimeon cried out. But this confused the crowd, for many of them thought he wanted us to listen to the dancers. Not so, for his intention was to bring about silence that he might speak.

Numerous voices in the crowd exclaimed, "Listen to the prophets, listen to the prophets! The spirit of the living God is on the prophets!"

"Return! Return!" sang the dancers in high voices. "Jerusalem, O Jerusalem! Soon we return! Soon we return! This year! This is the year of liberation!"

"Silence!" roared Shimeon in a voice of command.

The prophets dropped their arms and ceased dancing. They turned in a group toward the prayer house—the five prophets facing the five elders who had now gathered in the doorway.

Shimeon looked out over the people and said, "All of you have heard Jeremiah's letter, which has been read to you again and again."

Many in the crowd frowned, shifting their bodies uneasily.

"Jeremiah?" someone called out. "That man was of ill repute in Jerusalem!"

"He was a woe-sayer," said another, "with no words to lift the heart, only words to cast down."

"And was he wrong to warn us?" Shimeon asked. "Did his prophecies not come to pass?"

"Some yes, some no."

"Some fulfilled, some yet to come," Shimeon replied.

"How can you be sure of that? Half a prophet is no prophet."

"Wait and see," said one of the other elders, "before you cut the man in two."

"Waiting! Always we are waiting!" cried another objector. "Why drink the bitter water that pours from so dire a mouth?"

I raised my voice, saying, "I knew him. Though he was grave of countenance, there was joy in his eyes, for he saw a coming restoration."

"Ha! The days go on, the years stretch on, and still his restoration never comes."

Now the objector pointed to the prophets standing together in a cluster, looking solemn and spiritual. I could tell that they were listening to the debate even as they feigned indifference.

"These men bring us the voice of the Lord," he shouted.

"The spirit of the Lord is upon them, for the uplifting of our hearts and preparing us for return to Israel."

"You forget," said Shimeon in a tone of admonition. "You forget that all true prophets bring both warning and consolation. You would have consolations only, which bend your ears toward only those who do not disturb you."

Angry now, the debater huffed, got to his feet, and threw up an arm in annoyance.

"Seventy years, your Jeremiah said!" he exclaimed. "Seventy years! Nay, nay, it cannot be! Who could endure it?"

"We will endure it," Shimeon replied in his quietest voice. "For Jeremiah the true prophet promised that we would endure it. He has written that the Lord himself exhorts you to take no heed of false prophets who will arise among you. They will deceive many, even themselves, with their oracles in the name of the Lord, but their mouths will be full of lies. They will prophesy swift return to the Kingdom of Judah, but it will be a false hope."

The prophets stared glumly at Shimeon.

"Repent of the deception," he sternly admonished them, staring them in their eyes. And then looking around the crowd, he concluded, "Do not spread the deception."

The five elders now lifted their arms and bowed their heads, praying with their open palms toward the false prophets. These men abruptly turned away with irritable looks. One by one, they left the gathering with heads held high and moving with great dignity. Many others among the people rose and followed after them. Those who remained were by no means at peace, for a look of indecision was on most faces. I am sure that no one wanted to remain in captivity for another sixty-five or sixty-six years, but I think most of us sincerely wanted the truth.

In the months and years that came after, the false prophets never again disrupted the Sabbath gatherings, though they continued to influence people privately. I was told by Tzvi that the ones who originally had prophesied we would return within two years of our capture were not bothered by the fact that four years had now passed. In the same way, the more recent prophets of immediate return argued that the Lord had delayed our liberation because of our refusal to listen to *them*. Their influence gradually declined over time, but never entirely disappeared, for there were always people who would grasp at any hope, however false. As a result, the deceived ones remained inwardly in anxious expectation and did not abide by Jeremiah's exhortation to give their best service to our captors so that our lot in this land would steadily improve. Instead, they made it harder for everyone by neglect of their duties and by contemptuous behavior against the overseers, bringing about periodic regressions to harsh subservience. While such times were never again as bad as what we had suffered in the beginning, our lives continued to be overshadowed by the threat of fear.

There were other followers of the false prophets, mainly young and middle-aged men, who from time to time conspired among themselves to raise a revolt, which they believed would fulfill the prophecy by hastening our return to Israel. But they had no weapons, and they could agitate no common resolve among our people. They continued to grumble and foment rebellion in their furtive way, but fewer and fewer people would have any part with them, and in time this element dwindled to nearly nothing.

Finally I come to a third kind of bearer of falsehood, the ones who are now plaguing us in ways we could not have expected. They aspire to neither apostasy nor prophecy but have quietly developed a self-made role of influence, clothed with the mantle of conventional faith. They are not disrupters. They are not dividers. They are learned men who once held important positions in Jerusalem. Among them are four teachers who educated the children of Temple officials, three accomplished scribes, a translator of foreign documents for Jehoiachim's palace, an unordained adviser to the High Priest, and a private compiler of histories of the surrounding nations, who was writing a book on the subject when he was seized along with Jehoiachin—ten, all told.

The elders have thought it useful to draw upon these men's fields of knowledge by asking them to teach the people, that we might become better informed about the world and especially about our beliefs. Thus, from time to time, after meetings at the house of prayer, the learned ones will give talks to anyone who cares to attend. The numbers who do so are never very large, but intelligent people are glad for refreshment of their minds. Usually one or more of the elders are among the listeners, sometimes all five.

It seems to me that there is an inherent hunger for knowledge in human nature, and I am no exception. There is a pleasure in learning new things. I am especially eager to hear accounts of the beginning of nations in the lands between the Tigris and the Euphrates. I have learned about the first small towns that arose just south of here and about how the kingdom of Sumer grew from them. Then how Sumer spread its knowledge and customs farther north beyond its frontiers and, then, east and west. And then how Chaldea grew out of Sumer and how Babylon grew out of Chaldea. It is fascinating, and it helps me understand more about the ways of Babylonia surrounding us now.

In listening to the learned voices, I have often found that

what they say rings true to me and can even excite my heart. But there comes an evening when a sour note is played on the harp string, so to speak. The history teacher tells us with calm conviction that we should understand that the "legend" of Noah had its origins in a Sumerian tale written long before our Scriptures came into text by the hand of Moses. It is the story of Gilgamesh, an early king of Ur, and his travails during the great flood. The teacher informs us that Moses borrowed details from the old epic and adapted them to suit his concept of God and the religion of Israel.

This prompts some murmuring in the crowd, a general uneasiness. What is the teacher saying?

Shimeon speaks up and asks, "You do believe there was a Great Flood?"

"That is beyond all doubt," replies the teacher. "It was immense in scope and unequalled in depth. The tale of Gilgamesh is sometimes called *He Who Gazed into the Abyss* and *He Who Saw the Depths*."

Quiet reigns as this is absorbed.

"Long before Moses, you say?" asks Shimeon.

The man nods gently, as if with sympathy for our ignorance.

"Could it be that the epic you name is the legend?" Shimeon goes on. "If it was written long after the flood, the account of the flood may have been distorted as it was passed down generation after generation. Could it be that the distortions were further adapted to suit the Sumerian concept of God—"

"*Gods*. They had gods," the teacher patiently corrects.

"And is it not possible that Moses, though he was more distant in time from the flood, was given a true vision of what happened?"

"Ah, visions," replies the teacher with a tone of indulgent

regret. "Visions are of the imagination. Visions are not knowledge."

Tzvi speaks out. "But visions can be another way of knowing."

The teacher does not answer him. He smiles, says that this is enough for one night; it has been an enjoyable meeting, and he looks forward to seeing us again.

I accompany Shimeon back to his house. He shakes his head all the way there.

"Vision is of the *imagination*?" I say, trying to probe his thoughts.

"Visions can arise from the imagination, yes," he muses. "But when a vision is given from above, it shows the truth more clearly than a library full of book scrolls."

"Or a library full of clay tablets," I say, which makes him smile.

In recent weeks I have heard more of this kind of teaching. Not often, but enough to make me wonder what is happening inside the minds of these most intelligent men, among whom are ones knowledgeable in the Sacred Scriptures. They can quote with impressive memories, and their insights can be captivating. However, I feel a new uneasiness whenever this or that man speaks, even when the thing he says is good. I can see no wrong in these teachers; I can catch no fault in their words; I feel no dislike for them. Why, then, is my soul not at peace whenever they speak? What causes this disturbance within me?

In time, I begin to see that these men are little by little modifying the words of Scripture, taming them, easing their impact, and by implication weakening the authority of God's words, bending the faith of our ancestors into a pale reflection of reality.

The elders are becoming gravely concerned.

At the end of one meeting, Shimeon stands up and says, "By what authority do you give your teachings?"

The teacher retorts, "By what authority do you question us?"

Shimeon pauses to think of an answer.

Taking advantage of the silence, the teacher says, "In recent generations the best minds of Israel have searched the Scriptures and compared them with a host of documents from other religions and cultures. We have separated sinew from bone, so to speak, and discovered the hidden codes of meaning. Of late, we have been much encouraged by the Temple."

"Many diverse things come from the Temple," Shimeon replies. "It seems to me that you would make of the Lord Most High a legend like unto the legends of other peoples."

"No, certainly not," answers the teacher. "The people chosen by God were given a light—dim in the beginning, poorly understood by them—which they reshaped like clay according to their own hopes and needs at the time."

"So, are you saying that *you* see farther than Abraham and Moses?"

"It is the path of new understanding we offer. It is a new revelation. We do not deny the truths of the past, and yet we see the limitations of our people who lived in those times. They saw unusual signs and interpreted them as best they could."

"And what of Mount Sinai? The voice of the Lord spoke the Ten Commandments to Moses there, and the tablets were inscribed by the finger of God."

"Moses wrote the tablets."

"What?" murmurs Shimeon. Shaken, he steps back.

"I do not wish to offend you, Shimeon, but try to understand that it is a symbol, this finger of God, a figure of

speech that Moses used to relate what came into his mind
—an inspiration, if you wish."

So dumbfounded are the elders that for the moment none
of them is able to speak up.

"The commandments must be understood in a new
light," the teacher continues mildly. "Gone are the days
when life is ruled by 'shall' and 'shall not'. Now begins a
new era when all men will be free to decide how to use
their love and their energies."

This is a strange thought. What does he mean by *free to
decide*? That *we* may judge what is sin and not sin? And then
it comes to me that this may be the very thing that drives
these teachers to distortions.

A painful burning flares in my soul, and I am on my feet
before I know it.

"You would build a bridge that appears to lead to Paradise," I tell him. "But if our people were led onto it, the
bridge would bend little by little, and in the end it would
turn so far around that it would lead them to the fires of
Gehenna."

Affronted by this accusation, the learned one raises his
voice, "You slander me and my fellow teachers, for we desire nothing but salvation for our people. You fail to understand us, and you fail to understand God."

"Do you understand him?"

"We understand that in this time of trial he would make
the path easier for us. He is kind and loving."

"Truly he is kind and loving," I reply. "But his is the
love of a strong father, who fights off the wolf and lion,
lest they devour his children. He firmly guides and repri-
mands when needed; he never betrays his own word; he
always seeks what is good for us."

"It is not good that the people suffer."

"We brought this suffering upon ourselves."

"To feel shame and guilt is an evil oppression."

"Some kinds of shame and guilt are evil, but some kinds of shame and guilt are justified. In these times, *we* have brought shame upon ourselves because of our real guilt. And though justice has fallen upon us, behind this justice is the Lord's great mercy."

"His mercy?" the teacher replies with a dubious laugh.

"I say again, it is his *mercy* that has chastised us, for it is not merciful to permit evil to devour the good without end."

He throws up his hands in frustration. He is now joined by two other teachers who have been standing nearby, listening. They approach and stare at me with stern disapproval.

One of them says, "You, you with no children, dare to speak of fatherhood to us, we who have many!"

Stung to the core, I press on, replying, "Is a father merciful if he allows his children to eat nothing but honey or to play over the hole of an asp?"

Their grimaces and slitted eyes reveal how angry they are becoming. Why are they so angry? Are they angry at me simply for contradicting them? Is their anger about our difficult straits here in a foreign land? Or are they, most subtly and most ominously, angry at God himself?

"The Father of us all is a mighty God," I say to them. "Fierce and holy is his countenance. He cannot be tamed as a donkey is trained to the halter. We are created to serve *him*. Never should we be trapped in the spider's web of thinking he exists only to serve *us*."

"Spider's web! So far do you dismiss serious study? Do you not know that in this latter age, time and wisdom have led us farther than the laws of Moses, for men were not learned in his days, grasping little of the mind of the Most High."

"And you have grasped his mind?"

"Study has sharpened our sight beyond the eyes of desert dwellers. Moses was a great man, but he was simple and saw only his people's need for strict laws to bring them through the exodus."

"You think that Moses was simple-minded? Do you believe he invented those laws?" I shake my head in amazement. "And what of the parting of the sea?"

"It was the sea of reeds, very shallow, which a strong wind can part to make a path."

"And the pillar of fire by night and the cloud by day?"

"As Chaldean astronomers can testify, such 'pillars' are not uncommon in the night airs; they are a force of nature that plays in the upper regions above the earth. And under the desert sun, there are mirages. Add to this the hunger and thirst that inflame men's minds to misinterpret what they see, swelling it vastly beyond its true meaning. What they saw was *spiritual*, and in this sense it was true; yet those events could not have taken place in the way they were described."

"Out of your own mouths your words reveal you."

"Ha, so you would condemn us!"

"I do not condemn you. I ask how you come to be so certain."

"Phah! You are of the old ways, we are of the *new*!"

They shake the dust from the hem of their garments and stomp away. The crowd of listeners, who have been closely following this discussion, now get up and wander off to their homes, murmuring, confused, undecided.

Shimeon has been standing by, listening to the entire

exchange. He now turns to me and looks intensely into my eyes.

"Please pardon my interference, Shimeon. I said too much."

Without replying, he continues to assess me somberly.

"I am sorry. It was not my place to speak."

"A light was in you as you spoke, Yezekiel. What you said was hard but good."

"But my voice has no authority to change their blindness. Perhaps if I had accepted to be an elder—"

"No, you chose rightly. The hand of the Lord is upon you for a purpose you cannot foresee, and you must trust in this. You do not know where he will lead, but lead you he will."

Deep in the night, long after Leah is asleep, I climb up the ladder onto the roof and stay a while, contemplating the stars. My heart is sorely burdened by the strife of our people. Why are they so easily seduced? Why is it so difficult for them to resist falsehoods? Why am I so powerless to refute the lies of the enemy in such a way that people are called back to our true path? I believe what I said to those false teachers. There is no shadow of doubt in my mind, but why does this mysterious anguish persist?

I lift my arms and close my eyes, seeking the Kingdom that is above all created heavens.

"Out of the depths I cry to you, O Lord," I breathe into the night sky. Then, remembering a few more lines from the king-song, I continue, "If you, O Lord, should mark our iniquities, who could stand? I wait for you, O Lord, I wait for you! My soul waits for you more than watchmen for the morning, more than watchmen for the morning. O will you not redeem Israel out of all our iniquities!"

Then I fall silent, grieving and uncertain of the future, for still we are waiting for redemption. Fourteen generations have passed since the time of King David, and still we are waiting.

"O Lord do not abandon us!" I cry out. "See how swiftly we listen to voices other than your own. And thus have we become the least of all the nations, for we are scattered and despised throughout the world because of our sins. We have no true prophet in our midst, no holocaust, no place where we can offer you the first-fruits. But may the souls that trust in your mercy be an acceptable sacrifice unto you, and may it be your will that we follow you wholeheartedly, since those who put their trust in you will not be disappointed."

This is my prayer. This is my hope. I drop my arms and open my eyes, wondering if the words of my lips are heard. Wondering, too, if this prayer is no more than a spark from a dying ember in my soul. Does he who reads all hearts listen to me there—there in that hidden place within?

Why am I feeling so desolate? Where is the man of light who came to me long ago, in a time nearly out of memory? Will he ever visit me again? Does he still visit that boy I met on the road, the dreamer of dreams?

I think often about my four young friends whom I met on the journey to Babylon. I worry over their fate. What is happening to them in the palace of Nebuchadnezzar? Will they forget our God? Will they succumb to the allurements of the demon-infested city? It is likely that we will never again see each other face to face. Despite the promise of our bond when last we met at the temple of Marduk, man's memory is short and time is long. Will they remember me and pray for me? There are now so many of us here in this hateful land that it is impossible to keep track of them all, very difficult to remember more than a few when they have been taken out of sight and mind.

As I do each night, by force of will I murmur their names, lest I forget them. Hananiah, Mishael, Azariah, Daniel. I pray for them to stand fast in the face of all temptation. Their goodness will probably be known only in the heart of the Most High, for they will pass out of memory and remain unknown to the generations that follow ours.

Aye, this is a grief. It is a deep grief to see the flowering of such godly qualities in the young and to know that these can be swept away too easily by the power of a deadly culture and by force of circumstance. Man forgets. As our forefathers forgot the marvels the Lord had done for them to release them from captivity in Egypt, to bring them safely across the divided sea, to feed them in the wastelands. Even so did they hanker back to the melons and onions and stewpots of Egypt, preferring slavery to an ache in the belly. And worse, for they thought that idols would alleviate their hunger, and they fashioned a golden calf to worship in the desert. They forgot the One who sustained their very life. Forgetting, forgetting, forgetting.

I, too, must not forget. I must remember the man of light who came to me in a dream, the peace he brought, the courage and consolation he gave. I have not felt him close since my childhood and early youth, and felt only a breath of him, a brief touch, when I was leaving Israel. Since then, I mainly feel the emotions associated with our struggle to survive: food, shelter, laboring hard and well, cautious engagement with our captors, seeing to the needs of my fellow exiles. And, above all, my feelings for Leah. Because of her, I have been blessed with great riches of the *heart*, but even as I experience this new kind of happiness, there remains in me an abiding sense, quietly in the background, that something is missing—perhaps the priesthood to which I devoted my life until captivity. I recall the moments of joyous prayer when I served at the Temple, lost to me forever. Now in prayer I feel nothing. Year after year, I feel nothing. Is this interior desolation of *spirit* an extension of the desolation of our captivity? Or is it a lack in myself, a fault or a hidden sin? I do not know. As always, I fail to understand.

13

The Bridge

TWICE A YEAR, in the month of Elul and the month of Adar, the governor who threatened to burn me alive comes to Kebar for a day or two. It is a relief that I have not once seen his wife since then. He and his second-in-command have their seat of authority in Tel-abib, but of course they have their deputies who live here in Kebar. I presume that the higher officials come to inspect these men's audits of the town's accounts and to receive a periodic report on the activities of the Judahites. They seem to approve the expansion of our fields and commerce.

After the most recent visit of the governor and his retinue, the town authorities announce that Tel-abib has ordered the construction of a bridge across the river Kebar, between the town and our village, and that the *Y'hudi* must build it. This bridge will increase our prosperity, we are informed, as Kebarites do not enjoy wetting the hems of their garments or risking their purchases during a crossing. It is now midsummer, and the water is at its lowest. The project must begin immediately.

Without any reason comprehensible to myself, I am disturbed by the idea.

A bridge goes in both directions, I think. *What passes across it may be good or evil.*

Then I consider that it is always man who carries good and evil within himself. Good and evil dwell on both sides of the river. Moreover, bridge or no bridge, good and evil may be transported by wading back and forth across the ford. Do our unmarried men still frequent the women of Kebar?

Is this, then, the root cause of my disturbance—that the new bridge will make it easier for the passage of sinful intentions? And will the swifter passage be a dangerous thing in more than one way, enabling us to grow presumptuous as we walk dry-footed across the water? By saving us time and effort, will it train us to indifference regarding the continual need to discern our actions? Will it unite the town and village in such a way that they meld together into one thing, the union of the pagan nations and the remnant of Judah? At all times in the past, such intermingling has brought disaster.

Yet every progress in life comes with this basic problem embedded in it. How will we choose to use the new development? Will we master it, or will it master us, changing us beyond recognition and, in the end, bringing about the loss of our identity?

I ponder the matter this way and that, thinking of the different kinds of men who divide our people internally: the apostate become an idolater who longs for others to join him; then the believer who denies nothing of our faith but appoints himself a prophet, delivering false prophecies; and now these learned men who would never deny the one true God but seek to weaken his authority. Each of them in his way proposes a path he wants our people to follow.

Say, rather, that each proposes a bridge—bridges over an abyss.

Of course, a bridge between earth and Paradise would be a blessing way. And a bridge between earth and Gehenna would be a path leading to torment. But the bridge that appears to lead to Paradise but bends back toward Gehenna may be the worst bridge of all.

By the Rivers of Babylon

My mind begins to blur; I am desperate for sleep. Casting all these deliberations aside, I conclude:

The bridge on the river Kebar will be made of wood, and such a bridge is neither good nor evil in itself. The good and evil it will lead to depends on us, on how we choose to use it. This will be our test.

In the months of Elul and early Tisri, our workmen are involved in cutting poplar trees and transferring the fallen trunks to the riverside. Long are these boles and very heavy, but with twenty or thirty men carrying each one, it is not a backbreaking task. Some of us are appointed to build a brick pier in the middle of the ford, as the bottom is hardest there. Kiln-dried bricks in great numbers are dumped by the shore on the town side of the river. I am one of six bricklayers. After scooping the river bottom flat, we work quickly before the current and silting can undo our work. We lay large clay bricks underwater as a base, and for mortar we use bitumen, supplied by the Kebarites, brought in buckets by town slaves—not Hebrews. In the surprisingly short time of three days, the pier is completed. It is solid through and through, six feet to a side, rising eight feet above the water level, sufficiently high to ensure the bridge's survival in spring when the river is in full spate.

We pause in our labors for the Sabbath, which allows the mortar to dry still harder, and on the following day the poplar boles are lifted into place. It is a soft wood, smooth barked and very aromatic. With pleasure, many men use adzes, axes, and knives to flatten the tops. The chips float away downstream, and we are cheered to see children from both sides of the river leaping in and playing with them as toy boats.

To see children play! It is an unexpected delight for me. As I watch these little ones laughing and wading, briefly intermingling the two races, I think how blessed beyond all human joys is the gift of a child. In time, Leah and I will have one of our own. Many, I hope. Then comes the recurring worry: it is now nearly two years since our wedding and she has not yet conceived.

One evening I am feeling well satisfied, for I have at last captured a cockerel. Earlier in the day, as I was pounding pegs to secure logs on the bridge, I spotted a half-mad bird racing past me, pursued by a cat. I blocked the cat and then scurried as fast as I could on my own pursuit. I captured the cockerel where it was hiding in the thicker bushes by the river bank. It raked my forearms with its spurs and stabbed me with its beak, but I was jubilant nonetheless. It now resides in the wicker pen with our little rust hen.

It is very beautiful, with shimmering black feathers, red comb, and a purple fan-tail. Ruth and Leah laugh and clap their hands when I show it to them. The bird struts about pompously, crowing and fluffing its feathers, and then applies itself to the business of mating.

"Ah, see how the Lord has blessed us," exclaims Ruth. "Fertile, fertile, those two, with plenty of chicks to follow!"

A few hours later, I have just laid the final brick to the floor of our house. Leah is moving quietly about the kitchen side of the room. I am amazed as always that this wondrous woman is my wife. I am so happy to have something to give her.

"Twice blessed is this day," I say to her. "A cockerel of our own, and now the floor is done."

"The floor is very fine," she replies with a quick smile. "The bricks fit so tightly, and you have laid them so smoothly. Thank you, my husband."

As she turns away to resume whatever she was doing, I

notice a certain tilt of her head, a moisture in her eyes, her slight frown as she busies herself with inconsequential tasks.

"Leah, I sense a hurt in you. Has someone given you insult or—"

"No, nothing. Neither slights nor harm," she says. "It has been a good day."

"Yet something troubles you. Please tell me."

At first she will not answer. Finally, she places her hand on her abdomen.

"Still no child, Yezekiel. With my whole soul I yearn to give you a son or daughter."

I put my arms around her and hold her closely. I can feel her sorrow in the trembling of her flesh.

"If it be the Lord's holy will, one day a child will be given to us," I murmur soothingly.

"But it may not be his will for us," she says with a sob in her throat.

Lacking an adequate reply, I cast about in my mind to find reasons why the Most High would withhold fertility. Then, foolishly thinking it might console her, I say: "Leah, at times I ask myself if it is wise to bring a child into the world in these darkest of days."

She covers my mouth with the palm of her hand. "Never, my husband, never speak this way. It is not ours to judge his giving and not giving. Even so, Yezekiel, he is the Lord of Life."

"He is the Lord of Life," I say, ashamed of my momentary doubt.

"Perhaps the fault is mine."

"I see no fault in you—you, the flower of Israel. If there be faults, they are all mine."

"I may be barren."

Now it is my turn to gently cover her mouth.

"If barrenness is to be our lot, it would not be the end of all hope. Think of Sarah, our mother in faith. Think of Samson's mother and the Shunammite woman visited by Elisha—all barren, and in the end all fruitful beyond measure."

She smiles, and we step apart.

"I have made a special bread for you," she says, bustling about her kitchen. "It is well risen, sweet with honey and nutmeg. Come, let us eat it together."

"Let us eat it together."

Months pass. The hen broods on her nest, the cockerel strides about imperiously, guarding her. I have seen it harry and destroy a snake that crept into the pen. It has torn a scorpion apart without being stung by its tail. The gleanings from the fields provide ample feed for the birds, but they are also voracious for insects, and thus our lives are becoming easier in this regard, too. Daily, Leah brings them water in a jug, pouring it through a gap in the wicker into the clay bowl I fashioned for them. When I return from work at the end of each day, I bring them handfuls of grass, for they are avid for greens as well. *I am your servant*, I tell them.

Full moon gives way to star-filled nights, and then comes another moon. The peeping of chicks is now constant music outside our window. Life is the primary rule of the Lord's creation—life succeeding unto life unto life unto eternity. Though death entered the world, corrupting the garden we once knew, driving us east of Eden, I pray it may not enter here.

One morning I cross the bridge with my crew and our overseer, on the way to dredging a canal. As we approach the town gates, three servants emerge, dragging what look to be three dead bodies wrapped in sackcloth. Nearby stands a waiting pair of donkeys harnessed to a cart. The bodies are dropped to the ground, and the servants hastily retreat, holding their noses. One of them calls out to our overseer. I have learned enough of the Babylonian language to know that he is asking for the loan of one of the Hebrew *wardu*, to help with some task. The overseer points to me and beckons me over.

"You, *Y'hudi*, get these bodies loaded. Go with the driver to help him at the dump."

He and my crew head off down the road.

I am heartsick as I lift the first body onto the cart.

"Hurry, hurry," says the driver. "Why do you make my life a misery, you foot-dragger?"

Though he is speaking Babylonian, I hear a strong accent in his diction.

After lifting two more bodies, I am done, panting for breath and trying not to inhale the odor of decay. Though they are wrapped in sackcloth I can tell that two of them are men and one an old woman, with wisps of white hair showing through the loose weave.

"Come, step up now," the driver insists with his gnawing voice. "The smell is bad and will get worse, so let us finish this as quickly as possible. The valley of the dead awaits its food."

I climb onto the seat beside him. Now I note that he has only one complete arm, the other amputated below the elbow. He flicks the reins with his single hand, and the donkeys pull the cart forward on creaking wheels. He drives it across the bridge. Arriving at the edge of the Portion, we turn and follow a lane that heads downriver.

"A grim task we are given today," I say.

He shrugs. "No more than usual."

"Who are these people we bury?"

"Wardu. Sick ones, old ones."

"Are you a servant of Kebar?"

"No, I am a slave like you."

"From which land do you come?"

"Assyria, in the north," he says with a jerk of his head to indicate the direction. "Sixteen years ago I was taken prisoner, when Nabopolassar, the father of Nebuchadnezzar, besieged and conquered my city."

"What is your city?"

"Harran."

"Harran," I say with interest.

"Yes, it is east of Karkemish. Do you know it?"

"I know of it, for it is a city important to my people."

"Aye, a mighty place on the trade routes. But who are your people? Are you the Habiru? They say the Habiru of times past were bandits and runaway slaves, the lot of them."

"No, we are the *Hebrews* of the Kingdom of Judah."

"So many slaves these days, so many! People from nations near and far, seized by the Babylonian hand."

He shakes his head, puzzling over the matter a while, then proceeds to name a few nations that have been brought captive into this land. I am surprised that he is not fully aware of who we are. But then, by the look of his face, the dullness of his eyes, I see that he is not a man given to reflection —or perhaps through long servitude he has ceased to think at all, no longer caring about anything other than his own wants and duties.

After passing the last of the Portion's fields, he clicks his tongue at the donkeys and reins them left onto a dusty cartwheel track leading to the swell of hills on the horizon.

"Judah," he murmurs at last, coming to some conclusion.

"I have heard mention of it. Ah, yes, now I remember. You Judahites were brought here four years ago. I was then in Mari, cleaning canals."

"A hard task with one arm."

"I had two at the time. Last year I was caught thieving from my master, and lost this one as punishment." He lifts the stump to show me. "Then I was sent to Nippur to work for a camel merchant, feeding the animals one handful of straw at a time. He soon grew tired of my slow ways and sent me south to this lowest of low places." He sighs. "Such an end for me, me with my mighty name."

"What is your name?"

He looks askance at me. "Tell me first, rude one, what is *your* name?"

"I am Yezekiel ben Buzi."

"They call me Saggo, which comes from Sargon, and I am son of Shamash, my father named for the sun god."

"When you lived in Harran, did you ever hear of Chaldeans from Ur who dwelled long ago in your city, or lived near it? They had cattle and a flock of sheep. Their names were Abraham son of Terah, and his wife, Sarah."

"No, I never heard of them." He wrinkles his brow, and a long silence ensues as he chews on an elusive thought.

"I do remember a stone someone put up in ages past to honor an Abram and Sarai. We Harranites remember because if you touch the stone, it will give you good fortune." He sighs. "Well, I touched the stone, and look where I am now. If my mind does not cheat me, the legend says old Abram and Sarai went westward to a land called Canaan, and there they became a big tribe. That is the story told about them. I do not believe it myself."

"You should believe it, because it is true. I am of the

tribes that came from them. And some of these tribes have become a nation called Judah."

"Huh, so Harran has spawned a nation! Ah, this old head of mine, always forgetting, forgetting."

"It is how we are, Saggo bet Shamash, as much in my land of Judah as in Babylon and Assyria."

"You say true. We grow old, we grow old, and none can stop it. The seed sprouts, blossoms, bears fruit, and withers." He laughs to himself and jerks his head to the cartload behind him. "And then it goes back into the soil."

"We Hebrews bury our dead in caves or make a stone cairn above the bodies of our deceased."

"Nary a cave or stone in these parts. That's why we are going where we are going today."

"The valley of the dead, you called it."

He laughs. "The noble Tombs of the Wardu!"

"I have not seen it."

"Not a pretty place, that. But surely you know of it, for your people die like everyone else."

"During the first years after our arrival, some of our dead were laid to rest there, but the Kebarites now allow us to make burials in the soil. We have a place near our olive orchard."

"A waste of good land!"

"Is not the valley a waste of good land?"

"It is barren soil, nothing grows there, too far from water, and the gods are grudging with their rain around here. In my homeland, where we have hills by our sides and mountains not far away, clouds grow heavy and often weep on us, because our women are good at wailing when the god dies, and they jump and laugh when he pops back up out of the—"

By the Rivers of Babylon

I can no longer bear listening to the man. The cart is now climbing a low rise, and I am suddenly full of unnamed dread.

When we arrive at the crest, the driver yanks the reins, bringing the donkeys to a halt. I stare without moving at what now appears before me. Carrion birds lift from the valley floor, rising and circling. Clouds of buzzing flies fill the air. Skulking dogs are snarling at the base of the slope below us, rummaging in a heap of torn clothing and partly devoured human bodies. Beyond them is an expanse of bleached bones. My gorge rises, the stench is sickening.

"Just toss them off," growls the driver as I get down from the cart. "Quickly now, quickly!"

Suppressing my revulsion, I pull each of the bodies off the cart and lay them carefully onto the ground, trying to preserve what little dignity they have. There is nothing more I can do. A swarm of flies immediately covers them.

"Kick them down the hill!"

Ignoring him, I bow my head, invoking the Lord's mercy on the souls of these dead strangers.

This is how we all end, I think. *Slaves and kings, elders and prophets, poor and rich, none excepted.*

"What a fuss you make, Hebrew!" Saggo sneers. "The dogs and jackals will be feasting before our dust settles on the road."

I climb back up onto the seat beside him and turn away from the valley of horror.

The false teachers have declined in number, half of them dispersed to cities where their learning will be put to use by Babylon. Enough of them remain in the Portion to erode the people's faith, but they no longer conduct public lectures approved by the elders. Indeed, the elders have warned the people against their teachings. Nevertheless, I see evidence that these subtle underminers continue to spread their ideas, instructing followers in their own homes.

The elders have invited me to be more active at the house of prayer. Standing before the people, I often recite from the Sacred Scriptures, whatever I recall from the five great books and also from Isaiah. More than ever, I am grateful for the "punishment" the master at the house of studies once gave me, for my memory of the prophet's words awakens with unusual clarity. How unique and powerful his prophecies were! How far-seeing! And why should it not be so, for the spirit of the Lord himself was speaking through him.

After prayer one night, Shimeon and I are seated by his fire.

"Yezekiel, you have told us that Isaiah said the Lord would refine our people in the furnace of affliction. It seems to me that we are now living the prophecy in part, but not in whole, for the great majority of our people remain in Israel, and their lives continue much as before."

"This is true, and yet we must not forget that a prophecy may unfold over a span of many years, the parts slowly becoming the whole."

"Forgive me, I should have remembered that. And when I come to think about it, Jeremiah surely agrees with Isaiah."

"Generations ago, Isaiah foretold what would happen to us at the hands of Babylon. Even so, he promised that the Lord would fulfill his purpose on Babylon, for his mighty arm would be against the Chaldeans."

"This has not yet come to pass."

"Not yet. Not yet, but if we are true sons of the Most High, we must place our trust in the promise—however slow in coming it may be."

Shimeon bows his head with a woeful look. "Babylon

goes from strength to strength, wickedness to wickedness, ever swelling the numbers of captives. O Yezekiel, there be times when I fail to see the mighty arm of the Lord."

I am surprised by this, for throughout these past years it has always been he who strengthens *us*.

"Shimeon, was it not you who rebuked the false prophets who foretold a swift return? Do you now doubt Jeremiah's prophecy?"

He shakes his head. "No, I do not doubt it. Yet, if truth be told, Yezekiel, I grow weary, I grow weary."

"Fear not, for the restoration will come. Isaiah foretold that a man named Cyrus, far in the future, will conquer Babylon and return us to Jerusalem."

"Cyrus? A Persian name?"

"That is what is written. It is a wholly mysterious passage, and thus I cannot explain how or when it will come about."

"Write it down, Yezekiel, write it down!"

Thus, at the elders' urging, I accept to undertake the task of writing Isaiah's prophecies, feeling much worry that my memory may play me false. They go so far as to purchase well-cured lambskin hides at no small expense. I make rude ink from a mixture of bitumen, olive oil, and ashes, and I whittle a twig to a fine point. Before writing the first word, however, I hesitate with the point of the stick poised over the vellum, flooded with fear. Perhaps it is a necessary fear of the Lord, a holy fear. I do not know for certain, but when I close my eyes and pray for inspiration, a strong light appears in my mind, and with it peace. *Begin*, it seems to say, *just begin!*

I open my eyes, dip the twig into the ink pot, and write: *Hear, O heavens, and give ear, O earth, for the Lord has spoken:*

The Bridge

Sons have I reared and brought up, but they have rebelled against me.

Then the rest follows.

Shimeon asks me to teach him to read and write. From his younger years this old fisherman has known a few letters of the *aleph-bet*, but he cannot put them together into words, still less connect the words into streams of thought. As the lessons get underway, he learns with agonizing slowness. Then one night when we sit together in his dooryard, I use a small pottery shard to inscribe a line in the moist cake of clay at his feet:

Hear, O Israel, the Lord our God, the Lord is one.

As if a key has turned in a lock, Shimeon erupts in jubilation, his eyes lighting up, his hands leaping to the sky. Now he understand how it works. I smile with him in this shared success, and smile to myself, thinking that this very wise man has until now had no formal education in the ways of knowledge—another proof that intelligence is not wisdom.

The annual rains return. The field work eases off for a time. The river is rising. Soon we will be flooding the cropland, and after that will come sowing of seed. Until then, I work daily in Kebar's brickworks. It is less onerous labor than the toils of canal and field, though it taxes my muscles in new ways and can give me burns if I am not careful when removing newly fired bricks from the kilns. All in all, it is a welcome respite, renewing my body and spirits.

On a morning near the end of the rains, the clouds part and a many-colored bow in the heavens appears, arching gloriously over the place in the west where Jerusalem lies. Kebarites run out onto their rooftops, the people of the Portion hasten to gather in the village commons, both communities delighting in the display, exclaiming and pointing. It is a perfect arch. It is very beautiful. It reminds me of the promise to Noah after the Great Flood.

After the bow melts away into the sky and the last of the clouds disperse, I work for another two hours until the overseer tells me and my crew that we can leave. He informs us that in honor of the return of the god Tammuz from the dead, tomorrow will be a day of rest. As an additional favor, we are permitted to take home sprigs of grapes, a heap of which are overspilling a copper vat.

"Were these grapes consecrated to the god?" I ask him in Chaldean.

He snorts, saying, "Not these. They are fresh-cut, for next season's wine, for making staggering and happiness."

I wait until the others have taken theirs, and then I select two large sprigs, heavy with their fruit, to bring to Leah and Ruth. Gladly bearing this burden, I walk from the town gates to the bridge, noting that Kebarite women are returning from the Portion carrying bundles of bread and other purchases.

Just as I step onto the bridge, I notice a woman ahead of me, walking my way with a rug over her shoulder and a bundle of bread clamped under one arm. With the other she is dragging a child by the hand, a girl of about ten years who looks very irritated, insolently scolding her mother. They are passing the middle of the bridge, where there sits a small girl from our village, with her legs dangling over the water. She is singing to herself, paying no attention to the Kebarites.

In an instant, the insolent girl yanks free from her mother's hand, and with an expression of pure malice she pushes the younger child off the bridge. I drop the grapes and run along the bridge, arriving at the midpoint just as the woman begins screeching at her daughter. I look over the edge, hoping to find the victim unharmed. But she is nowhere to be seen. The water is deeper where she has fallen, for the river gouges a hole where it spills over the ford. Now I see in the muddy whorls the shape of a child floating away, face down and sinking. I jump in after her, plunging until my feet hit the silted bottom. I do not know how to swim, but the water is not yet deep enough to drown me; my head stretches upward, breaks the surface and gulps air.

I grope with painful slowness toward the place where I spotted the girl, reaching blindly until finally I catch the edge of her garment. The current is pushing me, trying to topple me, but I am able to take hold of the girl's body and lift her higher. When her head breaks the surface, it lolls sideways, with water spilling from the mouth.

Now I push desperately toward the riverbank, and even as my feet touch the shore I hear screeching on the bridge above me:

"Look what you have done!" shrills the mother's voice. "You have killed one of them!"

I sit down on the bank and hold the drowned child to my chest, rocking her.

Now the girl on the bridge is kicking her mother, even as the mother seizes her by the rope of her hair and tries to yank her away from the scene.

"It is just a *wardu*!" shrieks the child. "It is a stupid little one!"

"It would have grown into a valuable servant! You have destroyed someone's property!"

"It is a nothing person!"

But I can listen to no more of this. Heartbroken, I lay the child's body on the ground, and then, without thinking, perhaps impelled by denial that the *ruach*, the breath of life, can be so easily, so wickedly snatched from an innocent one, I open her mouth and with my mouth upon hers I force a strong breath into it. Her chest swells then collapses. Again I force air into her mouth, and again the chest inflates and collapses. Once more, and then on its own the chest rises and falls and rises again. A cough sends a gush of water out of the child's throat. More and more coughing and spurting follow until finally the child cries out in a feeble voice, *"Ee-mah, Ee-mah!"* She is calling for her mother.

I help her sit up, and then I carry her in my arms to the village. A frantic woman runs toward me with arms outstretched, takes the child into her arms, and carries her away. I note with relief that the child is now crying loudly as she tells her mother what happened.

"I fell into the river, *Ee-mah*. I was singing, and then I fell."

The year passes with the changing seasons—plowing, flooding, planting, harvesting, storing. Sun and rain, heat and coolness, wind and silence.

One evening, an overseer comes to the door of our home and enters without knocking.

"You, the one they call Ben Buzi, a visitor to Kebar will speak with you tomorrow. Go to the city gates at the midday hour."

"I will be at work in the brickyard and cannot leave it for more than a moment."

"I will speak with the brick master."

"Who is the visitor?" I ask.

"That is none of your affair. Just do as you are told."

The Bridge

"I will be there."

He sniffs and curdles his face. "And wash before you meet the visitor."

Next day, I work throughout the morning, then ask permission to leave. The brick master dismisses me, I ladle water from a barrel and wash my face and hands as best I can, dry myself with a rag, then walk to the town gates.

There I am met by a Babylonian servant whom I do not know. He leads me through streets I have never walked before to a house backing onto the northern wall, not far from the high-storied house of Kebar's administration.

The servant directs me through the doorway into a wide room with one window. A breeze is billowing the indigo curtain inward and outward; it is decorated with tinkling brass bells at the hem. The light is dim.

"Come, if you please," says a voice in a courteous tone. As my eyes adjust to the gloom, I see before me the form of a man seated on a rug. Beside him on the floor is a tray with baskets of sweet pastries and fruit, alongside a carafe and two cups.

"Sit by me," he says, patting the rug.

Warily I sit down, wondering what this is about.

"You are well, Yezekiel ben Buzi?" asks the man.

Now I recognize him. It is the law-teacher I conversed with some years ago.

"I am well, Abil-ilishu," I reply.

"You remember me."

"As you remember me."

"Our conversation was memorable. Have you recounted it to others?"

"No one."

"That is good."

I wait, still ignorant of his purpose in summoning me.

"Please," he says with a host's gesture to the food. "Have some food. Wine?"

I am both grateful and suspicious of this largesse. Abil-ilishu says nothing as he watches me eat and drink. I try not to bolt it, hungry as I am. The noon distribution of bread at the brickyard is never copious.

When I am finished, he pours himself a cup of wine and a second for me.

"Have you come to better understanding of the Babylo-nian mind?" he asks as I sip from my cup.

"No," I answer.

"Neither have I," he replies with a wry smile.

As once before, I am struck by how very unusual this man is, so unlike his countrymen. I recall that he travels widely among the nations.

We have been speaking in his language, but I now remem-ber that he is conversant in mine.

"I thank you for this generous meal," I say in Hebrew, "though I am intrigued by your reason for bidding me here."

With a thoughtful look, he replies in kind. "Ah, of course you are. Doubtless in the secret places of your thoughts, you ask yourself if I intend to plumb the hidden affairs of your people."

I say nothing, taking another sip.

"Rest assured, I am not seeking that." He pauses and ex-amines my eyes closely. I resist the instinct to flinch away.

"Two reasons do I lay before you. But let us ponder the first. It is this: I would ask, if you agree, that we speak to-gether openly, as we did at our last meeting."

"To speak of what matters?" I inquire.

"I see you misread me. It is not the subject that concerns me so much as the openness."

"But why me, a slave?"

"I do not think of you as a slave."

This is startling. How can he or any of his people not think of us as their slaves?

"I hope that you do not consider me one of your masters," he adds.

He waits for me to respond, but I can produce no reply. Of course they are our masters, and he is one of them.

He continues. "You have obtained a surprising fluency in the Chaldean language. You are a man of education and intelligence, endowed with clear perception."

"My education is limited, so too my intelligence. As for perception—"

"I would add to your qualities the rare gift of humility."

"You flatter me, lord."

"Do not call me *lord*. Let us speak as men equal under the sun."

"We are not equal under the sun, as you well know."

"Yet you are free in your mind and soul." He pauses and sighs.

After considering a few moments I say, "Throughout four years in Babylon, never have I met a man like you."

"I think you mean that never have you met a Babylonian like me."

"Yes," I say, "if we are speaking openly."

"We are, and I am glad of it. But do not think too highly of me."

For the first time I smile, and am forced to suppress a laugh. He presumes that I think highly of him? In their humblest moments, even the best of Babylonians cannot leave aside their sense of superiority.

"Of what, then, should we speak?" I ask.

"Tell me more about the one you call Most High God. Does this not imply that there are lesser gods?"

"No, for us the name means that he is highest above all created things. Of him we know only his dealings with us through ages upon ages since the time of Abraham—even farther back unto the time of Noah. Have you heard of Noah?"

"I have read the flood account."

"You surely know the story of Gilgamesh. Which of the two do you believe is the truer version, your Gilgamesh or our Noah, written by Moses?"

"I have heard the stories of Gilgamesh all my life," he replies. "It is a fascinating tale—or I should say a compilation of early Assyrian and Sumerian legends and poems, transmitted in the Akkadian language. But when I studied your book of *Genesis* during my time in Jerusalem, I knew beyond all doubt that I was reading an account of actual events. The epic of Gilgamesh is a poem of great significance, containing some truths pressed through a filter, ever changing as the ages passed one after another, containing inventions and mirages. For example, he was not only a hero, he was semi-divine."

"Our Noah was not divine. The One who spoke to him and guided him to make the great ship is the only God, the living God, the true God. He is invisible. He is wholly spirit, and thus we are commanded to make no graven images of him."

"Ah, that is why your Temple is empty."

"It is not empty. His presence fills it."

"That may be so. In truth, I did feel something there in the outer court, something entirely new to me. I did not know what it was, but it drew me. I felt a yearning that had no object, no name. This was before the conquest, of course, and thus I was prohibited from entering the Temple. I could not explore farther . . . say, rather, *deeper.*"

"You are a man who seeks truth, Abil-ilishu, this I know."

"Am I? I dare to hope so."

"He is real," I say. "He *is* who he says he is. We call him *He Who Is*, for he existed before the beginning of time and will exist forever. His name for himself is *I Am*."

"But why no multiple gods to assist him?"

"He has countless servant spirits to assist him. We call them *malakh*, which means *messenger*, though they are far greater than simple messengers."

As I continue to describe at length the richness of our faith, and the composition of the divine order in creation, Abil-ilishu leans closer, listening with an expression resembling that of an eager child. There comes a moment when he seems surfeited. He leans back and inhales deeply, pondering what I have told him. Staring at the rug, he shakes his head, and yet it seems to me that this does not express rejection of what I have told him, but, instead, reveals a state of wondering amazement.

Sitting straighter, he looks at me and says, "More wine?"

"Thank you, no."

"More food?"

This, too, I decline.

He pauses for a few moments over some private thought. Looking up at me he says directly and sincerely, "I realize how difficult it is for you to trust us. We hold you in exile by force, even as we welcome you as if you were free guests. This is a contradictory message, which of course is repugnant to you and which you must dismiss as blatant falsehood."

I refrain from replying directly to this statement of the obvious.

"You said you have two purposes," I say.

"Yes. What you have just told me about your God, and

the manner in which you related it, convince me that the second is more urgent than I thought."

"Urgent?"

"Yezekiel, it is within my power to remove you from this hard place. Do you have family here?"

"I have a wife and mother-in-law."

"No children, then."

"No children."

"I ask now whether you would like to live in a city, where your duties would be more suited to your knowledge and character."

"A city? Do you mean Tel-abib?"

"Here you are about three hundred, is that correct?"

"Little more than three hundred, yes."

"Tel-abib has a thousand Hebrews, perhaps more. They live in their own town just outside the city. While the strong are mainly engaged in our fields and canals, a sizeable number pursue less arduous tasks. They have developed considerable industry and commerce of their own and have built a small library and houses of study."

"Do they have a house of prayer?"

He nods. "A house of prayer as well. I can arrange that you be moved whenever you wish."

I fall silent, my blood racing, my mind spinning. To have an opportunity to study, to pray without anxiety and exhaustion, to leave behind the endlessly draining labors, seems too much to hope for.

"I see that you desire it," Abil-ilishu continues. "I should say that it need not be Tel-abib. You may choose from a number of places."

"Such as?"

"Babylon the Great itself."

I think, *Never, never that evil place!*

"There are several other fine cities along the Euphrates, and a few on the Tigris as well. Even so, I would suggest that you consider Ur."

Ur! Abraham's city!

"Ur is where I was born and raised," he says. "I have my home there."

"But what would I do in Ur?" I ask in a choked voice.

"You might work as a translator and scribe. You would receive no wages for that, at least not from the government or other employers. If you agree, however, you could work for me in those capacities. In payment, you would receive a small wage and a house to live in, attached to my house."

"Are there Hebrews living in Ur?"

"Many. They, too, have their own commerce and houses of prayer and study. You would not be alone."

"Your offer is generous in every way, Abil-ilishu. I am staggered by it."

"My house has a pleasant prospect, close by the river. It is cooler there, with breezes flowing inland from the port, for the waters of the gulf are not far away. The quarter in which I live is quiet compared to other sectors. I live on the street of a temple dedicated to a god once revered by the Philistines of Ekron. Do you know Ekron?"

"A city west of Jerusalem, I recall."

"The Philistines were your enemies of old, were they not?"

"Yes, very terrible enemies," I say, thinking of David facing Goliath and his army.

"They were traders, mainly upon the sea, and once kept merchant-agents in Ur, though few now remain. They built the temple to their god Baal-zebul in those days."

"Baal-zebub," I mutter.

My host smiles in appreciation. "A clever play on words.

You change Baal-zebul, the 'Prince Baal' to Baal-zebub, 'Lord of Flies'."

Lord of death, lord of the devouring flies.

"Well, no matter. You will meet with no enemies in Ur. Devotees are few now, and, as I said, it is a quiet street. Please consider it, Yezekiel. I know you would be well contented there."

I look up from my musing, thinking that what he offers is so immense a promise of liberation that I can scarcely refuse it. In fact, I intend to accept.

"I am grateful beyond words, Abil-ilishu. Yet I must first discuss this with my wife."

"Do discuss it, and then give me your answer. I leave Kebar for Nippur two days hence, returning shortly after. Then I will bring you and your family to Ur."

As we bid each other farewell, he tells me, "You may go home now. I have arranged with your overseer that you work no more today."

Walking in a happy daze toward the bridge, I note that both he and I have presumed my answer will be positive and that Leah and Ruth will be enthusiastic about the offer. That it is an offer and not a command is encouraging.

I walk onto the bridge with a light step and have just come to the middle when I stop and stand still. I do not know why I do so. There is no compulsion, no inner doubt or hesitation that paralyzes me. No, my body is simply immobile. A measureless peace descends upon me. I close my eyes and feel it flow into every part of me. This peace is like a river of oil, warm and very gentle. And with it comes a knowing—a knowledge sent from beyond the frontiers of all feeling and thought:

We will not be moving to Ur. My place is here.

14

The Archer

O N THE DAY OF PREPARATION for the feast of Passover, I am regretting that I cannot afford to buy a lamb for my family. I go to the butcher, hoping to beg a little meat for tomorrow's meal. I stand with several other people watching the slaughter. Though I have seen this many times in my life, my heart is strangely heavy as I observe the lambs' silence before the sacrifice of their lives. They neither writhe nor cry out. It brings to my mind that time when I was a boy and our family brought a lamb to the Altar of Sacrifice at the Temple, the warmth of the lamb in my arms, its pitiful bleating as it smelled the blood of other victims. I remember my prayer to the Most High, beseeching his mercy to fall upon Israel.

Grudgingly, the butcher allows me to dip my fingers into a bowl of blood. After hastening back to our house, lest the blood dry on the way, I anoint our doorposts and lintels. I do not know what moves me to do it, but the sign I make with the blood is two strokes that cross each other. Perhaps it implies arms embracing the directions of the earth, north, south, east, and west, for the Lord is master of all the world. It may be that such a sign points with one stroke to the world around us, and with the other to the heavens above. Man's soul is where the strokes meet. I do not know if this is a fanciful illusion. I hope it is not unpleasing to the Lord.

By the Rivers of Babylon

The *shofar* trumpets, heralding the beginning of the Sabbath.

On the holy day, Leah and I and Ruth eat our meal standing, according to the ritual ordained by the Lord when our people were captive in Egypt. There are bitter herbs and unleavened bread and, blessedly, a piece of roasted lamb, which Ruth has obtained by trading one of her weavings. After giving thanks, we walk through the village to the house of prayer.

Because the house of prayer is densely packed for the Passover, we sit down on the ground outside with hundreds of other village folk ringing the open doorway. I earnestly hope that the "prophets" will remain silent. I pray that the spirit of the Lord will illumine them with truth. I ask, as well, that if there be any secret or open idolaters among us, they will repent and turn to the one true God. I pray for my own deeper conversion. I pray for blessings upon Leah and her mother and for all of us.

There are about a dozen new faces tonight, men whom I have never before seen in the village. It is not uncommon that Hebrew slaves from other places are brought here to swell the work force, sometimes after there have been deaths or accidents, but more often when our overseers are planning a major expansion of fields and canals.

Among the newcomers, I see a face that strikes me oddly. I feel the intuitive sense of recognition, though I cannot place where I might have seen him before. He is listening raptly to Shimeon's account of the scourges that struck Egypt to make pharaoh let our people go.

The more I look at this newcomer, the more I become certain I know him. Yet nothing about his appearance prompts a memory. He is about my age, short and thin, garbed in a rough sackcloth robe. His face is set in an expression of gravity as he listens attentively, and, unlike his restless companions, he remains without any movement of head and limbs. Strangely, his skull is shorn of hair.

Then the certainty comes: It is Issa ben Ephraim, whom I knew when I began my studies in Jerusalem. He made me a pair of sandals before departing for his home in Idumea.

At the end of the recitation of the story of the exodus, all of us rise and sing in loud, deep voices the king-psalm praising the Lord for our deliverance from Egypt, while Eli and others strum mightily on their harps and lyres. Soon after, a stream of people emerge from the prayer house, mingling with those outside, sharing greetings and beginning to disperse in every direction. In the crowd, Issa is lost to my sight.

And then he is suddenly standing before me.

"Issachar ben Ephraim!" I exclaim.

"Yezekiel ben Buzi," he answers quietly.

"Who is this?" asks Ruth, examining the poor fellow dubiously.

Leah says nothing, merely gazing at Issa with interest and her habitual kindliness.

I introduce him to my family.

"This is my friend Issa," I say, "a servant of the Lord."

Issa lowers his eyes.

We bring him back to our house and sit down together by the fire. Though he has said nothing further, he seems pleased by our reunion.

"Did you have your Passover meal?" I ask him.

"No," he murmurs with a tone of regret.

With motherly concern, Leah and Ruth bring him unleavened bread, herbs, and the last morsel of lamb. He stands to receive the food into his hands and raises it above his shoulders, silently invoking a blessing. He continues standing while he hastily consumes it, according to tradition. I notice that his legs are trembling. He is extremely weary or else he has not yet eaten today—most likely both.

After giving thanks to the Lord with open palms, he sits down again on the ground. Leah offers him a sprig of grapes. Ruth places a piece of risen honey bread on his lap. Leah brings more flatbread and a bowl of olive oil in which to dip it. After this, they give him smoked fish, cheese curds, and six boiled eggs. He refuses nothing, communicating his thankfulness with a glance.

"Are you traveling through this place, or are you here to stay?" I ask him.

"To stay," he says.

The women ask him more questions, but he replies only with a word or two, not really giving any information. Nevertheless, his eyes again send streams of gratitude to them, each in turn.

For my part, I am eager to know how he has come to be here. But I keep my questions in repose until he has finished his meal.

I offer him wine from a skin. He declines and asks for water. Leah brings a cup and a jug. Again he responds with glancing eyes, shining now. Some color has returned to his cheeks, which look less sunken.

"Where will you sleep the night?" I ask him.

He slowly shakes his head. "The guards sent us across the bridge and told us to find our own shelter. They said that an overseer will assign our tasks in the morning."

"Where have you come from today?"

Issa lowers his head and rubs his eyes with the knuckles of his hand.

"A long way."

"You will stay with us, Issa," I tell him.

"I cannot," he replies.

"But where will you sleep?"

"On the ground. I must not be a burden to you."

"Nay, nay," the women protest. "You are no burden. We will put you on the roof with blankets."

Again he shakes his head and stands.

"I must go."

I rise with him and put a restraining hand on his shoulder.

"Where would you go? I have a place for you, Issa, a little brick house that is empty now, a poor thing but it will be warm and safe. It once was my house before I married."

Hesitantly, he nods his acceptance. He bows to the women and wordlessly turns to depart. I walk with him, lifting high a burning splinter of wood to light the way.

Leah runs after us and gives me a blanket, which she insists is a gift for Issa.

My first house has not yet fallen into ruin. The walls and roof are intact. The old door cloth is still there, though full of holes. When I go inside, I smell the staleness and note that animals have been rummaging here; the pigeons in the rafters have left droppings on the floor. Passing the blanket and torch to Issa, I clean the house as best I can, clearing out the debris with my bare hands and feet.

"Come in," I say when it is done. "You may stay here as long as you need."

"It is very large," he murmurs.

"It is the smallest in the Portion, which is the name we give to the village, and now this house is your own little portion."

He is swaying on his feet, and he can scarcely keep his eyes from closing.

"Lie down and take your rest," I say. "We will speak more in the morning."

With a sigh he sinks to the floor and rolls onto his side. I drape the blanket over him. Within moments, he is asleep.

Returning to our home, I find the women still awake, seated by the dying fire.

"He sleeps," I tell them. "Tomorrow he will fare better."

"That man says nothing with his mouth," Ruth remarks.

"I hope his manner is not offensive to you," I say.

"Offensive? Never. Your friend speaks much with his eyes. Deep waters are his thoughts."

I am moved by her astute observation.

"This is true," I say, "more true of him than of any other I have known."

"A prince of Judah, that one."

"He is from Idumea," I say with a note of apology.

"Out of Edom comes a sprig of Judah. This Issa redeems Esau."

Astounded, wondering how she has arrived at such a thought, I say, "May it be so."

Leah, seated beside me, puts her hand on my arm.

"See how the Lord sends you a brother in this land of desolation. He takes away your beloved brothers and now gives you a fine one in their stead."

Here is revealed my wife's extraordinary perceptions. There is no fineness in Issa's appearance. He is dirty and ragged, and his butchered hair is appalling. Though dignity is inherent in his face, his lips utter hardly a word. He is the farthest from being a prince as one can imagine.

I place my hand over Leah's, and she leans closer, resting her head on my shoulder.

I say, "Though the Lord has taken me from my family, he has given me the great treasure in you."

At dawn, before the workday begins, I hasten to my old house. Overseers have not yet arrived, so Issa and I are able to talk a while. Now, after a full night's sleep, he seems disposed to answer my questions. The tale he tells is both consoling and shocking.

"Three days ago, I and the other laborers were taken by escort from Erech, a city on the Great River, a three-day journey south of here. From before daybreak until after dusk, we were driven, resting only a few hours each night. Some of us fell on the way and will never rise again."

"I have heard of Erech," I say, recalling with a shudder the chant that the law-teacher sang to me.

"It is north of Ur, a long day's march, and southwest of Nippur by another. It is an exceedingly wicked place, being a sacred city devoted to the rites of their gods. Erech is more ancient than the city of Babylon and more evil by far."

"More evil than Babylon?"

"Legend recounts that it was one of the cities built by Nimrod in the time of the tower of pride and the scattering of language."

"What were your tasks there?"

"Work in their fields and canals, for even in the south the need for grain never ceases. All Hebrews live in mud-and-reed huts outside the city walls, close to the water and not far from swamps. It is a pestilential place. So you understand, Yezekiel, why I am overwhelmed by this splendid house." He gazes around the room with a sincere smile.

"I think of it as a rude cave, Issa."

"It is beautiful, Yezekiel, and I am very grateful for it."

"How long did you live in Erech?"

"Four years."

"Four years! But that is near the time of my own capture. I thought you were in Idumea."

"Yes, and now I must give an account of how I come to be here. Moreover, I have very good news to tell you."

I cannot imagine any good news coming from his woes.

"Just before the fall of King Jehoiachim," he begins, "your family sought refuge with mine."

"They found you!" I exclaim.

"Yes, they found us. Your father and mother, your brothers and their families and flock came by an arduous way through the mountains, from Hebron, by diverse paths down to the valley of the Sea of Salt. Sore afflicted were they by heat and thirst and lack of pasture for the sheep, as it is a desolate way and springs are scarce on that side. Even so, they lost no people and only a part of their flock, coming at last to the mountains of Seir by passing around the base of the lake."

"Why did they not go by the eastern shore, which is more verdant?"

"There are hostile towns there, as it was in the time when Moses brought the people out of the desert and began his march northward to the Jordan."

"I am overjoyed by this news, Issa."

He nods and smiles. "All praise belongs to the Lord! Our village is a little place, you understand, a few houses, a shallow water well, pasture enough for goats and a few sheep. Among ourselves we call our village 'the shelter of Moshe', for we like to think he stopped there a while, weary from his travels and needing to revive his people before moving on to confront the Moabites."

"A good name, historical or not, and indeed it was a shelter for my family. Do you know where they went next?"

"I believe they are still there. My father and mother welcomed them, inviting them to remain in our village. Long had they known of your family."

"How so?"

"They had often heard my stories about you from our days at the house of studies. You did rightly, Yezekiel, to send your family to us. Your brothers dug a new well nearby —thirty cubits in depth—and found a spring, providing enough water for us all. Also, they and my brothers worked to make a grainfield. So you see, they prosper and are safe. When the invasion came, no Babylonian troops penetrated that far south."

"I am filled with gratitude beyond words, Issa. But now tell me how you come to be here in Babylon?"

He pauses before answering.

"When news reached us of the death of King Jehoiachim and that the city was largely unharmed, we thought that soon the storm would pass and life would return to normal, that it would not be long before your family might return to your home village. Then, months later came reports that the new king, Jehoiachin, had been seized and taken away into captivity, along with large numbers of the city's populace."

"More than ten thousand."

"Your parents were sore troubled with worry over you. And it came to me that I might find you and bring you to safety. My own parents gave me their permission, and I set off around the lake, following the path by which your family had come. In time I reached Hebron, and though it was occupied by alien troops, I passed by unseen and continued northward to Jerusalem."

"Where were you captured?"

"Not far from the city. I had avoided all roads until then, keeping to the hillsides. I carried dry bread with me but was often very thirsty. Then one day I came upon a little green valley just south of Bethlehem, with a brook winding through it. Seeing that no people were about, I crept down to drink my fill and to replenish my waterskins. While I was lying on the ground with my mouth in the brook, a troop of Babylonian soldiers came up over a rise and spotted me. Foolishly, I ran. I was weary from the journey, slower of foot, and they ran faster. That is how I come to be here."

"Issa, Issa," I groan. "Forgive me. Forgive me for this burden I brought upon you."

"You brought no burden upon me. I *chose* it. I chose to go in search of you."

"Still . . ."

"Nothing is hidden from the eyes of the Lord," he says with a light in his eyes. "Our lives are in his hands."

But no more can be said, because the overseers have arrived, shouting for work crews to gather in the village commons, where the day's tasks will be allotted.

That night I recount to Leah and Ruth the story Issa told me. They are glad that my family has survived, but sorry for him.

"Poor soul, poor soul," Ruth laments. "See how he suffers for the sake of an errand."

"Unjust has been his treatment from the day I first met him," I say.

Leah considers this in her thoughtful manner but says nothing, still absorbing what I have told them. But Ruth maintains her grievance against the unfairness of life.

"That is a skin-and-bones prince, Yezekiel. Undersized and underfed."

"Keep offering him your bread, good mother," I say, breaking the mood and making the women smile.

But it is Issa who feeds *us*.

Four times a year the Babylonians grant a full day of freedom from all work, for on those days they are abandoned to revelry in honor of their gods. On those days, too, there is much slaughtering of pigs across the river; we see men chasing them and catching them, trying to hold their thrashing limbs as the knife cuts into the throat. Their squealing is a mad, demonic thing.

On one such day—I do not want to think about whatever god they are honoring, do not want its name on my lips—Issa finds me sitting in our dooryard.

"Let us go hunting," he says with a smile.

"Hunting? What would we catch with our bare hands?"

"Come and see."

I get up and walk with him to the end of the village, and from there he leads the way along the edge of our fields. Beyond the last one, we pass the small graveyard where a few of our people are now buried. Old Chaya-Ayala the bread-maker is interred there, alongside Eli the harpist and a few others. Clay tablets with their names inscribed in Hebrew letters ensure remembrance of them. It is not an assured matter that we may bury our dead here. If someone dies during work across the river or dies in the village alone and unclaimed, the overseers will hastily dispatch Saggo to cart the corpses away to the valley of death. There is not always time or opportunity to petition for the better way.

Now Issa and I are passing through the olive grove, which is thriving with an abundance of fruit. We wave to men tipping baskets of olives into a brickwork press, and they wave back. After we have left the last tree behind, Issa stops and drops to his knees beside a pile of pruned branches. From beneath it he pulls a bow and a woven quiver full of arrows.

Standing, he shows them to me with his slow smile.

I am unable to return the smile. "Issa, it is a serious offense to possess this."

"Our people are poorly fed, Yezekiel. I must take the risk."

"It is no small risk," I argue, "in fact, a grave one."

But this elicits no response. For him the matter is settled.

"These have been weeks in the making," he says, stroking the bow with the loving hand of a craftsman. "Finding the right bow-wood and arrow-wood was the main challenge, and then curing them for hardness."

He pulls an arrow from the quiver. It is very straight, notched at the hilt, with a whittled point.

"No arrowhead," I say, "but it might do for small game."

Reaching into his carry-satchel he removes a metal arrowhead, rusty, very old by the looks of it.

"Can you not use this?" I ask.

"Nay, Yezekiel. I do not want to risk losing it. Surely you remember it?"

"No. Where does it come from?"

"You gave it to me many years ago when I was sent away from the house of studies in Jerusalem."

"Ah, ah, now I remember."

"I treasure it as a memorial of our friendship and ever as a sign of hope, for you showed me on that day that I was not cast out by the Lord Most High, that I was not hidden from his eyes, and that, though our ways be hard or easy, long or short, his love endures forever."

This is one of the rare times when Issa has spoken at length and I, by contrast, am silent.

From his satchel he extracts a rough stone and hands it to me.

"What is this?" I say, surprised. "Where did you get it?"

"If one digs into the river mud, a stone can be found now and then."

He breaks a twig and walks forty paces farther into the wasteland. There he pokes the twig into the ground and walks back to me.

"Go ahead, Yezekiel. Think of it as a wolf or lion."

Aiming with care and a squinted eye, I hurl the stone hard and fast. It thumps into the ground with a puff of dust, about three paces from the twig. He runs to retrieve the stone, then brings it back to me.

"Again," he says.

Again and again I do my best, but the stone refuses to obey me, landing sometimes nearer, sometimes farther from the twig.

"My aim has become poor, and my arm is slower," I say with a shake of my head.

"Aim and speed will improve with practice. But you are far stronger than you once were."

"Stronger?" I answer with a sigh.

Once more I hurl the stone, and at last it shatters the twig into a spray of fragments.

Issa leaps in the air, crying jubilantly, "See, with what impact it hits the target!"

Not so enthused, I murmur, "Whenever it *happens* to hit a target."

We go searching for the stone, but somehow it has become lost in the sands.

Undaunted, Issa says, "Now, let us go hunting."

"We have no more stones. They are rarer than gold in these parts. But you with your bow have aim, speed, and force."

"Regard that quail," he says, pointing.

"I see no quail."

"Look, there!"

And then I see its speckled feathers blending into the ground around it.

"Many a time I have tried to capture those swift creatures, Issa, with no success. If only I had my old sling and my Jordan stones."

It now strikes me that during these past years I have given little thought to my boyhood sling or to making a replacement for it. I think it may be due to my way of seeing myself as a beast of burden and no hunter.

He takes another shard of river stone from his satchel and hands it to me.

"Just try," he says.

I do my best, missing the bird by a finger breadth. It scurries away into the bushes. Issa hands me another stone. And then another, and another. Finally, the seventh stone fells the quail, and I am laughing with the amazing success of it. We will have meat tonight! Issa easily could have brought it down with his bow, but stood back to give me first place. I understand anew how considerate he is. The habit of humility in him that I encountered years ago has not diminished.

"Seven throws," I say. "Yet a throw is not the hurl of a sling."

"I will make you a sling, Yezekiel."

"With what would you make it, Issa?"

"The Lord will provide."

As we walk back to the Portion through bushes and shallow ravines, we keep low lest our profiles be visible to any Kebarites who might be wandering about on our side of the river. Along the way, Issa pins a hare and two moorhens.

The Archer

When we come to the village's olive grove, he buries his bow and arrows beneath the pile of pruned branches.

That night we feast.

During the following days, I wonder if Issa will try to make a sling from hare-skin, though I know that such skin is too thin and brittle when dry, the kind of plaything I made when I was a child and just beginning to learn. It is good for a few throws before it tears and becomes useless. Even when oiled, it has little strength and does not last long.

One evening, two weeks later, Issa comes to our house, and without ceremony he hands me a sling. Its saddle and thongs are solid hide, soft and supple, smelling faintly of willow smoke, tanned by a method I cannot guess. To Ruth and Leah he gives a heavy sack.

"I brought down a desert gazelle," says Issa. "The meat is smoke-cured and must be hung from your rafters for preservation. It should last many weeks."

"We will eat some now!" cries Ruth, bustling about to make a fire.

"This sling," I say to Issa with wondrous gratitude, "is better than any I had when I was a lad."

Reaching into his satchel, he now presents me with five smooth stones. They are the usual rough river stones, but chipped by hand and ground to a shape that is close to a sphere.

"You give me gold, my friend," I say, and he smiles with satisfaction.

"Soon you will practice, Yezekiel, and then your aim and speed and strength will be as if it had never left you. Better, in fact."

A month, two months, and into a third we go hunting together many an evening. The light is dim, but our eyes adjust, and though we do not find game every day, we are successful more often than not. With this additional good nourishment, I can feel my strength increasing further than I had thought possible. We share much of the meat with others in the village, especially those in greatest need.

From time to time, Issa will join our family for an evening meal, but only when pressed to do so. He eats none of the delicacies Ruth prepares, contenting himself with basic sustenance. And still no wine. I often wonder why he keeps his scalp shaved, why he has continued to dress so penitentially after all these years. One evening he accepts an invitation, and while food is being prepared, I ask him about it.

"I have taken a vow," he says with a thoughtful look. "As with the *nazirites* of old, I drink no wine or strong drink, and I wear sackcloth as an offering to the Most High."

"Did not Samson, who was *nazir*, grow his hair long, with no razor ever touching his head?"

"The Lord has not called me to be Samson," he replies with a whimsical smile, lifting a bare arm and flexing the muscle.

"But why do you shave your head?"

"I do it as a reminder that our strength is not in hair but in obedience to the Lord. Above all, I do it as reparation for the sins of our people."

Issa shows me a little piece of iron he has honed into a sharp knife. He then demonstrates how it can scrape away a few bristles from the crown of his head.

"That looks a painful process, Issa."

"One grows accustomed to it," he says, gazing fondly at the knife.

By chance or providence, on this same night Ruth chooses to give Issa a gift, a linen robe for wearing on the Sabbath.

At first, he is reluctant to take it, but my earnest mother-in-law argues that if he refuses, he will dishonor the Lord.

"Dishonor the Lord?" he says with a frown.

"To rejoice on the holy day is to honor him. To dress yourself in a decent robe on that day proves you believe you are the son of a generous king."

He considers this, looking doubtful.

"Issa, do you wish to proclaim to all the world that the children of the Most High are wretched beggars?" she says in a wheedling tone.

Issa tentatively smiles, and then he laughs. It is the first time in my life I have seen laughter in him.

"I *am* a wretched beggar, good lady."

"Well, be the wretched beggar for six days a week, if you wish. But the seventh is not yours to rule."

Burying his nose in the fresh-smelling cloth, he relents.

"Thank you," he murmurs with a look of gratitude.

"Good. Now let us eat!"

I am in a canal, dredging and leech-harried. Despite this, I am consoled as always by the thought that within a few hours I will arrive home to be greeted by the light in my wife's face, her good food, and her great love. I am not worthy of her—may I become worthy of her!

At end of the work day, I burn off the leeches and walk back to the village with my team. Today, Issa has labored side by side with me.

"Eat with us," I invite him.

"I am glad of your welcome, Yezekiel," he says, "but my soul tells me to rest. I will sleep early tonight."

"As you wish. But know you are always family to us. Come whenever you choose."

"I know and I will."

We wash in the river, and then he is off to his hut and I to my home.

Arriving at our dooryard, I find Ruth baking flatbread on top of the oven. I greet her and ask her where Leah is.

"She is resting now, my son."

"Ah."

"Do not worry, I will feed you soon."

"I never worry about that."

I see that she looks very tired, her eyes red-rimmed, her aged spine hunched more than usual.

"Are you well, Ruth? You seem exhausted."

She does not answer at first. Using her fingers, she deftly flips the bread to bake the other side. Then she says:

"I prayed throughout the night for light on a question."

"What question is that, may I ask?"

"I sought the Lord about you and Leah." She looks up from her bread and peers at me somberly. "Leah told me this morning that she lay all night sleepless beside you, though I did not know and you could not have known, for you were lost in your dreams. Like me, she asked for light about you."

Now I feel a quickening of concern. "What is wrong? You must tell me."

"More than a year has passed since she had the woman's monthly showing of blood. Do you not understand?"

"I understand very little about those matters."

"If a woman has no blood flow for a time, it means one of two things. Either she has conceived a child in her womb or . . . or she is unable to conceive a child. And Leah is surely without child."

Now I sense the approach of a new sorrow invading our lives.

"Do not think the fault is with you, Yezekiel. She has told me that from the beginning of your marriage there has always been great love between you, in the way of man and woman, in the way of the laws of nature the Lord wrote into our flesh."

I look away, embarrassed.

"All three of us have prayed for a child," she goes on. "None has been given. Thus I spent the night in prayer, begging the Lord to answer us, one way or the other."

I look into her eyes again, noticing tears welling.

"The light was given, Yezekiel. And when we spoke together this morning, my daughter and I learned that the same light came to both of us."

"What light is this?" I ask, doubting, hoping.

"You will be the father of many, many children—children beyond counting."

She closes her eyes and raises both arms to the heavens. In a fragile voice she continues. "They will not be the offspring of the flesh. I saw your name, ages and ages from now, your life grown great in memory and revered beyond your own understanding, for a gift is coming to you."

Trying to dispel the pain I feel, I ask myself if this dear woman, one whom I love very much, is playing the prophet or voicing her own imagination in order to console me.

As if reading my mind, she cries out, "Oh yes, I know, I know, I am dim-sighted and my head is a tumble of silly thoughts, but even Balaam's donkey spoke prophecy, did it not? And when the voice of the Holy One speaks, you know who it is and you know it is true!"

Uncertain, I say nothing.

"There is more, Yezekiel. He showed me that out of grief will come vision, out of poverty will come richness. This wealth will be given from above, but it will not be for you. It will be given *through* you for others."

I put my hand on her arm and gently hold it. "What will be given?"

"It was not for me to know. I saw a terrible storm rising,

with flashes of lightning and a wheel of fire, but it was only the beginning of what will come. Then the spirit left me, and I saw no more."

Shaken, still disbelieving to an extent, I remain silent.

Drying her eyes on her sleeve, Ruth sighs and says, "In Paradise, Leah will dance and sing with rejoicing. Now she is weeping. Go, console her."

In the days that follow, the deep and private grief between Leah and me does not diminish. At night, hearing her weeping in the darkness, I hold her closely, and only then does sleep eventually come to us. Though I do not know what to make of Ruth's thoughts about lightning and a wheel of fire, it is certain that, barring a miracle, my wife is barren. Her heart is nearly broken over it. Even so, as week gives way to week, I see her effort to overcome her sorrow by turning to the serving of others. She is well loved by village children, whom she continues to teach—their letters, weaving and cooking skills, the stories of our people. I notice her mending their small cuts and bruises or simply playing with them. I hear her laughter when she is among them, yet I know that she laughs for their sakes.

From time to time, I will whisper into her ear, "After affliction comes blessing."

I seldom see Issa throughout this period. Of an evening he will still wander over from his cave to greet us as we sit by our fire. He says little and never stays long. Now and then he will deliver a quail or a hare and then leave without waiting for our thanks. Perhaps he senses that something has changed with us, and he keeps himself at a distance in order to ponder the matter, not wanting to intrude with questions.

On the eve of the Sabbath, after the women have gone to

sleep, I get up in the dark and go to visit my friend. Standing by the door of his shelter, I call his name quietly, hesitating to waken him. But he is awake, for straightaway he comes outside, and we sit down facing each other beneath the light of stars.

The faint embers of his cookfire emanate a little added light. He bends over and blows on them. As they glow brighter, he feeds them with bits of thornbush. Flames take hold, and the fuel crackles as Issa adds chips of aromatic poplar.

"Issa, I would plumb your thoughts," I begin. "You were the most learned of us all in Jerusalem. In your studies, did you ever come across any Scripture passages that have to do with lightning and wheels of fire?"

A long silence ensues, perhaps because he is searching in the library of his mind. I wait.

At last he says, "There was Elijah, who was taken up to heaven in the fiery chariot. A chariot has wheels, and thus it must have had wheels of fire."

"Yes, but what does it mean?"

"Why this question about wheels of fire, Yezekiel?"

"I am just curious."

"Curiosity does not arise out of nothing. Nor does curiosity alone drive a man from his bed to seek another's counsel in the middle of the night."

I tell him about Ruth's vision—if vision it was. I can hear him silently weighing the matter.

"We know how feelings can play with our minds," I say, hoping to prompt a response.

"And how our minds can play with our feelings," he replies.

"True. But then where are we? Can we trust anything that flashes through our inner thoughts?"

"Caution is best," he says in a sober, rabbinic tone. "Even

so, if a word or an image is sent from the Lord, it will bring with it a spirit of certainty. Was your mother-in-law certain about what she described?"

"She was certain. Never have I seen her more so."

Issa lapses into silence.

"Well, I am sorry to have disturbed your sleep," I say, rising to my feet.

As if in answer, he throws more wood onto the flames.

"Yezekiel, from time to time a straight sapling will grow up among its brethren. From such a sapling an arrow length may be cut and dried and tempered over fire."

These words seem familiar to me. Where have I heard them before?

"Over fire? Surely it risks burning a good arrow?"

"One must know the character of the wood. As it dries, one senses how much fire it can endure without setting it aflame. Heat and cold, heat and cold, again and again, make it ever stronger."

Now I remember. These were the very words he spoke at the time he was cast out from Jerusalem—his last words to me.

"You are that sapling," he says gently, and then pauses. "After these many years do you still not know it?"

I bow my head. "I understand nothing, Issa, nothing."

"Yezekiel," he says with a sudden firmness, unusual for him.

I look up. "Yes?"

"Captivity is not a matter of exile in alien lands and kingdoms and empires."

"How so?" I ask, straining to discern his meaning. "Surely we *are* captive in an alien land."

"Yezekiel, the only true sanctuary is in the heart of the soul."

The Archer

"What do you mean?"

But he will say no more.

Again comes a day when the Babylonians worship one of their gods. On the far side of the river, the squealing of dying swine and the shouting of revelers pollute the air. Issa and I go hunting, as usual seizing the opportunity, for it is fairly certain we will meet no guards or overseers on our side.

While he retrieves his bow and arrows, I revolve my sling with great speed, making a whirring sound. Then we set off on a track parallel with the river's course, an hour's walk inland, I estimate. Beyond the last grainfields and orchards, we enter into the semi-arid zone of scrubbushes where small animals live and where larger creatures such as the antelope and fallow deer sometimes rove. It is extremely difficult to bring one down, because they can spot movement at a distance, beyond bow shot, and will instantly spring away at great speed. The land is unevenly broken by dry wadis bordered by thickets of stunted trees, and we keep close to these because deer especially like to browse there.

By midafternoon we have seen no game. We are following a winding wadi, shallow enough that only our heads and shoulders show above the plain. There are bushes to help screen our passage. I observe how Issa moves as lithely as a gazelle, his steps making no sound, and I try to copy him. Suddenly he stops, hunches low, and points to a flicker of tawny hide foraging in a thicket upwind from us. We freeze, and Issa slowly lifts his bow, fitting an arrow to the string. He lets fly the shaft with a twang. The bolt shoots true, striking the animal just behind its shoulder. We race forward and find that our quarry is a small fallow deer, a half-grown yearling. It is already dead, its eyes wide open. With his knife Issa cuts the neck and lets it bleed dry, then he opens the animal's belly and guts it.

Unthinkingly, we have been rejoicing over the kill, talking aloud, and neglecting to keep ourselves low. Without warning, two figures appear over a heave of the land and come to a halt, staring in our direction. From this distance, I see that they are the shape of men, glittering in the reflected light of the sun setting behind Issa and me. They are Babylonians in helmets and carrying spears.

"They have spotted us," I whisper.

"Yes, but they do not yet know who we are, for the sun is in their eyes. Their hands are over their brows in order to keep from being blinded. It may be they cannot yet tell if we are one or two. Drop to the ground."

"It is too late. We should run."

"Drop to the ground, Yezekiel," Issa commands.

I do as he says.

"Roll under the thorn tree."

This, too, I do. But he is still standing in plain sight.

"Issa, get down. They may not find us."

"They will find us—or one of us."

Now the Babylonians are striding in our direction, lifting their spears.

"Let us fight them, Issa. Make ready your bow. I have my sling."

"Nay, this is the land God gave to Cain. Are we to become killers of men?" He pauses for a breath and then climbs up out of the wadi, with the deer slung over his shoulder.

From the side of his mouth, not looking at me, he murmurs, "This is the way I go."

Without a backward glance, he walks briskly in a direction that leads the soldiers away from my hiding place.

Lifting my eyes above the rim of the wadi, I see them

break into a run, chasing after him. He neither slows nor quickens his pace. Within minutes they have him, shaking him and threatening him with their spears. One makes him drop the deer, the other lifts it and packs it onto his own shoulders. They seize his bow and quiver. When they have bound his wrists with thongs, they take him away, heading in the direction of the river.

With my heart hammering, I duck down and wait. When dusk has slipped into deeper darkness, I climb out and walk stealthily back to the village. There I tell Leah and Ruth what has happened. Tears spring to their eyes, and they cover their mouths with their hands.

"We must pray," says Leah.

We pray for Issa's safety. We pray that he will be given no more than a beating for possessing a bow. We pray that he will not be blinded. Long we pray into the night, and even after the women have gone off to an uneasy sleep, I remain awake. I climb up to the roof and pray more. Again and again through my mind there passes Issa's last words to me.

"This is the land God gave to Cain," he said. And I think, *Yes, the land bequeathed because of murder, the land where murder still reigns.*

Three more days pass, and still he has not returned. Why do they not just beat him and cast him out? Will they blind him? The elders have received no word about Issa; the Babylonian officials they speak to merely shrug off the inquiries and tell them to go away. It may be that Issa has been sent to another colony of Hebrews as punishment, one harsher than our own. Constant is my anxiety, fitful my sleep.

By the fourth day, fear and anger are wrestling continuously within me. A trickle of hatred has begun to rise in my heart, a foul thing that I have never felt before, a leech

on my soul. As I walk heavily back to the village after a day
of harvesting in Kebar's fields, I feel my face flaming, my
fists clenching open and shut as in my mind's imagination I
am beating Babylonians to death. Recoiling in horror, I race
across the bridge and run upstream beside the river, seeking
to flee these unclean thoughts. I do not know where I am
going or why I do what I do. My feet lead me at last to the
hidden place where I bathe. There I wade in up to my shins
and kneel. I cup my hands, letting water fill them, and then
I pour it over my head. *Create in me a clean heart, O Lord,
renew in me a right spirit!*

But my spirits are too far cast down, and the waters of
Babylon can neither soothe nor heal this wound. Finally, I
wade back toward the shore. When the toes of my right
foot bump into a hard thing, I bend and pick it up. It is an
uneven stone, half covered with silt. Beside it is another,
and yet a third. Each of them is as large as my hand. For no
reason, I pull them loose from the mud and tie them in my
head scarf, making a sack to carry them to the village, I do
not know why. In the wildness of my thoughts, perhaps I
am planning to hurl them at the soldiers who captured Issa,
if I chance to meet them.

Approaching the bridge, I notice the one-armed Assyrian
rattling across on his donkey cart.

He spots me and yells:

"Ha, Judahite! More food for the jackals!"

Gleefully exposing a mouthful of broken teeth, he turns
the donkeys onto the path that leads to the valley of the dead.
The body on the back is wrapped in sackcloth, but the crown
of the skull is exposed, bristling with short brown hair. In
horror, I realize who it is and hasten after the cart. Looking back over his shoulder, the driver cackles and lashes the
donkeys, spurring them into a trot. I begin to run, weighed

down with the stones—why I still carry them I do not question. No matter how fast I run, the cart keeps drawing ahead. Up the last rise in the dirt track I go and arrive at the crest just as the driver is pulling away, cracking his whip and giggling in his high-pitched *he-he-he*.

Issa's body has been kicked off the edge and rolled down the slope, losing its sackcloth on the way. He lies in a heap of carnal refuse, corpses half stripped of their flesh by carrion birds and animals, the dismembered bones of decomposing bodies strewn all about. Vultures have just settled on Issa's body as I hurry down the slope, forcing them to flap away with screeches of protest.

I can scarcely recognize the body, so ruined is it and covered with dried blood, but the face is his. I stoop, lift the body in my arms, and carry it back up the slope. Arriving at the top, panting from the exertion, I lay it down on the ground. Now the cruelty of what they have done to him is fully revealed. His flesh is not only covered with lash marks, there are countless cuts—no part of him has been spared.

I cannot leave his mortal remains thus exposed. I pick up the body again and carry it toward a hill that rises in the east, higher than all others in the surrounding terrain. How long this journey takes, I cannot measure, for I am immersed in mindless grief beyond all thought. Coming to the base of the high hill, I look up and hesitate, my arms and legs already strained to the breaking point. But again I climb. At the height I drop to my knees and lay the body down, and there I begin to scoop out a burial hole with my bare hands. Beneath the surface, my fingers come upon old potsherds, more and more of them as I dig lower. Using one larger piece as a scoop helps me to excavate the soil without tearing my flesh. When the pit is around four feet deep, I stop.

I place the palm of my right hand on Issa's forehead. Then with my forefinger I trace upon it the four letters for the name of the Lord.

"Fare you well, little brother, O best of friends," I whisper. "May you be welcomed into Paradise; may the Most High robe you in royal garments and prepare a feast for you—"

My voice fails, I can say no more.

I take one last look at this face and body, which have known little else but toil and trial since birth. A poor and ragged semblance of manhood, covered in the marks of torture. Now before the eyes of my heart there appears the inner man who once was, living and breathing, speaking with his eyes, thinking, praying, giving. I see his goodness, his greatness, his silent sacrifices—and now the final sacrifice he made for me.

"Wear this degradation like a crown of glory, Issa ben Ephraim," I say, the words arising from the inner reservoir of my soul, as if a few drops of water have condensed from a desert dew.

Dragging his body by the shoulders, I let it fall into the pit, and then I climb in after it. I arrange the body as if on a bed of rest. I cover his nakedness with my head scarf. I cross his arms over his chest. I climb out and begin to fill the pit with scoop after scoop of soil, leaving the face for last, allowing me a final glimpse of a soul so noble that no one in this world knew his full worth. His face is no longer contorted with the traces of agony; it has now settled into an expression of profound dignity and repose. Blindly, I open my palm and pour a handful of loose soil over it.

When the grave is entirely filled, I build a little altar beside it, made of the three stones I brought from the river. With the edge of a potsherd I scratch the letters יהוה on the top stone facing the sky. Perhaps the eyes of the Lord will see the holy name and know that this small life, this Issa, honored him and looked to him for salvation, though the salvation did not come to him in this world.

I stand up but cannot yet leave. Gazing at the little mound of soil and the small altar, I remember Mount Zion and the Temple. Into my mind come scenes from the time we spent together in our student days. I see again those two youths hurling stones in the streets, laughing and competing with each other as if we were young Davids. I remember that he was the most intelligent and devoted of all the students, though he was ever humble. I see him being unjustly cast out because of his righteousness, which offended the unzealous and the compromised. Then his silent penance for the sins of the people of Israel and the sins of the nation's elders, though he spoke not a word of recrimination. Finally, after a length of years, there came the generosity of his family, giving shelter to my family until the storm passed by. And at the last, his words spoken as a kind of authoritative counsel:

"Captivity is not a matter of exile in alien lands and kingdoms and empires. The only true sanctuary is in the heart of the soul."

And though I still cannot grasp his meaning, I know that we have lost the best of the children of Abraham.

15

The Anointing

I N OUR HOME, after I tell Leah and Ruth the story of Issa's end, omitting the details of his torture, they weep copiously and pray with me the mourner's *Kaddish* in memory of the dead. I cannot weep.

Through her tears, Leah tries to console me, using the words I once spoke to her: "After affliction comes blessing."

That night at the prayer house, I tell the whole story to the elders and the few people who have gathered there, and together we recite the *Kaddish*. Still I cannot weep. A portion of my heart has died.

Nor can I sleep. Sensing my awakeness in the dark, Leah whispers once more, "After affliction comes blessing."

The following day is the Sabbath. At the conclusion of morning prayers with the community, I quickly leave. Walking in no particular direction, I peer at the world around me, seeing everywhere the beast that hides behind the mask of normality, as the life of village, town, and empire continues as if nothing has changed.

I wander out beyond our fields, and soon I find myself entering the arid zone. Weaponless, indifferent to anyone who might see me, I follow dry wadis, ignoring the gazelle and antelope, the moorhens and quail. Then I realize that my feet have brought me to the place where Issa killed the deer. From there, I pace in the direction he went as he led the soldiers away from me. When I arrive at a spot that I think is where they bound him, I look at the ground, hoping to find his footprints, but the wind has blown all traces away. Only a small chip of rust-colored stone remains. I bend and pick it up, discovering that it is not a stone but the ancient arrowhead I gave him many years ago.

Now I see that he must have dropped it deliberately, knowing that he would be seized, and, I think, knowing that we might not see each other again. He left it as a sign for me to find.

The desolation stretches onward week after week. I perform my duties, I try to love where love is possible, try to ignore the spirit of malice that surrounds us, poisoning the very air we breathe. I continue to write down the prophecies of Isaiah, faithfully I hope, though my heart remains numb. There are no consolations from above. No tears flow unbidden from my eyes. The cracked cistern within me remains dry. No wind comes from the eternal Promised Land, no man of light to reassure me or to explain why the very best of us die alone and in pain, while the wicked prosper and prosper.

What is left is patient endurance. And prayer of the will, *choosing* to pray in the face of darkness, though heaven remains silent. I know it is not allotted to me to understand anything more than the humblest things, and thus I force myself to be faithful to worship, lifting my voice in praise to him and thanking him for what is good in the world, though the world is filling with confusion and darkness, the plaything of the serpent. And all the while my prayers feel like dust thrown upward into the wind, invariably falling back to the earth.

I think to myself how consoling it would have been to take Eli to Issa's grave and there to sing with him a king-song and hear him plucking his homely five-string harp, making beauty in honor of our lost friend. But Eli, too, is buried. I have asked other harpists to accompany me out into the wasteland, but all have declined my request. In recent times there has grown a reluctance to sing in places other than the prayer house or in private homes.

Then comes a Sabbath morning when I happen upon a young man sitting in the reeds by the riverbank, his feet in the water. He is bent over, his face in his hands, sobbing. Hanging from a nearby willow branch is a very fine ten-string harp. I kneel down beside him and ask what is the trouble.

He dries his eyes and looks up at me in a state of misery. It is David, the son of Abner the shepherd.

"An overseer who heard me practicing demanded that I go to Kebar and make music for a banquet," he says. "He promised coin reward and rich foods. And so I went. When I began to play, the banquet guests clamored for me to sing one of our songs and to look more merry, to join in their mirth. Then my heart fell within me, and I wept and could play no more. I ran from them, and here I am."

"I would have done the same," I tell him.

"O how can we sing!" he cries out. "How can we sing one of the songs of Zion in this alien land!"

"Do not sorrow, David, do not sorrow. The songs and the music live within you. They cannot take this away from you."

I ask him if he would play his instrument and sing with me for a friend of mine who has died, buried far out in the hills. He accepts to go there with me later that day.

The Anointing

I return home and ask Leah and Ruth if they will come with me to Issa's grave, where we might try to sing together for him. I have not sung since his death. I have not grieved, not truly mourned. Leah immediately lays aside what she is doing, washes her hands, and finds a scarf to cover her head for the journey, as the sun is beating hot today. Ruth pleads that she is unable to walk far and will join us in her spirit, sorrowing privately within her own four walls.

David arrives carrying his harp. Leah takes my hand and together we three begin the long walk toward the distant hills. I lead them by a roundabout way that avoids the valley of death. When we reach the height of land, we stand beside the little altar over the mound of soil where Issa is buried. As the harpist begins plucking his strings most beauteously, I feel my inner self begin to melt, and then when he opens his mouth and sings full-throated one of King David's lamentations, at last I weep.

Three months have passed since Issa's death. It is now the first month of the fifth year of our captivity. I scarcely dare think of the long years ahead—sixty-five more years according to Jeremiah. I know that I will die in this land, never again seeing my home, never again gazing upon the glory of the Temple, never again feeling the holy consolations that were given to me there. I resolve to persevere until my dying breath, refusing to permit the eyes of the serpent to mesmerize me or to lure me into the seductions of Babylon. I will offer all my burdens and deprivation in reparation for the sins of our people, that this sacrifice might play a role in bringing about the restoration prophesied by Isaiah and Jeremiah. Though I will not live to see it, I will have done my part.

Toward the end of the first month, I am trudging wearily home to the village after a day of planting fields. As I pass Kebar's gates and approach the bridge, a donkey cart rumbles alongside me. It halts at the bridge. Three old men get down from the back and stand there, waiting. A guard jumps down from beside the driver and goes to them. He seems to be instructing them, pointing with his spear to the bridge. With uncertain steps, the old men head onto it and begin to cross over the river toward the Portion. I follow close behind, listening to them speaking in undertones. They are Judahites.

"Who are you, good fathers?" I ask.

They stop and tell me their names. They are Aaron, Gershon, and Obed. I tell them my name. Aaron is very old, white-haired, with a sunbaked wrinkled face. Gershon and Obed are also well advanced in years but grey-haired.

"Where have you come from, and where are you going?" I ask.

"We have come from the city of Babylon," answers Obed. "On the morrow we will be taken onward to Tel-abib."

Gershon says, "We are told to find shelter and food among the Hebrews of this place."

"Come with me," I say. "We will speak with the elders, and they will give you food and a place to rest for the night."

At the house of prayer, I find Shimeon sitting on the ground outside the entrance, practicing writing words on a piece of wet clay. He stands when he sees us approaching. I introduce the three visitors, and he warmly welcomes them to the house and village.

"You may sleep here," he says. "I will go find food and blankets for you. Yezekiel, make a fire for our guests, if you will."

The Anointing

I borrow embers from a neighbor's house, carrying them in a pan back to the fire pit near the entrance. After gathering sticks, I set them ablaze, while the three men sit down and gaze at the rising flames. Shimeon returns with an armload of blankets, which he arranges into three makeshift beds within the prayer house. Shortly thereafter, Tzvi and Amos and their wives bring a meal of bread and fruit, ewe's cheese, and small strips of smoked mutton. After covering their heads with their shawls and giving thanks to God, the old men eat. As they do so, they explain their situation.

"We are priests of the Temple," says the one named Obed.

"Until five years ago, we were priests of the Temple," the white-bearded Aaron corrects.

I say, "Yet you will always be priests, even in this foreign land."

They nod in agreement.

"Are there priests here in your village?" asks Aaron.

"None," I say.

They seem familiar to me, though I do not recall seeing them before. But of course there were hundreds of priests attached to the Temple in the days when I assisted there, and many of them came seldom to Mount Zion or only once a year.

Gershon says, "We are originally from the thousands brought to Babylon when Jeconiah was deposed by Nebuchadnezzar. And you, Yezekiel, when did you come?"

"Three months earlier, at the murder of Jehoiachim."

"Your people have made a sizeable village here, I see. And a house of prayer."

"We were at first only a hundred, and then later an additional two hundred captives were added at the time of your deportation. With marriages and children, we have grown a little since then."

"It seems a good place."

I say nothing. With a stab in my heart, I am thinking that no place in this world lacks its span of good and evil.

"During your deportation," I say to change the subject, "more than a thousand were taken onward to the city of Tel-abib. Is that where you dwell?"

"Yes, for the most part. We have resided the past year in the city of Babylon. We are scholars and were required to work temporarily in the law courts as translators. We also began a translation into Chaldean of the Five Books. This is now completed, and we are being sent home."

"*Home.* It is painful to use that word," says Obed. "Never will it be truly home."

"The only true home is in the heart of the soul," says Aaron. The other two incline their heads to him, and in this gesture I see that they revere him. Indeed, he is not only the oldest, he appears to be the wisest.

The Portion's elders and their wives now bid the visitors a good night, and I am left alone with them.

"I know your face, young man," says Gershon. "Have I seen you before in this land?"

"I have never visited Tel-abib."

"Was it in Judah that we met?"

"I cannot say, as I do not recognize your face or those of your companions."

"Ah, ah, now I know you," says Obed. "Though you have aged a little, I remember you serving at the Temple."

"My face was often besmeared by charcoal in those days."

They smile. "That may be so, but later you assisted at the Altar of Sacrifice, did you not?"

"I did. I was in studies for the priesthood then."

The Anointing

You deserved better, O my Lord. I should have given you more,
listened to you more, studied harder when plentiful books were by
my hand in Jerusalem.

"I remember the way you turned your face to the open
door of the *Hekal* and bowed like no other, when you need
not have done so. I saw you put your face to the paving
stones at times. Of all the students and acolytes, you alone
did this."

"How close to ordination were you?" asks Aaron.

"I had five more years of studies ahead of me," I tell him.

"And five years have now passed since then."

"That is correct. It is a grief to me."

"Aye, a grief and a double grief," says Aaron in a quiet
voice, barely above a whisper. "You did not receive the
anointing of priesthood at the proper time, and thus Israel
in captivity suffers from one less priest."

"Even so," Obed interjects. "Even so, we priests no
longer can offer a fitting holocaust so far from the Temple."

"Yet you may offer the sacrifice of acceptance," I say,
"acceptance of our chastisement."

Aaron looks at me with a solemn expression, saying nothing, pondering.

"Have you continued your studies?" asks Gershon.

"I lack any scrolls of the Holy Scripture," I say, then ask,
"Do you have books?"

"None that accompany us on this journey. Numerous
scrolls have been brought to Babylonia secreted in clothing
and baggage. We are many Hebrews in Tel-abib, far greater
in number than in this place. There, we gather for prayer
in our town outside the city walls. It is no longer necessary
to hide books, for Nebuchadnezzar permits us freedom to
practice our religion."

"The promises of kings," I say with a worried sigh, "are as changeable as the wind."

"Let us hope and pray that the wind does not change. For now, we have collected all the manuscripts brought by our fellow exiles, and we are struggling to master the skills of making papyrus, on which one can copy books, as do the Egyptians." He points south-westerly. "Papyrus plants grow in abundance farther along the rivers."

I nod in dejection. I cannot go wandering in search of this papyrus plant. I do not know what it looks like, or where it might be found by the River Kebar, or what to do with it if I were to find it.

"We have made copies on lambskin," I say, "mainly passages remembered from the Torah and Isaiah. It is slow work, and I worry that memory is not always accurate."

"We will try to send you correct copies, if time permits and our skills with papyrus improve."

"This would be a blessing beyond measure," I answer with wonder at their generosity.

"Then you may resume your studies," says Aaron.

"Until that time, it might be said that I study still, for when I was in Jerusalem, I read far in advance of my required reading."

The two younger priests now proceed to ask me many questions about the content of the Scriptures known to me. Aaron remains silent, though he is regarding me with great attentiveness to my replies. Soon I see that I am being led step by step from Genesis to Isaiah. As if from a deep well, my mind brings forth crucial passages from each of the books.

The hours pass. These men must be very tired after their long day of travel. Nevertheless, they do not seek the restoration of sleep, but in their gentle, persistent manner they maintain their inquiry until the sky in the east begins to pale.

When a streak of rose appears on the horizon, I say in conclusion, "Much of it remains in my memory. Daily I ponder these holy accounts and messages from the Most High, and I pray that the seed of them will not die in this barren soil."

"For what purpose do you desire to preserve this seed?" asks Aaron.

"That it may sprout and flower and bear fruit", I reply. "That the Word of the Lord may not fall into neglect and final disremembering."

The three men nod their heads and murmur, "This is good."

"Do you teach the Word to others?," asks Gershon.

"I teach in small ways, mainly in conversations. I recite certain passages for the people when asked to do so by our elders. I am not an elder or a Scripture rabbi." After pausing a moment, I say, "This is a house of prayer, and thus the life of our people's faith continues. Yet, I lament that no burnt sacrifice can now be offered to the Lord."

"You may offer your very self as a living sacrifice," says Aaron in his quiet way.

I am startled by this thought, which I had come to on my own and have silently practiced, though I am uncertain if it is acceptable to the Lord.

The east grows brighter. I explain that I will be called to my labors a few hours from now. I must sleep a little. We all rise to our feet.

"May the Lord bless you and keep you, Yezekiel," says Aaron.

"May he protect you on your journey and make you fruitful unto eternity," I reply. "I hope that the Most High permits us to meet again one day."

Aaron answers, "We will return."

At home, I find Leah mixing freshly ground flour into her bowl of sour dough, preparing for the day's baking. She smiles at me.

"Welcome, wanderer. Are you hungry?"

"Very hungry, my wife, and very tired."

I explain my absence as she brings me boiled eggs and a disk of flatbread.

"Despite your fatigue, Yezekiel, your spirits have risen. The visitors were good for you."

"They were. In what way, I cannot say with any certainty. It reassured me, I think, that our faith goes onward into the future, that exile cannot destroy it."

"But it cost you your night's sleep. It will be a hard day for you out in the fields."

I go to her, make her put down the bowl, and embrace her.

"You are the delight of my eyes," I whisper.

"You are the delight of my heart," she answers.

"You are the delight of my eyes *and* my heart."

"You are the delight of my heart *and* my eyes."

The cockerel crows, the sun rises, the overseer yells from the village commons.

Six weeks later, in the third month of the fifth year of captivity, the three priests return. They are being taken back to the city of Babylon to do additional work for officials there, and their guard and driver will stay overnight in Kebar. I first learn of it after my evening meal, when Amos comes rushing into the house.

"Yezekiel, the priests from Tel-abib are here! They ask for you."

I find them standing outside the open doorway of the prayer house, murmuring together with the village elders. There is baggage at their feet.

The Anointing

"Aaron, Gershon, Obed, I am very glad to see you again."

"As we are glad to see you, Yezekiel."

"You stay the night? Will you have time to talk more with me?"

"We stay the night, and we will surely have more time to converse with you."

Aaron steps forward and says, "We bring you a bidding that you are free to accept or refuse."

"What bidding is this?" I ask with curiosity.

"We have prayed much about you since last we met. We feel certain that the Lord desires you to become a priest."

My breath leaves my mouth, and my eyes blink rapidly.

"Do not look so stricken, Yezekiel," says Gershon.

"I am not stricken, but overcome, good fathers. You should understand that I am not worthy of what you ask."

"Your feelings are as they should be," says Aaron, "for it is no small thing to be a priest of the Lord."

"Besides, it is not we but the Lord himself who asks it," Obed says.

"Have you brought books?" I say. "I will pray about the question and study hard."

"We have brought you no books as yet," he answers. "However, we bring you a gift of another kind."

Obed bends, opens the baggage sack, and removes from it a slender bronze jug. He stands and holds it out before him.

Aaron speaks in a tone of recitation:

"Five hundred *shekels* of free-flowing myrrh, two hundred and fifty *shekels* of cinnamon, two hundred *shekels* of fragrant balsam cane, five hundred *shekels* of cassia, blended into a *hin* of olive oil."

Then I begin to understand. He has quoted the Lord's instructions to Moses in the desert, the formula for making the oil of anointing to the priesthood.

Gershon says, "It would need a cart to carry the full weight of anointment as commanded during the exodus. Even so, we have made this oil in the proper proportions."

"Are you ready? Do you accept?" Aaron asks.

I bow my head and feel my hands begin trembling.

"I accept," I reply in a shaken voice, "though I fear I will never be ready."

"Fear not."

The other two repeat, "Fear not! Fear not!"

Aaron turns to Shimeon. "Please bring Yezekiel's family here and gather all the people."

The elders hasten away throughout the village. We wait. Still I cannot look up, for I am rooted in a silent space between heaven and earth.

In time I hear the whispering of hundreds of voices encircling me. I feel the touch of Leah's hand upon my arm, a press of her fingers and then withdrawn.

"Look up, Yezekiel ben Buzi," says Aaron.

I look up and meet his eyes. There is a solemn joy in them. Gershon and Obed stand beside him. Aaron takes the bronze flask from Obed's hands.

"Bow your head," he commands.

I bow before him. Warm oil pours over the crown of my head, runs down my brow and cheeks, as if the glad waters of heaven have opened, filling the world with intoxicating perfume. And with it comes joy almost beyond endurance. I lift my arms before me, and the three priests anoint my open palms.

Aaron cries out in a strong voice:

"The Lord sees not as man sees; man looks at the outward appearance, but the Lord looks upon the heart!"

"Amen! Amen!" shout the two other priests.

"Amen! Amen!" shout the elders and all the people.

The Anointing

In the silence that follows, Shimeon raises his deep, powerful voice, singing the words of King David's song of anointing:

"The Lord is my shepherd . . . he restores my soul . . . You anoint my head with oil . . . I will dwell in the house of the Lord forever."

All the elders join with him, and finally the whole gathering of the people.

Then comes an outburst of festive singing and dancing, as timbrels and drums and harps are brought out from the shadows, and for the first time they are played with mighty rejoicing.

And thus in my thirtieth year, in the third month, my life is anointed for service unto the Lord, my being consecrated to him forever. And though I will never be able to offer holocaust or oblation of first-fruits, even so I may offer fit praise and thanksgiving and teaching in the house of the Lord, for the sake of all my people. Mine is a priesthood of the soul.

In the fifth year of my captivity, in the fourth month, on the fifth day of the month, I am awakened long before dawn by I know not what. A strange inner movement stirs my soul, compelling me to get up and dress myself in my work-robe and go out. The sky is clear, radiant with stars.

My feet lead me toward the river, and when I come to the trail that follows beside it, I walk northward. I pass thickets of reeds and bulrushes, I pass the bathing place, and then the stands of willow trees where our people have at times wept, their songs turned to wails of grief.

I come to an open space beyond the river and the fields and head out onto the plain where the whole sky is visible. Before I am aware of it, before I choose to do so, my body is kneeling and then laying itself face down on the ground, my arms stretched out before me. My hands are cupped open and empty. My mind, too, is empty. My heart is calm but empty. I present all that I have been, all that I am, all that I will become.

What service can I offer you, O Lord Most High, I who am so poor in holiness, who can offer no sacrifice, who have so little learning, who am a ragged remnant of your Temple here in this desolation!

"Do unto me according to your holy will," I cry aloud —or think or exhale with the breath of life.

A black snake untwines from a dead tree and winds closer and closer toward me. Yet I do not move, for my life is in the Lord's hands. The serpent halts and coils its body upon itself, a foot from my face. It stares into my eyes, hissing, flickering its forked tongue. When I whisper the name of the Lord, it averts its eyes, uncoils, and slithers away into the darkness.

Still my arms are stretched before me, still my hands are open like empty cups. A scorpion crosses my field of vision, scuttling toward my hand, its tail arching as it prepares to sting me. Again I whisper the name of the Lord. The scorpion halts and lowers its tail. It changes its course and scurries away into the darkness.

Now the sunrise is near. I close my eyes and wait. I wait and wait, for I know that this is what is required of me, if I would accept it.

Then into the empty reservoir of myself comes the sound of water. Water trickling into a jar, water rising within me until it overflows, becoming a brook that grows into a river. Rising with still greater force, the river swells and deepens, and as this happens I am impelled to stand and raise my arms to the sky. Now I see before the eyes of my soul a shepherd boy digging a spring on a hillside. The spring fills its pool, spills over, and runs down, growing in strength as it goes, joining with other brooks and making a river, uniting with other rivers that become one great river coursing onward toward the sea.

And then all these waters turn and flow upward to heaven, beseeching, beseeching, offering, offering, and I open my mouth to let the torrent pour forth, for the river is within me. Now the great river changes to music—it is both water and music—at first it is the sound of a boy playing a flute to his sheep, and then the flute becomes the *shofar*, but unlike any I have ever heard, for its notes are trumpeting deep and long, and in it there is love and joy and lamentation— all one! And then I know that *this* is the great song I was created for:

"O You whom I cannot see, cannot hear," I sing as the river pours forth from me. "O You whom I love, O You who have poured out upon me in my desolation the love of she who is the delight of my heart, and he who sacrificed himself for me, and the messengers whom you sent to anoint me as your servant, I praise you! Thus shall I forever lift up my poor hands to you, and my blind eyes to you, and my deaf ears to you, and from out of the depths I will cry unto you, and praise your glory!"

And as I look, behold, a great storm wind comes out of the north and a mighty cloud with brightness around it, and flashing forth from it there is fire.

There is fire.